RUSH

Kim Wozencraft

IVY BOOKS • NEW YORK

Rush is a work of fiction. Any resemblance its characters
may have to persons living
or dead is purely coincidental.

Ivy Books
Published by Ballantine Books
Copyright © 1990 by Code 3 Communications, Inc.

Grateful acknowledgment is made to the following for permission to reprint previously published material:

EMI Music Publishing: Excerpt from the song lyrics "Heroin" by Lou Reed. Copyright © 1966 by Oakfield Avenue
Music Ltd. All rights controlled and administered by Screen
Gems–EMI Music, Inc. All rights reserved. International
copyright secured. Reprinted by permission.

MCA Music Publishing: Excerpt from the lyrics to "Do't
Take Me Alive," words and music by Walter Becker and
Donald Fagen. Copyright © 1976 by MCA Music Publishing, a division of MCA Inc., 1755 Broadway, New York, NY
10019. Rights administered by MCA Music Publishing, a division of MCA Inc. All rights reserved. Used by permission.

Library of Congress Catalog Card Number: 89-29117

ISBN 0-8041-0789-0

This edition published by arrangement with Random House,
Inc.

Manufactured in the United States of America

First Ballantine Books Edition: June 1991

For John

PROLOGUE

THERE ARE TIMES, WHEN I'VE SLIPPED AWAY FROM concentrating on something specific, that I suffer a rage which takes my sight away, closes off my vision, makes the air around me turn the color of bloodless muscle.

I try to believe that I would not really do it.

I have been in this place, the Beta Unit, nearly six weeks now, while the prison shrinks prepare their evaluation. I must not tell them.

Nothing they might say would change what I'm feeling, and I cannot admit to them how many times each day I lose my focus and find this thing, this raging unwanted something, assaulting my brain.

I must not think about it. I don't know how not to. But if I tell them, they will decide I am dangerous. They will call Nettle and warn him. They will run straight to Dr. Mossman.

He is the one who will decide whether I am sane. If he feels that I am, he will send me back to the population so that I may do my time. But if he certifies me, time stops. He can keep me in here for as long as he wants, for the rest of my life, and it won't count toward my sentence. If I am insane, then legally I am incapable of recognizing the fact that I am in prison. Therefore I am not being punished, and the time served doesn't count. It's Dr. Mossman's decision.

I'm not innocent. This I understand no matter what the doctor decides. But when I attempt to comprehend what it is that put me in here, why I complied, it always comes back to Jim Raynor and Donald Nettle. But Nettle is the one.

It wasn't Jim's fault. I fell in love with him quickly, the way a schoolgirl falls in love, and with the same unbending loyalty. That was my own weakness. Jim was my boss, my mentor. He believed in me when I wasn't old enough to know how to believe in myself.

He'd been a cop for six years when we met. He was mean when the situation demanded it, and was strong because of it. He knew how to deal with brutality, and he believed in what he was doing. On some level, he believed. But he understood the *realpolitik* of buying dope at street level, that the survival of self was right in the big middle of it. He went in specific directions. "You do the best you can with what you've got at the time," he said. But his was not the philosophy of optimism.

He made me aware that you have to bend the rules to be effective. He made me a cop. He made me feel, for the first time in my life, that I was functioning as an adult. And from the start, from that first day, he brought to me an understanding of need.

If I had known what it took, that you have to be able to turn your feelings off, just shut them down completely, I might never have filled out that application. It happens gradually, so slowly that you don't realize it. The injuries and deaths and lies pound away at you until, finally, you reach down inside yourself and find nothing. Empty space. And it feels pretty damn good not to hurt.

I must not think about Nettle.

*   *   *

I try to concentrate on what I will tell the Parole Commission, if I get past the shrinks.

I will tell them that I was an athlete. That I ran track and played basketball and church-league softball, that I belonged to the Drama Club and the Spanish Club and wrote for the school paper. That I spent Saturdays at the stables down the road, bathing horses on the off chance that I would get to ride. I'll explain to them that I believed in God, and that my parents were decent people who struggled like hell to stay together and give their children a home.

I will tell them that when I was in fourth grade I didn't go to Communion one Sunday because Rory Larson had passed around some Sweetarts ten minutes before Mass, that I stayed on my knees and suffered the stare of Sister Mary Joseph rather than mix the Body of Christ with a piece of candy.

I will try to make them understand that my intentions were honorable. And I will admit that I loved Jim Raynor more than was good for either of us.

And they'll say, "Cut the crap. Why are you in?"

I am not innocent. It comforts me now, in here, to tell myself that if I hadn't believed to excess, if I hadn't loved Jim, I would never even have encountered Nettle, never have learned the extremes of hatred I now know so well. There are moments, in the middle of the night, when I cannot stop the awful thoughts of vengeance that make my stomach a sodden sponge, that turn the walls red in the dark.

I try to forgive myself. I work at it. Some nights I try to pray.

My cellmate has a wood-burned plaque above her bed. It says: AND HOW DO WE PUNISH THOSE WHOSE REMORSE IS ALREADY GREATER THAN THEIR MISDEED?

I'm not sure of the answer, but when I go deep inside myself, to places we are taught to be afraid of, I realize with fear, with disgust, the strength of my hatred for Nettle. I fight not to be consumed by it. It punishes. Some nights it hurts as though there is an abscess in my heart.

He feels no remorse for what he did to Jim, or to me. No remorse. What I want from him is an admission.

Nights in here, I sit backed into a corner on my bed and listen for the guard on his 2 A.M. count. There is the clinking metal echo of keys hitting his hip as he walks on rubber-soled shoes down the corridor, and then a shadow pauses behind the wire-mesh window in the door of this room, this cage. A spot of light hits the bed and searches the covers, finds my feet and jerks upward to my face. It burns quickly, this sudden white glare in my eyes, and then it is gone and the keys clank down the hall. I am left staring at shimmering yellow orbs that float in the middle of the room, like ghosts playing tag in the dark.

And I despise the need I have to find Nettle and put things right. I don't want to feel this.

But I do. Jesus God I do.

ONE

I DIDN'T GROW UP THINKING I WOULD BECOME A COP. I don't suppose I thought I would become particularly anything. My grandmother called me a tomboy, and I was, but I got the message early that I would someday be expected to assume the female mantle, and I was raised to do that which was expected. I couldn't see past the crisp green lawns of suburban Houston, and I refused to acknowledge that I was uneasy about the possibility of spending life as a Mrs. Mommy. Perhaps I was playing Cinderella: studying part time at the University of Houston and waiting tables part time at Wild Bill's Rootin' Tootin' Ice Cream Saloon in the Alameda Mall, hoping for someone to dash into my life and change it forever.

It was Alton Sharply, a regular Friday evening customer, who suggested that I take the exam for the Pasadena Police Department. Though Alton had been coming in for months, I'd never suspected that he was a recruiter. I was standing beside his table, balancing a tray full of sundaes, when he said, "You ought to get out of here, Kristen. This is nowhere." I put his hot fudge malt on the paper placemat and went about delivering the rest of my orders. When I came back with his check, Alton handed me an application.

"Think about it," he said. "Pasadena is growing like mad, you could make sergeant in two years easy."

I was twenty-one, barely old enough to be considered for the job. I knew thirty dollars was an outstanding amount of tips for a Saturday night. I knew frivolous evenings with friends who, like me, were biding time, studying this or that and waiting for something to happen. And I knew I'd been almost good enough, in high school, almost fast enough, to go somewhere as a runner. I'd had good form going over the hurdles. But no matter how hard I worked, how much I practiced, I couldn't shave that last essential two-tenths of a second off my time. I won frequently, almost constantly, until the big Invitational Open at the Astrodome. And two-tenths of a second can look like forty miles when you've just cleared that last hurdle and there's an Olympic contender in front of you leaning toward the tape.

Alton kept on pitching and made it sound good, like my life would suddenly have purpose. I would be doing something that made a difference, and could stop serving chocolate sundaes and singing "Happy Birthday."

I met Jim the day I was hired. Alton escorted me past a row of cubicles filled with secretaries who couldn't have been much older than I was. He pointed into an office and left me there, sitting next to a wall covered with certificates of merit from every civic group I'd ever heard of and some I hadn't.

A few minutes later Jim Raynor walked in. He didn't look at all like any cop I had ever seen. He was tall and of medium build, wearing a tailored olive-green suit. His hair was black and wavy, reaching almost to his shoulders. And his deep-set eyes were of such a pale blue that they appeared almost white around the pupils, the irises rimmed with a kind of gray-blue ring and flecked with amber green.

When he reached across the desk to shake hands, his jacket fell open to reveal a shoulder holster. He seemed intense even while he was only standing there smiling, and when I felt his warm, dry palm press against mine, I knew. He was a captain, in charge of the Criminal Investigation Division, and his confidence astonished me. He moved with a matter-of-factness that made me believe he knew what was happening and it was all under control.

The job he had in mind for me was undercover narcotics. Pasadena, Texas, with not quite a hundred thousand residents, had a drug problem. The police department was supposed to be doing something about it. Wedged tight against the eastern limits of Houston, dragging a slender tail of land from its own southeast corner all the way to the edge of Galveston Bay, Pasadena was more small city than suburb.

I was not known on the streets. I was ignorant of police procedure and jargon. And I was female. I was just what they were looking for. A natural, Jim said. Made for it.

I didn't know if I could handle it, but I knew for certain that I was sick to death of selling ice cream and tired of sitting in classrooms listening to professors who were bored with their own lectures. I wanted to try.

I looked like just what I was: a woman jock. I had inherited my mother's blond hair and green eyes, and my father's cleft chin. Though it didn't show, I was physically very strong. I still ran daily and could bench-press nearly my own weight, which hovered around one twenty-five. I looked younger than I was, so much so that on those rare occasions when I bought beer, I always got carded.

I liked the quivering knot of apprehension that grew inside me while Jim warned me that the job could be dangerous. I knew that somewhere there were things happening that could give me back the feeling I had when I knelt at the starting line, ready to race, ready to explode. I wanted risk. I wanted excitement. And even though Pasadena wasn't Houston or New York, it was there, and I could start in two weeks.

I was too naïve to stop and think it through, too young to consider consequences. My eagerness was pathetic. Yes, I said, let me do this. Like a fool I said it. Like the ignorant, unthinking, and ridiculously sanguine little optimist that I was. I wanted the job.

Jim drove me to the shooting range so that I could be qualified to carry a weapon. I'd never even touched a gun before that muggy April afternoon, but he was a good teacher. Of the hundred rounds I fired, I missed the black only four times, and then only by centimeters. When I'd finished shooting, Jim pulled the target sheet down and looked at the holes clustered evenly in the midsection of the human-shaped silhouette.

"You're steady," he said. "You've got a great pattern. You don't pull to one side like most beginners I've seen."

He rolled the paper into a cylinder as we walked to his Plymouth, and when I reached for the door, he slipped his hand past mine and grabbed the handle.

"I've got every confidence in you," he said. "You'll make a good cop. All the same, when you're with me, I hope you'll permit me to be a gentleman." He opened the car door and stood holding it until I was seated, and then shut it carefully. I watched in the rearview mirror as he walked back to lock my target sheet in the trunk, and found myself thinking that the dates I'd been on in high school and college had all been with boys.

He came around and leaned in the driver's side window.

"So," he said, "what was that bullshit on your application, about a couple of joints in high school?"

"I tried it a few times," I said. "Everyone did."

"We're talking just between us now. You and me. Out front."

"That's it," I said. "Three or four times."

He popped open the door and slipped behind the wheel, and then leaned across me to open the glove box. He pulled out a palm-sized pistol and handed it to me. I was surprised by its weight.

"Twenty-five automatic," he said. "Easy to stash."

"It looks like a toy."

"You get hit and one of those suckers will bounce around inside you until it finds something solid enough to stop it. Friend of mine, ex–state agent by the name of Denny Dennison, got damn near blinded by one of those. Still carrying fragments in his head. It'll do damage all right."

I slipped the pistol into my purse, trying to seem calm.

"I hope you don't have plans for this evening," he said. "We'll drive into Houston. We've got plenty to talk about, and we might as well do it over dinner."

Things happened faster than I could keep track of during that first investigation. The Pasadena P.D. installed me in an apartment on the east side of town and Jim introduced me to my first informant, a speed-freak scooter nasty named Skip who was looking at automatic time for violating probation.

He was to introduce me to dealers, who would take his word that I was okay and sell to me. Jim would come by, usually well after midnight, to pick up evidence and fill out the paperwork. That was the plan. Jim estimated that the investigation would last about ninety days. The defendants would be arrested only after it was finished, after I had testified before a grand jury and indictments were issued.

I hadn't even been to the police academy yet.

*　　　*　　　*

Skip had to show me how to roll a joint. He brought an ounce of pot over the night after Jim introduced us and showed me how to sprinkle the leaf into a cigarette paper and roll it up. I was trying not to let him see how nervous I was, but I kept tearing the paper.

"Keep practicing," he said. "You got to be able to do this." Eventually, I managed to roll the entire ounce into joints.

"So you've passed Doobie Rolling 101," Skip said. "Wanna burn one?"

"I'd better pass."

"Captain Raynor said you knew what was happening."

I didn't know anything. Jim had said Skip would show me the ropes. He'd mentioned simulation, but hadn't explained how it was done.

Skip lit a joint and held it out at me.

"Relax," he said, "it's practice."

He watched carefully as I drew smoke into my mouth and held it there while I passed the joint back to him. I let the smoke out slowly, blowing air through my nose to make it look like I'd inhaled. I thought it was convincing. Skip took another hit and shook his head at me.

"You do that on the street," he said, "and I guarantee we'll both be up Shit Creek without a paddle."

Skip drove, leaving patches of rubber at each red light on the way to the Londonderry Apartments. His car was his life: a black '57 Chevy, heavily chromed, polished so bright it would burn your eyes on a sunny day.

The girl who answered the door was plain but pretty, about nineteen or twenty, with a pale, freckled face and long brown hair. She was dressed much as I was, with flared Levi's and a pullover top.

"Hey, Skipper," she said, opening the door wide and motioning us in.

"How's it going," Skip said. "I got a friend here who's in the market."

When the girl handed me the pot, I tried to look like a connoisseur, opening several baggies and sniffing at their contents. The smell was sweet, like fresh-mown hay. Finally I chose one and twisted up a joint as if I'd been doing it for years. I handed it to Skip, who struck a match against one seam of his jeans and inhaled so deeply it looked like he was trying to suck some kind of relief out of the thing. He took three or four quick small hits and passed it back to me. I held it in what I hoped was a casual manner, and put it to my lips.

When Jim came by late that night to pick up the evidence, I told him what Skip had said about my attempted simulation.

"The dude's exactly right," he said. "You'll get made in a stiff minute. Listen to what I'm saying here. *Simulation* is a word that comes in handy in court. We're out there to buy dope."

It was nearly three in the morning when Skip dropped me at my apartment. We'd been out on a deal, scored hash and some kind of speed. We were making buys regularly, and as the weeks went by I was starting to enjoy my job. I didn't have to think about what would happen after, and I chose not to. I went with Skip and bought dope and turned it over to Jim. I was one of the good guys, convinced that I was doing the right thing and working hard to take it all so easily in stride.

When I walked into the living room, there was Jim, sitting on the mattress beneath a *Wizard of Oz* poster I'd taped to the wall, rattling ice cubes in his empty glass.

I had done the apartment in post-hippie funk: the mattress on the living-room floor, posters of Humphrey Bogart, Blue Oyster Cult, Omar Sharif, a couple of cinderblock bookcases holding candles and paperbacks. I lit the candles and turned off the overhead light.

"Scored hash," I said. "And some speed. Brown and clear capsules. More scotch?"

"Sure." He handed me his glass. "Brown and clears? Probably Dexedrine." He lit a cigarette and tossed the pack to the mattress. "And bring me a side of water with that, would you?"

I stood holding his empty glass.

"Yeah," he said. "You look like you scored a little hash. Any good?"

"Seems to be," I said. I was cool about it. Stupidly cool. He knew I was high and I knew I was supposed to be high. It was part of my job.

"Wait'll you make a junkie," he said. "That's when things get real."

When I brought his drink back from the kitchen, he was pulling a small plastic package from his sock.

"You'll need to know about this," he said. He put the package on the coffee table. "You got any cotton balls?"

I brought some from the bathroom.

"Think you can handle this?" he asked.

"Handle what?" I said.

"I'm going to put a needle in my arm."

I was so calm it was disgusting. I wanted to handle things. I wanted to prove myself. He unwrapped the package and took out a syringe and a small cellophane packet of yellowish powder.

"A spoon," he said. "I forgot my spoon.

"A tablespoon," he called as I walked to the kitchen.

He bent the handle so that the bowl rested level on the

table and then he drew water into the syringe and squirted it into the spoon. He mixed some of the powder in.

"This is called cooking," he said. "The spoon and cotton and rig are sometimes referred to as works. If you don't have cotton you can use a piece of cigarette filter."

He struck a match and ran the flame under the spoon a few times, until the water bubbled.

"Okay," he said, drawing the word out long and slow. "You cook heroin, you don't cook coke. Some people cook speed, but mostly they don't."

He finished preparing the shot and then turned the syringe upside down and flicked his middle finger sharply against the plastic cylinder until air bubbles rose to the top. Then he slowly pressed the plunger until a small drop of liquid appeared on the tip of the needle.

"There it is," he said. "Ready to run. But it's a good idea to let it cool a moment. Shoot that shit now and you'll parboil your damn heart."

He looked around the room, focused on the braided leather belt I was wearing.

"Give me that," he said, shaking his head. "You're a fucking natural."

I watched as he strapped the belt around his biceps and pumped his fist. Large, ropelike veins rose up on his inner arm.

He picked up the syringe and slowly pushed in the needle.

"Okay, take the belt off," he said. His voice was husky.

Circulation. I had memorized it for biology class. A few months ago? Arteries and veins, capillaries, the heart. Gas and nutrient exchange. It would come in through the superior vena cava. Oxygen-depleted, carbon dioxide–loaded blood. To the pear-shaped, fist-sized heart. Heroin-rich blood to the heart. Cocaine-laden blood to the heart. To the lungs. To the brain.

"This I'm about to show you," he said, "is called registering."

He pulled on the plunger until bright red blood swirled into the cylinder, mixing with the cloudy fluid already in there.

"It's how a junkie knows he's got the needle in a vein. If you put the thing in too far, or not far enough, you just shoot the drugs into tissue. You'll still get a little buzz, much later, but nothing at all like you do on a mainline. Junkies get awful pissed if they miss."

He sat there like that, with the needle in his vein, his blood in the syringe, the syringe resting on his arm, for a very long moment. I looked carefully, saw the spiked ridge of the needle below the surface of his skin, saw the syringe moving ever so slightly with his pulse.

The process fascinated me—the ritual preparation, the religious intensity with which Jim laid out the instruments in order of use on the glass-topped coffee table, the anticipation of pleasure showing clearly on his face. I, with all of the enthusiasm and phony omnipotence that goes with being a rookie, persuaded myself in that moment that I could handle it, could handle anything. I sat there in the candlelit living room, staring at the needle, and refused to let myself be scared.

"What's in there?" I asked.

"It's just Cremora, but it looks a little like heroin and a lot like crystal meth. I thought it would be a good demonstration."

"Come on," I said. "You can't possibly inject that."

"No way. But I might, in a pinch. I might. I usually carry some with me."

Smooth, milky, Cremora-rich blood to the heart. Something was wrong, it would have to be fatal. Have to be. But Jim was a captain; he knew. The lesson was outrageous enough that I accepted it, though it left a queasy uneasiness floating in my stomach. I didn't know enough to judge for myself and could not help feeling that I did not want to know. Cops and dope. For the greater good.

"It ain't no lightweight thing," he said. "You're getting there. Sooner or later you're gonna run into this."

He looked at me closely, and then at the rig, and slid the syringe out. A dark red drop of blood beaded on his arm. He wiped it off with his forefinger and licked the finger clean.

"Let me just go wash all this stuff up," he said.

"There's alcohol in the bathroom." I got up to show him.

"Keep your seat, keep your seat, I'll find it."

He locked himself in and I heard water running. He was in there for several minutes, for what seemed to be a very long time. Finally I went to the door.

"You all right?" I asked.

He cleared his throat. "Fine, fine. Be right out." The same husky voice.

A few minutes later he sat back down on the mattress.

"One more refill," he said, raising his glass.

I brought him a scotch and he leaned back against the wall, one knee up, arm across knee, drink in one hand, cigarette in the other.

"Listen, this shooting business is heavy," he said, "but it's a thing where knowing how may save your life. You find yourself looking at a rig or a .45, you gotta take the rig. If you see that it's the only way to get out of a deal alive. It happens. You fix it yourself, and you let the dealer go first. A hot shot's as fast as a bullet." He reached to crush his cigarette into the ashtray. "All this crap about addiction, it's only a matter of how strong you are. I've seen agents been brought up after six or eight weeks hanging in shooting galleries and the dudes are plenty strung out, but you gotta get strong. You kick bedcovers for a week or so. You run a little temperature." His hand trembled when he set his drink on the carpet. "Then," he said, "you stand up on your feet and walk."

I must have looked like I didn't believe him.

"Hey," he said, "it's how it's done. Fucking heroin dealer won't split down with anyone, nobody, less he *knows* they're cool. It's business. It's the way it is. But you're stout for a chick, man, plenty stout, I know you'll handle it.

"You been putting in some long days, you just keep after it and you'll find the heavies." He leaned toward me, his shoulder so close to mine that I could feel heat. "You look really tense," he said quietly. "Why don't I give you a little old massage."

I hadn't been exposed. I didn't know the symptoms. I wanted him to know that I was strong, I was standup, that I could take anything. Part of me knew that it hadn't been Cremora, but he seemed okay, he hadn't metamorphosed into some strange and dangerous monster. He was sitting next to me on a mattress in my living room, sipping scotch. His eyes seemed more sharply focused, and he swallowed frequently and seemed ready to talk forever, but that was all. I wanted to believe it had only been a lesson, a little on-the-job training.

For weeks he'd been coming over almost every night, to pick up evidence, or else, as he put it, to make sure I hadn't been dragged off to Mexico by some dealer. He was protective of me, and I liked that, but, more important, I felt he believed in me. He told me he was getting hassled for putting a woman undercover. He didn't care, he said, he had confidence in me. When he left me each night to sleep there

alone, I lay in my bed and drifted off while thinking of him,
hoping he would enter my dreams.

I wanted the massage. I wanted him to touch me.

He began rubbing my neck, moving his hands in slow
circles across my shoulders and then down my back, and
his touch was even stronger than I had imagined. When
he reached my hips he turned me to him and began kissing
me, softly at first, biting my lips gently, then deeper, and
I couldn't stop what was happening, I couldn't and didn't
want to and knew I should and Jim kissed me until thought
was gone, until he had stripped away resistance and I was
falling, and he took my face in his hands and went gentle
again, kissing softly, with care, and then I felt the mattress
give next to me and he stood up quickly and walked to the
kitchen bar.

I sat up, trying to recover, feeling like I'd been pushed
out of a window. He stood silently for some time, his back
to me, his fingertips tucked into the pockets of his jeans.
I took a sip of his drink.

"Well," he said finally, turning to stare at me, "tell me
what we've got ourselves into here."

"It doesn't matter," I said, and then I was letting him
undress me, and he was kissing me again, and then inside,
inside and driving, and he raised himself, reached with one
arm to brace himself against the coffee table and watch our
bodies move.

"We'll bring the state boys in on this one," Jim said. His
tone was strictly business, as it always was when I called
him on the straightline. "I know just the man. Tell the asshole you're bringing your boyfriend with you. Best agent
in Texas."

"It's set up for tonight," I said. "At seven."

"He'll be at your place by six. Tall guy, big brown beard.

Rob Johnson. Good friend of mine. Call me when it's finished."

I had met Hayden, the dealer, a couple of days earlier, standing at the mailboxes beneath the stairwell that led to our shared landing. He told me he was studying theology and art history, and then he dropped his mail all over the sidewalk. When he bent to pick it up, a vial fell out of his pocket and I took a chance. Jim had told me, at dinner that first night in Houston, to ask for chemicals. I did, and Hayden went for it.

"Sure," he said. "If you're in the market for snow or acid, I can help you out."

Just like that. Ask and it shall be given to you.

The state man was indeed smooth. He walked into Hayden's apartment with me that night wearing six-hundred-dollar gray ostrich-skin boots and finger-combing his beard.

He sprawled on the couch like he owned the place, his boots shining to the point of glare, and patted the space next to him. I stood a moment longer, pretending to look at the religious prints that hung on the opposite wall, but actually trying to gauge Hayden's height and weight. Rob would be writing the report, and if he should ask, I wanted to be able to give an accurate description.

When I sat down, he slipped an arm across the sofa back, playing the boyfriend role, letting his hand rest gently on my shoulder. Hayden brought a Ziploc full of powder from his hall closet.

"Not trying to brag," he said, "but this is some of the best I've ever run across."

"Let's check it out," Rob said. He wrapped his arms around my neck and nibbled on my ear, whispering, "Follow my lead, I'll walk you right through."

Hayden took a framed print from the wall and set it carefully on the coffee table. He spooned some powder onto the glass and began forming it into lines, following the curvature of the robes worn by the saints in the painting.

"This was done by a guy named Giovanni Di Paolo," he said. "I mean, it's only a print, a poster, you know, but it's called *Paradise,* and I dig it."

Rob raised his heavy brown eyebrows at me, and then shrugged and began rolling a hundred-dollar bill into a tight tube. He edged forward on the couch, leaning toward the table, twisting and retwisting the bill, and then he looked over at me and winked. I had to have looked frightened. I must have. I was trying to hide it, trying to act like this was something I did all the time, but I was flat-out scared of this stuff, this cocaine. Scared, but I wanted to try it. I wanted to know why it was such an item, why everybody was talking about it. And on top of that I was wondering if this were some kind of test, if Jim had brought in Rob to find out whether I could handle the buy. I felt incredibly thick, and wondered if I was perhaps being a bit paranoid about things, but we weren't dealing with pot here. I was sitting next to a state cop, scared out of my mind and wondering if it was a trap, if he was going to watch me do the stuff and then *arrest* me for it.

And I was doing my best to be so very, very cool about it all.

Rob lifted the print to his lap, leaned over and snuffed up two of the lines. I watched him and I didn't believe what I was seeing. I thought he must have been simulating, but I saw the stuff go into the cylinder of the C-note, I saw the little flakes of cocaine that started to fall out of his nostrils before he tilted his head back and sniffed deeply. And I saw the pleasure in his eyes.

Then he handed the print to me and I saw that he was

as nervous as I was. We didn't know each other, we'd only just met that evening, and here he had laid himself wide open.

The powder hit the back of my throat and numbed it almost immediately. Even before Hayden had finished his lines, I was feeling the first overwhelmingly pleasant rush of what psychologists call euphoria.

And Rob was sitting there next to me with the slightest kind of smile on his face, almost hidden by his beard, but very much there.

Back at my apartment, he spooned some powder onto the kitchen counter and used a credit card to form the lines.

"You were great," he said. "I don't know what all Raynor has told you, but I think you'll do just fine."

"What he's told me," I said, "is be anything you have to be to make the case and keep your ass from getting shot."

He ran his eyes over me and pointed at the rails.

"Yeah," he said, "we damn sure don't want that."

"I was quoting him."

"I'm sure you were," he said, smiling and handing me the C-note. "I'm certain that was a direct quote."

I rolled the bill until it was tight and leaned toward the cocaine on the counter. I'd never felt anything like it. Ever. The Immaculate Conception in powder form. And I was doing it because someone had to. I was making this personal sacrifice. I was rationalizing my ass off.

"You see," Rob said, cutting out more rails, "it's like this. We're out here risking our lives to keep the fucksticks off the streets. But the job has a few fringe bennies."

TWO

DEEP NIGHTS ON PATROL, I STRUGGLED TO STAY awake and tried not to scrape too much rubber off the squad car tires. The investigation was finished, the arrests made. I'd been to the academy, and now I was learning what ordinary patrol meant. It was impossible, some nights, not to nod behind the wheel. Cruising down some quiet nighttime residential street, I would feel the bite of my tie clip in my neck and then, from the other side of dream, hear the tires scudding gently against the curb. The slow, scraping sound usually woke me before I actually bumped onto the sidewalk, and I would stop the car, get out, and walk around it three or four times, shaking my head and squeezing my eyes rapidly, trying to get conscious.

Deep nights is the shift when the law-abiders are tucked safely in their beds, abandoning the streets to those who move in shadow with burglary tools or weapons in their pockets. It was a thing felt, like a change in air pressure, a busy hum of activity beneath the black morning hours trailing quietly after midnight.

It took almost a week to adjust to the nighttime workday, and shifts rotated, from deep nights to days to evenings, every four weeks. The first three days after a change were a lesson in disorientation, my body didn't know if it wanted

eggs for dinner or pizza for breakfast. Whenever I patrolled
a district close to my apartment, I took my meals there
rather than at restaurants. I found the stares of civilians
disconcerting.

In the months since the department had rounded up the
defendants on the dope buys Rob and I had made, I'd seen
Jim only in the hallways at the station. He had called once,
the night before my academy graduation, to say he would
attend. I spent an hour that night polishing my shoes and
the next day went through the ceremony with twenty-nine
men, searching the small crowd of spectators for Jim's face.
He never showed.

Whenever I chanced to meet him at the station, he always said hello, courteously, but as though he were acting
in an official capacity or something. I took it to mean that
those nights in my apartment had been, for him, a matter
of opportunity seized. It left me aching and confused, but
I kept quiet, I gave him no clue that I was feeling abandoned. He was a captain in CID, and I was now a lowly
patrolman, unwilling to risk humiliation in the pursuit of
what I had hoped was a relationship. I felt sometimes as
though he were testing me, waiting to see if I would stay
straight after spending the first three months of my employ-
ment smoking dope and snorting coke. That wasn't really
a problem. I kept it in perspective, looked on it as having
been part of my job. I really didn't miss the drugs. But I
missed working dope. I missed being with Jim.

If we passed in the hall he would wince a brief sort of
half wink at me and say, "Keep your head up, Officer." I
would give attention to some aspect of my uniform, shift
my Sam Browne or straighten my tie, and nod politely.
"Always," I would say, and then he would be gone, talking
in low tones to a lesser detective at his side.

*   *   *

I had rotated back to deep nights when the first of our drug cases went to trial. The D.A.'s office had spent months trying to plea bargain with Hayden Smith's attorneys. I was no longer part of it. Most of the other twenty or so defendants had taken probation deals, but Hayden wanted his day in court.

I finished my shift at seven, went home to shower and dress and sit on the couch, waiting for Jim and Rob to pick me up. I should have been exhausted, but the idea of actually going to trial had my eyes wide open.

On the way to the Harris County Courthouse, I sat in the backseat, listening to Jim and Rob talk about some deal or other. I envied them. Patrol, I'd discovered, was boring, mind-bendingly pedestrian.

Jim stopped talking suddenly and turned to pass Rob's case reports back to me. "You might want to take a look at these," he said. I took them and began reading. They were clean, very clean, with no mention of mirrors or rolled C-notes or cops with the sniffles.

We waited in the state's witness room, a closet-size place empty but for five light green chairs and a huge floor-stand ashtray. The air smelled of dried sweat and wet cigars. Rob was pacing back and forth while Jim sat next to me, tapping his fingers lightly on a wooden chair arm. I concentrated on the reports, memorizing dates and times.

"Relax, girl," Jim finally said. "The D.A. will ask you exactly the same things he talked about this morning."

"And the defense attorney?"

Rob kicked a chair.

"Fuck him," he said. "He's trying to keep a damn dope dealer out of jail. He's as much a scum as the dopers themselves. Ought to put them all in Huntsville." He adjusted his tie and sat down.

A few minutes later an ancient bailiff rapped on the door and poked his face into the room.

"Agent Johnson," he said, "you're up."

Rob tucked a few loose hairs behind his ears. His ponytail trailed halfway down the back of his navy pinstripe jacket.

"Time to put old Hayden in the joint," he said, and gave us a vague salute as he ducked out.

"Too bad you can't be in there," Jim said. "You want to see someone who knows how to testify."

"I'll be happy just to get through it."

"Hey," he said, "take it easy. The dude sold to you. He's the one on trial. You get up there and answer the questions and then you walk out."

"But what about, you know, doing the stuff? Does that come under lawful discharge of duty or something?" I wasn't sure why I was asking. I knew the answer, that much I had learned, but still I wanted to hear it said. Perhaps I needed to be relieved of responsibility.

He stood up and propped a foot on the chair. "Look," he said, "everybody knows what goes down. All the way up to the judge, they know how it works. But nobody wants to hear about it. You walked Johnson in, this guy Smith sold you the dope, you paid for it and walked out. You'll have everything right in front of you, and if it's not in the paperwork, you just say you don't recall."

"I'm concerned a little," I said. "Perjury."

"Baby," he said, "let me tell you something here, and by the time you come out of there you'll know what I'm talking about." He rubbed a hand across his forehead, pinched his eyebrows tiredly. "They're going to ask you some questions. The D.A. will be all polite and courteous and everything. The defense attorney may be the same. Or he may be a real asshole and come with a full frontal attack.

Either way, you sit there, you answer professionally, and you don't lose your cool."

"Somehow I feel like I just did six lines of pink Peruvian."

"Talk about get-down testimony." He patted his suit pockets. "Hey, you'll handle it. Everybody in there lies. They've all got something to hide. The goddamn attorneys lie, just by the way they ask questions. We're here to put this boy in the joint. You go in there, and you answer. And no, it isn't the whole fucking truth so help you God, but it takes the dealers off the streets."

He lit a cigarette and sat down again and things got quiet. An airplane passed somewhere overhead, droning in the winter afternoon. I felt sweat curling down my sides.

I would walk into the courtroom and sit down in the chair and lie. Not about the deal, but about taking drugs with Hayden. We'd bought the dope, he had sold it. I'd seen twelve-year-olds coming out of his apartment, tucking things into their pockets. I would lie because it was necessary. I concentrated on the reports.

When I looked up, Jim had his elbows on his knees, his chin resting on one fist, and he was watching me.

"How's patrol?" he asked. "You liking it okay?"

"It's been five months of dull."

"Yeah, well, you got spoiled. Anything's dull after narcotics. You'll be in Criminal before you know it. But you got to do your time in the harness."

"I'm taking courses again. Only part time, six credits this term. Criminal Investigation and French."

"French?" He shifted in his chair. "Who you planning to *parlez vous* with?"

"Nobody in particular."

"Hell, girl, you ought to go on and try for law school. Some of the D.A.'s I've seen, you'd put them to shame."

He started to light another cigarette, but changed his mind and slipped the pack back into his coat pocket. "So. You're staying busy?"

"I work, I sleep, I go to school."

"No romance? Come on."

"I miss working narcotics, if you know what I mean. I have lunch with Rob every once in a while."

"I thought so," he said. He took out a cigarette. "I had a feeling he might be hanging around."

"Nobody else is. The guys on my shift act like I'm some sort of pariah. Like they're scared of me."

"Well what'd you expect? You made more felonies in your first three months than they have in their entire careers. They're jealous."

"They're okay about it," I said. "Most of them anyway. But I am not one of the gang. Not sure I want to be." I realized that I had rolled my copies of the reports into a cylinder and began trying to flatten them back out.

"What the hell," Jim said. "Rob's wife knows all about him. Couldn't care less. Nothing wrong with an occasional lunch."

I got up and walked to the windows. The January sky was cold blue and crowded with the glass and steel of downtown Houston. Ant-people below, winding along sidewalks. I turned to Jim. "Pardon me, Captain," I said, "but sometimes you can be a real bastard."

"Yeah," he said, "you got that absolutely right. Sometimes I really can." He leaned back in his chair and let his arms fall over the sides. "What the hell. It keeps life interesting."

"What was that about?" I asked. "What we had going there for awhile, was that just, I don't know, what was it?"

"I've got three big cases working right now. Things have

been busy. And I'm catching heat from the Chief." He slid down and kicked his legs out in front of him.

"What kind of heat?"

"You know Sergeant Quill?"

"He's been at a briefing or two."

"Yeah, well he 'suggested' to the Chief that I'm dipping into evidence. Claims he's seen me high. The asshole. Never made a decent case in his life. Hell, he couldn't track a damn bleeding elephant across a flat acre of fresh-fallen snow. But he wants to be a captain, he wants to run CID."

"That has nothing to do with what I'm asking you," I said. "Do you even have a clue what it's been like?"

He stood up and draped his arms over my shoulders and backed me toward the corner of the room, next to the door.

"I know exactly what it's been like." He lifted his arms and put his hands against the wall on either side of me, and then he leaned down and kissed me. "It's been like not having enough air," he said quietly. "It's been like choking." He kissed me again and then I felt his fingers pressing something into my palm. "You just swallow this," he said, "and you'll do fine up there on the stand."

The door opened and he stepped away abruptly and walked toward the windows, leaving me standing there in the corner, like a child hiding. I forced the Valium down as Rob walked in, kicking the door shut behind him.

"Man," he said, "the dude calls himself a district attorney. He's worthless. Screwed the evidence up completely." He was hopped up, rolling on the balls of his feet and swinging his arms front to back. "Couldn't keep the cases straight, had the dates all confused, it was pathetic." He walked over and slapped Jim on the back. "Be glad you're not testifying on this one," he said. "The man is incompetent." Jim glanced at me and turned to stare hard at Rob.

"What the hell does it matter, Johnson, as long as you're taking good care of my trooper here."

"Hey," Rob said, "how about a little slack?" He took a step back and jammed his hands into his pockets. "It's not like you've been around or anything."

I was saved by the bailiff, who leaned into the room just then and said, "Cates. Officer Cates."

I followed him down the hall and through the heavy courtroom doors. I hoped that I looked composed. I hoped that the Valium would kick in quickly.

Jim was asleep when I returned, folded into the chair with his chin on his chest. Rob stood at the windows, drawing miniature suns into the corner of each pane, using his fingertip to carve short, jagged rays in the grime.

"We're excused," I said.

Jim pulled his head up slowly and rubbed his face, blinking. He stood and stretched, saw me, dropped his arms. "What the hell's wrong with you?" he said.

Rob began wiping his finger on a chair back.

"Nothing," I said. "You were right."

"About what?" Rob asked. "What happened? That piss-poor excuse for a prosecutor lose it for us?"

"No," I said, "I don't think so."

"So why the face?" Rob asked.

"Unbelievable," I said. "Hayden's attorney got up and accused me of, are you ready for this, being a temptress. He said I *lured* Hayden to a dope party and did a striptease so he'd sell me drugs."

Jim glanced at Rob and then put an arm around my shoulders.

"You survive it otherwise?"

"Did he try to say you'd slept with the dude?" Rob asked.

"No," I said. "Just used the temptress bit. I didn't know people still thought that way."

Jim was smiling as he walked to the door. "Sounds to me," he said, "like you got off light."

At my apartment, I called the evening dispatcher and asked her to phone me at ten to make sure I was awake for my shift. I set my alarm for nine thirty and buried myself beneath the sheets, trying for a few hours sleep before I had to go out again.

When the phone rang, I was in the middle of a dream featuring a jazz band in the jury box, and there I was, up on the defense table, dancing and peeling off my uniform while the lawyers and judge applauded and Hayden Smith sat staring at the handcuffs on his wrists. Jim was toward the back of the courtroom, trying to climb over the benches, but was stuck there somehow, calling out to the judge, "Objection, Your Honor, objection. I have an objection here."

I took two cups of coffee into the briefing room and sat drinking them numbly while the sergeant read out assignments. When he'd finished with instructions, he said he had a special announcement.

"The first of those drug cases made by our very own Officer Kristen Cates went to trial today," he said. "I got word this evening that the defendant, Hayden Smith, was found guilty of V.S.C.S.A.—that's Violation of the State Controlled Substances Act for those of you who don't know your penal code. The jury gave him a total of fifty-seven years."

There were applause and whistles, and the sergeant raised his coffee cup to me. "Congratulations, Cates," he said, "hell of a job."

I thanked him and drained my cup; I nodded quietly to

the men around me, but inside of me, inside I felt something shift, something slip off center. A man. What *man,* a guy my own age, was in prison looking at fifty-seven years for being a minor-league dealer, selling a few grams of powder. And I had helped put him there. Our lives had collided, and I had knocked him into a world full of dirt and grinning ignorance, a place of gleaming metallic violence and nightscreams. I could not fathom what he must have been feeling toward me. But it was there and it was real. Sitting in the briefing room being applauded, I could feel his hatred seep into my body like disease, become part of me. And the fold in my brain that was bent on emotional survival knew that the only way to defend against a rage that strong was to return it in kind.

Deep nights became days, days became evenings, evenings became deep nights. Pasadena, Texas. What was I doing in Pasadena, Texas? Every twenty-eight we rotated shifts. Month after month. In the women's locker room, we referred to the change as the period from hell. There were three of us, one for each shift. We didn't know each other; we passed in doorways at seven, three, or eleven.

I worked enough overtime to be able to take a few hours off to go to classes in Houston when I needed to. In the Criminal Investigation course, a detective from the Dallas Police Department visited and told war stories about the Kennedy assassination.

"The crime scene was a bust from the start," he said. "Cops were running all over the Depository, stuffing things in their pockets, trying to grab souvenirs."

I drove home after class remembering fourth grade and how the nuns had herded us all into church to get on our knees and count rosary beads while we prayed for a dying president. Monsignor O'Brian stood on the altar and told us how at that very moment High Mass was being said all over the world, no matter the hour, and I pressed the beads into my fingers and prayed as hard as I could, and thought maybe God would pay special attention because every Catholic in the world was asking for the same thing at the same time, asking him to save one of their own.

When I got home I studied French for a few hours. It was almost nine when the sun was gone, and then it was ten and time once more to buckle myself into uniform and head to the station.

The shift was dead, the radio quiet. The moonlight reflecting off the pale cement streets and beige lawns turned everything gray-white, the color of caliche rock. I drove down alleys with my headlights out, searching for burglars and conjugating French verbs.

Midway down one alley, I passed an unfenced backyard strewn with sleeping bags. A group of teenage girls sat wearing nightgowns at a picnic table on the patio, their hands fluttering about their faces as they talked and giggled in the April night. One of them saw my squad and pointed and the others turned to stare. I waved and rolled by, letting the car idle slowly down the alley.

I was sleepy, and felt decades away from slumber parties and teenage romance. I wanted to be home in bed. I thought it might be nice to smoke a joint. Just one. Just this once. Hit the streets and score just for the fun of it. My belt was cutting into my back and my face was getting that 3 A.M. numb feeling that meant wake up or start hitting curbs.

I requested a 10-10 and drove to my apartment. I was thinking about a can of ravioli and a twenty-minute nap, but when I walked into my room there was Jim, sitting on the bed, leaning against the wall, a half-empty bottle of vodka resting against his thigh. I noticed a screwdriver shining on the carpet next to the bedroom window.

"Good evening, Officer," he slurred. "That uniform looks damn good on you. Wanna frisk me? I feel like being frisked." He let out a sad breath and his head fell forward. He was a mess, his hair frizzed and dank, one shirttail hanging out, his gun stuffed down the front of his jeans. I pulled it out and put it on the nightstand and eased him away from the wall until he was lying on his side. He opened his eyes suddenly and reached up to touch my badge.

"You haven't heard," he whispered loudly.

"I don't hear much from your direction these days," I said.

"No," he moaned quietly. "I wanted to see you. I wanted to talk to you. Do you know?"

"What I know is that you seem to come strolling in whenever you want. And then you disappear. I mean, when did we last talk? At the Smith trial? You were concerned about Sergeant Quill I recall. How're things with Quill?"

"He didn't prove shit. Nothing to prove." Jim struggled to sit up. "But I resigned today. Quit. Had enough of this bullshit department."

I didn't know what to say. I unbuckled my gun belt and put it on top of the dresser.

"It must really be easy for you, huh? Everything just easy. A matter of taking a hike."

"Hey," he said sharply, "don't tell me about easy."

"Then what should I tell you about? What do you want to hear?"

"That you're with me. That you understand why I'm going. I have to. I know a few things, girl. Maybe my daddy wasn't always around, but I respected him. And one thing he *did* teach me about was taking care of my name."

He offered me the bottle and I sat down and took a swallow, enjoying the burn.

"Yeah," he drawled drunkenly. "My old man. Worked his ass off throwing chain on the rigs, until one day he missed his timing." He dragged a hand across his mouth. "Lost it. Chain broke, flew loose like a bat out of hell and just flat killed his best buddy."

"What does that have to do with you quitting?"

"Big Spring's a small town, people started speculating, saying he was drunk and that's why it happened. He couldn't live with it. So he split." I passed the bottle back to him and he took a long swallow. "Said he was going someplace where his name wasn't muddied."

"You're telling me you're leaving because some lard-ass sergeant is on your case? You expect me to believe this?"

"I'm getting the hell out of Pasadena," he said.

"Letting Quill chase you off."

"Listen. Rob tells me they're hiring in Beaumont. He spoke to the chief over there, a guy named Nettle. Looking for somebody to put under. Long-term investigation. Wants to interview me."

"So shoot straight, Jim. You're going because it's a chance to work undercover. Don't come at me with this muddied-name garbage."

"It's ninety miles east," he said. "You could be there in an hour and a half."

I didn't answer.

When my thirty minutes were gone I picked up my radio and checked back on duty while sitting on the bed with Jim's head in my lap. He didn't say he loved me, or would miss me, or anything. Maybe he thought I didn't need to hear it. Maybe he thought I knew. I stroked his hair and rubbed his back until he began to snore softly, and then I walked back out to my car to drive the deserted streets and rattle shopping-center doors until dawn.

THREE

I N A DARKENED CLASSROOM IN AUSTIN, I SAT WATCH-ing colorful slides as they flashed onto a large screen.

A round yellow tablet, speckled golden, an autumn kind of yellow against a warm orange background.

"Oxycodone," the lecturer drawled from the rear of the room. "Brand name Percodan. Used as a painkiller. On the streets, a downer. No illicit manufacture that we know of, most dealers get it by walking scripts, but there's probably cartons of the things being sold out the back door at the factory."

On the screen, large, round, white tablets spilled out of a brown pharmaceutical bottle onto a field of blue.

"Methaqualone. A sleeper. Very popular, goes for as much as twelve bucks a tablet on the street. Might be called Ludes, or Quays. Supposed to knock you on your ass." A muffled laugh filled the room.

A mound of shiny pink tablets scattered on a white table, briefly, then a close-up of a lone bright pill, Day-glo pink against a yellow background.

I shifted in my chair and saw a line of male faces glowing in the pink light, staring at the screen from the row of desks behind me.

"Phenmetrazine hydrochloride," the lecturer said. "Pre-ludin. This one can bring fifteen, sometimes twenty on the streets. It's a diet pill, very potent speed. Supposed to be an aphrodisiac. Used intravenously after a very elaborate process to extract the ingredients into liquid. Only connoisseur junkies know how."

Two hours of this stuff. Alton had been right. With one investigation under my belt and a scant ten months in patrol, I was headed for detective. And this time they were actually giving me some in-service training before I took on my new job.

A pile of yellow powder, small wax-paper packets, a syringe, red plastic cap off, needle shining against a green background.

"Diamorphine hydrochloride. Heroin. Sold by weight. We'll be devoting an entire class session to this one later on in the week."

Slides and lectures. I knew of these drugs, had bought some of them. But that first investigation had been, except for the cocaine buys on Hayden, mostly pot cases, embarrassments. I'd made a couple of acid buys, and some Valium and diet pills. The one heroin buy I'd managed didn't involve using the stuff. I'd sat in a kitchen until the connection showed with the dope and then I paid the city's money and ran. I'd been scared of it.

Then, white powder on a triple beam scale. Behind it, plastic baggies full, powder spilling out of one torn baggie onto a smooth black surface. Stark. Clean. This I recognized immediately. This I knew.

"Benzoylmethyl ecognine, a white crystalline alkaloid used by such luminaries as Pope Leo XIII, Massenet, Gounod, Herman Goering, and Sigmund Freud."

Someone behind me whispered, "What's a luminary?" A voice answered, "Fuck if I know."

"Cocaine. Fast becoming the drug of choice. Some folks

mix it with heroin and shoot the blend. It's called speedbal-
ling. A regular chemical roller coaster."

The lights came on.

The captain said, "Let's take a break, get some coffee.
We'll start again in fifteen minutes."

We stood blinking and squinting from the sudden fluorescent brightness, and filed slowly out toward the vending
machines in the cafeteria.

"I wouldn't mind trying some of that Preludin shit,"
someone said, laughing nervously.

In the late afternoon, after a lecture on the illicit manufacture of methamphetamine (Mix phenyl-2-propanone, hy-
droxyl amine, methanol, hydrogen, sodium acetate,
palladium black, potassium hydroxide, ether, sulfuric acid,
lithium aluminum hydride, and formaldehyde, shake well,
hope it doesn't explode, and come out with a pound or two
of crank, crystal meth, yellow dog, one-tenth of a gram will
wire you up for a good twenty-four, and you can sell it for
two grand an ounce when the market's up), I sat in the dayroom at the north end of the dorm.

It was a semimilitary set up, the Department of Public
Safety Academy, where the State of Texas trained its Highway Patrol recruits and conducted special seminars for city
police officers and sheriffs' deputies from throughout the
country. Visiting officers were assigned two to a room, each
room furnished with a pair of army bunks and a small writing table. Because I was the only woman in the class, I had
a room of my own.

In the dayroom, an oblong lounge with a ceiling-
mounted color television in one corner and four or five
couches scattered about, I sat below a sepia-tone picture
of Lone Wolf Gonzaulles, who made a glorious portrait in
his battered brown Stetson, wearing ammunition criss-

crossed on his chest. On a brass plate, bolted to the bottom of the wormwood frame, were the words ONE RIOT, ONE RANGER.

The man who sat next to me in class, a blue-jeaned sheriff's deputy from Midland, walked in and saw me staring at the portrait.

"Good old Lone Wolf," he drawled. "Those were the days, now, weren't they."

"When men were men," I said. "Shoot first and ask questions later."

He shook his head and chuckled. "A few of us are going over to The Chase for a beer or two. Wanna come?"

"No thanks," I said. "Have fun."

I listened as their voices faded down the corridor. Then I went to my room and wrote a letter to Jim, telling him of my promotion and how I hoped soon to be working narcotics again. I told him how I missed him, that I wanted him to come back. And when I had told him everything, I sat staring at the letter for a long time. He wouldn't want to hear it. He was in Beaumont, on the streets, doing what he loved to do. I ripped it into the smallest pieces possible and tossed the whole mess into the wastebasket.

I grabbed my keys and drove to Memorial Stadium at U.T. The track was crowded with joggers, most of them wearing some combination of orange and white, trotting easily in the June evening. I took off my tennis shoes and walked slowly around lane eight. The springy, nubbed rubber surface was still in perfect condition, as it had been at the state meet near the end of my senior year in high school. I'd never been on a rubber track before, and it had been like running on a giant pencil eraser. If the rules hadn't forbidden it, I'd have run my event barefoot. I used to imagine, when I was doing the distances in training, that I was an Indian, a woman warrior clad in animal skins and running without effort across the plains of Texas, carrying a message to the chief of a distant tribe, a warning that would give him time to prepare for the attack of the white man.

They were killing themselves that summer in Pasadena, the workingmen, the ones who earned a living by laying bricks, unloading ships, pouring pavement that would become highway number something to somewhere. They were swallowing pills, shooting themselves, dangling from rough-hewn nooses in their garages. I was learning that suicide, like the common cold, is highly contagious. Somebody gets a bright idea and suddenly everybody's doing it. They always seem to come in bunches.

One electrician even rigged up a contraption that zapped him into a state of heavenly bliss via 220 volts. There were nine of them in the space of six and a half weeks, and all but one had been white males, ages forty to fifty-six, all but one of them lived in the north part of town. Around the office we started calling it Lemmingsville.

The incident reports listed each and every one as a suicide. I was not so sure, although I had followed up some of the cases myself. I didn't think anyone was murdered, but I wasn't convinced that they were all victims of intentional self-slaughter.

The Fourth of July was the final big bang for two of our good citizens. That was the day the electrician strapped a couple of copper panels to his bare skin, just about kidney level, connected the wires to a plug, sat down on his living-room floor and pushed the plug into the wall outlet. This was no sloppy job. His electrical work would have borne the UL stamp of approval.

My third day in CID, I had worked what appeared to be a suicide, but the detective who was training me had explained that the victim was one of that special breed of autoerotic: folks who chose to enhance their sexual pleasure by shutting off their oxygen supply while jerking off. In that case, the slip knot had failed. But since this guy still had his trousers on, I had to assume I was looking at a straight suicide, not a sexual accident.

With victim number two there was no question of intent. He stood in front of his refrigerator and bit down on the barrel of a .357, splattering a large portion of his parietal lobe onto the kitchen wall.

I smelled the blood as soon as I walked in the front door. All of the lights were on, and someone in the back part of the house was whistling "Good-night, Irene." The strong scent of blood does something to your body. It is nothing you can control, it just happens. And no matter how hard you try to convince yourself to stay calm, the physical reactions come. I walked toward the whistling, trying to prepare myself for what I would see, and even though I knew there was no danger I could feel the hairs on my scalp rising, I could hear my own pulse above the whistling noise, I swear I could feel air pressing against my skin and I couldn't swallow fast enough to keep up with my own salivary glands. The smell of blood doesn't burn the nose, it invades your whole body, takes it to a separate level of mortal awareness.

Coy Mason, the Crime Scenes man, was doing the whistling. He was standing on the kitchen counter, leaning on the top of the refrigerator with a pair of tweezers in his hand, plucking a single black hair from the acoustical tile of the kitchen ceiling.

"Amazing," he said, and scratched his balding head. "It is just amazing what a .357 can do. Drove a single goddamn hair clean into the ceiling."

The body was slumped against the refrigerator in a puddle of blood that almost covered the white linoleum kitchen floor. Most of the back of the guy's head was gone. He was wearing jungle fatigue pants and a green T-shirt.

"How'd you get here so fast?" I asked.

"Oh, you know," Coy said, "heard it on the radio."

I was certain that Coy spent every waking moment clutching his radio, praying for deaths to investigate. He was never happier than when he was in a room with a dead body.

The ambulance crew arrived a few minutes after I did and loaded the victim onto a spotless white stretcher. When they had gone I walked through the house. There was an empty bottle of Seconal on the nightstand, prescribed to Todd Williams. Next to that was a picture of the body in the kitchen, presumably Todd, taken at some moment in the past when he was posing with three other guys in fatigues in front of a thatch-roofed hut. On the floor of the closet I found a grocery sack half full of dirt-brown marijuana. Other than that, everything looked as it should. His toothbrush and razor were on the counter in the bathroom, a bottle of shampoo sat opened on the edge of the bathtub. There were wrinkled clothes folded on a chair in the corner of the bedroom, some ironing maybe. A recent *Playboy* was tossed on the floor next to the bed, opened to Miss June. It was a lived-in room. I walked back to the kitchen.

"There's a note," Coy said. "Next to that package of Mr. Chips on the counter there. The cookies are stale."

I picked up the note.

Sorry about the mess, but you cops are nothing but glorified garbage collectors anyway.

Todd Williams, if he was in fact victim number two, was a keen observer. A real poet. I hadn't quite been able to tap into it until that moment, hadn't understood what it was about what I did for a living that left me feeling like a highway trash-picker, stumbling around bar ditches stabbing at gum wrappers with a nail-on-a-stick while happy motorists whizzed by emptying their litter bags onto the road. I found tracking burglars and rapists fascinating, but Todd was exactly right. I was a garbage collector, scraping waste off the streets and dumping it into a system that prospered on trash.

I was part of it, and suddenly it all seemed very small.

Apart from the suicides, which involved little or no investigation, the hottest case going lately was The West Side Weenie Wagger, a white male, mid-thirties, who got his kicks displaying his penis to sixth-grade girls on their way home from summer vacation Bible school. This guy was waiting around at just the right times and in just the right places to catch the kiddies as they skipped home, Bibles in hand. He never said anything, at least nothing that the young witnesses could remember, and the truth is it wouldn't have mattered much if they had been able to quote him. The detective working the case didn't care if he ever caught The Wagger. "Investigator" W. I. Whilaby, as he preferred to be called, was the man who sat at his desk with an I'D RATHER BE FARMING bumper sticker stuck on the wall behind him while he listened to C&W and shuffled papers from one pile to another. There were twenty-eight cases of indecent exposure fitting the M.O. of The Wagger, and W.I. kept them in a neat stack on the left side of his desk. He said it was harmless. No one got hurt, and the schoolgirls seemed able to laugh it off. It was their parents who wanted something done, and a nice Saturday afternoon lynching would have suited them just fine.

I wasn't on the case. Sergeant Quill was using his authority to keep the bane of the office, his only female detective, tracing stolen hubcaps and writing suicide reports. But I knew that sooner or later the lieutenant would step in and tell W.I. to get off his duff and do something. He might even call him by his given name, Welcome Israel, the mention of which in W.I.'s presence was good for at least a minor scuffle.

It turned out that I missed the fireworks, but when I got back to the office after working the suicides I found the stack of Wagger reports on my desk. There was a note from the lieutenant also: *Need to close this one out.*

I was scheduled to be off for the next two days, but had nothing planned. I stayed late, well past eleven, fiddling with paperwork until the office was deserted. When everyone was gone, I dictated the report on Todd Williams's suicide, wondering as I did so if the Black Cats, Roman candles, and cherry bombs exploding all over Pasadena would be audible on the tape. I was labeling the cassettes when the phone rang.

I could hear when I picked up that someone was on the line, but there was no response when I answered.

"Detective Cates," I said again. Still no answer. I listened for a moment longer, and was about to hang up when Jim's voice came over the line.

"What are you up to?"

"Paperwork," I said.

"No, really," he said, "what's happening."

"Two suicides and a mess of indecent exposures. Thrilling stuff."

"You should come down."

"You making any cases?"

"A few. Nothing major yet. It's beautiful down here. You'd like it."

"You're inviting me?"

"I miss you."

"I'm off tomorrow," I said. "See you then."

We hung up and I finished labeling the cassettes and left them on the secretary's desk. And then I did something I had never before even considered. I went to Coy's office and pulled a handful of pot out of the brown paper bag I'd confiscated from Williams's closet. On my way home, I stopped at a 7-Eleven and bought a packet of rolling papers.

The next day, I caught The Wagger, but not through skill or hard work. I had planned to be on the road to Beaumont by nine, but the dispatcher called just after seven to say that Patrol had a peeping tom in custody, and that he fit the description given by the schoolgirls. She connected me to book-in and I asked Coy to get me a good picture of the guy before they released him on bond.

"I'll have it for you this afternoon," he said.

I called Jim, trying to keep disappointment from my voice, and told him I couldn't make it until the following week. He sounded as though I'd woken him.

By four o'clock I had positive I.D. from four different victims. I had selected seven photos of men who resembled The Wagger from the big box of shots that Coy kept in his office. Each witness pointed immediately, with absolute certainty, to the peeping tom, who turned out to be a peeping Albert Ashbey, computer consultant.

I did the required paperwork, went to the city magistrate and got the warrant. I went to pick up Mr. Ashbey in an unmarked car, but brought along a harness bull in case there was trouble.

There wasn't. His wife stood on the wall-to-wall carpet in the living room of their home, weeping quietly while the patrolman handcuffed her bear-size husband. I read Miranda to him and we ducked out of there before Mrs. Ashbey could comprehend completely what was going on and get vehement. At one point I almost started to believe her.

She touched one slender finger to her husband's cheek and looked at him with tears rolling unashamedly down her face and I began to wonder if, after all, the schoolgirls might be mistaken. It could happen. It happened all the time. My reliable eyewitnesses might have been feeling pressure to identify, might have talked themselves into certainty.

When patrol finished booking Ashbey, for the second time in a single day, they brought him to my office. He sat quietly in front of my desk, in tennis shorts and sport shirt.

I thumbed the stack of offense reports and offered him coffee. I wondered what Jim was doing.

"No thank you," he said.

"Mr. Ashbey," I said, "we'd like to get this cleared up."

"I didn't do it," he said. He ran a hand up his face, chin to eyebrows, and then pushed his mud-brown hair back off his forehead.

"I've got a positive I.D. from four people already," I said. "It's only a matter of bringing the others in to look at the pictures and then I'll have more."

He started to cry, a thin puddle of tears appearing at his eye rims, but he pressed his thumbs across them and then blinked several times quickly before folding his hands in his lap.

"Look," I said, "I know you didn't mean any harm to anyone. You never hurt anyone. But we've got a situation here and we've got to get it taken care of."

He leaned forward across the desk and stared at me. Brown eyes. Pocked face. Just like the victims reported. There was something about trying to get him to cop out that made me feel scummy. Always, after soliciting confessions, I felt in need of a long hot shower. It made me itch all over, this interrogation business.

He put his hands on top of the stack of reports, as though

the papers were sacred, and looked at me. He looked at me for a long moment and then whispered, "Do you know God's name?"

I did know, having more than once opened the front door of my parent's calm suburban Houston home to find a dark-suited Jehovah's Witness standing on the front porch. But I'd have said yes whether I knew or not, in the hope it would help him to confess.

"I do," I said.

"Then we can pray together."

"Mr. Ashbey," I said, "I'm here to help you." He would believe me, the moment was right. Like almost everyone, he was ready to unburden himself. He merely wanted to do it in a way that wouldn't paint him as Satan.

He clasped his hands over the reports and closed his thick-lidded eyes. After a moment, he opened them and said, "If you'll pray with me we can find the answers."

I didn't know if that meant he would cop, and I wasn't sure exactly how we wound up with Mr. Ashbey sitting in my chair and me kneeling next to him, my left hand clasped between his sweaty palms while I listened to him pray and wondered if he had been standing in an alley a few hours earlier, holding his dick. Midway through the prayer I heard a noise in the hallway just outside the office door, and when I edged my eyes open I saw W.I. with his Houston Oilers coffee cup, rolling his head in circles and smirking.

When Mr. Ashbey finished praying, I got up off my knees and brought him a cup of water.

"Let's see if we can get rid of this paperwork," I said.

"I'm ready," he said, but even with all his calm and bulk he looked like a lost two-year-old.

By the time we finished, around midnight, I had a signed confession to twenty-five of the cases. That was my fault.

If I had done the job right, he would have taken every last one, whether he'd done them or not. I had practiced carefully the fine art of interrogation and come up short.

I walked him over to the holding cells where he would spend the night unless a judge could be found who would come out at this late hour to set his bond. After I turned him over to the jailer I went back to my office and taped the clearance report. I kept losing track of what I was saying and had to backtrack the recorder several times to straighten things out. I couldn't help thinking that in spite of his religious fervor, I had no sense that Mr. Ashbey was in any way malicious. He had secured a pretty good chunk of the dream: a family, a nice house, some children, a decent job. But I had the strong feeling that all in the world Mr. Ashbey truly wanted was for someone, somewhere, to pay him just a little bit of attention. Maybe say a prayer with him.

Sergeant Quill had taped a sign on the front of his desk: COWS MAY COME AND COWS MAY GO, BUT THE BULL IN THIS PLACE STAYS ON FOREVER. W.I. referred to it as agri-humor.

"He took twenty-five of them," I said.

Quill kicked his putty-colored sea turtle boots up onto the desktop and leaned back, his belly listing to the left as he shifted his massive bottom in the chair.

"What about the other three?"

"He didn't do them."

"Damn," he said, "and you couldn't convince him to take three more lousy cases? Looking at twenty-five, three more won't make no difference at all."

"Sergeant," I said, "he is a religious man."

"Yeah, old W.I. told me about you in there on your

knees last night." He let out something that was half snort and half laugh. "Damn, I wish I could've seen that."

It was all over the station in a matter of hours. I didn't mind. It helped me, in a way, to start trying to forget the waxen bodies and the blood smell.

It was that suicide note I couldn't forget. It was with me whenever I saw one of the city's spotless sanitation trucks mumbling down some manicured alley.

Sometimes, during those summer afternoons when the heat would bubble up the thin strips of tar that lay between the concrete sections of streets, I could picture it. Mr. Ashbey standing in the scorching afternoon sun at the end of a paved smooth driveway, sweating next to a section of six-foot cedar. Standing there in his tennis shorts, with his fly open and the horse out of the barn, his flaccid penis in the palm of one hand. There under the brilliant yellow sunshine in those kitchen-clean alleys, ducking the garbage trucks. Waiting for schoolgirls and whispering God's name.

FOUR

I SAT NEXT TO JIM, ON A BEATEN GREEN COUCH IN A
south Beaumont apartment, a dumpy one-bedroom with
a kitchen full of dirty dishes and a living room stuffed
with laundry-strewn furniture. Across from us sat Willy
Red, dealer in stolen merchandise and drugs.

"Don't give me no bullshit," Willy said. "Man, you said
you want brown, here it is. I want to relax, you know, like,
I don't *know* you. I want to *relax.*"

He was huge and coffee-skinned, with pale red hair
shaved close along his scalp. As he spoke, he pulled a
nickel-plated .38 from a stack of newspapers on the floor
next to his Stratolounger. He held the gun loosely, clicking
his thumbnail across the ridges on the hammer.

"Now you be showing me you ain't the man," he said,
flopping his hand back and forth, shaking the gun first at
Jim, then at me. I was scared, but psyched. I was with Jim,
I was Jim's partner, and we had a real street scum, ready
to make a sale.

I wasn't yet sure even what I was doing there.

I had driven to Beaumont for the first time the same morning I delivered the Wagger confession to Sergeant Quill.
Jim and I spent that afternoon in Tyrrell Park, wandering
from bridle trails to the edge of the golf course, watching

citizens at play. That evening, we'd gone to his apartment, his crib, empty but for a twin bed punched into one corner of the bedroom and a Mr. Coffee on the kitchen counter.

He'd waited until I was tossing clothes into my overnight bag before saying, "Come back next week," and it had gone like that for most of the summer.

I would finish my last shift of the week at eleven, grab a thermos of coffee and put the top down on the 442, plug Robin Trower or the Doobie Brothers into the tape deck and *move,* flying through the wide circles of gray-white luminescence that dotted the freeway during the first part of the trip, where there were still streetlights. Later, the sky took over, the deep-ocean blue-black Texas night sky, sliced by the cones of my headlights. And Jim would be in Beaumont, waiting.

Two days later, at the last possible minute, I would get back in the car and head for Pasadena, *the bull in this place stays on forever,* to slog through another five days' worth of trash.

When Jim finally asked, on an August afternoon that was so hot and sticky even the trees seemed to sweat, I didn't give myself time to blink. I had told myself I wouldn't, that I would not let myself cross over again, that I had no need. And until that afternoon, I had believed it. But I drove straight back to Pasadena, told Quill I'd see him in the next life, shoved my furniture into a U-Haul and headed back toward Beaumont.

I didn't think. It was what I wanted, this unwieldy something that was between Jim and me, pulling like rampant gravity, this thing that I fought against and struggled with and tried so hard to crush but couldn't. I wanted it to bury me. I wanted him whispering my name at midnight. I didn't care where he was living or what he was doing, I wanted to roll my cheek into the warm place on his pillow when he left the bed in the morning time. I didn't stop to think.

Jim reached slowly toward his ankle. Willy Red tightened his grip on the pistol.

"Easy, dude, just my works," Jim said, and pulled a syringe from his sock. He looked straight at Willy Red, who smiled at us, showing long yellow teeth.

Jim took out his pocketknife and scooped a small amount of powder from the packet on the table, delicately tapping it into the spoon Willy had provided. He carefully drew ten cc's of water into the syringe from a half-empty glass on the table and squirted it into the spoon, and then struck a match. While he was cooking the dope, I removed my belt and draped it over his thigh.

"Yeah," Willy Red said, smacking his lips once loudly and sucking his teeth repeatedly.

Jim put the needle in smoothly, expertly, and left the syringe resting on his arm while he loosened the belt from his biceps. He drew back the plunger and watched as his own blood mixed with the fluid in the syringe.

"Oh, yeah," Willy Red said. "Sweet heaven, here we come."

Jim pushed the plunger slightly, slowly, then pulled it back out, then pushed again, repeating this until he had gradually put all the heroin into his arm.

"Oh, shit, yeah," Willy Red moaned, edging forward in his chair. "Jack it off, man, shit! Shit yeah!"

Jim pulled the needle from his arm and sat back on the couch, his eyelids fluttering. I watched. I remembered the lesson. A junkie was when it got real, he had said.

"Damn," Jim whispered. "Good shit, Willy Red. Good fucking stuff."

"Mmmhmmm. You get the best from Red. Only the best."

Jim leaned back on the couch.

"So," Willie Red said, "what about you, sister, you wanna taste? Huh?"

"No, man," Jim mumbled, head nodding gently, eyes half closed. "She don't fix. The lady don't fix."

"Oh, man," Willy Red moaned, "she be missing the good thing in life. Shit." He sat staring at me through narrowed eyes. "I think she fix," he said. "I think she fix or she don't walk out of here."

"Hey, man, you wanted me to get down, I got down," Jim mumbled. "Don't be hassling a lady, she don't fix."

"Man, I ain't talking hassle. I be talking bullets in about a half a minute if she don't wanna get down. Like I said, man, I don't be knowing you."

Jim struggled to stand, gave up, fell back into the couch.

I leaned forward and looked at Willy Red's eyes.

"You think Durrell sent the heat in on you, man?" I asked. "He told us everything was cool, he told us you said come on by, everything was all right."

"Durrell cool as the other side of my pillow, honey, but you ain't showed shit. Durrell say he know some folks want to get down, want some good brown. Now what you come here for, you don't wanna get down? You tell me that."

I picked up the syringe. The water I drew into it turned milky red, residue from Jim's shot. I squirted the liquid onto the wall to his right. It made a scribbly pinkish line, bloodwater on dirty yellow plasterboard.

"Then fuck Durrell," I said, and copied what I'd seen Jim do to prepare the shot. I was shaking, trying to control my hands and not let Willy Red see just how scared I really was, and I wanted to do it, that's the truth of the matter, I *wanted* to. I wanted to know what it felt like out there on the edge and I wanted Jim to be able to say that I was standup, that I handled it. He opened his eyes when I took the belt from his lap. I didn't know how I was going to get that needle through my skin and into my vein, and I didn't know whether or not it would kill me. I knew it could, but I knew it only in the way a kid knows. Not *me*. Never *me*.

"Here man, wait man, wait, let me do you," Jim said. He took the syringe from me and leaned in close over my arm. He eased the needle in so gently I didn't feel it, pulled the belt loose, and slowly pressed down the plunger, straight in this time, slowly, evenly, no back-and-forth.

I sat motionless, waiting, trying to feel it inside me, flowing, and then my body was melting and my eyes were closing. If things were happening around me, I was not a part of any of it. I was only a tiny shimmering existence, a glowing, softball-sized globe of being, located somewhere inside this body that was so warm and delicious and so far far away. Pieces of talk floated around me. This was nice. This was very, very nice.

"Yeah," Willy Red falsetto-drawled. "Yeah. The bitch caught a rush. Dreamland. Yeah. I taste it myself, man, sitting right here watching. Just watching. Yeah."

I was silent on the couch. I watched, from far away, Willy Red fixing a shot. Everything was soft, wonderfully soft. He had the needle in his arm, playing with the plunger, in and out, slowly, a little less out and a little more in each time.

"Jack it off," he whispered, absorbed, intent.

I pulled myself forward, looked slowly around the room, wondered at the distant discomfort swelling in my stomach. Everything was so far away. I watched my hand reaching toward an aloe vera plant next to the couch, watched my hand pull the plant out of its pot and hold it, root ball dangling, dirt on the floor. I heard myself vomit, effortlessly, into the green plastic pot.

"Shit's sure enough good, ain't it?" Willy Red said, still smiling, running one finger gently over the tiny puncture wound just below the bend of his elbow. He turned to Jim. "You pretty stout. You the first white boy I seen didn't puke after doing this stuff."

Jim opened one eye and smiled at Willy Red.

"I'll be wanting more of this," he said.

Willy Red bent forward toward Jim, chest almost on his knees, face thrust upward.

"*Mañana,*" he said. "See me at three."

Back in my car, Jim leaned close to the steering wheel and stared hard at the solid white stripe along the outer lane of Interstate 10.

"You all right?" he asked.

"Never better," I heard myself say.

"All right then. You snapped real good."

"Never better."

"You're a natural," he said. "A fucking natural."

"It was great," I said. "The look on Quill's face when I handed him my resignation."

"Wish I'd seen it."

"Effective immediately. He asked me why I was leaving."

"And?"

"I told him school."

"Whatever you want," he said. "But this guy Nettle'd hire you in a quick minute."

"You think so?"

"Yeah," he said. "And I think I'm gonna kick Durrell's ass when I find him. Hainty motherfucker ran us smooth into a trap, thinks I'm the heat or something."

"That Willy Red," I said, "he had maroon eyes. Fucking maroon eyes. Did you see that?"

The persistent, almost rhythmical banging of kitchen cabinets woke me up. I had been dozing on the couch, waiting for Jim to get home. I sat each night in his apartment, reading college catalogues that advertised the fall '78 semester and waiting for him to come home. Some nights he brought dealers with him. I smoked their dope and laughed with them, and watched, after they were gone, while Jim wrote his reports.

There was a week yet before registration, but I wasn't sure I'd go back. I was enjoying being in limbo.

Jim was hanging on the refrigerator door, staring blankly at the empty shelves before him. I looked up, still not fully conscious, saw his face lit white by the glare spilling out of the refrigerator, and turned over to get some good sleep, real sleep. He was home.

I could hear him pacing, then the rattling started. I got up to see what was wrong. He was in the hallway, hunched over the bathroom doorknob, jiggling the lock with a screwdriver.

"I locked myself out I don't know how," he said, his voice oddly monotone.

I looked at his eyes. There was a virtual roadmap of swollen capillaries jagging out from the thin ring of blue surrounding his dime-size pupils. He had made a case. Or had at least been working on one. I took the screwdriver from him and popped the lock.

He looked at the tool in my hand and marched past me into the bathroom, closing the door between us. I went back to the couch and sat down, trying to rub my eyes awake. The heater kicked on with a muffled rattle and I felt a stirring above my head as warm air began flowing from the vent near the ceiling. It wasn't cold outside, it was September, but Jim insisted the heat be left on.

From behind the bathroom door came the clatter of banging cabinets, then silence, and then the awful echo of Jim violently retching.

He hadn't locked the door, and as I entered the bathroom he rolled away from the toilet, began crawling in circles, round and round, spinning and moaning. He grabbed my feet, clutched at my ankles, but when I bent toward him he jerked back and pulled his head sideways, as though ducking a punch. He darted a look at the wallpaper above the sink, a brilliant blue-and-green floral print, and shielded his face with his hands.

"Stop!" he yelled, "make it fucking stop!"

"It's okay," I said, "it's okay." I reached toward him, moving slowly. "You're fine, you're safe." He jumped around and grabbed the shower curtain, yanked it in front of him, and then fell to the floor, pulling the shower rod down with him.

I threw the curtain into the tub and leaned over him. No breathing. I pounded his chest, hard, jerked a towel from above the toilet, swabbed out his mouth and started CPR. I pounded and blew and pounded and blew and thought, over and over and over, "Breathe." I tried to will it to happen and tried not to remember all of Jim's tales about how many times agents had O.D.'d and the panic you feel when you think you're about to have a body on your hands and how to God are you going to explain why, or how, or anything. Right at that moment I hated loving him. But I did. I put my lips to his and forced my breath into his lungs. I think I prayed.

I was trying to figure a way to keep breathing into him and at the same time get to the phone for some kind of help when he choked and coughed and opened his eyes. He squinted, then opened his eyes wide, then squinted again. And then he moved and the back of my head smashed against tile and white light exploded in my brain. I felt my eyes bulge against the tops of their sockets and heard Jim's rage everywhere, his screaming fear.

"I'M DEAD I KNOW IT ALREADY YOU DON'T HAVE TO SPELL IT OUT MOTHERFUCKER I'M HERE TO DO THE DIRTY WORK! HIDE THOSE RIGS THEY'LL BE HERE ANY MINUTE! FUCKING FEDS DON'T KNOW THEIR ASS FROM A HOLE IN THE GROUND BUT THEY GOT THE STROKE BROTHER, THEY GOT, THEY GOT, THEY GOT . . ."

His voice slowed to a crawl and when I could see again he was on his knees in the bathtub, mumbling, bent over and holding the faucet with both hands, tears running down his face.

I pulled myself up and slipped my hands under his arms, moving slowly, talking gently while the pain built in my skull. I was dizzy, but got him out of the bathroom, draped his arm over my shoulder and lugged him to the couch. I could smell the chemical in his sweat, as though his body were tainted with battery acid and it was seeping out through his pores.

"I don't know what you're on," I said, "but you got a dose and a half." Talking to myself. Jim slumped onto the couch and I pulled a blanket over him, tucking it tightly under his shoulders.

I took his face in my hands, trying to force him to look at me. He jerked his eyes in every direction but mine, and then gave up and simply closed them.

"Jim," I said.

"I don't know I don't know," he sighed. I thought about an ambulance, and about the storm that would follow when the powers at the police department got the call. I should wait, as long as he remained conscious, I should wait.

He was suddenly calm, wide-eyed again and stretched out on the couch like a cadaver, staring through the ceiling. I sat rubbing the welt that was rising on the back of my head.

"Rob," he finally said.

It was nearly two in the morning, but I dialed the number. His wife answered, sounding resigned when she heard a woman on the line, but she woke him.

"Sorry," I said. "Jim's been O.D.'d. I need a little help."

"What's he on?"

"I don't know. Maybe acid or maybe dust. Whatever it is, it's stout."

"On my way."

I turned to see Jim ripping his clothes off, scattering them across the living-room floor as he headed for the front door. I caught him as he struggled with the chain lock and eased him back to the couch.

"Just lie here," I said, "Rob's on the way over."

I took his gun from the coffee table, and my own from under the couch cushion, and moved them and the screw-driver to the far end of the L-shaped sectional, stuffing everything back under the end cushion. I gathered his jeans and shoes and shirt and underwear from the floor and tossed them in a pile next to the couch. They were objects he might start seeing as alive, lurking on the floor, waiting to hurt him.

I sat down to watch him, hoping he would stay calm until Rob could make the thirty-five-mile drive from Saratoga.

It was almost an hour later when at last Rob walked in the door. He'd stopped to pick up his ex-partner, Denny Dennison, before driving in. Jim was hunkered on the floor

in the corner of the living room, staring at the ceramic grey-
hound next to the stereo.

"I know, I know," he was saying, "she told me that the
day I left. But she's dead now." He paused, tilting his head,
chewing on his tongue while he waited for a reply. He
squatted before the dog, leaning forward on his hands, the
curve of his back dotted white where the knobs of his spine
pushed against his skin. "Mother is dead," he said.

Denny looked at me and then at Rob and shook his head,
chuckling softly.

"I'm sorry," he finally said, "I'm sorry. We all been
there, but sometimes it's just goddamn funny. What's he
on? Did he come home naked?"

"No," I said. "Disrobed after arrival. My guess is PCP
or acid."

"Well this is one hell of a way to get together," Denny
said, "but I'm pleased to finally meet you." We shook
hands. His left eye seemed to be in a permanent squint.

"What do you think?" I asked Rob.

"I think he's a fucked-up motherfucker. I told the dude
to be careful around here."

Denny got Jim back onto the long part of the sectional
and sat down on the shorter end. Jim was blathering on
about rigs and dope and heat and handling it, but he was
talking calmly, almost to himself. We watched him without
speaking.

"How about some java?" Denny finally said.

We moved across the room to the tiny dining table next
to the kitchen bar. Denny dumped four big spoons of sugar
into his cup and almost filled it with milk, adding coffee
last, until the liquid hung at the rim of the cup. He leaned
down and sipped loudly. Rob, as always, took his black,
and held his little finger extended straight out when he
drank, as though it were at attention.

"So," Rob finally said, "you think old Jim done himself?"

I looked at Denny. He kicked one black-booted foot up on the empty wooden chair next to him and shrugged.

"It's happened," he said.

"No way," I said. "There is no way. Somebody slipped him something."

"Hey man, I'm not accusing the dude," Rob said. "Just asking a question."

"And there's no way he'd do it accidentally," I added. "He knows from just a taste how much to take. He knows." I didn't want to admit to them that the possibility had simply not occurred to me.

We sat there, sipping coffee and staring at Jim. His eyes were closed, but I could see the blanket moving in time to his breathing.

"You gonna call his sergeant, what's his name, that Dodd feller?" Denny asked.

"I don't know," I said. "I don't even know the man. I met him once, for about ten minutes, when I went with Jim to drop off some evidence."

"He's not the sharpest dude I've ever run into," Denny said.

"Say that," said Rob. "Maybe you should go straight to the chief."

I walked over and checked Jim's pulse. It was steady, though fast.

"He'll be okay," Denny said. "Let him sleep it off."

"He stopped breathing on me once already." I rubbed a hand over the back of my head. There was a silver-dollar-size bump there, tingling, like somebody was using it for a pin cushion.

"Look," Denny said, "long as he ain't foaming at the

mouth he'll be all right. Relax, girl. If he was gonna die he'd already've done it."

"Anyway," Rob said, "You can't take him to the hospital. He's buying morphine off two nurses, at least, that he's told me about. Maybe more. Blow his cover in a minute."

When 5 A.M. finally rolled around, Denny flipped on the "Farm and Ranch Report."

"Got to see what's doing," he drawled. "I'm a farmer now, you know."

"Some farmer," Rob said.

"Hell with you too, boy." Denny pushed a wad of blond hair off his forehead. Most of his left eyebrow was missing. Instead there was thick white scar tissue.

"How about I go after some breakfast?" Rob said.

"Do that," said Denny. "I'm just about hungry."

"Got some cash?" Rob asked. "I ran out without my wallet."

Denny handed him a twenty and he stuffed it into his jeans pocket.

"In a few," he said, and slipped out the door.

"So what do you think?" I said. "You don't think he did it."

"Darlin'," Denny said, "I don't think shit. The man's still breathing, right? I'll tell you right now I think the whole damn deal is about as screwed up as a thing can get."

"His working here?"

"Not just that. I damn near got killed by a dope dealer. I have no use for any of it. No use at all."

"Jim said you were ambushed."

"Been half blind ever since. But I can still see a heifer good enough to get a rope around her neck and I can find a barn door. I can even get my truck down the highway if it's not cloudy outside."

"I never heard exactly what came down."

"It was a rip-off, a smooth out-and-out burn. Me and Rob was working down around San Angelo, supposed to buy two keys of brown off some Mexicans out of Coahuila." He took a sip of coffee and held the cup as he talked. "We were down there sweating our asses off in this hole-in-the-wall roadside motel on the edge of Ozona, down Crockett County, figuring they're bringing it in somewhere between Del Rio and Langtry, or maybe, hell, who knows, we didn't know. It's about a hundred and four that afternoon, and this motel hadn't even got a name. Even three hours after sunset you could feel the heat coming up out of the ground. One thing it did have, though, that room had a fucking back door. And Johnson damn sure found it.

"The beaners showed up without the dope, said it would be along in a few minutes. I go in to take a leak and the next thing happens is a fucking gun comes through the bathroom door and there I am holding my dick, no heater, not even a fucking nail clipper to defend myself, I am on the floor and scrambling. I didn't hear a damn thing when they popped the first cap. Not a goddamn sound. Silence. And then I couldn't see. I was fucking *blind*. I heard footsteps going out that back door and all I could think about was my kids. Just my kids.

"I'd been shot in the face, right here." Pointing to his eyebrow. "Johnson, I don't know how he did it, he hooked 'em out that fucking back door and ran off into the desert. Ran smooth out of his shoes. The sheriff's office found the fucker's shoes about forty yards from the back door. The Mexicans caught him, and they started beating the shit out of him when they did. Hell, one of them had a blade and was three-quarters of the way across Rob's face before he badged them, and they stopped with the beating and ran off their own selves."

There was a tap on the door, Rob's special three-two-three knock. I got up to let him in.

"Chocolate, sugar, or blueberry," he said, tossing a dozen-box of doughnuts on the coffee table. Denny waved him off.

"Rangers tracked them," he continued. "Found them in Pandale, three days later. They're still in Huntsville, picking cotton and getting butt-fucked, God bless the Texas Department of Corrections, and they'd best hope they never get out of there."

"You talking about those Mexicans again?" Rob asked.

"They won't. Back-to-back lifes. Forget about it."

"No shit, Sherlock." Denny looked at him and started to say something else, but reached for a doughnut and then pushed the box toward me.

Rob had run. I couldn't understand why he and Denny were still so tight, but I knew that they were. It was Denny who had talked Rob into moving from Houston. He wanted his partner around, he said, even though he'd been retired for nearly five years.

"I moved out near Saratoga right after I got out of the hospital," Denny said. "Heard there was medicinal springs there. Hell, they ain't been used since Spindletop blew, but the fishing's good. I take my boy fishing every Saturday, up at Livingston or Toledo Bend. Got forty acres and some heifers, a barbecue pit in the back yard. A few laying hens and a rooster that thinks he's the best-looking thing this side of Memphis. It's cool in the shade."

"Yeah," Rob said, "bragged about clean air and pine trees until he talked me out into the countryside. It's dull as dishwater and now I got damn near a seventy-mile commute to the office. Is there any more coffee?"

Denny moved to the couch and squinted at the television, trying to get some kind of image through his damaged ocular nerve, but mostly just listening to the newscaster squawk about the price of pork bellies. Jim slept, tossing every so often on the couch.

Rob began pacing the living room, scattering blueberry doughnut crumbs until Denny told him to sit his white-boy ass down and be still. He tossed a half-eaten doughnut at Denny, poured himself another cup of coffee, and joined me at the dining table.

"Been working a coke case on some dudes in Houston," he said. "Jam-up stuff."

"And?"

"Just thought you might be tired. Offering a little help."

"I could use a little help," I said.

He pulled a baggie out of his shirt pocket and began cutting rails on the tabletop.

"Did you ever think things would go this direction?" he asked. "When you first signed on?"

"I had no idea."

"Yeah. Well sometimes you just got to go with your instincts." He snorted a couple of rails and handed me the tooter. "You know," he said, "I watch the weather on TV and hear that joker talking about barometric pressure and think, fine, that's fine, but what effect does it have on *me*? Is there anything out there controlling this scene, or what?"

I snuffed up the lines and passed the tooter back to him.

"Thanks for the bump."

"Anytime," he said. "Anytime at all. From me, you just say the word."

I looked over at Jim. He was still asleep, one foot twitching slowly beneath the blanket.

Just say the word. The night before the bust-out in Pasadena, I'd been in my apartment, staring out the back window at a large field in the June glory of weeds, trying to gather myself for the return to real life, for the arrests, wondering what Hayden Smith would think when he discovered I was a cop, what all of them would think. Wondering if what I had done was right, and what it would feel like to be marked, to wear a uniform, or if it would make any kind of difference at all, attempting not to think too hard about any of it. And Rob, his body taut, lean like an Indian, blowing into my living room at two in the morning with roses in one hand and champagne in the other. Not saying a word, laying out lines, opening champagne, moving quietly and efficiently, no time to waste, this was it, our final night as partners. All those weeks we'd been playing the role of lovers, and there was a hint of desperation in the way he slid his hands under my blouse. No wasted motion, lifting me to him, carrying me, and then the cool of white plaster against my back and the heat of him inside me, and the sweat-slick warm of his skin, his breaths coming faster, and mine, and the scent of him, the overwhelming strength of him.

I sipped my coffee and looked at the man across the table.

"You down here to stay?" he asked quietly.

"I think so," I said. "I may go back to school. I don't know. Jim said come on down. Here I am. But I didn't realize this was quite what he had in mind."

"Raynor will be all right." He put his cup down gingerly and leaned back in his chair. "He'll be all right. But I'll say this. When my kids get a little older, I'm out of this end of the business. I see these bastards knocking down major bucks and I wonder what I'm doing. You know? I think about joining the winning team for awhile."

"Do you know an agent who hasn't?"

"Hell, baby, dudes I know working the border patrol say their job isn't busting dealers, it's eliminating the competition." He pulled at his beard. It was trimmed close, but coming in dark enough to cover the scar on his jaw. The agent's cycle: grow the beard and hair, get down and dirty, make cases, cut it all off, keep the appearance changing constantly, the thing to be avoided was recognition. His hair was down over his earlobes and shaggy on his collar, dark as ever, straight and brown.

"I've thought about it lots of times," he said. "But then I get home and see my little girl playing kickball out in the back yard. It's hard, man."

"I guess we could get all philosophical," I said, "and decide that's the reason why. Easy to do at five in the morning. But when you get right down to it, see what it does to people, you can't fade that kind of action."

"Who the hell knows." He leaned back and clasped his hands behind his neck. "You going to call that chief?"

"In a few hours. No sense dragging him out of bed. Not much to do except wait it out."

"Listen," he said, "I'm not trying to tell you how to run your business, man, Jim's a good dude, but, he's working right now, you know. You know how it can get. Things happen. You wonder whether to shit or go blind."

"I think I'll settle for letting this guy Nettle know what's going on."

"Good idea," he said. "Very good idea. Cover Jim's ass. And your own." He plucked a doughnut from the box on the table, took a huge bite, and threw it back toward the box. It landed in the middle of the cocaine on the tabletop.

"Oh, Christ," he said, "look what I did. No slack anywhere. Jesus H." He carefully lifted the doughnut and began licking it, dropping powdered sugar all over his beard. I used a matchbook to try to scrape the sugar away from the coke rails.

"Man," he said, "I fucked this up real good, looks like to me."

"It was probably already full of sugar," I said.

He handed me the tooter.

"Yeah, probably," he said. "Ain't much pure around these days. Not on the streets anyway."

FIVE

HIEF NETTLE'S KITCHEN WAS AJAX CLEAN, *BETTER Homes and Gardens* neat, and smelled overwhelmingly of Lysol. His wife answered the door and waved me inside. She had on a pale pink jumper with an antique lace collar, and wore her blond hair braided, wrapped in a neat bun at the back of her head.

"Donald will be in in a moment," she drawled lightly. "You'nt some ice tea?"

"No thank you," I said.

She walked toward the sound of a sitcom, which came from somewhere in the front part of the house. I sat down at the table, a round, pine thing in the middle of the large kitchen. Jim hadn't said exactly why his boss wanted to talk to me, only that it was something about the overdose, and that I was to see him alone. It had been nearly two weeks since I'd called Nettle and explained what had happened. He hadn't seemed terribly concerned. "Keep an eye on him," he'd said. "Let me know if he gets any worse." Though Jim seemed to be recovering, there were still days when he had a rough go. One morning I'd found him sitting on the landing outside of the apartment, staring through the wrought-iron railing. When I'd asked what he was watching, he looked at me oddly and said, "I'm not sure.

Some days I look around me and it's like the whole world is shivering."

There was a picture of Mrs. Nettle on the wall next to the window. She was in a blue formal, holding roses, wearing a yellow sash with silver glitter that spelled out MISS BEAUMONT. Standing in front of an oil derrick. Beaumont had been carrying on a long-running love affair with the stuff. When the Lucas Gusher blew at Spindletop in 1901, spewing liquid dinosaur remains hundreds of feet skyward, Beaumont, like most of East Texas, was overrun by all those who would get rich quick. In a single month, the village became a town of thirty thousand, entrepreneurs all. It must have been chaos. And muddy. Very muddy. Enter Texaco and Mobil. Du Pont Chemical. The ship channel. The unions.

I had been deep into East Texas once before, in high school, for the track and field regionals. I was the white girl on the mile relay team. When we stopped at a Chicken Shack in Lufkin to get lunch, the six black women on the team refused to leave the van. I was astonished that they were actually scared; I'd never seen that kind of fear up close. But when I finally got them into the restaurant, I saw why they'd wanted to wait outside. The whole place got suddenly quiet when we entered, and people leaned across tables to talk and glance over at us and then talk some more. The waitress had an ugly sneer in her voice when she took our order, and when our food arrived, it looked like it had been thrown at the plates from a great distance.

Why Jim had chosen to come here I didn't know, except that Rob was close, and Denny, and it was a chance to work undercover, start clean.

When Nettle strode into the kitchen, he jerked his head once in a military nod before sitting down opposite me. He was slick like motor oil, shiny and tall, and even in his own house didn't take his suit coat off. His tie, a loose-knit strip of light blue polyester, was hitched tightly around his skinny white neck, and he sat with his tiny fresh-from-the-manicurist hands folded neatly on the table between us. Every hair on his head was in its place, every single red hair, and his mustache was trimmed pencil thin beneath his rounded nose. He had on translucent black ankle-high socks and black patent loafers with gold clasps, and picked, every so often, at an invisible piece of lint on his suit.

"Thank you for coming," he said.

I nodded, not sure how to respond. I wanted to trust this man, it was important to me that he be someone I could speak honestly to, but he was giving no indications. I got the feeling that protection from the elements was what he desired, like the furtive white-male Christians who scream Jesus and weep in front of television cameras so people will send them money.

He folded his hands and rested his pointed chin on the tips of his fingers. He sighed his very best world-weary sigh.

"Perhaps you're aware," he said, "of the considerable effort, and expense, the city has put into this investigation. I initiated it, I'm responsible for its success. I need to know how my number-one agent is doing."

"I told you already," I said. "And Sergeant Dodd's seen him twice since the O.D. Why ask me?"

"You're his woman, aren't you? You're with him every day. You know him."

Jim's woman. That's what I was to Nettle.

"I guess you would say that," I answered. "Or you might say we're engaged, or almost. That's why I'm here. Not to babysit."

"I'm not asking you to. You've got experience. I'm asking for your opinion."

"My opinion is that not only does he need rest, he needs

to be pulled up. Look at the case log, he's barely made a buy in the last two weeks. You should end this thing now and take the cases you've got."

He shifted his chair and crossed his legs, looping one elbow over the carved wooden chair back.

"That's not possible," he said. "We do have a primary target. Jim doesn't even seem to be close to him yet."

"Gaines."

"You're familiar with him."

"Not really," I said. "I know he's supposed to be some kind of pornographer."

"At least. He owns four clubs, two here, two in Houston. That health spa out near China is his, and he's got two car lots out near the edge of town. You know that place, Lovelace, that underwear store?"

"Frederick's of Hollywood goes Western Wear. Yeah. I've seen it."

"That's his, too."

"None of that sounds terribly illegal to me, Chief."

"He's got legitimate fronts." He pulled a paper from his inside coat pocket, unfolded it carefully, and began reading. "T.C.I.C. Two assault, three exhibiting obscene materials, two obstructing police, one D.W.I." He refolded the paper and slotted it neatly back into his pocket. "No convictions. In addition to that, we understand from the Lubbock P.D. that some 'known associates' of his are suspects in two murders. One in New Mexico, one in Texas."

"How long ago?"

"The most recent? About a year and a half ago, April of 'seventy-seven."

"Well if they haven't got the case together by now, they're not going to."

"They got close, very close. The victims did some work for X-tra Special Video, that's one of his companies too, and were found in the desert, single shot to the head, .357, entry at the rear of the skull. The ring and pinky fingers on their left hands had been broken."

"Nasty stuff."

"Every agency in this county, clear down to the damn constable's office, wants Will Gaines. And I said I can deliver him. I stood up at a task force meeting and said I had a man under. And that man is going to stay under and this investigation will come to a successful conclusion. There's a lot riding on it."

From what I could gather, what was mainly at stake was Nettle's confirmation as chief of police. He'd been an assistant chief for three years before his boss left the scene. It was common knowledge that Chief Duane Anderson had come home one night, drunk as usual, but in such a bad mood that he threatened to kill his wife. His four-year-old twins sat on the floor with their brightly colored blocks while Anderson made his feelings known and then they watched as he staggered over the Early American couch and out the patio door to get his MAC 10 from under the front seat of his car. When he came back through the sliding glass door, his wife cranked off a single round with the .357 he had given her for Christmas. She hit him smack in the left eye, ending his screaming, alcoholic life right there in the living room of their home. A jury saw the merit of her self-defense argument.

Assistant Chief Nettle had been immediately promoted to Acting Chief Nettle, and everyone knew that Acting Chief Nettle wanted nothing more than to drop the present participle from his title.

"Look," Nettle said, "whatever the reason you came down, the important thing here is you can help Jim out. He told me himself that he'd like to have you on board."

"I'm doing what I can," I said. "I'm there for him. But I want to go back to school."

"What if I said you could go to school and work for us at the same time? And resign as soon as this thing's over. Do you really think a man like Gaines needs to be on the streets?"

"Of course not," I said.

"All right then. We make a porn case on him he'll get a couple of years. If we're lucky enough to get a conviction. But if you and Jim buy cocaine from the man, we can put him away for a long, long time."

"Jim's not well," I tried. "He needs a rest."

"Genesis two, verse eighteen," he said. " 'It is not good that the man should be alone; I will make him a helper fit for him.' "

"Amen," I answered. "What are you saying?"

"Jim needs you. I want you to come to work for us."

"What, I just do this thing and resign whenever I want?"

"When we have the case. If you still want to by then. Absolutely. No strings." He shifted his chair back around and leaned across the table toward me. He had tiny gray eyes. "But you know, this isn't such a bad little city. It's a great place to raise kids. We intend to keep it that way." He smiled. "Jim said you're a runner."

"Used to be."

"Well, Beaumont is the birthplace of a very famous lady athlete. You've heard of Babe Didrikson, I'm sure. And you can't tell me the countryside isn't beautiful."

"I didn't come here for scenery."

"You should understand," he said. "I'll write you a recommendation that will get you any job you want. I have friends at the university. School could be a breeze, a matter of a little paperwork. I can get things done." He picked at his lapel and flicked his thumb against his index finger, frowning. "And you could make a big difference in this investigation. You could help us get this guy off the street."

There was that. And there were the Willy Reds of the world. If I decided to do it, well, this time around I would know how. I thought I understood what discretion was. I thought I could do a good job, do some good in general. And I would be Jim's partner. I didn't want to think about the rest of it, I wanted to believe I could maintain my balance. That I could go under and make the cases, make the sacrifice, and come out and clean right up. It would be one hell of a party. I wasn't sure exactly what I was trying to prove.

"Give me a yes or no," Nettle said. "Either way, Jim is staying under until the job is done. That's all there is to say." He leaned back and snugged the knot of his tie up tight against his collar.

I sat there for a moment, wondering if there were any way I could talk Jim into quitting. Absolutely not. What else did he know? He was a cop. He loved it. And part of me did too, whether I could really admit it to myself or not. This guy Gaines sounded major. It would be a thing worth doing.

"Well?"

"I guess I'm in."

He cleared his throat and clutched his hands on the table.

"We have to run you through the hiring procedure. You can take the test and the obstacle course next Wednesday, out IH-10 at Pine; the end of Happ Street. Be there at ten. I'll get you before the Review Board first thing Thursday. And I'll arrange for your polygraph. Don't worry about anything. In your case it's all just a formality."

I'd had a few brief doses of Sergeant Larry Dodd since moving to Beaumont, mostly when Jim had to drop off evidence. He was genuine good old boy, originally from Arkansas, newly appointed by Nettle as head of Vice. I put my seat belt on after he busted his third red light on the way out of town. He had a voice like a wrecking ball.

"I tell you," he yelled, shouting over the noise of the engine, "I could have done it, but it was just too damn hot. I mean ass-blistering hot. About the third day of getting my dick knocked in the dirt and sweating my skull off beneath that helmet, I said that's enough of this. Fuck training camp. Fuck the Houston Oilers. Ain't worth it. Been policing ever since."

He was big enough to be a defensive end, or maybe a tackle. He drove hunched over the wheel, his curly, hillbilly-blond hair touching the roof of the Dodge, mashing his foot on the accelerator as though he were trying to grind it right through the floorboard. It sounded like we would either become airborne or blow up any second.

"One of these days though," he said, "I'll find out what I was put on this earth for. I ain't gonna hang around Beaumont all my life."

We were doing an even hundred, scenery breezing by in a brown blur, when I spotted a Visibar sticking up from the bar ditch off the highway and yelled, "Hi-Po!"

"Huh?"

"Too late. Highway Patrol, we're busted."

"Aaawwww sheeeyut!" he moaned.

He pounded the steering wheel and braked down to forty while we looked for the troopers. They were down the highway about three-tenths of a mile, standing well off the road, on the shoulder. One of them struggled with an enormous black woman while his partner stood with his thumbs tucked in his Sam Browne and rocked backward with laughter.

Dodd pulled over and hung his badge case in front of him as he got out of the car.

"Police!" he shouted. "Beaumont! You fellers need a hand?"

I sat feeling the wind rock the car until Dodd waved me out. It blew the door back when I opened it, yanking it from my hand and slamming it open until the hinges groaned. I crunched across the gravel into the weeds where Dodd and the trooper were standing with the woman. She was a heavyweight to be sure, up there around two eighty, and easily six feet tall. Her hands were cuffed behind her and her pants were down around her ankles. She had on huge white bloomers, and even with the wind I could smell booze when I got within a few feet of her.

"Damn," said Dodd, "she'll blow a point-two-oh easy." His hair was flattened against his head by the wind. It was blasting so hard that it seemed to suck the breath right out of my lungs. I stood leaning into it until Dodd feinted back and threw a pulled punch at my arm.

"Help them out. She can't file no harassment charge on you."

I bent down and pulled the wad of red plaid doubleknit from around her ankles. I got them up, but there was no way the zipper would close. I raised my palms to the trooper.

"Best I can do."

"Thank you," the woman slurred. He pulled her toward the squad and folded her into the back seat and slammed the door.

"Y'all slow down now, hear?" he called.

"You bet," Dodd said.

He held the car to sixty until we were down the road, but the minute he had a few mild hills between us and the radar trap, he gunned it again.

"We're late," he explained.

"Not even the police yet and already I'm dressing drunks," I said. "I don't need this."

"Aw, hell," Dodd yelled, "she didn't puke or nothing. But I don't like handling niggers either."

"Do me one favor," I said.

"Sure," he said. "Name it."

"Don't say that around me."

"Say what?"

I closed my eyes and pretended to sleep the rest of the way to Houston.

The waiting room was decorated in nouveau funk, the floor a dirty beige linoleum. There were a few chrome and white Naugahyde chairs scattered about, and several ancient magazines tossed on a rust-spotted chrome coffee table, mostly antique copies of *Law Enforcement Today.*

Eventually the examiner came out. He was short and round, and seemed to sort of roll forward in bursts, short spurts involving many tiny steps.

"Cates!" he said, and led me to a closet-sized white room with a small desk and two chairs set in the middle of it. The cop-out box was open on top of the desk, the wires from the graphing mechanism tangled over the back of a chair.

He skipped the pretest interview, which was what most examiners used to try to get their subjects to tell the truth. I sat down and right away he strapped the equipment onto me: blood-pressure cuff on the left biceps, an accordion-pleated, round plastic hose around my chest, metal plates Velcro-ed around the index and middle fingers of my left hand.

He hit a switch on the wall and the main light went out,

leaving the room filled with a dull orange glow, like that of a photography darkroom.

"Sit very still and look straight ahead please," he said. He spoke softly, but his voice had a flat kind of whine to it.

I had visions of answering the first question and seeing the needles sling red ink all over the walls.

"Relax, now." He adjusted some knobs on the instrument.

When I had taken my first polygraph, for Pasadena, I had walked into the room believing the machine could read my mind. That was then.

"The test will begin in three minutes," he said. He made more adjustments.

I picked out a white paint bump on the wall in front of me and concentrated. There was nothing else. Only one little bump of paint on the wall. Only now, this minute, this one tiny instant of existence, and the littlest sliver of gray shadow cast in the orange light by a bump of paint on the wall.

"Answer yes or no please," the examiner said. He touched a knob. "Is your first name Kristen?"

Control question. My responses to the other questions, the real ones, would be measured against the response to this one. I thought about the time I had walked into the suicide's kitchen, what was his name, Todd, yes. Todd with his brains all over the refrigerator. I needed to get a few neurons popping, give a strong reaction to this question so that when he asked about drugs, the difference in the ink waves flowing onto the graph paper might not be obvious.

"Yes," I said.

My real name is Kristen. I wondered if I was lying.

Toward the end, he asked the standard question about

supporting the Constitution of the United States, and then finished up with a catch-all.

"Have you ever engaged in any behavior which is a felony against the laws of the State of Texas or the United States of America?" He said "America" just the way Lyndon Baines used to, "aMURka."

"No," I said, and I believed it.

Dodd sat reading a magazine while we waited for the results. Finally the examiner bustled out, a cigar in one hand and the other trailing about twelve feet of graph paper. He tapped the paper with the soggy end of his cigar and squinched his face up until he looked like a squirrel with a mouthful of pecans.

"Something's wrong," he said flatly.

Dodd's eyes got big and he stared first at the examiner and then at me. The examiner broke into a big lopsided smile and toked on his cigar and a croaking noise came out of his throat.

"Hell," he said, "she's too damn clean to have been a police for two whole years. She ain't never done nothing wrong in her whole damn life."

Dodd smiled at me and said, "Pheeyoo! I thought we had us some trouble there for a minute. Well girl, congratulations! Welcome to the Beaumont P.D.!"

Later that night I stood in Dodd's kitchen, waiting for him to dig paperwork out of his briefcase. The whole house was dark but for a small light over the gas range, which was pale green, like the refrigerator, dishwasher, and sink. Finally he pulled out the papers.

He turned to face me and lifted his right hand. He really was big. Maybe a defensive lineman.

"Raise your right hand," he said. I looked at him.

"Aw, fuck it," he said. "We don't have to do this shit. By the power invested in me by the assholes that run this town I hereby appoint you police in the City of Beaumont in the County of Jefferson in this here great State of Texas. Kick ass and take names. Amen." He put the papers on the kitchen table. "Sign here," he said, pointing. He pulled out another form and said, "Pick an alias."

"Jim's been introducing me to people as Florence," I said.

"What the hell kind of name is that?"

"Assumed."

"Huh?"

"It's a name," I said. "I go by Flo. Nobody would believe a cop would choose a name like that, right?"

"Damn straight. What's your last name going to be, Nightingale?"

"Wright," I said.

"No way. No fucking way."

"W-r-i-g-h-t. Wright."

"I got it," he said, nodding sheepishly and scribbling something on the form in front of him. "Okay, Florence Wright." He shook his head. "Jesus Lord. Take this down to the D.P.S. tomorrow and they'll give you a driver's license with your new name. And by the way, I don't need to know if you've been living with Jim to this point. All I need to know is that you have your own place now. So find yourself an apartment. And kick ass out there, now. We want some cases."

Walking up the drive to Jim's apartment, I looked around at the pine trees surrounding the parking lot and smelled their cold, clear scent and asked myself what I was doing. Jim was always saying, "What goes around, comes around," and walking up that quiet drive in the dark I had the feeling that things might just come around with a vengeance. I laughed at myself, tried to shake it off. You're being emotional, I said. It's only a feeling. The afternoon wind had turned into a nighttime breeze, and I listened to the pines creaking and tried not to imagine the witchlike whispers of haints perched in the branches. But things were different here, as in a good fifty years behind the times. The races didn't mingle. A man worked hard, played hard, and took care of his family. If he got to drinking with the boys on Saturday night and broke a few windows, well, that was just life. His woman would try to glue things together until the next time it happened. And then she'd try again.

Beaumont. The outer limits of East Texas, hard against the southern edge of the Big Thicket National Preserve. The locals were always sighting UFOs and having personal encounters with aliens out there in the piney woods.

SIX

SHOULD HAVE LISTENED. I SHOULD HAVE PAID AT-
tention to the part of me that was whispering Be Carefuls
from somewhere near the base of my skull. I hushed the
voice, told it to be quiet, go away, leave me alone. I was
determined to know what I was doing.

Jim was asleep when I got home from the midnight
swearing-in ceremony at Dodd's house. When I slipped out
of my clothes and crawled in next to him, he rolled onto
his side and pulled me close, his body warm beneath the
covers.

"You the police now?" he asked sleepily.

"Call me officer," I said.

"Love you," he whispered, and I turned to press my face
against his chest. The scent of his skin mingled with the
smell of clean sheets as he wrapped himself around me and
took me into sleep.

In the dream, I was lying naked in a snow-covered field,
but it wasn't at all cold. Snow floated around me like music,
purest white and melting warm against my skin, it surrounded me, was covering me, and then suddenly there was
ice on my breast.

I started awake and when I opened my eyes, there was
Jim's hand, pressing a cold glass to the center of my chest.

"You're cruel," I said. He laughed.

"The ceremonial cup," he grinned. I sat up, wide awake, and saw that the bedroom window was still dark. He handed me the glass and raised his own in a toast.

"To my partner," he said. "Drink heartily and prepare to do battle."

The champagne exploded icily down my throat, and Jim was draining his down in one long swallow. I tried to keep up and then he handed me a green bottle, uncorked and sweating water. He grabbed a second bottle, pressed his thumb over the opening and began shaking it, staring at me like I was a target. I jumped and ran, or tried to run, there was no place to hide, and he got me square in the back just as I reached the bedroom doorway. I rounded the corner and pressed myself against the wall, laughing and shaking my bottle furiously, and when he crouched into the living room, I let him have it. Suddenly we were wrestling, the bottles were somewhere on the floor and we were slick-wet with champagne and he had my arms pinned to the wall, straight up, and he leaned down and began kissing my neck, frantically licking champagne from my skin, and then quietly, and kissing again, pressing his chest to mine, in circles, and guiding my hands, wrapping my arms around him and pulling me to him, he took us to the couch and started slowly, deeply, with a gentleness I had not known he possessed.

Someone was knocking, banging on the door. I was halfway to the bedroom before I woke up, scrambling to find clothes. It was still dark outside, or gray with morning, I couldn't get my bearings, I had no idea what time it was or how long we'd slept.

I tossed Jim a pair of jeans and he stepped into them on

his way to the door while I dug through the bedclothes, looking for my pistol.

I heard the door open and listened for alarm in Jim's voice. There was none. I tucked the gun back under my pillow, calmed myself, looked for something to wear. When I walked into the living room, my shirt sticking to the dried champagne on my back, Jim was sitting on the couch, smoking a joint with a neighbor.

"Flo," he said, "meet Walker."

Walker stood up, shaking his light brown hair from his eyes, and nodded at me. He was tall and stocky, wearing a Blues Brothers T-shirt and faded jeans.

"I've seen you around," he said. "I wanted to ask if you needed help with those groceries last week, but . . ." He shrugged and sat down. He had a low, soft voice, full of the yes-ma'am courtesy of a shy cowboy. His steel-toed work boots were black, crusted with red mud, and he had the winter tan of one who works outdoors.

"You know that Blue Hawaiian last week?" Jim asked, "this is the guy who had it."

"Good stuff," I said. Walker nodded again.

"We knocked off at lunch today because of the rain," he said. "I got some more coming in and just stopped over to see if y'all were interested."

"Always," Jim said. He passed me the joint. I noticed that Walker looked carefully when I took a hit.

"What time is it anyway?" I asked.

"Close to three," Walker said. "I apologize for waking you." I went to the window and pulled back the drapes.

"No problem," I said. "I don't usually sleep all day, but I was ambushed with champagne about four this morning." I could feel Jim smiling at me. "It's really dark out there."

The clouds were blue-gray, the color of egg yolk beyond hard-boiled, and seemed to be hanging only yards above

the rooftops. Everything was wet, water dripped rhythmi-
cally from the branches of dark green pines in the court-
yard.

"Well it's been raining like a cow pissing on a flat rock
for the better part of an hour," Walker said. "I don't see
how anyone could've slept through it. Thunder and everything."

When I turned from the window I almost tripped on an
empty champagne bottle. I picked it up and aimed it at Jim.

"Be forewarned," I said. "The attack will come when
you least expect it."

Walker put a joint on the table and stood up.

"I'll let y'all get back to whatever it was you were doing."
He smiled. "And I'll stop by when that comes in. How
much do you want?"

"Quarter pound should do for now," Jim said. "You
wouldn't have any of that other, would you?"

"White stuff?" Walker asked. "It's coming in with the
Hawaiian. Interested?"

"Like a hawk on a June bug," Jim said.

The rain started again a few minutes after Walker left,
coming down hard and steady against the wood-shingled
roof and pouring in sheets off the eaves and past the window.

"Looks cold out there," Jim said. He got up and flicked
on the television, leaving the volume off, and turned on
some music. A black-and-white John Wayne was peering
through some bushes at a circle of young boys who were
passing around a bottle and laughing, this to the sound of
Eric Clapton.

We sat on the couch and Jim picked up the joint Walker
had left.

"If nothing else," he said, "the boy deserves slack for
having such jam-up smoke."

"Try running that at the D.A.," I said.

"He'd probably ask for a pound himself. Anyway, I figure everybody's got at least one probation coming."

"Get real. This guy, yes. Everyone, no way."

"I had Dodd check him. No record."

"Technically this joker Gaines doesn't have a record. Zero convictions."

"Rob's got a snitch in Houston says Gaines started out as a bouncer in Atlantic City, Fat Willy they called him. Dude's six five, two hundred thirty pounds and bragged all over New Jersey that the thirty was swinging."

"Prince Charming incarnate."

"You got it. Fat Willy. Jesus. Snitch says he saw him beat the shit out of a skinny-assed card-counter one night. Carried the guy out to the parking lot behind the casino, knocked most of his teeth out and stomped on his chest until he heard ribs cracking."

"Doesn't sound like the kind of guy who'd respond to tea and sympathy."

"Only thing he'll understand is a gun in his face. But we've got to figure a different route."

"Check it out," I said. Jim looked at the TV.

"John Wayne saves the day," he said. "I grew up believing that shit."

The Drillers Club was pumping heavy metal cranked so loud that the walls of my stomach rattled. At the far end of the room-length bar was a miniature oil pump that would squirt beer into your cup in exchange for a few quarters. Walker was leaning next to it, talking to a guy who looked like Charles Manson. Jim and I had a table near the back wall, waiting to see if Gaines would make his appearance.

He always showed at one of his clubs, strutting around,

checking out the local talent, ordering another stinger when his glass ran dry. He was huge, bordering on fat, but looked pretty solid. He was indeed six five, six five at least, with thick blond hair rimming his earlobes and porkchop sideburns coming in yellowish-gray. His face had the look of a heavyweight fighter who'd been K.O.'d one time too many. His nose had been mashed for sure.

Each night, night after night, Jim and I made the rounds until we found him. We had to let him see us, Jim said. We needed to be "regulars." After Drillers came Ace's and Ate's, where we would sit sipping gimlets and playing backgammon, trying not to listen to disco. The Yellow Rose was our last stop, we drank Lone Star and watched dancers two-step their way through the night, ending always with a C&W version of the William Tell Overture. It started slowly, getting faster and faster with each verse, until finally the bodies whirled around the floor, out of control, while multicolored lights above flashed rapidly in time to the music.

Jim leaned close and spoke straight into my ear.

"Maybe we should split, check someplace else."

"It's early," I said. "Let's give him a few."

It wasn't yet ten, it would be another hour or so before the roughnecks would be drunk enough to start throwing beer around and cracking each other across the back with pool cues.

I went to the "Heifers" room and when I got back Gaines was ambling through the club, greeting customers and rubbing one large hand in circles over his belly. He had on a V-neck blue velour pullover and gray slacks, and when he walked past our table he slapped one huge hand on Jim's shoulder and said, "How you doing, man?" He smiled quickly at me and walked toward his office, pausing at the bar to say a word to a couple of scooter nasties.

He had spoken softly, without emotion, in monotone. Hadn't even slowed to wait for a reply from Jim.

"The dude is hainty," Jim said, leaning toward me to whisper. "Tagged us for his men. Far end of the bar."

I looked slowly around the room, taking in the guys Gaines had nodded at. One of them was rather slight and had pure white hair that hung to the middle of his back. No facial hair. Not even eyebrows. The other was bigger and wore a Fu Manchu. Both had on bike-gang leathers— pants, jacket, boots.

"Maybe I'll go get a couple of refills," I said. "Say hi to Walker, get a better look at those two."

"Do that," Jim said. "We leave now and Gaines will know for sure we're the heat."

The man talking to Walker saw that I was coming over and said something to him before turning away, heading toward the men's room. I took a cup from the stack on the bar and dropped a few quarters into the derrick.

"You know that's Lone Star coming out of that thing," Walker smiled. "I'd rather drink sheep dip."

"I'd rather have some snow," I said. "You've made yourself scarce."

"Minor delay," he said. "It'll be around in a few days. I'll have the other tomorrow. Come by if you like. I'll be home after six."

"See you then," I said. The scooter nasties stood a few feet away, sipping their beer, and as I turned from the bar I thought I saw the one with white hair wink at me.

Jim was halfway through a margarita when I brought the beers back.

"That thirsty?" I asked.

"I set up a score for later tonight. That red-headed waitress over there. Crystal meth."

"She looks like a scab," I said. "Have you no scruples?"

She was a walking skeleton in black lycra tights, her skin almost yellow, her hair dyed the color of a rotten tangerine.

"If she's easy that's her problem. I didn't flirt."

"She looks anorexic."

"She's just another speed freak."

We drove around for awhile after the club closed to give the waitress time to get home. It was almost one when we got there. The apartment complex was shabby at best. It was a single building, two stories, made of wood and in need of paint.

"Give me twenty minutes," Jim said. "I don't expect trouble."

"Wait a minute," I said. "I'm not going in? What's the deal?"

"I'm okay. I'll do this one."

"No witnesses."

"If I'm not out in twenty minutes, come in after me." He pulled a napkin from his coat pocket, looked at it and stuffed it back. "Apartment twenty-three," he said.

"Hey," I said. "Shoot straight."

"Just let me get this done," he said.

"This is not cool."

"She's a needle freak, okay, you saw what happened with Willy Red."

"Yes," I said. "I saw. You think I didn't handle it or something?"

"You handled it beautifully," he said. "That's what I'm afraid of."

He weaved across the parking lot and took the stairs slowly, checking and rechecking the napkin. I left the engine on and the heater running. Twenty minutes. *You're stout for a chick, man, I know you'll handle it.* Right. So what was I doing waiting in the car? Fuck him.

I got out and sat on the hood, which was warm against the cold night air of November. I counted ten faded red doors, spaced evenly along the ground floor, separated by sets of windows on either side. Television-blue light flickered from some. A man's voice flared from behind a door, then a woman's, screaming back at him. The sounds of their rage pulled at my stomach. I wondered how far they would take it, if glass would be broken or blows exchanged, but it didn't sound like it would turn into full-scale Family Disturbance. I could tell by their yelling that they were trying to vent steam, attempting to get rid of the pressure that builds quietly between couples until it either blows them apart or sucks them under, pulling them so close together that they forget how to breathe without one another.

The yelling stopped as suddenly as it had begun, and when Jim came down the stairs his footsteps were loud on the wooden slats.

He filled out his report as soon as we were home, initialing the tiny triangles of plastic and sealing them in a manila envelope. He wrote the date and time and his initials across the flap, making sure the letters and numbers crossed the seal to show it was delivered to the lab intact. The chemists would slit the top open, test a sample, and reseal it with red tape, adding their own initials last.

"Your turn," Jim said, handing me the envelope.

"I didn't see the buy," I said.

"You saw me go in, you saw me come out with this. Now you're seeing me seal it. I doubt this one will go to trial anyway."

I took the envelope and added my initials. If he'd done speed, I couldn't tell it. He seemed calm, a little high from another evening of drinking, but not at all wired.

"So," I said, "the mighty Gaines spoke tonight."

"We have to be very patient. He's not the kind of man you can press."

"Walker said he'll have some smoke tomorrow. Told me to come by."

"I've been thinking we ought to flip that little bastard."

"I'll check his pulse," I said. "Right now I'm tired." He stood up and stretched.

"I think I'll read the paper awhile, catch up on the news."

I picked up the envelope.

"Leave that," he said. "I'll stash it later."

I was almost asleep when I heard him ease the front door open and lock it quietly from the outside.

SEVEN

I SLEPT UNTIL ALMOST ONE THE NEXT DAY, AND WHEN I woke up Jim still wasn't back. There was a note on the table: Had some business, see you at dinner. I made some calls to set up buys and spent the afternoon flipping channels.

At seven, when I was leaving for Walker's, Jim showed up looking like forty miles of bad road.

"Where you headed?" he asked.

"Walker's," I said. "He's supposed to have smoke."

"I'm bushed, I'll wait here." He kicked his shoes off and fell onto the couch. "Ran into some armed robbers last night," he said. "Sorry motherfuckers. One of them just got out of the joint yesterday. Said they'll have crystal by Saturday."

"Can't wait to meet them. I'll be back shortly."

I had to bang on Walker's door with my fist. His sound system covered most of the north wall of his living room, and he had it cranked. He was pulling in KOKE FM all the way from Austin: Traffic doing "The Low Spark of High-Heeled Boys."

When I sat down, he plopped next to me on his couch, lip-synching while he twisted up a joint. When he finished, he picked up the remote and muted the sound.

"It's not the Hawaiian," he said, "but it's pretty good."

I lit it and passed it back to him, and we smoked in silence for awhile. He seemed antsy, tapping his boot to some imaginary tune.

"I think," he said finally, "we should like, talk about something."

"What's that," I said.

"Some of my friends and me," he said. "Well, they're kind of concerned, we're kind of concerned about your boyfriend." He looked at his watch, then rapped the face of it with his knuckle. "Worthless," he mumbled.

"Broken?"

"Just slow. Every day winds up forty-two minutes slow. Rolex my ass."

"Take it back," I said.

"I can't. Guy gave it to me for some blow."

"Anybody I know?"

"Naw. He split out of town, can't find him. Anyway."

"So what's the deal, what's the problem?"

"Some of us are kind of, uh, some of my friends think Jim might be a cop." He pulled a fleck of marijuana from his tongue and wiped it on his jeans, holding the joint out to me.

"I've known Jim for ten years," I lied. "Your friends should be careful about who they tag as heat."

"I'm not saying he is, just that some folks are wondering. I mean he moved into town last May, doesn't work, and been steadily buying dope from damn near everybody he meets. Folks are talking, and that's not good. A man could get hurt."

"That's the thing," I said. "Someone could get hurt. Jim doesn't need a bunch of lightweights starting up about cops. It's not smart."

"Well I don't *think* he is, but I'm in a goddamn deep pile of shit if the rumors are true."

"You got nothing to worry about," I said. "Not from Jim's direction. You should tell your friends to think about what they're saying. Jim does business, you know. He doesn't want any heat of any kind from any direction. Tell them that."

"Hell, I ain't so worried. I mean, I just figure you're the one to talk to. I know you're cool, hell, you're a woman, and I know you're tight with Jim, and, well, if he is the heat, you know, I'm in a bind."

I wasn't sure, but it seemed like Walker was running way out front, looking for a deal. He knew something was up. I could see invitation in his eyes. He was scared, looking for the way out of a maze he wasn't entirely sure he was trapped in. It sounded like he was flat out offering to snitch.

"Why don't we just go upstairs and talk to Jim," I said. "He's home. Let's get this cleared up."

He let out a sigh and said, "Let me roll one more."

"Do that," I said. "Jim will appreciate it."

I sat there watching him try to be calm while he twisted the joint, and I remembered my first night with Skip, when I'd struggled to roll an entire lid into cigarettes and had no idea what I was doing or what I was getting into. Then, I'd wanted a few pat answers to my vacuous little questions, and now I was foolish enough to believe that I had them. This guy did not need to go to jail.

He was in trouble, he didn't know how much trouble, and I was incapable of mustering the cold efficiency that Jim seemed born with. I liked Walker. Whether he knew what he was asking for or not. But it would be better for all of us if he worked off his cases and avoided arrest. Jim had mentioned flipping him. I lacked the predatory instinct. Perhaps this is what drove me to try all the harder.

Perhaps it was the lure of illusion: I'm separate from all of them, morally superior, I tell them how to behave. It was a sham. Working undercover on this kind of defendant made me feel like a meter maid.

Jim was on the couch, wrapped in the blanket even though the heat was on. The temperature in the apartment had to be pushing eighty.

"Hey, man," he said, struggling to sit up when Walker and I entered. "What's happening?" His eyes were sleep swollen, his face creased from a wrinkle in the pillow.

"Walker here wants to chat with you."

"Oh," he said. "Damn. Made some coffee and dropped off to sleep before it was brewed." He tossed aside the blanket and stood up to snap the button of his jeans. "What time is it?"

"Close to eight." I motioned to the kitchen table and Walker sat down.

"Excuse me a moment," Jim said. He shut the door behind him as he went into the bedroom. I brought cups from the kitchen and set them on the table.

"He probably went in there and fell asleep again," I said. "I'll be right back."

Jim was combing his hair in front of the mirror on the closet door.

"He'll snitch," I whispered.

"He just jump up and volunteer?"

"Practically. There are rumors. He's concerned. Says he wants to do whatever he has to in order to keep himself clear. He's scared you're the heat."

"I guess he should be, shouldn't he," Jim said.

"You mentioned flipping him. I think he's ripe."

"What about Nettle?"

"He'll go for whatever gets him his cases. We should just do it and tell El Jefe after."

"El Jefe," Jim said. "You damn sure got his number." He stepped into his shoes and leaned against the dresser. "Yeah. He wants the cases. He'll go for it."

"You said Walker's connected. He could make life easier. And we could keep him out of the joint."

"You be the good cop, baby. Be polite now. Stay calm and ministrate to the boy's emotional needs. He's about to have a heap of them."

Jim waited until I was clanking dishes around, setting out the sugar bowl and spoons, before he came out of the bedroom and sat down next to Walker. He had his .45 stuffed down the front of his jeans and his eyes had a look I hadn't noticed for awhile, a certain eagerness that pulled his eyebrows down and hardened the muscles of his jaw. The last time I'd seen it, he was standing on someone's front porch, getting ready to kick a door in.

"What's on your mind?" he said.

Walker sat silently for a minute, cleared his throat, and sat some more.

"He thinks you're a cop," I said.

"That right, motherfucker?" Jim asked. "You been running around town yapping that I'm the man?"

Walker stared at the gun and shook his head no.

"I ain't accusing you of shit, man, I just think you should know that some folks are concerned. Just around, you know, people are talking."

"Well, hey, little boy," Jim said, "let me just get something real clear here." He stood up, pulled his gun out and stuck it against Walker's lips. Walker straightened in his chair and sat trying to blink his hair out of his eyes. His T-shirt was black and the Aerosmith logo on the front was peeling.

"You ever tell one solitary motherfucker a single word about what I say to you here tonight and I swear to God I'll kill you. It's that simple. I'll drop the hammer on your ass so fast you'll be dead before you got here. You understand?"

I watched the blood drain slowly out of Walker's face, his flesh going gray-white in distinct stages. He barely nodded. Jim stood there in a low-burning rage, and in that moment I knew what he was capable of, that he would do as he threatened.

I kept my hand steady as I poured coffee. Jim still had the gun at Walker's face, staring at him as though pulling the trigger would redeem both their souls.

"Not a word," Jim said. "To anyone." He pulled the gun away and stuffed it back in his jeans.

"I need the john," Walker said.

"Down the hall," I said.

I listened for the sound of the bathroom door closing and turned to Jim.

"Prosecutor, judge, and jury."

"No need to drag the thing out in court," he said. "I know he's guilty. He knows he's guilty. Hell, he takes the deal it's the best thing could happen to him. That boy wouldn't last ten minutes in the joint."

Walker came back and fell into his chair, landing hard enough to knock a gust of breath out of his chest.

"What made you snap?" Jim asked.

"What?"

"Why'd you think I was heat?"

"I don't know," Walker said. "Not exactly. I don't know." He shook his head. "I guess that nobody could do as much dope as you've been buying. And I ain't heard yet of anybody buying from you."

"Yeah. Well, you got it right."

"No way," Walker said. "No way you're the man."

"Well, hell, boy, if you don't think I'm the heat, what the fuck did you come here for? Are we a little bit bored on a Friday night, decide to stir up some amusement?"

"This isn't happening," Walker said.

I brought some blank offense reports from the bedroom closet. If Walker argued, Jim's gun would come out again.

"See these?" I said. "There are two of them filled out with your name right there on the top line. They're in a filing cabinet at the Vice office downtown."

Walker stared at the reports. Neat blocks for name, address, description, date and time of offense, a space for details of the crime.

"Man, what's the deal?" he said. "Come on, Flo. Enough already. Man. Let's smoke a joint."

"Walker," I said, "we're cops. Undercover. As in narcotics agents. Yes, it can happen in your town. Get it?"

He let his head fall back and closed his eyes.

"Damn," he sighed. "And all this time I thought you were from France."

"What?" I asked.

"Yeah," he said, "you look really French." He laughed to himself. "I don't know, man, I just always thought of you as French." He rolled his head back and forth, his Adam's apple jutting from his neck. "I was trying to decide if I could hit on you without Jim here finding out."

"Hey," Jim said. He sat down again and leaned toward Walker. "I got to have some answers now, boy."

Walker pulled his head up and looked at him.

"You want to slide on these cases?" Jim asked. "You want to work for us? You cool things down, you make some introductions, you'll walk on the cases. What'll it be?"

"Man, don't I get a lawyer? I mean, I want to talk to

a lieutenant or something, man. I want to know what the fuck is going on here. You can't do this."

Jim reached for the phone, dialed the Vice office.

"Sergeant," he said. "Working late on a Friday night?" He listened for a moment.

"Got somebody wants to go to work for us."

He paused, said okay, and hung up.

"Let's go," he said.

"Where?" Walker asked.

"To meet the chief of police. He'll be waiting for us behind the Piggly Wiggly. Ten minutes. You'd best think straight on the way over."

"I want a lawyer."

"You want a lawyer?" Jim was on his feet again. "Okay. There's the phone. Here's the deal. You call a lawyer and we forget about walking you. We'll take you to trial. We'll tell a good solid drug-hating Jefferson County jury that you have been out on the streets of their fine town selling cocaine and LSD. You know what they'll do, boy? They'll lock your ass up for forty years. Maybe life. Go ahead. Call your fucking lawyer."

I stayed behind the wheel when Jim and Walker got out. Halfway to Dodd's Plymouth, Jim turned.

"You're not coming?"

"I'll sit tight," I said. They climbed into the back seat, and I could see their silhouettes through the windshield as they leaned toward one another and talked.

The alley behind the supermarket was narrow and dark, lit by a single, mesh-enclosed bulb above the truck dock. There was a large green dumpster near the side of the dock, the asphalt around it littered with crushed containers and pieces of cardboard. I noticed a large jar of Bosco near the base of the dumpster, cracked.

They talked for some time. At one point I turned the ignition to accessory and let the heater run for a few minutes.

Jim held Walker's arm in the classic suspect-in-custody grip as they walked back to the car, a gesture that said, "He's ours." Nettle and Dodd pulled slowly out of the alley and Jim got into the back seat, motioning Walker to sit up front.

"Let's go score," Jim said.

"Right now?" Walker asked.

"This minute. Who's that dude, your running buddy, the one drives the maroon hearse and thinks he such hot shit. He holding?"

Walker began cracking his knuckles in the silence.

"Hey, boy," Jim said, "you gonna do it, let's go. Show me where your loyalties lie."

"Grady," Walker said. "His name's Grady Carter."

At an Exxon station, Jim handed Walker a quarter and stood next to the phone booth while Walker dragged his boot heel back and forth across an oil spot on the concrete and stabbed at the pushbuttons on the phone.

I watched him talking, and then Jim brought him back to the car and leaned in to ask if I wanted a Dr Pepper. Walker got in and sat next to me, staring at the glove box while I watched Jim feed coins to the machine, his face glowing red when he bent close to pull out the cans.

"Don't freak out," I said. "I know it seems pretty bizarre, but don't lose it. You'll be okay."

Walker slammed a hand against the dash and twisted in his seat to face me.

"What the fuck does okay mean?" he yelled. "I'll be okay?! The fucking chief of police tells me he wants thirty cases and you're taking me over to help you buy drugs from my best friend and you're telling me I'll be okay?"

"Hey," I said, "you won't even see the inside of the

courthouse if you do what's right. Jim and I are in a position to help. We can help you, and we can help your friend. But you've got to work with us. Do you hear what I'm saying?" I felt ill.

Jim came back with the Dr Peppers and stretched out across the back seat.

"You said Fourth Street?" he asked.

"Yeah," Walker said. "There's a store down there. He'll meet us."

I pulled into the lot and parked under the bright yellow "Wag-A-Bag" street sign. Beneath red lettering was the image of a smiling dachshund, standing on his hind legs holding an open paper sack between his teeth. There were curved brown slashes painted near his rear end to indicate that his tail was wagging.

"He's here already," Walker said. The hearse was parked next to the south wall of the store.

"Dude carry a heater?" Jim asked.

"Not usually," Walker said.

"Okay. Flo will go with you. Before anything changes hands, you get out of the car. Long as you don't actually see the deal they can't call you as a defense witness. Got it?"

"I think so," Walker said.

"We're buying Demerol?" I asked.

"Yeah," Walker sighed. "Demerol or smoke."

"We'll take Demerol," Jim said.

I followed Walker across the lot and as we got close to the hearse I could see that the back of it was loaded with all kinds of junk, mostly stuff from Mexico: patio lanterns, wrought-iron bookends, piñatas, and a few adding machines and typewriters.

Grady leaned out the window and smiled when he saw

us. His left front tooth had a gold cap with a bas-relief peace symbol in the middle of it.

"How they hanging man?" he asked.

"This is Flo," Walker said. "She's moved in across the walk from me."

"Good to meet you. Where you from?"

"Houston," I said.

"Oh. Too tough for me, man."

"Walker says there might be some Demerol around somewhere."

"Might be," Grady said, and dove down toward the floorboards. He came up holding a Batman lunchpail, his tooth glaring from the darkness of the hearse.

"Here we are," he drawled. Walker patted his shirt pocket.

"Damn," he said, "out of smokes. Be right back."

Grady pulled out a bottle of pills and shook them.

"How much?" I asked.

As we walked upstairs to Jim's apartment he leaned close and took my arm. "We'd better get this boy good and fucked up," he said. "He got no idea how you spell relief."

Walker went immediately to the living room and sat in the corner of the sectional. Jim handed him a Demerol and offered the rest of his Dr Pepper.

"Relax," he said. "It ain't the end of the world."

Walker handled the tiny tablet of Demerol as if it were a communion host, using both of his shaking hands to set it gently on his tongue.

Jim and I took up places at either end of the sectional and he tossed me a tablet.

"A friend of mine," he said, "swears that the first time he had Demerol he thought he was floating on a sea of titties." We tried at one point to smoke a joint, but couldn't keep it lit.

"How old are you?" I finally asked Walker.

"Twenty?" he slurred. "Yeah. Twenty. And I have fucked up big time."

We nodded through the night, sometimes talking sense, sometimes just saying words. He heard the gospel according to Jim, "It's every citizen's duty to do all they can to help keep the streets safe for children." I dozed behind the Demerol and listened to Jim's drunken passion in the night. It was the same song he and Rob had sung to me when I first started undercover, the pathetic little tune that sounded so good the first time I'd heard it.

I struggled with my eyelids while Jim talked, watched Walker's head rolling on his shoulders as he fought the drug and tried to make sense of what he was hearing. I saw white squares and triangles floating in the dark around his narrow face.

"How old are you?" I asked.

"Twenty?" he said. "Didn't we do this already?"

"Maybe we did." My tongue felt like gelatin. "Don't feel bad," I said. Who was I pleading with? "You shouldn't, you know, you shouldn't feel bad at all. You think Grady wouldn't do the same? I'm telling you. They all do. Everybody. Wake up and roll over, man, talk and walk."

"Don't get ahead of yourself," Jim said to me. "Dude might get out there and tell the whole damn town what's coming down." He leaned toward Walker. "I hope you do, motherfucker. I really hope you do. Been too long since I killed anybody, I'm kind of in the mood, you know?"

"Would anyone like some chocolate milk?" I asked. "I'm getting up now."

At dawn, Walker picked up his boots and stumbled home, sock-footed. He was out there, out there and knew the score, but the rules had all changed. I watched as he staggered down the steps and lurched across the sidewalk to his patio door.

"Don't worry," Jim said. "We got his attention."

EIGHT

AS I TURNED INTO DODD'S DRIVEWAY, THE GARAGE door opened slowly and he waved me inside, hitting a switch on the wall as the back of the Olds cleared the entrance. There was an electric hum beneath the sound of gears grating as the door came back down. Dodd was in jeans and a dirty white T-shirt, wearing an Astros baseball cap. He looked like a pig farmer.

I got out and handed him the evidence envelopes, a dozen new cases thanks to Walker. I'd just come from making a coke buy, and was wired enough to hope it didn't show.

"Kickin' ass and taking names," Dodd said. "Closing in on fifty cases. Any news on Gaines?"

"We're letting him see us," I said. "I'm so sick of the Drillers Club I could puke."

"How many cops you know would love to get paid for partying? Got your own place yet?"

"No," I said, "and it's hardly a party when you're watching your back every minute."

"Just start watching the classified section," he said, "and get yourself a goddamn apartment, girl. Nettle's on my ass about it."

"I haven't had much time for personal business."

"It's not personal, it's department regs." He leaned

104

against my car. "What's Jim doing, I haven't seen him lately."

"He's okay," I said. "I've mostly been working Walker, Jim's in with a bunch of pill dealers now."

He shuffled through the envelopes.

"Buying a shitload of crystal."

"Yeah," I said. "There's a lot around."

"That and coke, looks like."

"Those are mine. From Walker's circle."

"I've seen a lot of these names before. Burglars. Some of them still on probation. That'll save time in court." He ran his eyes over me. "You're losing weight, girl."

"I've dropped a few pounds," I said. "We're only working about twenty-three hours a day."

"And doing a fine job," he said. "Don't slow down."

I signed a year-long lease on a one-bedroom in the Elysian Fields apartments, across the street from Jim's place. The telephone man looked at me oddly when he came for installation. He worked silently for awhile and finally said, "No furniture? No dishes?" I told him I hadn't quite moved in.

I wasn't going to. The address would suffice. On some afternoons, when I found myself home alone, I would walk over there and sit on the beige carpet in the middle of the living room, smoking a joint while I tried to imagine what things would be like when the investigation was over. We were buying lots of dope, plenty of it, but I kept telling myself it was all under control. Pulling up would be no problem. I was strong enough. I could handle it.

Rob cruised in the front door in his full-length black leather, looked around the room and said, "I'm sure there's some smoke around here somewhere."

Walker had brought a whole crew over, reeled them in

like fish and landed them in our living room. Jim's place was the place to be in town. No rules. Loud music. Plenty of booze, plenty of smoke. The place to hang out after the clubs closed, taking turns on the telephone, looking for more cocaine. One more time. Tonight we had a room full of lightweights, disco cowboys and their girlfriends, the party crowd, not serious dealers.

"This is Jim," I said to the defendants when Rob walked in.

"Where's Jim?" Rob said to me.

"I thought you were Jim," someone said.

"The other Jim," Rob said. "Where is he?"

"Gone after groceries," said Walker.

"At two in the morning?" Rob asked.

"He got the munchies," someone said. "You're Jim too?"

"Yeah," Rob said, "I be Jim. Now why don't you motherfuckers splitdown with the smoke."

Someone gave him a joint. Someone else took J. J. Cale off the stereo and put Supertramp on. Rob toked on the joint, flaring his nostrils as he inhaled.

"Damn," he said suddenly, "I forgot. I have someone in the car."

"Bring her in," I said.

"It's not a her."

"Anyone I know?"

He smiled. "It's Jim, I'll go get him if Jim's coming back soon. He didn't want to come up if Jim wasn't here."

"Tell him Jim will be right back."

Walker stared at us. Rob took another hit, handed the joint to him, and headed out the door.

"Save that," he called. "I'll be back in a few."

A skinny defendant talking on the phone motioned for Walker to bring him the joint.

Rob came back and introduced Denny. "Everyone," he said, "this is Jim."

Someone said, "What's going on."

Someone else took Supertramp off the stereo and put on Marvin Gaye.

Denny sniffed the air and said, "You got anything around here that ain't illegal?"

I brought him a bottle of Wild Turkey and a shot glass.

"That'll do just fine," he said. He fingered the scar where his eyebrow used to be and blinked a few times, as though trying to wake up. Walker nodded toward the bedroom and I followed him.

"Who are these guys?" he asked, closing the door.

"They're Jims," I said.

"Come on. Really. What's the real deal?"

"Current and ex-State boys."

"Agents?"

"One is, one used to be," I said. He looked at me, half-stoned, half-drunk, and still confused. I fell to my knees and raised my palms to the ceiling, felt the room rolling around us, heard my wasted voice bounce off the walls while I sang: "When the smack begins to flow/Then I really don't care anymore/About all you Jim-Jims in this town/And everybody putting everybody else down/And all the politicians making crazy sounds/And all the dead bodies piled up in mounds." I staggered up and fell against the wall, took a bow, laughing, giggling, stoned silly. Walker stared at me.

"Sorry," I said. The walls were shimmering.

"I don't get it," he said, collapsing onto the bed. I tried to focus.

"It's a Lou Reed kind of thing."

A short blast of Rod Stewart and loud voices came through the door with Rob when he ducked into the room.

He eased the door shut behind him and the music pounded against the bedroom wall.

"Walker," I slurred, "meet Jim."

Walker managed to stand up and shake hands.

"How you doing, man?" Rob said.

"I'm doing," Walker said. "Just doing."

Rob pulled a pill bottle from his coat pocket and began tossing it in the air.

"Who am I meeting here?" he asked.

"Not-Jim," I said. "Un-Jim, dis-Jim, but not anti-Jim. Semi-Jim. Working for us."

"That right?" Rob rattled the pills and slipped the bottle back into his pocket. "You wouldn't know anything that might be happening in Houston, would you? I work the greater Houston metropolitan area."

"I might," Walker said. "I know some people there. Depends what's in it."

Rob threw his head back.

"Oh, yeah," he squealed in falsetto, "this boy be *doing.*" He brought his voice down and talked fast. "In the way of slack, my man? There be plenty of slack for a poor white boy got himself in a little old jam. Lots of slack from the state's direction. When you finish up here, you know. There's folks who do it professionally, and make a good living at it. You'll be relocating, I assume, when this thing's done." He took out the bottle and poured pills on the bed.

"Look there," he said, pointing, his voice rising with wonder, "someone left dope in this room."

Walker picked up a pink tablet and inspected the markings. "What is it?"

"It looks like speed," Rob said. "Like Preludin maybe. I've heard that's some damn good shit. Maybe somebody around here should try it."

*   *   *

Jim was out on a deal when Walker stopped by after work the next day, covered with red dirt. His eyes looked wired, but he was moving slowly as he fell onto the couch and dug in his pocket.

"Blue Ringers," he said, handing me a capsule. "Dude's got thousands."

"Never heard of them," I said.

"I hadn't either."

"You try it out?"

"Took the edge off that pink thing y'all gave me last night. Must be a damn good downer. Dude's name is Monroe, and he's expecting your call. I told him you'd be interested in a couple hundred at least. If they were good."

I drove out early in the evening, finally found the right numbers on a mailbox and pulled into the rutted drive. The house was made of cinderblocks, a perfect square, set way back off the road and surrounded by trees. I dug into my purse and made sure my gun was on top of everything. The setup was hillbilly spooky, and in moments like these I realized exactly how vulnerable I was. In the middle of nowhere with a dope dealer I'd never met before.

He came outside before I was out of my car, and I recognized him immediately. He was the man who'd walked away the night I approached Walker at Drillers. Even up close he looked like Charles Manson. Same weasely hair, same Holy Ghost eyes.

Except for a bathroom, closet, and small kitchen, the place was one large room, filled with gaming tables—blackjack, poker, even a roulette wheel. The floor was concrete, with an industrial drain set in the center, and there were a couple of leather couches against the back wall, large brass spittoons on the floor next to them.

"You want a beer," he said, his voice scraping through

the room like a wet shovel on dry cement. It wasn't a question.

"I guess I do," I said. "You have a party or two here?"

"Every Friday," he said, "and every Saturday."

I followed him back toward the kitchen. He took a couple of beers from the refrigerator and handed me one. Then he pulled open the flap on a cardboard box next to the stove and stuck his hand in, coming up with a palmful of tiny white capsules, each marked with a bright blue ring around the middle.

"How many you want?" he asked.

"Where's the break?"

"Three bucks each, up to a hundred. More than that, two fifty." I sipped the beer.

"Hundred sounds good."

He dumped a handful on the counter and began knocking them off by twos into a bottle. When he finished he capped it and picked up two capsules from the leftovers, handing one to me.

"Let's get fucked up," he said.

"I've got people waiting on these," I said. "I have to drive back into town."

"I said let's get fucked up."

I tossed the pill in my mouth and took a gulp of beer, handed him the cash. I figured I had twenty minutes to make it home before the thing kicked in.

"Look," I said, "I'm gonna be in a real jam if I don't get back. I've promised a lot of people I'd have these to them tonight. It's been real, but I've got to go."

He turned and walked to the closet, and came back holding a potted baby marijuana plant.

"Peace," he said, making the gesture.

"Yeah, peace," I said. "Right. I'll see you around."

Just as I was about to get in my car he pinned me to the

side of it and planted a skanky kiss on my mouth. I eased sideways and slipped into the front seat.

"I really have to go."

"Happy motoring," he whispered. It must have been the Ringers, but his eyes seemed to glow in the dark.

I remember the first ten minutes of the drive back. After that, it was all headlights. I knew I was in my car, I didn't know on what road, I didn't know who was steering.

I remember a phone booth, I don't know where. I was standing there shivering, punching at buttons, listening to an operator's voice. I think I passed out. I remember sliding down the dirty glass wall of a phone booth, seeing a gray plastic receiver dangling helplessly at the end of its metallic cord, feeling it tap against my forehead.

Then I was walking in the door to Jim's apartment and I remember seeing Jim and Rob and Denny stare at me as I fell over the couch. Laughing. I remember tossing the bottle of capsules to Jim. Passing out again.

There were trumpets, four of them, and they blasted out something that sounded more like a call to battle than an introduction to Christmas Midnight Mass. The processional came up the center aisle from the back of the church, a troop of altar boys led by Monsignor O'Brian, resplendent in white-and-gold vestments, followed by two priests I didn't recognize. The monsignor had aged incredibly, his hair gone white, his skin sallow and deeply creased around the mouth. Too many years of dealing with sin, of unanswered rosaries, of baptisms and last rites. He had sounded so sure of himself the day he'd prayed for Kennedy. I gripped the back of the pew in front of me to keep my hands from shaking.

The smell of frankincense preceded them up the aisle, battling the scents of women's perfumes, men's aftershaves, and, over it all, the collective breath of the parishioners. I was afraid of what I looked like.

They, we, were gathered, all in a row, fifth pew from the front: Dad, Mom, Valerie, Michelle, me. And Jim. High Mass at the Church of the Good Shepherd. Yes indeed. Jim and I had scored a quarter ounce of coke that afternoon before making the drive to Houston.

"In the name of the Father, and the Son, and the Holy Spirit." The monsignor's voice, even with the aid of the microphone, was barely audible and shaky with alcohol.

I stood between Michelle and Jim, wearing my court clothes, a conservative gray suit that had gotten at least a size too big for me.

My sisters had pleaded over the phone. We're a family, they'd said, we should act like a family. It's only once a year, they said. It's Christmas. You can make it for the day.

I did my best to look like I was participating. My father sang beautifully from his seat on the aisle. I mouthed the words and tried not to sniff too much. I watched them go to Communion. I felt tacked on, an ingredient added at the last minute by a cook trying to salvage the stew.

When we got home, I led Jim to my old bedroom. The single twin bed was still in the corner, wearing its light blue spread and matching dust ruffle. Above the small desk next to it, a bulletin board covered with medals, and ribbons of red and blue. First Place, Mile Relay, First Place, 220 Yard Dash, Second Place, High Jump, First Place, 80 Yard Lows. What did Babe Didrikson have on me, except that she'd gone the distance. On the dresser was a trophy from church-league softball, a monument to the sandlot league.

"Man," Jim said, "it's like a fucking museum in here."

"Yeah," I said, "my mother keeps talking about turning it into a study." I stood staring at the ribbons, remembering. I had quit the team once, during my junior year, telling the coach that running around in circles no longer appealed to me. I'd managed to stay away for three weeks.

Jim closed the door and came up behind me, pressing himself close and slipping his arms around my waist.

"They gonna let me sleep in here?"

"No way," I said. "The folks are not big on mortal sin."

"Come on," he said, "they know."

"Knowing and admitting are two different things. I'll show you the guest room."

He reached next to the ribbons and took down a framed photo. There I was in high school, clearing a hurdle in front of seven other runners. Winning had been easy, had always been easy, because I'd loved running the race, I'd loved the race itself.

Jim came out of his pocket with a vial and began tapping out lines on the photo.

"First time I've been to a mass," he said. "Preacher I grew up around said we'd rot in hell if we ever set foot inside a Catholic church. Said the pope was the Antichrist."

"Which pope?"

"All of them. The position itself, doesn't matter who holds it."

"So what do you think, think you'll burn?"

"I've known that since I was eighteen," he said, bending to snuff up a line. "I packed a bag and walked out the front door, headed for Austin, and that was the last thing my mama said to me. You're going straight to hell. Yelled it from the porch, in front of God and everybody. Didn't matter. She went kind of crazy after my dad ran off. Spent the next five years in the garden, pulling weeds and quoting from Corinthians. I didn't know where I was going, but I knew I had to get out of Big Spring." He handed me the tooter.

I didn't want any more cocaine. I had the shakes, a bad case of the shakes. We'd gotten a batch laced with crystal, I could taste it, and it would not leave me alone. My family was in the living room, waiting to say good-night. I didn't want any more. I wanted rest. I leaned toward the photo. I didn't want it. *I did not want any more.*

Oh yes I did.

I lay awake most of the night, my eyes too tired to read, the rest of me wired to the point that sleep was out of the question. I finally drifted off just as dawn was coming up.

I was awakened by kitchen sounds, my sisters laughing about something while they set the table.

The turkey was perfect, golden brown. My father said it looked succulent. He sat at one end of the table, Jim at the other. My mother and Michelle were opposite Valerie and me. We wore the new clothes that we'd wrapped in brightly colored paper and given to one another the night before, when we got back from mass. There was even a dog, an arthritic collie named Herbert who'd been brought into the family a year or so after I moved away to campus. Herb sat at the dining-room doorway, his front paws planted on the imaginary line that he had been trained never to cross, his nose lifted to catch the aroma of dinner.

I felt surrounded, as though I should be the one begging at the doorway. They were such good people, such believers, so very American. Michelle was on break from her biology major at SMU, Valerie a senior in high school. My parents? Nine-to-fivers. They kept the lawn trimmed and paid their taxes. They bought groceries and cheered, with restraint, for the Oilers. They voted Democratic, regularly, even in the primaries.

They believed in law and order, and like all decent parents, were terrified about the drug problem. They thought my job was honorable. I couldn't begin to explain.

I watched my father carve the turkey meticulously, the way he did everything, and tried to muster an appetite. When he finished, he smiled around the table and said, "Jim, would you like to offer grace?"

Jim gave me a glance that said, What the fuck have you gotten me into, then he smoothed his face over and said, "Certainly. I'd be honored."

During Jim's prayer, I looked up to see my mother studying me, felt my mouth trying to smile at her, and looked quickly back down. I had her eyes. What did my eyes look like?

"Amen," Jim said, and the family echoed him.

"Dig in," said my father, reaching for the dressing. He spooned some onto his plate and handed it to Valerie.

"So things are well in Beaumont," he said, speaking to Jim.

"Fine," Jim said, "just fine. Have you been following the Oilers?"

"What can you expect," laughed my father, "from a team who's head coach is named Bum?"

I put food in my mouth and I chewed. I think at that moment I wished that my father would jump up and slam a hand on the table and make some demands. Demand to know why his daughter looked like death warmed over, why she never called, why her eyes looked like they were coated with egg-white. Why she wasn't laughing and joking at the table the way she used to.

I wished for it and was afraid of it. But he wouldn't. He wouldn't because he never had, had never questioned anything about his family. I wanted to deserve his concern. I wasn't sure why I didn't.

I remembered the day I was hired in Pasadena. I'd gone

to the house to tell them what I would be doing. My father asked only one question, if that was what I wanted. I'd said yes, and he said, "I'm not thrilled about it. But you are, as they used to say, free, white, and twenty-one. It's your decision." That was it, it had been my decision, whether I was ready to make it or not.

I looked around the table, at all the closed mouths politely chewing food.

"Kristen," Valerie said, "you've got to meet Steve. He's *sooooh* cute, you can't believe it. We're going to see Rod Stewart next Saturday, and he got third-row tickets and everything, and he's in a band, too, he plays drums."

"That's nice," I said. I took a bite of turkey and chewed. It tasted like nothing.

"What's the name of his band?" Jim asked.

Thank you, I thought. Just keep talking. I don't know these people anymore. Everyone just keep talking, and I'll sit here and force down this food and try to maintain.

I rinsed the plates and handed them to Michelle, who put them into the dishwasher.

"You don't look so hot," she said. "Mom's worried."

"She said something to you?"

"She said you looked bad."

"Why'd she tell you?"

"Why does she always tell me? I don't know. We talk."

"She shouldn't worry," I said. "It's just long hours. Very long hours. It'll be over soon and I can take a break. What's happening at school?"

"I'm not sure I like him," she said.

"Who?"

"Jim. There's something about him. But he dresses nice."

*   *   *

Later in the afternoon, we watched football. That was safe, sitting around the television, listening to Jim and my father trade comments on plays. Michelle brought out the dress she was wearing to an upcoming New Year's party; it was chic and black and stunning. Everything Michelle wore was stunning. She knew how to direct her efforts.

"I think you need satin pumps with that," my mother said. She turned to me. "What do you think, black satin pumps?"

"I guess," I said. I had no idea.

"Would you like some cake?" she asked. "Or there's pecan pie."

"I'm still full from dinner," I said. "Maybe later."

"All right then," she said quickly, tones of hurt in her voice.

I offended her without trying. I wanted to talk. I wanted to get the hell out of there.

When evening came, good-byes were said and gentle hugs exchanged. It had always been that way, hands placed lightly on shoulders, as though if we squeezed too hard something might break. I watched my family standing on the front porch, waving at us as Jim eased the car away from the curb. I wanted to stay. I wanted to talk. I didn't know them.

When we rounded the corner, Jim's whole body seemed to sigh. He draped an arm across my seat back and said, "Girl, your family's a class act, but damn are they ever straight. I mean it's 1978, for God's sake, and you're hardly sixteen anymore. I can't go for that separate-rooms shit."

Maybe that was true, or maybe it was just that the vials were almost empty.

NINE

*I AM SO DAMN GOOD AT WHAT I DO, I AM CRAWLING
on the floor, crawling on the fucking floor, wearing the
lovely black silk kimono that Jim gave me before he left
me in his living room with a quarter ounce of coke and went
out on "business." Business is what we are about.*

*I am crawling on the floor, scuffling, looking for one tiny
speck of white, hoping for a rock, hoping for one more heart-
slamming rush, wanting to get up there where I can smile
eye to eye at the Holy Trinity and say, "Hey, boys, what's
happening?" My body wants to go there and my body is
crawling on the floor and my brain is trying to keep up,
there's a continent between my body and brain, there are
light-years between my eyes and hands, there is a nanose-
cond between where I was twenty minutes ago and where I
want to be now. One more rock. One speck of white. So tiny.
So little. Such a small space between misery and joy. I pick
up white pieces from the brown carpet. My knees burn as
I crawl. A bit of cotton, pieces of lint, a speck of white paint
from the wall. Trash.*

*I want to watch Jim put the needle in my arm, slide it
smoothly into the vein, I love that little piercing pain that
comes right before the ocean hits my heart.*

I am such a damn good narc.

Jim and I, we could walk into a club cold and come out with three deals set up that same night and four more for the next day. We knew how to buy dope. We knew how to work our snitches, work the streets.

So I pick up a little old jones, so what? We are the good guys. What we do is right.

Right. I am crawling on the floor. There must be more cocaine here. If there isn't more we have to get some. It's evidence. We have to have something to turn in, even four percent will do. There must be more here. Somewhere. Have to find more.

It's like smelling blood, the way it takes over your body, the reactions, the smell everywhere, the pure, clean, smiling smell of cocaine.

Jim stood in the doorway, wearing his own kimono, maroon, with a dragon on the back. I saw his legs, the fine black hairs on his legs.

When there is enough cocaine, too much cocaine, when I am kicking myself just a little bit higher every twenty minutes, watching the clock between shots, pressing my fingers to my neck to count the pulsebeats, waiting for them to come down from one seventy-four, down below ninety so I can do it again, sometimes hair starts to grow out of everything. Leg hair grows right before my eyes, on the pillows, on the walls, out of the carpet. Fine pale hairs or thick black hairs. I close my eyes and hair grows from the insides of my eyelids.

We scored, scored cold a couple of nights ago, or weeks or months or years ago, I don't know, from a scuzzball in a cowboy hat who said he had been the youngest bank robber ever in the history of the whole country. Gave Walker the night off and hit the clubs. When he was a kid, a nine-year-old kid, this cowboy, he helped pull a bank job. And his friend, standing there next to the cowboy, leaning on a pinball machine, got out of Huntsville yesterday and he's got that look in his eyes like he's waiting for somebody in a uniform to come snatch him up and take him back to the joint. Three grams of coke, not even a speck out of the tons that pour in, but we've got some real sorry asses here, some genuine fuckups, and a dope case is just as good as a robbery case when it comes to getting them off the streets. The baby bank robber, the cowboy, he said, "Hey, man, like we got to know you're cool, man, like here's my rig. Let's get down." And while he said it he's got his hand wrapped around the pretty walnut grip of a Colt Lawman. So we do it, Jim and I, we run the dope right in front of his squinty red eyes, and it's my first time with cocaine, and what did Willy Red know about a rush, this is a rush, I have never felt anything like it before, not even the heroin. I nod at God and whisper "It's nice up here," and Jim is smiling at me because we're both thinking of how this asshole will be screaming in court, "They shot dope! They fucking shot dope!" and when the prosecutor asks us did we ever take drugs we will say, "No sir, certainly not, we're police officers," and we will look so clean and All-American and the jury will just love us for taking armed robbers and dope dealers and fucking third-time recidivists off the streets. For making it safe for children. I find it right somehow, that we beat the sleaze at their own scummy game. I am still capable of appreciating irony.

I am crawling on the floor.

Jim looked down at me, took the rigs from the coffee table and said, "I guess I'd better clean these up."

They came to our door at any and all hours, staggering, stumbling, looking for sanctuary, a place where they could fix without getting hassled. Sometimes with Walker, sometimes because they'd heard on the streets. They gravitated to the scene, *there's a new kid in town.*

We bought their dope and wrote our reports, paying attention to times and dates and physical descriptions, omitting the details that might make them seem human to a jury: Nadean, a burned-out sixties azalea farmer, who also happened to grow marijuana and who delivered her pounds with a complimentary houseplant and recollections of Woodstock; a guy named Buzz Saw who showed up to sell Quaaludes to his old friend Dice who "used to live here, I'm sure," and I, who had six coke deliveries on Dice, calling to tell him Buzz Saw was looking for him and then myself scoring a dozen Quays from Buzz, whom I had never heard of until that moment.

And then there were those like Lester the Mo-lester, who came by one day to show off his brand-new Smith and Wesson .38 Chief Special, which fit so nicely in the pocket of his baggy white pants and which he swore he would break in by shooting "the first pig that steps across my doorway," leaving us to wonder whether he was trying to get a message across or just being his usual psychopathic self.

He brought us to his home, come check out the latest merchandise, in a red '56 Galaxy, bruising down Highway 10 like it was time to die, and we spilled dopesmoke and vodka all over a Sunday afternoon. We looked at hot TVs and stolen shotguns while Lester danced around the kitchen with a loaded syringe in each hand, getting ready to fix his not-so-sweet-sixteen girlfriend who had pulled jiggers that morning while Lester and his young brother Douglas broke the back windows of a couple of nice brick custom homes and went in to see what could be had while the owners were at church. We watched Lester tie Lisa off and inject the meth and we watched Lisa's eyes get big and heard her gasp when the speed hit her heart. She made it to the kitchen sink before she puked, but came up smiling and looked on with fascination while Lester did the deed

to younger brother. They wanted to party, and party we
did, and yes I had a problem, I got the hard rush and
smelled the chemical smell and tasted that burning acid
crystal meth taste right there in the back of my throat even
while I was just watching them fix.

Two days and how many cases later Jim was in the kitchen,
what day was it, what month was it, how long have we been
doing this, holding a Preludin under the faucet, washing
the coating off. Five pink tablets in a row at the edge of
the sink. A test tube, a glass stirring rod, two new syringes,
and a pair of pliers.

He looked up at me, his mouth curled into a question.
The medicine smell rose up the back of my throat, oozed
from my tongue, the Preludin taste, different from coke or
meth, and the needles were on the counter, begging.

And this was what Jim liked, leaning over my arm,
watching the blood mix, stopping to look at my eyes before
he pressed the plunger. *I'll take you there.* It came in slowly,
teasing my heart for a single long instant before it slammed
like a head-on collision, standing me up, and I was cough-
ing, spewing air, too much, he'd given me too much, and
everything was red, Jim was red as he bent over his arm,
and pink molecules danced in the room's dead air, and then
the burn in my lungs, up the back of my throat, between
my legs, and I went to my knees, and my arms were beneath
me, bracing, waiting, my face on the floor, I smelled the
carpet against my cheek, and Jim knelt behind me and
grabbed my hips and it was nothing but fucking, pure and
sweat-soaked and desperate, until we screamed, until we
lay raw and gasping on the floor.

*   *   *

I stood in front of the bathroom mirror and let my robe fall. The bruises ran from the elbow almost to wrist, big blue-and-yellow blotches on the inside of each arm.

I ran the shower too hot, watched my skin turn pink as I stood under the scalding water. I scrubbed until it felt as though I were taking off, layer by layer, my own skin. I breathed in steam. I tried to understand.

It changes you. You can tell yourself you are doing it because you have to, so you can make the case. Because it's better than sex or it makes sex better. Because you feel like it today. But no matter what you tell yourself, how you explain it, there's only one reason.

You are after the rush.

And no matter how many times you go for it, no matter how many times, you'll never hit it again. Some people look all their lives. They steal for it. Don't know how to give up. Murder for it. Chase after it until it turns on them, roaring. Lumbers onto their backs like a bear, ripping flesh from bone, killing. They've been dead a long time by then.

TEN

MUCH LATER, YEARS LATER, THEY WOULD ASK WHY didn't I do anything. As if I hadn't. I suppose that in their eyes, not doing enough is the equivalent of doing nothing. It's easy, afterward, to make all the right decisions. Why didn't you? What about? Couldn't you have? Spectacular hindsight.

I got home from some club or another and found Jim's front door kicked open. It should have stunned me, should have scared me, but I was still so wired up from the cases I'd made that evening that when the adrenaline mixed in my blood I was taken to a state of calm. I pulled my gun, peered in. He was passed out on the couch, his arm hanging off the edge, sticking out from under the navy blue blanket that covered his body up to the eyes.

I checked the bedroom, the bathroom, the kitchen, the closets, moving silently, carefully, ready to shoot, hoping I would get the chance. The shrinks say there is a thin line between homicide and suicide, that it is only a matter of which direction you send your loathing.

I knelt next to the couch. Looked at Jim's arm. He was good, I mean he could hit and leave only the faintest kind of track, a pinpoint puncture wound and the next day only a trace of bruise, but that was when he had it under control.

The marks were there, the indications of self-inflicted disease. Bruises, big ones, blue and green and yellow, and dozens of scabs dotting the skin. Around that, swollen redness.

I tried to shake him awake. He moaned and turned over in his sleep.

I jammed a chair under the doorknob, dragged the bedspread into the living room, and stretched out on the smaller section of the couch. I listened to the pulse that throbbed in my ears, I waited patiently while my body worked to purge the toxins I'd been forcing into it all day and all night. I watched Jim sleep. Even now, at rest, the muscles of his jaw were taut, his teeth clenched tightly. I had never seen his face slack with the innocence of sleep, but it must have gone that way sometimes. I wondered if the world he slept in was as vicious as the one we were fighting against and conceding to every day, and I wanted to be in there with him, to enter his dreams and take both of us to a place where we could have just a few hours of peace. I wanted to feel the way I had on the summer Sunday mornings of my childhood, when I would wake up early with my soul still perfectly clean from Saturday evening confession, and put on a sundress and grab my sandals and tiptoe out of the house while my family slept. The mornings I remember were always brilliantly sunny, but the air would be cool still from the night, and full of the smell of trees. I would walk past the green quiet of lawns mown yesterday and onto the hard-packed dirt path that led through the woods and was solid and cool against the bottoms of my bare feet. The woods opened onto the elementary-school playground, where my sixth-grade friends and I played kickball during afternoon recess, and there it was, the basketball court, a rectangle of rough black asphalt, already soft from the heat, waiting. I would stand for a mo-

ment at the near end, with my head bowed, and recite, "Oh
Blessed Virgin Mary, accept this as my offering, it is right
and just that man should suffer on this earth, for God gave
His only Son so that all people might be saved, and pass
from death into a new life. Accept now my own meager
suffering in honor of your blessed name, and that of your
son Christ Jesus, and ask God to look down upon me and
bless me, and forgive me of my sins." And then I would
walk with slow steps down the length of the hot asphalt,
the bottoms of my feet burning with each new step, until,
toward the top of the far foul line, they became almost
numb. I took that as a sign that my offering had been accepted, and I would step off the hot asphalt and onto the
cool of the lawn, where I would stand in a state of grace
and slip into my sandals so that I could continue on my
way to eight o'clock mass.

Jim sat up suddenly and looked around the living room
with his eyes closed.

"I don't understand the question," he said, and then he
lay back down and yanked the blanket up to his chin.

"Jim?" I whispered. "Jim?"

He was sound asleep. I got up and poured a shot of vodka
and stared at the clock. Four seventeen A.M., and there I
was, stuck in the middle of the small hour, the hour of
throbbing brains and quivering stomachs, the somnambu-
list's daydream. I was tired, so very, very tired. All I wanted
was for my eyes to shut. I went to Jim's closet and began
checking coat pockets, looking for a lost or forgotten stash.
I found matchbooks and toothpicks, spare change, crushed
cocktail napkins scribbled with doper hieroglyphics—
phone numbers, price lists, initials—and finally, at last, in
the pocket of his only wool suit, a couple of Quaaludes. I
ate one, and then another half, and went back to the couch

to wait for its effect, sleep so deep and dreamless that even the darkest nightmare could not crawl out of it.

I went under with my hand stuck down in the cushions, resting on the grip of my pistol.

The low curve of the sun rested on the rooftop of the apartments across the way and Walker was standing in the doorway, knocking loudly on the splintered wood frame. His body was a shadow against yellow glare. I moved in slow motion to pull the bedspread over my arms and saw the chair I'd wedged against the door lying on its side on the carpet. Walker fingered the doorknob.

"What happened here?"

I pulled at the bedspread. My arms were healing, but bruises were still visible. He was in his work clothes: blue jeans, steel-toed ankle boots, and a couple of sweatshirts. He had a black bandanna tied around his head. The chair on its side looked wounded.

"Well?"

I leaned over and slid the mirror from beneath the couch, keeping the bedspread over my arms, and pulled a glass vial from the pocket of my jeans. It was body temperature. I tossed it to Walker.

"Have a bump," I said.

He closed the front door as far as it would shut, darkening the room but for a thin wedge of sunset slicing across the carpet and the beige glow of daylight seeping through the curtains.

"I'll be right with you," I said. I stumbled to the bedroom and found a sweatshirt. UT, HOOK 'EM HORNS, GO TEAM FIGHT. The marks on my arms seemed to leer at me, yelling blue-and-green words about no self-respect, about what a weakling I was. "How low do you plan to get?" they said. "Gonna take the big dive? You're strung. Smooth fucking strung. LOOK AT YOURSELF."

"Flo?" Walker tapped on the door. "You all right?"

"Yes," I called. "I'm fine. Just trying to wake up." I pulled the sleeves down and wiped them across my eyes.

"Well come on out here," he said. "This stuff you gave me will sure do the trick. Who'd you get this from?"

I checked my eyes in the mirror and opened the bedroom door. Walker was in the kitchen, snuffling and making coffee. He pointed to the mirror on the counter. Precious white lines. Blessed relief.

"We're framing a six-bedroom over on the south side of town," he said. "Got two more, almost as big, lined up after. I'll have work clear into next July."

"Good," I said, "that's good. We'll be finished long before then."

I carried the coffee to the living room, needing the softness of the couch. My bones ached. I propped myself in the corner and wrapped the bedspread around my shoulders, leaving one hand free to hold my coffee.

"You look like Pocahontas," Walker said. "A blond Pocahontas." He pulled his boots off and put his feet on the coffee table. "So. Who wrecked the door?"

"I don't know," I said. "It was that way when I came in last night. Jim was here. He knows about it."

"Where's he now?"

"Out on a deal I guess."

"You seem down," he said.

"I'm tired. That's all."

"Well, do I need to go home and shower, get cleaned up? We working tonight?"

"I've got some stuff coming through from that Mungo guy you introduced me to last week. He trusts me. I'll ask him to bring it here. I'm not up to going out."

"Want me to stay?"

"I'm fine. You don't have to stay. Take a night off. Go on a date, do something."

"Is he bringing snow?"

"Said he'd have some."

"Maybe I'll hang out here anyway."

"If you want to," I said. "But I'm okay."

"I'll stick around."

He got up and browsed through the albums.

"Something quiet," I said. "Okay? Pick something quiet."

He put Patsy Cline on and came back to the couch.

"Flo," he said. "Your parents do that to you, give you a name like that?"

"Part of my cover."

"It's weird," he said. "Here I thought I knew these two cool people who'd moved in across the way. You know, good neighbors. I liked y'all. Come to find out I didn't have a fucking clue, don't even know your name."

"Yeah. Well, you won't have to put up with us after this is over. We'll be out of your life and you can go back to the way it was."

"Not exactly." He sipped his coffee.

"You going to leave town?"

"I don't think so."

"Don't rule it out," I said. "People get crazy when they're busted. I had a few threaten to kill me in Pasadena."

"Obviously they didn't."

"Didn't even try, that I'm aware of. It's usually just talk. But you have to think about it."

"How'd you get into this? Why'd you become a cop?"

"I don't know," I said. "I thought I did, but I don't. Not anymore." I pulled the blanket close. "Why are you helping, other than staying out of jail?"

"To protect my friends."

"That's kind of running yourself out front."

"Not really. I'd already sold to Jim and all. It was too late for me, I was just trying to find out for their sake. So they wouldn't get caught. If he was the heat, I mean. I never even suspected that you might be."

We didn't say anything for awhile. Dusk had come and the room was in shadow. I knew I was breaking rules, letting an informant be a friend, but I needed one. I needed a dose of friendship. The only people I was meeting in Beaumont were dope dealers, and even if I was one of them it was still a matter of playing roles. It was all surface, the illusion of communication. Rob would come by if he thought there might be dope around, but Denny had stayed away since the night he'd walked into that party. He said it scared him to be too close to undercover. He didn't like it at all.

"You gonna take care of Grady?" Walker asked.

"The best I can," I said. "Let me call Mungo." I got up and dragged the phone to the couch. "Is that his real name, or is it license-plate time?"

"That's all I've ever known him by." He started cutting out more rails.

"Listen," I said, "you wouldn't want to fix that front door for me, would you? Somebody could just creep in here."

He stood up and stretched lazily, groaning with enjoyment. His hair was starting to streak golden from the spring sun. It tangled into his eyelashes in front and fell straight and clean down to his shoulders.

"You're putting me to work on my night off?"

"I'm asking for volunteers," I said. "I can call a locksmith."

He let his hands slap against his thighs and sighed. "Okay," he said. "Okay. Let me get my tools."

Jim didn't come home and he didn't call and he didn't come home. I cleaned. Washed the place down from ceiling to floor, scrubbing, scrubbing, wiping reddish dust from tables, raking the carpet with the vacuum cleaner, pushing and pulling, eight times even, back and forth, invisible rows, raking. Ammonia biting the air around my face, disinfectant on tile and glass, I polished windows and mirrors streakless, my yellow arms shining back at me. I bent needles and threw out rigs and put the coke up my nose. I was glad it wasn't heroin I'd been shooting. I was not that strong, not that standup. I gathered clothes from chairs, from the closet floor, from beneath the bed, walked to the laundry, watched them tumble in circles, soap-soaked and wet, in clean-gleaming stainless-steel machines. He didn't come home. I put coke up my nose. I wondered if he was dead. I wondered how I felt.

Day one. Day two. Night three. I sat in the apartment. Answered the phone and answered the door. Drank quarts of orange juice, ate bananas, swallowed vitamins. I needed cocaine. I made promises to my skin, to my arms.

When the dealers came over, I broke out the mirror. If they fixed, if they brought rigs, I sat watching, tasting the taste, counting the seconds until it went away. I ached for it. Some days my brain screamed for it. I put the stuff up my nose to quiet the yelling inside me. I wondered where Jim was.

At the end of the fifth day, Dodd called.

"My chair's gone," he said.

"What?"

"I said my chair's gone."

"I don't understand."

"Yeah-boy," he said, laughing nervously, "it disappeared this morning." He paused. "I sucked it up my ass when Chief called to ask what the fuck was going on with you two. He's hot."

"About what?" I asked.

"Wants to know why there's no case on Gaines. You got a cold?"

"We're taking a breather," I said.

"He wants something done soon."

"We're working on him. We'll get next to him. Have you spoken to Jim?"

"No. Why? Where the hell is he?"

"Never mind, it's okay," I said. "We have some cases for you. I'll drop the evidence by this evening."

"Make it quarter to six or so. I've got places to go tonight."

I could barely see the road. I wound down streets, past people's Victorian homes, digging in the glove box for something I could use to dry my eyes, knowing that it wouldn't do any good. I had envelopes full of vials, full of evidence, or just barely evidence. More than cutting the coke with mannitol, I'd been cutting the mannitol with coke.

I spotted Douglas the Younger, Lester's little brother, holding his T-shirt in one hand and thumbing with the other. He saw my car and waved; I pulled over to give him a lift, taking a long time to brake so I could get my eyes dry. I didn't know if I was crying for Jim or crying for something stronger.

He looked good, blond hair just touching his shoulders, and his acne had cleared since I saw him last at one of the clubs. He'd sold me speed that night.

When I told him he looked healthy he said he'd gone straight.

"It agrees with you," I said. "Where you headed?"

"Lester the Mo's."

I turned up the radio. Poor bastard. Trying hard, trying too late. Eighteen and a believer, soaking up all of Lester's crap about being a communist and thinking that meant take what you want from wherever you can get it because your government owes it to you but they ain't delivering. Started pulling jiggers for Lester the Mo when he was ten and Lester was seventeen, before the Mo graduated from houses to banks and went to the joint for robbery.

He was sitting next to me smiling in the sunny afternoon and all the time I had the keys to his jail cell hanging around my neck, I had the envelopes locked in the trunk, the reports were written, he was down for two counts of delivery and ten or twelve Sunday morning burglaries. He and Lester knew how to work fast, that was a given. And for once so did Sergeant Dodd. The serial numbers from the stuff Jim and I bought that morning had already been traced. We knew what houses they'd hit and what they had taken. Time automatic, his dumb-for-nothing brother had led him into the home of the D.A.'s cousin and they stole everything they could carry, including a diamond-studded butterfly pin, which I bought for fifty bucks. And which the D.A.'s cousin's wife had recognized immediately when Dodd brought her in to claim property. It was all done and nothing could change it, not even the best of intentions. It was all done for all of them, all of the defendants. The sucker was riding along happy to be alive and didn't have a clue that it was my testimony which would send him to prison. My testimony and Jim's, so help us God.

And now, too late, he'd decided to straighten up. Drug enforcement. Who were we kidding.

"442," he said. "I really love this car."

"It takes regular."

I dropped him at the Mo's, a yellow frame crackerbox with dead pyracantha bushes under the two front windows. Some time later I stopped at a 7-Eleven for a Dr Pepper and called Dodd to tell him I was tied up on a deal and wouldn't be able to make it. I didn't feel like trying to explain to him why there were no cases from Jim.

I drove. I wished I were going somewhere. At some point I realized that the car was uncomfortably warm and I rolled down a window. The radio said, "Y'all ought to get outdoors on this beautiful Tuesday afternoon, March is in like a lamb and we may see eighty today. How 'bout those lying eyes? Here's some Eagles for you."

ELEVEN

I DON'T KNOW EXACTLY WHY I WALKED OVER. MAYBE I wanted to get away from the telephone calls and the knocks at the door. I went to my empty apartment, my address. The key was stiff in the lock, but when I got the door open, there he was. There was Jim. Sitting on the living-room floor, wrapped in a white sheet, holding a sawed-off shotgun, resting it in the crook of his arm. The shotgun was covered completely with duct tape, right down to the trigger. No fingerprints that way.

Something shining in the bathroom caught my eye. I looked past him and saw the U-joint from under the sink, lying on the floor in a puddle of rusty water.

He stared at the front door.

"Lock it," he said.

"You lose something?" I asked. "Something go down the drain, *Jim*? What kind of shit is this? I've been thinking you were dead, wondering what to do, who to call, not even knowing where to start looking. That's cold, man. That's very cold."

"The front door," he said, "lock it. People coming."

"No one is coming."

"Heavy dudes," he said. "Characters. Armed robbers. Lock it."

I walked past him to the bathroom. On the counter, a

test tube, opaque white plastic caked in the bottom, a glass stirring rod, a blood-tinted plastic syringe.

"Recover your Preys? They can get slick washing them down. Shame to lose a good rush."

He staggered up and locked the front door.

"Tricky business," I said, "trying to hold on to those slick little tablets under running water. But it's worth it, right? Washing that pretty, hard-pink coating off, all that time cooking them, stirring, stirring in the test tube, squeezing the juice out of the plastic. Yeah, that juice, it's worth it."

"What are you bitching about? I got heavy motherfuckers coming." He fell against the wall and slumped back to the floor. "They're coming." He licked his lips. "I know they're coming."

"What are you saying?" I asked. "Think about what you're saying. Every dope dealer in town is convinced you're the heaviest *dude* around. What are you talking here? They're all scared of *you*. Dude."

"The cowboy dude, him, and his running buddies. They're pissed. They're coming." He pulled the sheet around his shoulders, over his head, forming a hood. He was shaking. I saw sweat on his forehead. He set the shotgun in his lap and lit a cigarette, took two long drags before he tossed the match into a paper cup. Coffee dregs and cigarette butts.

"Have any evidence for Dodd?" I asked. "I'm taking some over." I pulled up my sleeves and stuck my arms out at him. Faintest traces of yellow. "Look," I said. "Look. I'm pulling up."

He stared up at two o'clock high and then closed his eyes and brought his chin to his chest.

"Let's get all righteous," he said, talking to the floor. "Let's show what a good and decent human being we are.

Who the fuck do you think you're talking to? You telling me you're suddenly straight? Grow the fuck up."

"I'm not doing needles," I said. "No more needles."

"What's it been, how long? We still have to get Gaines. We got a ways to go on this little deal."

"You saying Gaines is a junkie? I don't think so. No need for that kind of action with him."

"Check the closet, man, the envelopes please are in the closet."

I found them right where he said, scattered all over the floor, manila envelopes, evidence envelopes, offense reports taped to each one. They'd been sealed tight. And then torn open and emptied. I looked through the reports. He'd been buying lots of speed: Preludin, crank, Desoxyn, Biphetamine. I carried them back to the living room, tossed them next to him on the floor.

"Jim," I said, "there's no dope here. What are you doing? What in God's name do you think you're doing?"

"My job," he said. "I'm doing my fucking job."

I sat down facing him.

"Hey, *dude,*" I said, "talk to me. Tell me all about handling it. I need to hear that stuff about kicking covers for a few days, getting up on your feet and walking. Tell me that."

"All I can do is wait," he said. "They're coming."

I scraped up the envelopes and went to the kitchen sink. I burned them, one by one, envelopes and offense reports, holding them over the garbage disposal.

"Doing the Felony Rag," I said. He said nothing. The flames reflected dully in the brushed stainless-steel sink and flared up once or twice to lick the bottom of the cabinet.

"Hey," I said, "you told me a long time ago about the difference between chipping and going on a run."

He sat against the wall.

"You're on a run, Jim, this is no one- or two-day thing. You're on a serious run here." He shifted the shotgun to his other arm.

Finally there was nothing left but soggy bits of gray-and-black ash. I washed the remains down the disposal and hit the switch on the wall, listened to the blades grinding beneath the sink before I walked over and sat opposite him.

I did not know what to say, what words would reach. He lit another cigarette and rubbed his eyes.

"Not that I think you'll understand or even care," I said, "but I love you. I didn't come down here to watch this happen. Come home with me, back to your place. Please. Tell me how to help."

"Later," he said.

"Come by this evening. You don't have to stay. Just come by. For a few minutes even. You need to get out of here."

"Later," he said. "Later. Let me think."

"So where is he?" Walker asked.

"Over in my apartment," I said. "He's having a difficult time. He needs a few days."

"Is he sick?"

"He needs a few days."

"But he's all right," Walker said.

"I'm watching him. He might come over tonight."

"Man. Talk about your rough gig."

"That it is," I said. "You got any smoke?"

Walker had kicked his boots off and was dozing while I sat staring at the tube, not really watching. There was a tap on the door, and when I opened it Jim was on the landing. He looked through the doorway at Walker, who was stirring on the couch, and then he looked at me with a wildness in his eyes I'd never before seen. He blew past me, yanking his jacket off as he went toward the couch. Walker stood up and Jim didn't even pause, dropped his jacket on the floor, jerked his gun from his belt and slammed it on the coffee table as he passed, grabbed Walker by his shirt, just below the collar, and threw him against the living-room wall.

"Jim!" I screamed, "Stop!" I grabbed at his arms and he pushed and then I was on the floor. I shook myself, felt pain in my arm, tried to sit up.

"Okay, motherfucker," Jim snarled. He reached down to Walker, who had sunk to the floor and was sitting motionless, yanked him up to a standing position, and threw a fist into his stomach. Walker doubled over, but then caught his breath and stood back up, stood up with his lips drawn back and eyes narrowed, his own fists clenched. He circled away from the wall, around the front of the coffee table to the center of the room, where there was space. I saw fight in his eyes, his right hand drew back to return the blow, but then suddenly, he seemed to catch himself. The hatred vanished from his face, replaced by cold control. I could see it, Walker felt he could give Jim a run for it, he might even come out on top, but in the instant before he'd thrown the punch he had remembered who he was dealing with, recognized his situation, and his arm fell to his side. Jim saw Walker's submission and drew back his right arm. The blow knocked Walker into the coffee table and back against the couch. He slid slowly downward, clutching his face, and curled against the cushions.

"No more!" he yelled, "that's enough!" He wasn't begging. He was telling Jim to stop unless he wanted a fight.

Jim stood over him, so tightly wired that it seemed to me he might just explode where he stood. He was shaking with rage, breathing loudly, almost gasping.

I got to my feet and approached him slowly. I put a hand on his arm. I tried to be calm. I felt like I'd gone through a windshield.

"Jim," I said. "Look at me." He twisted his head sharply. His whole body was shaking. "Why are you doing this?"

"That's not the question," he said. "The question is what the fuck are you doing."

"Just what you asked," I said, "sitting here waiting for you."

"And what was he doing." He pointed at Walker, who sat bent over on the couch, clutching his stomach.

"He wanted to see that you were all right," I said. "That's all."

Walker raised his eyes to Jim.

"I'm fine," Jim shouted, pulling away from me. "I'm just fucking great!" He turned to Walker. "Now I want some cases from you, motherfucker, I mean *cases*, not this penny-ante bullshit you've been turning. You think I'm gonna sit back and take this crap you've been dishing out? You set up some real deals, no more of this pill bullshit. I want coke. I want brown. I want speed. And I want this bastard Gaines. Now you've got about the best deal there is, getting to party around with this lady. It ain't like you got to walk a dude into these deals. You know ain't nobody gonna suspect her of being the heat. So you start walking her in, boy, you walk her in and let her buy some *dope,* and you get me some goddamn cases before I personally deliver your ass to Huntsville."

"Walker," I said quietly, "go home." He grabbed his boots and stepped toward the door, stopping with one hand on the knob to glare at Jim.

"Go," I pleaded. "Now." He closed the door and I bent

to right the coffee table and began picking up stems of pot from the floor. Jim paced the living room, still shuddering.

When I'd cleaned up the mess, I sat down on the couch, rubbing my arm where I'd fallen on it. He stopped pacing suddenly and looked at me.

"You're fucked up," I said. "Walker's been busting his ass, giving me plenty of damn good cases. You are really fucked up."

"Talk to me about fucked up, baby. Tell me all about it. You got your head so far up your ass you must be seeing tonsils."

He walked out, slamming the door behind him. I wanted to go after him, try to bring him back, try to salvage something. I dug under the couch, looking for the mirror.

It was noisy in the clubs. Every night, the noise. The smell of beer-soaked carpet and rancid nicotine. The drunks. People trying to get loaded, fucked up, get wasted. Walker began doing his best to stay that way.

I sat in Drillers each night, waiting for him to stagger over with new defendants. I began sampling the dope right at the table. Fuck it. I would give Walker a taste, give the seller a bump of thanks, snort more myself, hoping Gaines might notice. At the end of each evening, I took myself to Jim's apartment and got out the grinder, cut the dope back to weight, wrote the reports. When I took evidence to Dodd, he would ask what Jim was doing, and I said Jim was working on Gaines. I hoped there was enough dope in the vials to satisfy the chemists at the lab.

I could see Rob through the storefront window, kicked back in a bentwood rocker, his boots resting on a large walnut desk. He was reading a newspaper.

Main Street in Saratoga was dark and dead, doors locked

for the night, owners at home sleeping, or maybe watching some late-night television. The lone light coming from the store spilled out of the floor-to-ceiling glass, casting a grayish pall on the sidewalk. A small sign overhead, in black cursive on tan, said DENNY'S ANTIQUES.

Rob looked up when my headlights hit the back of his car, the only one parked on the street, and by the time I reached the door he had found his keys and unlocked it. The smell of furniture polish floated past as I walked in.

"Glad you called," he said. "It's lonely out here."

"So this is Denny's shop," I said.

"In name. He's got cousins and sisters scattered all over the county, they work it for him. I don't think it makes him any money though. It's the same with the farming, just something to talk about. Hard to retire at twenty-seven." He took a corncob pipe from his shirt pocket and tapped it against the heel of his boot. "I really am glad you called," he said. "I'm bored out of my mind."

"A friend of ours is speeded out of his."

"What else is new. Let's go in back. The hazards of the profession, man."

We wound through the front of the store, past sixties-vintage couches and kitchenettes, to a small door in the back wall. The storeroom was full of junk, mostly old dressers and headboards, a few nightstands, some kitchen tables. The only light leaked over the three-quarter wall that separated the showroom from the storeroom.

I tossed him a baggie.

"Praise the Lord," he said, packing dope into the pipe.

"There's coke, too," I said, "if you're interested."

"Hell, baby, of course I'm interested. Been sitting here all night, wondering what a man could do around here except maybe fuck the dog."

I tossed him a vial.

"We been working a case on a statewide speed network," he said, "headquartered in San Antonio. It's all wiretaps and surveillance, no bust in sight, and things at the office are dry. Very dry.

"On top of that, we've got a new chemist on staff. Son of a bitch guards that evidence locker like it was Fort Knox. He's probably going in at night and cutting all the dope, taking home pure and leaving bags full of two percent or something." He looked around the room, spotted a mirror on a dresser top and began wiping a space clean with his shirtsleeve. He cut the rails, long ones, and then rolled up a twenty and knelt down next to the table.

"So," he said, "been working hard?" He stood up and tilted his head back, snuffling.

"Too hard," I said. "Made too many cases in the last two weeks. Very fast. People have to be talking. You want some Quays?"

"Damn, baby, you're better than Santa Claus."

"My little elf has been on overtime."

"How is that dude? Decent snitch?"

"Hard to keep up with. I think he was starting to get into it, considering a career as one of Beaumont's Finest. Until Jim slugged him around."

"Raynor kicked the dude's ass? When? What for?"

"One night last week. For no reason at all."

"Just went off on the dude?"

"Not serious, I mean no broken bones or anything, but he hurt him. Scared the hell out of me." Rob jerked his head back and began pulling on his beard, eying me carefully.

"You okay?"

"I'm fine," I said. "But he scared me. He went nuts. He's been buying too much speed, man, it's like he's somebody else. Had no idea what he was doing."

I stood up and leaned against a scarred desk next to the coffee table. Rob did more rails and then stepped over to face me. "Well, I'm glad you came out," he said.

"I wanted to talk to you," I said. "I'm kind of confused."

"I'm sure," he said. He wrapped his arms around me and I pressed my face against his neck, wanting him just to hold me.

"Take it easy," he said. "Just take it easy." We stayed that way for a long time, rocking gently. And then before I realized what was happening he was pressing himself against me, bending me back over the desk, kissing, pulling me toward him and forcing me onto the desktop at the same time.

"Missed you," he whispered.

I tried to stay upright, but he had me down on the desk, wrestling. And then I stopped fighting him, I felt myself go limp, tears were coming and I didn't try to stop them, he was kissing me and I didn't want to fight, I was tired of fighting, and then the tips of his fingers brushed my face, smearing wet, and he stopped suddenly and pulled back.

"I'm sorry," he said quietly, helping me to my feet. "I just thought . . ." He took out a handkerchief and dabbed at my eyes. "I'm really, I didn't, oh fuck, man, what on earth is wrong?"

I took the handkerchief and wiped my face.

"Everything," I said. "Everything is wrong."

"Easy," he said. "Take it easy." He slipped his hand into mine. "I'm sorry. I thought you came out because you wanted to see me."

"I don't know why it is," I said, "but you have positively got a gift for making me feel like I'm, like I don't know what. Things are really screwed up."

"Hey," he said softly, "Jim kicked a snitch's ass. What's

the big deal? It happens. Usually they deserve it. Who's side are you on?"

"That's just it," I said. "He's my partner. And more." I looked at the floor, around the room, finally faced him. "But he is one strung-out son of a bitch."

"Oh." He lit the pipe. "Go on," he said, "smoke it. Relax a little. You know how it goes, baby. I've worked with the man. He'll pull through."

"I'm talking about needles, Rob."

He didn't say anything.

"Methamphetamine, you know? Preludin. He's skitzed. He's been sitting on my living-room floor for at least the last two weeks, running up speed and waiting for someone to come after him. Before that, I don't know. I'm not sure how long he's been on it. Says he doesn't even remember coming to his place and smashing Walker. I go in there and it's like talking to a ghost."

Rob dropped my hands and took a few steps back.

"He's ripping into the evidence envelopes," I said. "After he's sealed them. I went by to get his cases so I could take them to Dodd and there was no evidence left."

"Bastard just don't care anymore, huh?"

"Only about where the next shot's coming from."

"And what about you?"

"I had a rough time for awhile."

"Really." He stuck his hands in his pockets. "Took a run down the old tunnel, huh?" He looked at me, his eyes glinting with suspicion. "Pull up your sleeves."

My face went hot, I could feel the flush creep up my neck and spread across my cheeks. I felt like I had just been slapped awake and had opened my eyes to find I was lying in the gutter. I felt like trash.

"Show me your arms," he said. "Let's go. Pull the sleeves

up. If I'm getting in the middle of something I want to know what exactly it is."

It was like in the dream, when I'd been up on that defense table stripping off my uniform. I recognized what I was feeling, but I'd never felt it like this. Rob was watching out for himself, but that didn't mitigate the shame that was crawling up my back, curling around my neck.

He took my elbows in his hands, turned my arms toward the meager light dripping over the divider wall. They were clean. The last traces of yellow had disappeared. My arms were clean, but I'd never felt so filthy. I was being inspected, checked for self-inflicted flaws, looked at like a side of beef.

"Hey," I said, "you asked me, I told you. It happened on a case. On a couple of cases. And for awhile after. I've pulled up."

He released my arms and I felt them drop to my sides. He rolled my sleeves back down and buttoned the cuffs, put his hands on my shoulders.

"Look," he said, "I've known Raynor for close to five years. For most of that, he's been a damn good cop. He's taken some sorry, dope-dealing bastards off the street. And he's gotten this way before. He made it through, he can do it again. But stay away from him. Make your own cases, handle your own business. Denny and me, we'll talk to him."

"Rob," I said, "I can't just bail out on him."

"You're not," he said. "You're not bailing out. I've seen it too many times. You hang with him, you'll go right back to it. You got to get some distance. For him, and for yourself. Give him room to come around."

He hugged me, held me tightly, and I put my arms around him and rested my head on his shoulder. I wanted us to stand there like that until it all went away.

"You know," he said, "I've worked a case or two, and the first thing you're supposed to understand is that one good reason for having snitches is so they can deal with the rig and you don't have to. It's a one-way ticket to hell, man. Some agents think that's a chickenshit attitude, but I'm telling you, stay away from it." He stood holding me, rocking gently.

"You call me," he said, "I don't care when it is, if you need *anything*. Understand? Anything. If you need me, you call." He squeezed. "God," he said, "I've seen some shit in my life but this beats it. Motherfucker had no business, man, no business at all."

"He needs help," I whispered. Rob sighed.

"Don't we all," he said.

The next morning, when I led Rob and Denny to my apartment and unlocked the door, Jim saw them and froze.

"Hey, man," Rob said, "what's happening?"

"Heavy shit," Jim said. "I told her." Pointing at me. "Dudes are coming." Denny tossed me the keys to his truck.

"You owe me a tank of gas," he said.

I left them there and took Denny's truck, driving to nowhere, driving to kill time, driving and thinking about Jim, hoping that Denny could reach him if Rob couldn't, knowing that I had failed. They were talking. Maybe Denny. Jim was talking. Maybe Denny.

I believed I was clear of it, clear of the needle anyway, just snorting, swallowing too many pills, but only on cases, or mostly on cases. Doing it sometimes when I didn't really have to for the buy, doing it because it was safe, because it put the dealers at ease, because it spread a layer of strength over all that fear.

*   *   *

When I got back to my apartment, not my home, not someplace safe, just an address for regulation's sake, they were sitting in a circle on the floor, not saying anything. I gave Denny his keys and sat down against the wall.

Jim looked around the room, then at each of us. "Hey," he said suddenly, hatefully, "why don't you motherfuckers just take care of your own goddamn business. I can handle mine." He got up and walked out the door. Denny went after him.

"Just like you described it," Rob said.

"What did he say?"

"Not shit. Listen to me. You get a call in to that sergeant and you tell him straight up what's coming down. You make them get Jim some help."

"And if they don't?"

"They will," he said. "They have to."

TWELVE

DODD POINTED THE WAY DOWN HIS HALL TO THE guest room.

"I'll be right there," he said. "Gotta take a leak."

The room was white, the four-poster bed covered with a white lace spread. The cushions on the rocker matched it, and above the headboard was a framed picture of Jesus, a silver globe resting in his palm, yellow light shining from behind the purple and red of his exposed heart. I sat in a rocking chair in the corner and listened as Dodd's wife sang to their little boy behind a closed door down the hall. I felt like a burglar who'd stumbled into the middle of a fairy tale. I had forgotten that this sort of thing existed.

I heard her ease a door shut and then she came in and asked if I cared for iced tea. Dodd walked in behind her.

"Not now," he said, "we got stuff to talk about."

The first thing he said when I told him was, "Oh, Jesus Lord, man, I gave him some goddamn balloons of heroin and some hits of speed to start out with, he told me he needed them. Jesus Lord." I think my mouth dropped open.

"Sergeant," I said, "we're talking about a life here."

"I'm trying to think."

"Forget about the dope," I said. "It was metabolized long ago."

"What?"

"He's strung out. Whatever you gave him went straight into his arm."

"We'll have to take his badge. He can't be carrying the badge."

"Hey, fuck the badge, man! He's killing himself."

"He still can't be carrying the badge. How many cases are bad?"

"I don't know. I have no idea. Probably most of those he's made in the last month or so."

"We'll have to meet with the Chief. Can you get him to come to a meeting?"

"I'll try," I said. "I don't know."

"Chief'll want to talk to you first. I'll call you later and set up a time. You sure about this now?"

"You know," I said, "there's this concept that got drilled into me from the day I became a cop. It's called taking care of your partner. I believe in it. If I thought there was a way to get Jim over this without telling you or Nettle or another single soul, I would do it. I've tried. I can't. The man is killing himself. Now get us some goddamn help."

On the side of Farm to Market 105, just west of Sour Lake, Rob and Denny and I stood leaning against Denny's truck, waiting for Nettle.

"I don't like it," Denny said. "I don't like it at all."

"What was I supposed to do?" I asked. He kicked at the sand with his boot.

Nettle pulled up in his department Chevy, got out of the car twisting his head back and forth, checking it out, looking for observers.

"Kristen," he said, "what exactly is going on?" I started at the sound of my own name.

"What you've got," Denny said, "is one plenty fucked-up agent. Your man is firing up daily."

Nettle cleared his throat and looked at Rob.

"We tried talking to him," Rob said. "He's paranoid as hell."

Nettle looked at me, a grim smile on his wormy lips. Even in the afternoon breeze his hair stayed glued in place. I almost expected him to bow his head and offer a prayer for Jim's recovery.

"What do you think we should do?" he asked.

Denny scuffed his boot again, cupped his hand over his crotch, and spat onto the roadway.

"Shit," he drawled, "we ought to just chain the son of a bitch to a toilet and leave him there till he kicks this thing."

The Chief laughed, Rob laughed, we all laughed. Nettle stopped suddenly and looked hard at me.

"Bring him to Dodd's house tonight at seven. Tell him those are my orders."

"I'll try," I said.

"Bring him." He turned toward his car. "Thank you men for coming out," he said over his shoulder.

When he was down the road Denny looked at me and said, "Hell, girl, it's only noontime, you don't need to be spending all day looking forward to tonight. I know a damn good barbecue joint just down the road. Let's get some dinner."

"Thank you men for coming out," I mimicked. I got in and slid toward the middle of the seat. Rob and Denny sandwiched me between them and Denny hunched over the steering wheel, squinting his eyes as he leaned to check the roadway.

"What's it look like?" he said.

"Holdup," Rob said. An old Falcon full of teenagers roared past and disappeared around a curve.

"Okay," Rob said.

Denny eased the pickup out and we puttered along at about twenty-five. He kept the truck mostly in his lane, but occasionally wandered across the double yellow stripe. Each time he did it, Rob would tell him to pull to the right.

After about the fifth time, Denny turned toward Rob and said, "Ease up, man, I drive all over the county by myself."

"Well you goddamn shouldn't," Rob said. "Hell, you're blind. Don't even have a damn driver's license."

"Long as I don't hit any cows or children I'm happy."

I listened to their banter, knowing it was for my benefit, but I couldn't stop the dread that was working away inside me. Tucked in there between them, shoulder to shoulder in the dusty cab of Denny's farm truck, a lariat curled on the floorboard under my shoes, the scent of pine coming in through the windows, I searched for something, anything, to think about. But all that would come was the image of Jim wrapped in that sheet.

I could feel the muscles in Denny's arm as he drove along in his world of shadows, looking for movement that would signal something living, something to steer away from, on the roadway.

The aroma of burning mesquite wood hung over the parking lot, and the tang of barbecue made my mouth water even though my stomach felt as though it had been inflated with helium. I couldn't remember what it was like to have an appetite. The restaurant was an old barn, with sawdust-covered wood floors and red leatherette booths scarred with black electrical-tape patches. There were miniature juke-boxes at each one, listing Merle and Hank Jr. and Willie,

Waylon and Tammy and Patsy. Ray Charles was on when we got there, singing "Georgia."

"Ever been there?" Denny asked.

"I grew up in Atlanta," Rob said. "You know that."

"I was talking to Kristen," Denny said.

"No," I said. "You grew up in Georgia?"

"Six brothers," Rob said, "three sisters. On the edge of Atlanta. I hightailed it out of there at eighteen. Worked offshore out of New Orleans for awhile, got tired of busting my ass. Joined the Highway Patrol in San Angelo. Then transferred to Narcotics."

He dropped a quarter into our jukebox and punched up "I Fall to Pieces."

"Play some Johnny Paycheck," Denny said.

"Sometimes I think about going back. Working those oil rigs. Paycheck ain't listed."

"What about Mel Tillis?"

"Yeah. He's here."

"Play him."

"But those oil rigs," Rob said. "Dangerous. A man can lose body parts."

Denny put his menu down and stared at Rob.

"You little son of a bitch," he laughed, "you don't usually get shot at on the rigs."

Rob looked at his menu. "Hey," he said. "I got kids to feed, you know?"

The waitress took our order and returned a few minutes later with large oval platters piled high with ribs and potato salad and ranch-style beans.

"I guess a man's gotta do what he's fit to," Denny said. "Maybe I was the lucky one. Least I got retired out of it."

"You just don't know, man." Rob put his fork down and stared at Denny. "You got no idea." He picked up a rib and bit it viciously. "Pass that sauce there," he mumbled. "No, the tabasco."

I picked at some potato salad while Denny and Rob attacked their platters, sucking the ribs down to clean white bone and licking sauce from their fingers.

"You better eat, girl," Denny said.

"I can't," I said.

"On account of you fucked up."

I looked up at him. "What do you mean?"

"I mean you shouldn't have got Nettle involved in this. Mistake. I'm sorry, darling, I love you to death, but I think you fucked up and I feel like I should tell you. It don't mean I don't love you as much as ever. I just think you're in for some grief."

I looked over at Rob, who sat gnawing on a rib.

"I had to," I said. I wondered why Rob didn't say anything.

"You just watch yourself," Denny said. "Nettle strikes me as the kind of man who would put your ass in a sling without even blinking."

He was just as I'd left him, leaning against the wall, wrapped in the sheet, holding the shotgun and staring at the door. How many days growth on his face, greasy hair, the smell of speed in his sweat. I sat down facing him.

"You've got to stop," I said.

He stared past me.

"Jim."

"I'll handle it." He nodded slowly, weakly, his eyes narrowed. "I'm here waiting for the dudes. I'm ready."

"Right," I said, "you're ready."

I stood up. "I'm sorry," I said. "Really sorry. I didn't know what else to do."

"What the hell are you talking about?"

"What am I talking about. You wouldn't talk to Denny, you wouldn't talk to Rob."

"Fuck Rob. Fucking motherfucker, fucking coward. He ran. Dude ran when Dennison was down. Topwater floater, don't know what down is, fucking lightweight, fucking hot dog motherfucker. Fuck him. Yeah, you know all about that, right? Fucking Rob."

"Damn it, Jim, don't twist it!" I yelled. "Nothing's going on. Jesus Christ, nothing's going on. Not with Walker, not with Rob. Do you understand strung out? Paranoid? Can you hear me? Am I talking to you?"

"Dude's partner ought to stand by him when there's a hassle coming down," he said.

"That's right," I said. "But the only hassle coming down is in your head. You're skitzed out. Walker's got his finger on the pulse, nobody in town is after you. Nobody even suspects you anymore. Jesus!"

He hugged the shotgun to his chest and looked at me with syrup-coated eyes.

"Walker's a punk boy, he don't know shit." His cheeks were cavernous, his skin flushed red.

"I brought you some ribs," I said. "You need some food."

"I want my partner here with me when the shit starts."

I sat down, took the shotgun from him, laid it next to me and pulled him toward me until he gave in. He settled himself on the floor with his head resting in my lap and one bony shoulder digging into my thigh. I stroked his hair. I waited until I felt him relaxing against me.

"We have a meeting," I said. "This evening."

His eyes popped open and he jerked his head up.

"With who?" he asked, "about what?"

"I didn't know what to do," I said. "I talked to Dodd, and I talked to Nettle."

He was on his feet instantly, headed for the front door, but stopped halfway there and reeled to face me. I stayed seated, tucked the shotgun behind me.

"What the fuck do you mean," he screamed. "What did you tell them?" He circled toward me, his eyes white with shock. "What did you tell them!"

I sat silently, staring at him. He crossed his arms and stood trembling, looking at me, his nostrils flared, his eyes pinched.

"Tell me," he said sharply.

I sat, saying nothing, looking at him, waiting. I don't know how much time passed. Finally he went into the bathroom, the water ran, he came out calm. He sat down across from me.

"Damn it, girl," he said. "Talk to me. You owe me that much. You owe me. Let me know what I'm walking into."

"I told them everything," I said. "I told them cases were bad. I told them you were strung out."

His head dropped and he pressed his palms to his eyes.

"Why?" he asked.

"Because I had to," I said.

"You had to," he said. "Hell of a deal. What a hell of a deal."

"Yeah, it is," I said. "Indeed it is. At last I get your attention. We're supposed to be there at seven."

"Seven," he said. "You know what you've done? He pressed his fingers against his temples, shook his head slowly. "Do you know what you're doing?"

"Yeah," I said, "I know. Just like you're always saying, man, I'm doing the best I can with what I've got."

"Like hell," he said. He raised his head and looked hard at me. "You've probably just landed both our asses in the joint."

"That's bullshit and you know it," I said. "You were

overdosed, Jim, that wasn't your fault. Nettle hired me to look out for you, to help you. I'm doing it. All you have to do is tell the man the truth. They can't put us in jail for that."

In Dodd's living room, just at dusk, I sat at one end of a furry purple couch. Jim sat in the matching chair, frowning, tapping his foot rapidly against the carpet, rubbing the fingers of one hand against the palm of the other. His hair was still greasy and hung in sloppy curls, but he'd put on a fresh shirt, the cuffs buttoned tightly about his wrists.

Dodd was between us, at the other end of the couch, and Nettle was a few feet away, catty-cornered to Jim, in an upright recliner. The lamp in the room lit a small circle that included the couch and Jim's chair, but only Nettle's legs were outside the shadow which hovered over the rest of the room. I saw his knees, the trousers stretched tight over them, and in the gap between his ankle-high socks and the cuffs of the trousers, the fishbelly white of his legs.

He cleared his throat with a tiny dry cough.

"So we have a situation," he said.

"Well, Chief," Dodd said, "you've worked undercover, you know how it can get."

I edged the drapes back. Some kids were playing touch football on the lawn across the street. Nettle undercover. Busting a black guy for a matchbox of marijuana. Fifteen years in the joint. Hell of a deal.

"How bad is it?" Nettle asked.

I let the drape drop back into place and looked over at Jim.

"Since that overdose I guess I've had a rough time," he said. His voice was shaking. He glanced over at me. I have betrayed my partner, betrayed my lover.

"Exactly how bad is it?" Nettle asked.

Jim sucked in a breath, leaned forward in his chair, rolled his sleeve up and extended his arm toward Nettle. It was worse than when I last saw it. There on his arm was a four-inch track, bright red and swollen, like some nightcrawler had slithered under his bruised, scab-dotted skin.

Nettle leaned to look at it, shook his head slowly, and then sat back in his chair. He raised a hand to his face and rubbed his cheek.

"I think," he finally said, "that you could use a few days off. Go to Houston, get some rest. And then get back here and make the goddamn case on Gaines."

Jim cocked his head back and glared at me: See there, bitch, I can handle it. He nodded at Nettle.

A few days off. I couldn't seem to get my breath.

"Right away," Jim said. "Thanks for your confidence."

"It's not confidence, Raynor," Nettle said. "I want Gaines. That's why you were hired and that's what I expect you to deliver."

Jim flashed a look at Nettle, but caught himself.

"Clear as can be," he said quietly, standing up to leave.

"Larry," Nettle said, "why don't you give Jim a lift to his place. I'd like to talk to Kristen for a few minutes." He turned to me.

"Just follow me down the road a ways. We can talk in my car and then you can head back."

He drove slowly down a blacktop two-lane road heading south from Dodd's house. The pine trees came right up to the road shoulder, looking black against the night-blue sky. There were hundreds of stars, thousands and millions of them, stars you couldn't see when you looked at the night sky in town. I could see a glow above the tree line a mile or so down the road. Nettle drove slowly, carefully, as though feeling his way along.

I rounded a curve in the road and saw a church, solid

white, spotlessly, brilliantly, white. Set on black asphalt in a large clearing among the pine trees, surrounded by floodlights, glowing in the night. The asphalt lay clean and level and black, with hard-edged white lines marking the parking spaces on its surface. The steeple, tall and traditional and shining, was a stark white point jutting into the air before the jagged blackness of the tall pines which cut the night sky behind it.

Nettle pulled onto the road shoulder just before reaching it. I eased over behind him, killed my engine, and walked across the gravel to his Chevy.

I got in and clicked the door shut, surrounded by the smell of new car, of vinyl and plastic and ultraclean carpeting. I sat staring at the church, wondering if I was about to be fired. He turned toward me, draped his arm across the seatback.

"I just wanted to tell you that I know how hard it was for you to come forward," he said. "It took a lot of trust, and I want you to rest assured that you can talk to me whenever there's a problem."

"Three days off isn't going to do the trick, Chief. You know that." He turned in the seat and leaned toward me. Such even, white teeth he had, so polished, so spotless, so perfect. I despised his teeth.

"I can't tell you," he said, "how important it is to me that I know there are officers in the department who are willing to be straight with me, to tell me what's happening. I value that. I'll remember come promotion time."

Then he lunged, grabbed my face and pulled me toward him. I don't know exactly what happened next, I felt an arm around my waist, pulling, and another, his forearm across my neck, trying to push me down on the front seat. I scrambled, twisting away from him, something ripped, his lips mashed wet against my cheek. And then somehow

I was outside, slamming the door against his reaching hand, hearing him yell something as I ran toward my car.

I cranked the engine, turned the wheel hard to the left and slammed the accelerator to the floorboard, screeching onto the roadway, slinging gravel against his car. I heard the metallic pinging as the stones hit his trunk; in my rearview there was Nettle, stomping in circles next to his car. Bastard.

I held the pedal down until my speedometer was pegged and fought the car around the curves. Damn him. Got a woman in his car on the side of the road at night and holy Jesus, she has to want it. Has to. Worthless fucking East Texas egg-sucking playboy.

I didn't slow until I reached the edge of town, and then I sat most of the way through a green light, wiping his dried spit from the place on my cheek. I made it through the intersection on yellow, wiping my hand on my jeans until I felt friction heat on my thigh.

Jim was at the apartment when I got there. Sitting at the kitchen table drinking a beer. I went to the kitchen sink and washed my face, scrubbing hard, then to the bedroom to change my clothes.

"Hell of a deal," he said when I sat down. "I've never copped to anything. Nothing. No matter what the accusation was. Now that bastard has a rope tied right around my neck. All he has to do is tighten the fucking noose. Hell of a deal."

Something was rushing up inside me, and I looked at the floor, tried to shake my head clear, couldn't, falling, drowning, couldn't stop it. I stood up and slammed him in the chest, nearly knocking him from his chair.

"Who the fuck are you," I screamed, "to tell me hell of a deal? Hell of a deal? Yeah, bastard, it's a hell of a deal!

Come on down, you said, come on down and marry me, be my wife, love me. And I do it, and I get down here and you've turned into a worthless sack of shit that can't do anything but stick needles in your sorry-ass arm. Curl up and die! Fucking shrivel up and blow west!"

He stood up, his mouth half open, eyes wide with alarm, and reached for me. I pushed past him and slammed at the wall, feeling the soft plasterboard give beneath my fist.

"Just fuck you!" I screamed. "You and your self-righteous lawman bullshit, you're a fucking junkie, that's all, a strung-out punkboy needle freak!" I slumped against the wall and closed my eyes. "You aren't even worth pitying."

He put a hand on my shoulder, wrapped himself around me. I felt the wet warmth of his tears on my neck, his body pressed tight against my back.

"I'm sorry," he said. "I'm so fucking sorry."

THIRTEEN

WE DIDN'T GO TO HOUSTON. WE DIDN'T GO ANY-
where. Both of us knew that three days wouldn't
make any difference. We stayed right there in the
apartment, and after a night without dope Jim took to his
bed.

When I walked into the bedroom with a cup of beef
broth, he was under three blankets, sweating heavily.

"Just take a little," I said. He turned his head away.

"I can't." His voice was weak with fever, his jaw trembled spasmodically.

"All this from speed?" I asked. His teeth chattered
loudly in the morning silence.

"Not speed," he said. "Brown."

It was as though he'd just confessed to having a secret
lover, a woman on the side. I felt like someone had finally
ripped a blindfold from my eyes after leading me around
sightless for weeks. I'd thought he was strong enough to
recover from the overdose, believed all this time that he was
doing okay. I'd been so busy making cases that I hadn't
noticed how badly it had shaken him.

"I thought you knew," he said.

I had no answer. I was relieved when someone knocked
on the door.

"Tell them I'm sick," he said. "Tell them I have the flu

or something." He clenched his mouth shut and I closed the bedroom door behind me.

It was Jammer, a scooter nasty, an ex–heroin addict who'd switched to speed because, he said, he got more done that way. He was thin and tiny, with greasy brown hair that hung in uncombed strands to the middle of his back, and a scraggly goatee of the same drab shade. The only real color left in his Levi's came from gray-black oil stains streaked across the thighs. His irises were fierce blue, glaring out of Mongol eyes, but he was one of the gentlest of our defendants.

"Flo," he stammered, "I don't want to be a bother, but, could I maybe use your scales for a few minutes?"

I waved him in and brought the scales to the dining table. He sat down and began pulling things from his boots.

"Got any baggies?" he asked.

I brought the Ziplocs from the kitchen, and the other things he would need: the mirror, the grinder, the razor blades, a pack of matches.

"I'm so broke," he said. "Got no place to crash even, gotta get some cash. I been sleeping in the railyards."

He smelled like it, the odor of poverty clinging to his clothes, scents of layered dirt and sweat.

"You want something to eat?" I asked. "Jim's kind of sick and I was going to try to get some eggs down him."

"That'd be good," he said. "I ain't really had much to eat for a week or so. What's he got?"

I could tell him and he would understand, it would be real, not the way it was with Nettle. In the narcotics course, they'd told us always to choose a cover that was close to our real lives, that there was less chance of slipping up that way. That bit of advice was N/A to Jim and me now. We couldn't slip up. We were no longer playing roles.

"He's been chipping some," I said. "He's trying to pull up."

"Oh, man," Jammer said, "I been there. What a drag."

I scrambled some eggs while Jammer cut the last of his stash and sealed the powder into tiny plastic triangles, which he would sell for ten bucks apiece. He stopped long enough to wolf down the plate of eggs I put in front of him and then he went back to work, his hands shaking so badly that I was amazed he didn't spill crystal meth all over the table. He didn't drop so much as a single grain.

When he finished he asked if I wanted any and I said of course. Of course I wanted some. What I didn't say was: Yeah Jammer I want some, but not because I'm going to put it in my arm, I want some so I can have another case on you, so the D.A. can prosecute you and the State can lock you up. I need another number, Nettle wants lots of cases, yeah, sell me some more dope.

I bought three dimes from him and he pocketed the thirty bucks like it was a real stake, enough to put him on the road to success.

"Think I could use your shower?" he asked.

"I'll get you a towel," I said. It felt good to be kind to him. Maybe he would remember.

I put the scale away and made more eggs while Jammer was in the bathroom. Jim was sitting up when I brought them in. He hadn't touched the broth.

"At least try," I said.

"At the moment," he said, "I feel not unlike trampled dogshit. Who's in the bathroom?"

"Jammer. I bought some speed from him."

"What for?" he asked. "We've got two on him."

"Because he needed the cash. Besides, just because Nettle says get Gaines we're suddenly supposed to stop buying from everyone else? That'll raise some eyebrows for sure."

"He wants that case."

"I was there. I heard."

"I'm getting too old to do this shit. Keep it up, I'll wind up sitting out on the highway next to a truck full of vegetables, quoting the price of okra."

"Hey, Jim, you're barely thirty. It's not exactly time for the home yet. Now eat this."

He opened his mouth and I put a forkful of eggs in. He closed his eyes and struggled to swallow.

"They're pretty dry," he said.

"The rate you've been going they won't stay down long anyway."

"I shouldn't have brought you in on this, girl."

Jammer tapped on the bedroom door and stepped into the room, standing awkwardly next to the dresser. His wet hair was pulled into a ponytail and draped over his shoulder, leaking water onto the front of his still filthy shirt.

"How you feeling, man?" he asked, slipping his hands into his back pockets.

"Like I got run over by a truck," Jim said.

"Yeah," Jammer said. "Well, I was strung on heroin for a good four years. Switch to speed. It's not so hard on you."

"Whatever," Jim said. "I'll find you when I'm back on my feet, man."

"Sure," Jammer said. He looked at me. "Thanks for the meal and all."

When he was gone Jim just looked at me.

"Why'd you tell him?" he asked finally.

"He gets around," I said. "Now everyone in town will believe you aren't the heat. Including Gaines."

He clutched suddenly at his stomach and pointed to the trash can next to the dresser.

"Quick," he winced.

*   *   *

Defendant number seventy-eight, seventy-nine, eighty. While Jim slept it off I kept right on making buys: cocaine at five in the morning and Quays at eight-thirty; acid at two and Biphetamine at three-thirty. Day after night after day. My body was going so many different directions that I stopped trying to keep track. But I thought all along that I had it under control. I was doing my job. Jim had lost it, he'd let it get the better of him, but I was showing him that I was stout, I was strong, I was handling it. I would walk into the bedroom wired out of my mind and talk calmly to him, give him progress reports, tuck the blankets around him and tell him I loved him. I thought about moving him to my apartment so he could be away from all the activity, but the place was still empty and I did not feel like dragging furniture down the sidewalk.

I think a week or so passed before Jim got out of bed and put some clothes on. I didn't really keep track. I bought dope and tried to get him to eat and bought more dope.

When the day came that he finally felt strong enough to move around, he walked in and sat down at the dining table and stared at me. I'd just bought some coke, still had the mirror and vials out on the table, and was sitting there sniffling, trying to catch the last of the drip, hating myself for loving the taste of snot.

"Maybe I'll try a little lunch," he said.

"Excellent," I said. "I'll make you a salad."

"Just a little cereal." He picked up a vial and rolled it between his fingers.

"Bought it off a guy named Seymour."

"Walker set it up?"

"Yeah. We've got eighty-six defendants as of this buy."

"But not the big one," he said. "How many Fuhnew Lahnews?" FNU LNU, First Name Unknown, Last Name Unknown. Transients, people without names, dealers who slipped into the parks or the clubs, sold their stash and split quickly, leaving nothing in their wake but a physical description.

"Dodd told me only the third buy you made," I said, "at that Chicken Shack." My hands shook as I poured milk over his cereal and carried it to the table. Wired to the point of misery. I brought the Sunday paper from the couch, set it on the table in front of him.

"Check it out," I said. "The governor has declared a War on Drugs. Got a committee and everything."

"Run it up the flagpole and see if anyone salutes," he said weakly.

"They're talking about bringing in the military. They'll all get strung. Imagine the Marines on acid."

"Forget acid," he said. "Rob was telling me about some kind of shit called freebase. Mix a little coke with some heavy-duty chemicals, dry it out and smoke it. Said the first thing comes to mind when you do the stuff is homicide."

"Right. Like the first time you do LSD you're gonna jump out a window." I reached to touch his forehead. It was cool.

"I'm okay," he said. "Really." He tapped a finger against the newspaper. "Says here the governor's coming in May."

"You can bet Nettle will time the bust-out for that."

"Yeah," he said. "And he's not gonna let me up. We got about four short weeks to get the case."

"You think that stuff about the Cowboy Mafia is real?" I asked. Nettle had said Gaines was hooked up with them, a group of ranchers who supplemented their income by selling tons of pot. They had the space, the trucks, and strategic locations all over Texas, to say nothing of the ethic of the Old West: Don't fence me in, I'll kill any bastard who gets in my way.

"Who knows," Jim said. "Now he says he wants us to

make the buy out of one of Gaines's cars. So he can seize it."

"He think this is some kind of game show or something?"

"He wants the Cadillac. I told him we should go for one of the Mercedeses." He smiled. "We ought to set it up so we wind up with that dumptruck he keeps parked behind Drillers. That'd piss Nettle off but good."

"I'm glad you're up and around," I said. I reached for the mirror. Jim paused with his spoon halfway to his mouth.

"I'm just tired," I said. "Last one."

"Until when?" he asked.

"Until the next buy. Don't worry. I'm cool with it."

When Jim called Nettle that afternoon and said that we were getting closer to Gaines, I wondered if he had simply gone over the edge, lost touch completely.

"What do you mean, getting closer," I said when he hung up. "We haven't even seen him for weeks."

"I need some slack," he said. "I don't want Nettle getting antsy. We're talking about a heavy motherfucker here."

I'd never seen him so nervous about a case. In Pasadena, he'd always been the one to lead the charge. He was the one who kicked the doors, who walked cold into shooting galleries and came out with new cases. But he was no longer eager. He seemed almost desperate.

"Chief told Walker he would slide automatically if he delivered Gaines."

"Sure," I said. "Like Walker's in the same league. He's done a good job, and as far as I'm concerned he's already off the hook."

He stood up and began gathering the week's worth of newspapers that were scattered around the living room.

"What do you think about moving the furniture down to that crib you rented?" he asked. "Maybe operating out of there for the rest of this thing."

"It sounds like hard work for no good reason."

"There's too much traffic in and out of here," he said. "Be good to get someplace a little quieter. We're concentrating on Gaines now."

I thought about the afternoon when my track coach had told me he wanted me to learn the hurdles. He'd set them up on the football field, where there was grass and I could fall without scraping quite so much skin off. I argued with him, trying to convince him that I was a sprinter, but he'd said I wasn't fast enough. I had to either move to the mile run or learn how to clear the hurdles. We had faced off under the sweltering April sun and he said, "You're going places. You've got what it takes. Listen to me. I'm giving you good advice." It thrilled me that he had singled me out, decided to put extra effort into my training. I worked for him. I sweated and ached to make myself worthy of his attention.

The spoken word, the commitment to go after Gaines, made me feel the way I had at the track meets, when I stood at the line marking the start of the mile-relay hand-off zone, my body so charged with adrenaline that I had trouble getting the third-leg runner in focus as she hurtled down the stretch toward me, and then she'd hit the line that was my signal to take off, and my vision would go so suddenly clear that I could see the mole on her earlobe in that instant before I turned my head to run, and then I was listening for her footsteps to catch me, waiting for her command, "Stick!" and I would reach back, palm up, waiting, and the hard metal baton would slap into my hand, and then I had it and was running, pacing for the first two-twenty, and the coach was there at the pole, calling out times, and the third hundred and ten was just gutting it out, hurting, the air razor-laden, slicing my lungs, and then, then, the last hundred and ten, the final stretch, I was right where I wanted to be, two steps out of first place, and it was no longer a physical matter, it was a question of will, and then I was sprinting past the lead runner, kicking hard, forcing my legs to have strength, and there were the shouts from the stands, and the finish tape was glorious when I broke it with a downward slash of arms.

Gaines was major. He was a trophy worth having.

The phone rang and almost before I could say hello Dodd was yammering away as if he had news that Armageddon was scheduled for next Tuesday.

"The shit was all over the place," he shouted. "Reels of it! We'll put him away for forty years!"

"Where was it?" I asked.

"Out near the creek behind his house. Goddamn jury'll take a look at this stuff and want to hang the bastard on the courthouse steps!"

"Where'd you get your info?"

"C.I." Dodd said.

"You run a paper?"

There was silence.

"We just went and took it," he said quietly. "Hell, we didn't have time to check property lines and all. It was a good forty yards from his back door. Ain't no fencing."

"You had a confidential informant tell you there was porn on Gaines's property and you didn't get a search warrant?"

"Fuck, no, man, like I said, the shit was outside, reels of it, just dumped near the edge of the creek."

"No paper."

"No," he said flatly. "But you should see this stuff!" He

was yelling, excited again. "If it was capital he'd fry for sure. A warrant would have taken hours."

"Did he see you out there?"

"Hell no. Nobody was home."

"So you're going to pop him?"

"I don't know. Got to check with the Chief. He's talking now about a hundred defendants, wants some numbers for sure."

"For God's sake, Dodd, we've got over eighty now! We're not even making dealers anymore, we're down to potheads. What's the point here?"

"I'll talk to him."

"Yeah, well, tell him you've got one agent who's three-quarters wasted and another who's not too far behind. Like it'll make a difference."

"What do you mean?"

"I've spent the better part of the week watching my partner puke his guts out into a trash can by the bed, he couldn't even make it to the bathroom!"

Jim took the receiver from me.

"Sergeant," he said. "We've had a rough time here. But things are cool, I mean we could use a little help or something, but we'll handle it." He lectured Dodd about search warrants for a few minutes and then hung up.

"Damn, lady." He smiled at me for the first time in weeks. "You're liable to get us both on the carpet for insubordination."

"You think he even knows what that is?"

"Yeah," he said, slumping into a chair. "Our idiot sergeant. I feel like I been rode hard and put up wet." He tapped out a line and picked up the tooter. "A man ought to be able to get off this way once his tolerance is down."

I took the tooter from him.

"Hey," he said, reaching for it, "have a little faith." He took it and leaned over the mirror.

"The way you do?" I asked. But I was relieved when he did it. I hadn't liked the way he looked at me when I bumped up while he was eating.

"Dodd told me he'd call back," he said, absently fingering the vial. "To let us know if they're going to pop him."

"If that creek is on Gaines's property there's no way. Besides, you can't seriously think El Jefe will go for charging his big target with a misdemeanor."

When Dodd did finally call, it was to relay addresses and appointment times. Nettle was sending us to some doctors. A precautionary measure, Dodd said. Just to make sure we were all right. It was almost touching, except that I knew El Jefe didn't give a damn about Jim or about me, didn't spend so much as a minute worrying about our welfare. If he'd told Dodd it was a precaution, it certainly was not for our sake.

We sat in the barren waiting room at the county health center watching the junkies and poor pregnant black women traipse in and out until finally a nurse called for us.

Doctor number one must have been pushing ninety, with a beard down to his belt buckle and frizzy gray hair almost to his shoulders. He sat hunched at his desk, and when he stood up the bend of his shoulders stayed the same. I thought of Rumpelstiltskin.

He didn't so much as take our temperatures. When Jim told him we couldn't sleep he wrote out prescriptions for Valium and Quaalude, no questions asked.

Back in the car, Jim looked at the scripts and shook his head. He put on his best West Texas drawl and said, "Well, shit, darlin', El Jefe's taking care of us. Don't this beat all. A miracle of modern medicine."

From there we went to the psychologist's office for our three thirty appointment. The nurse led us to a four-by-six room that was entirely carpeted, the floor, walls, ceiling, even the benches along the walls, in a mealy, gray-colored plush pile. Pillows the shade of cream were tossed along the benches, and dozens of framed certificates hung on the walls.

"This place smells of incompetence," I said.

"Be nice," Jim said. "Maybe we'll score again."

"Wrong credentials," I answered. "The papers say psychologist. Check the diplomas. He can't write scripts."

We were still standing in the middle of the room when the doc walked in, tall and lumpy, wearing beige double-knit slacks with a navy-blue sportshirt and gray suede slip-ons. At first glance he appeared to have a reasonably full head of black hair, but when I looked closely I saw that it wasn't much more than a single black strand that was snaked around his pate and plastered in place with some kind of industrial-strength hair spray.

"Good afternoon," he said in a syrupy voice. "I'm Doctor Mawes. Jack, if you like. I just want to tell you that Chief Nettle is a personal friend of mine, and I've spoken to him at length. Rest assured that everything you say will be strictly confidential."

I took that as a sure sign that he would head for a telephone as soon as we left. He was practically quivering with excitement, thrilled to be in on a secret.

"Doctor," Jim said, "I'm not sure why we're here except that the boss said we had an appointment. I guess if you've talked to him you know we're under a lot of stress and all, and that I was overdosed a few months ago."

Dr. Jack sat directly across from us, pressing a pillow between his hands. He looked like he might drool.

"Let me tell you about my track record," he said finally.

"I've had wonderful success in the past. To date, I'm proud to say, I've saved thirty-three marriages and redeemed almost forty-seven alcoholics. I haven't lost a dope case yet. The treatment I have in mind would do you two a world of good."

"How long does it take," Jim asked.

"That's the beauty of it," said Dr. Jack. "It only takes a weekend. And you're in luck. We have our Christian Fellowship Retreat scheduled for this very Friday."

I looked at Jim and he looked at me and we both looked back at the doctor. For some reason I was tempted to break out a vial and offer him a line.

"The cost," he continued, "is only three hundred and seventy-five dollars, and that includes round-trip bus fare to Lake Livingston, a semi-private cabin, and all of our fellowship activities. But you needn't worry about that. The Chief said he would pick up the freight, pardon my expression, on this one."

"Doctor," I said, imitating the sweet notes of concern that dripped from his voice, "that's quite an impressive record. You say you've helped people get off drugs? What's your secret?"

"The power of faith, young lady." He pressed the pillow into his lap and beamed at us. "It's astonishing," he said. "The simple power of faith."

"Doc," Jim said, "we really aren't in a position to take time off right now. Maybe you could give us the info and we could get back to you."

The merest shadow of a frown fluttered past on Dr. Jack's smiling, complacent visage, but only for an instant. Then the mask of profound and supreme inner peace draped his face again, as though he were trying to imitate Gandhi.

"Why, of course, why, certainly," he said. "Just ask the nurse."

She gave us three pamphlets and folded her hands primly over her heart, her mouth stretched into an ear-to-ear grin while she watched us out the door.

Jim drove aimlessly, not headed anywhere in particular, not saying much as he drove. I plugged Steely Dan into the tape player and dug in the ashtray for a doobie before I picked up the pamphlets.

" 'What Every Christian Needs to Know,' " I read. Jim rolled his eyes. " 'Understanding Your Id and Reconciling It to Christ.' Ah, here we are. 'Dr. Jack Mawes invites you to spend a weekend Getting in Touch with Jesus. A fun-filled three-day retreat in the beauty and splendor of Lake Livingston for couples who want to strengthen their interpersonal relationships through Christ.' "

"Christian Fellowship Retreat," Jim said. "I bet those are real swinging deals." He passed the joint. "I can't figure this guy Nettle."

"It's probably a damn adultery club," I said.

He threw a glance at me.

"He hit on you or something?"

"Come on," I said. "Give me a break." I wanted to tell him. It would be sweet, watching him do a number on Nettle. I took a long slow hit. "Did you know," I asked, "that this band is named after a famous dildo?"

"Steely Dan?" he asked. "I'll bet you Gaines has more than a few in stock."

"So we're back to that."

"Hell yes, we're back to that. I mean, Christ, Nettle aside, what are you supposed to do if a dude's taking women and letting them drink free in his clubs, feeding them Preludin until they plenty fuckable and ripe for the camera?"

"Where's this coming from?"

"Hey," he said. "Right's right, wrong's wrong. Dude's flat-out wrong."

"There ought to be some way to take him down."

"No proof, man, he's done slid on those deals. But I'll say this. If the dude *ain't* wrong, I'll kiss your ass at noon in front of the post office and give you an hour to draw a crowd."

FOURTEEN

WE LAY ON THE CARPET IN THE EMPTY LIVING ROOM of my apartment, staring up at the whiteness of the ceiling. The drapes were open and the calmness of late afternoon whispered in through the screens, warm and sleepy. Now and then a breeze billowed the drapes, flaring them gently from the edge of the window, and slid along the floor to tickle at the bottoms of my bare feet.

Jim took my hand and ran his fingers lightly across my palm, barely touching it, then over my wrist and up my bare arm.

"Feel good?" he whispered.

"Very. It's been awhile, you know."

"Do I ever. Turn over."

I rolled onto my stomach and he straddled my back and began kneading my shoulders.

"The bra please," I said.

He reached under my shirt and slipped the hooks loose, began working his way down my back. By the time he reached my feet I was barely conscious.

"Don't drift off," he said. "This is strictly a split-down deal." He knelt up and unbuttoned his shirt and balled it into a pillow. "My turn." He stretched out next to me.

"I'm Jell-O," I said. "Haven't got the strength to blink."

I pushed myself up and rolled across him, brushing his hair away from his shoulders.

"Higher," he said. "Start at the neck."

I was working on his left hamstring when I looked up and saw him staring at his arm, rubbing the knotty mass under his reddened skin.

"I think I've done it," he said quietly.

I leaned across him and pressed the track. It felt like there was a tube-shaped piece of cartilage lodged under his skin. The bruises were mostly gone, there was only the faintest yellow tint at the very edges of the track.

"Too much scar tissue," he said. "Got one here that's permanent."

"Give it time," I said. I went back to massaging his legs.

"This'll take a year at least. And we'll be in court way before then."

"So we tell them we injected sterile water until a track formed. Part of your cover."

He lay there, pressing a finger against his skin.

"Maybe I should just go back to that screwball shrink and ask him if he does prayer healing."

"What we should do is make Gaines and get the hell out of here."

"To where?"

"Anywhere. Out in the country somewhere."

"And do what?"

"Whatever. We can raise guinea pigs as far as I'm concerned. Just something else."

"I would've done the deal a long time ago if I could figure a way."

"You're not in it alone, you know."

"That mean you've got an idea?"

"Maybe we should just wait it out until Nettle gives in, pulls us up."

"Ain't gonna happen. He's got a hard-on for Gaines and we aren't going anywhere until we give him a case. I don't have a clue how I'll manage to bail out of this one." He rolled onto his back beneath me and pulled me down onto him. "What the hell," he said, "it'll keep." He sighed quietly. "What do you say we hit a restaurant, maybe that Mexican place out near Vidor, take in a movie or something."

"A little later," I said, raising myself on my arms.

He reached up and began unbuttoning my blouse. I felt his lips against my earlobe when he whispered, "I didn't know how much I'd missed you."

When I woke up, early in the evening, I was alone. I dressed and walked back to his apartment, wondering where he'd gone, and why he'd left me there like that, sleeping naked on the floor of my empty living room.

He wasn't home, and there was no note. I tried Walker's place.

"I haven't seen him," he said. "Don't care to, either. I don't mind if somebody tries to kick my ass for good reason, but that wasn't right, man, what he did."

"He was fucked up," I said. "He's getting a lot of heat. He didn't mean it."

"Well, I probably shouldn't even mention this, but I've got a Quaalude case set up for you. If you're still interested in pills."

"Where and when?"

"Dude sells them at the Yellow Rose, out in the parking lot, around closing time."

"I'll be back at eleven," I said. I wondered where Jim was, but I wasn't nervous about it. I was sure he was all right.

* * *

The parking lot was jammed with cars, their radios and tape decks blasting everything from Sammy Hagar to Merle Haggard into the warm night air. The last customers were wobbling out of the club, swaying in small groups under the broad awning that ran the length of the building.

"Over there," Walker said, pointing to a dirty orange van parked on the south side of the acre-large lot. "We just tell him Monroe sent us."

"Wait here," I said. "No sense having you witness it." He got out of the car and wandered toward the front of the club. I wound the Olds past parked cars and clots of people, pulling up next to the driver's side of the van.

I didn't have to say a word. The 'fro-headed driver looked down at me for a long moment, then leaned out the window and said, "How many?"

"They're not that Canadian shit, are they?" I asked.

"Rorer," he said. "Guaranteed. Five apiece."

"What about two dozen?"

"I'll let them go for a C."

I handed him a bill and he tossed a baggie onto my lap. Then he leaned out and handed me a cold can of Dr Pepper.

"Appreciate it," I said. "If these are good I'll want more."

"I'm around," he said.

I drove off slowly, noting his license-plate number in my rearview. Anybody who was that easy deserved to get made.

I parked in a slot down the row from where Walker stood talking to a group of cowboys. Like all the clubs in Beaumont, the Yellow Rose was forced by city ordinance to close at midnight, leaving its patrons to gather in the parking lot until they got bored or a fight broke out and the cops came to chase everyone away.

I must have been staring right at them for the better part

of five minutes before I realized that Jim and Rob were standing near the front door of the club, talking to Gaines. Jim had his hands tucked in his pockets and was nodding his head while Gaines threw his huge arms around, obviously upset about something.

I felt betrayed. I didn't know why he'd decided to do it without me, and I didn't care. He'd cut me out, replaced me with Rob, even after his tirade about Rob running, Rob being a topwater floater. I thought about walking over, I had my hand on the door handle and was ready to go, but if Jim was actually making the deal and I walked up and blew it, there would be no peace. I tapped the horn and when Walker looked up, motioned him over.

"I had another deal," he said. "Some blow."

"Forget it for now," I said. "We have something to do."

"Like what?"

"Like move some furniture."

"Now? It's damn near one o'clock."

I handed him a Quay and the Dr Pepper.

"It'll be fun," I said.

Jim shook me awake the next morning, saying something about hurry up and get dressed. I staggered into the shower and gradually managed to get my eyes open.

He handed me coffee as soon as I hit the kitchen.

"Who did this?" he asked, sweeping his arm around the room. "And when? I got home last night and my fucking crib was cleaned out."

"Walker and I did," I mumbled. "You said you wanted to move, didn't you? I sure didn't have anything else going on. Being as my partner didn't seem to need me around last night."

"I was working."

"I saw."

"What do you mean?"

"I was at the Yellow Rose. Walker set up a deal, I went to buy some Quays. I saw you talking to Gaines."

"Yeah," he said. "Well, I had to try. He's not coming up for it. Rob flashed a shitload of cash at him and he looked at it like it was horse dung."

"When did we decide to bring the State in on this? Did Nettle change his mind?"

"I didn't ask." He poured some coffee and sat down. "Look," he said, "I was trying to get the thing done. I'm running out of options here. I'm trying to save my ass. And yours."

I sat listening to the pulse of one magnificent Quaalude hangover throb between my ears. He was trying to dig his way out of the hole I'd made for both of us. It didn't matter that I'd told him I was with him. He didn't want me to so much as hand him a shovel.

"We're meeting with Nettle today," he said. "And I'm going to tell him we can't make Gaines."

"He'll freak."

"Fuck it. We're not getting killed over a goddamn dope deal." He stood up and took a few steps toward the kitchen. "Rob should be by anytime."

I couldn't wake up. The sounds of Jim unloading the dishwasher came to me through fog.

"I flat out hit on him last night," he said. "Like I told you that night at Drillers, the dude thinks we're heat."

"You know he's got it," I said.

"Yeah, well, he ain't coming up for selling any to me. He was doing a tenth-gear backpedal."

I sat at the table and heard distinct metal clinkings as Jim tossed dinner knives into the kitchen drawer.

*   *   *

Rob handed me a bottle of Visine on the way to the meeting.

"Save me a little," he said.

Nettle was standing next to his car in the alley behind Kroger's grocery when we got there. He had on new shoes, black suede slip-ons with white patent tops.

"Pretty slick skids, Chief," Jim said.

Nettle saw what Jim was looking at and bobbed his head.

"Thank you," he said, "thank you." He looked at Rob. "Good to see you again. How've you been?"

"Fine, just fine," Rob said. The Visine hadn't helped much. He was high and he looked it.

"Listen, Boss," Jim said, "I won't waste your time. Gaines ain't dealing. At least not to us. I been trying to get next to him, hell, Rob was with me last night, and the dude ain't gonna come with anything. Nothing. Won't even talk about it."

"Wait a minute," Nettle stammered. "Will Gaines is a dope dealer. It's in our intelligence files."

"I'm telling you," Jim said, "he's staying clean. No way we can get a dope case on him."

Rob backed Jim up with a nod. Nettle turned to me.

"And you?" he asked.

"I wasn't there," I said. "I was out buying Ludes."

"This is crap," he said. "I know for a fact he's dealing."

"How's that?" Jim asked.

"We have our sources," Nettle said. "It's in our files." He looked at me, a brief head-to-toe glance. "I'll bet he'd give you anything you asked for."

Maybe it was my hangover. Maybe I wasn't hearing him right. But I was. Nettle's pale gray eyes were looking me up and down and he wasn't seeing cop.

"Chief," I said, "you can get someone else to screw him,

if that's what you're asking me to do. My job description says nothing about being a hooker."

He took a step back and leaned against his car, looking for all the world as though he might yawn.

"I didn't mean to imply," he said.

"Look," Jim said, "what would you say if I stood right here in front of you, like I'm doing right now, and told you Will Gaines is not dealing dope?"

Nettle looked around, checking out the alley.

"I would ask," he whispered, " 'When are you going to make the big case?' "

Jim was silent. Nettle stuck his hands in his trouser pockets and flexed his knees.

"By the way," he said, "how's that arm of yours doing?"

In the car on the way home, no one said anything for a long time. Rob turned on the radio, punching buttons so rapidly that we heard only disjointed scraps of music and voices.

"The man's telling you to stash," he finally said.

"Yeah," Jim said. "And he made it pretty goddamn plain what will happen if we don't." He put his arm across the seatback and rested his hand on my shoulder. "Shit, baby," he moaned, "here we could have a case on the dude in no time, if'n you'd only cooperate with El Jefe's plan."

I dug an elbow into his ribs and he faked falling over the steering wheel, nearly landing us in a ditch.

Toward the end of it, I began giving clues to the defendants. It took them only a few days to find the new apartment, to get the phone number, and as the investigation was winding down, I started to feel like an animal with one leg clamped in a trap. The options? Stay and get skinned, or chew off a foot and drag yourself into the forest, hope you don't bleed to death.

All we needed was Gaines. Nettle had his magic number. Close to two hundred cases on a hundred defendants. And counting.

When the defendants came over, I put on music for them. Sometimes I played "Everything That You Do Will Come Back to You." I had a favorite, by Steely Dan, *Agents of the law, luckless pedestrians, I know you're out there somewhere* . . .

Some hours and God knows how much tequila later I was one of them, thinking fuck it all, we're here together and that is what matters. We didn't get killed in a jungle, we don't have to worry about the stock market, we have no need for *haute couture*. I will not spend my life writing speeding tickets. I cross lines, but even I have a few shredded scruples left, hanging inside my chest like torn rags, and I will not fuck Will Gaines for the sake of a case. That's what Nettle wants, that's what he expects of me, all in the sweet line of duty. I refuse. I could, I wouldn't die from it, and yes, I thought about it when he mentioned the possibilities, and I should have pistol-whipped him then and there. Caught him off-guard and felt the wondrous crack of stainless steel against his brainless skull. That would have been nice. It would have been nice to see his hair messed up. I can see him, El Jefe, standing outside with his megaphone, *saying all is forgiven, mad dog surrender* . . . The defendants and I are sitting in this room, together, still breathing and warm with Cuervo. I understand now, after living in their world, why they hate cops. I know how cops think, or don't think, about the laws they have sworn to enforce. Cops don't have time to ask questions, they're too busy trying to stay alive. They respect authority because they have been selected to uphold the status quo. The power is on their side, the power wants them out there on the front lines, separating the haves from the have-nots.

I despise the defendants, but I pity them, too, playing in the dime-store league instead of on Wall Street. Late at night, when they have gone, Jim and I will sit on the couch and talk about which ones we will try to flip. *Throw back the little ones and pan fry the big ones.*

But for now, light the candles, roll a joint, pass the bottle. Here we all are. One sunny tomorrow I will betray you in the name of the law. But for the moment, let's get high and listen to music.

The report, scrawled in Jim's skinny, straight-line script said:

> At approximately eleven forty-two on Wednesday, April 26, 1978, Agent Jim Raynor of the Beaumont Police Department purchased EXHIBIT 1, a plastic baggie containing a white powder substance believed to be COCAINE from defendant, GAINES, WILLIAM ROBERT, W/M, 3/16/42, in the alley behind the Drillers Club, a bar located in the city limits of Beaumont, Texas. Agent Kristen Cates witnessed the delivery.

We didn't so much as say hello to the man that night. When Walker trotted in the front door and said there was a guy dealing ounces out of a room at the Best Western on IH10, Jim called Dodd and said the deal with Gaines was set, we needed buy money. We met Dodd and picked up the cash and then Walker and I drove over and scored an ounce from the FNU LNU in Room 144.

When we got back, Jim was pacing the living room, smoking one cigarette while another burned in the ashtray on the coffee table. I dumped the whole ounce onto a plastic cafeteria tray that came from somewhere and cut out some grams for Walker.

"Have fun," I said. "Things will get tight real soon now."

"And start thinking about where you're going," Jim said.

"Going?" Walker said. "I ain't going nowhere. This town is my home. I'm staying right here."

"You're crazier than I thought, boy," Jim said.

Walker stuffed the vials into his jeans pocket and went out the door smiling.

"So," Jim said. "Probably ought to step on this stuff. No sense wasting good dope."

I cut out eight more grams and we mixed them with twenty of mannitol. When we finished, we sat for awhile, staring at the bag of evidence. I played with a line on the mirror, shaping it into an *S*, then straightening it, then curving it again.

"It'll be weak," I said.

"Long as it's dope." He used the butt of his cigarette to light a fresh one. "Listen to me, girl," he said. "Listen carefully. If we do this, somebody's gonna get hurt."

I leaned over and snuffed up a line. *Come on, man, come right ahead on and give me a little courage here.*

"It'll be him, or it'll be us," Jim said. "But somebody's gonna get hurt."

I heard him. I tried to absorb his words. I guess at that point we wanted to end the thing, no matter what it took. Wanted out. And believed Gaines needed to go, whether righteously or not. I thought I had achieved, at last, the larger perspective.

Jim sat back in his chair, stretched his legs straight out before him.

I nodded at his arm. "What about that?"

He stared at the track. "Not sure yet." He rolled his sleeves down. "He'll probably make bail."

"I know," I said.

"It'll be get-down time in court, too."

"Jim," I said, "I'm here. Okay?"

"Rob's faded heat for it plenty of times. And Denny, and every goddamn narc I've ever known."

That was part of it, too. Still, after everything, I wanted to show him I was strong enough.

"You know," he said, "several years ago, I was in Houston, working with a state agent. Just hanging out with him one evening, really. He'd just bought an ounce of brown off a dude, and on the way back to the office we drove past this old house. There was a Mexican sitting on the front porch, just drinking a beer.

"So this agent looks out the window at him and says to me, 'You know, I think that sorry-ass just sold me a half ounce of brown. Let me just jot down that address.' It was a wrong stash, man, just out-and-out wrong. I still don't know why he did it.

"Three months later I get a subpoena. The son of a bitch had put me in his report as a witness."

"You testify?"

"Yeah, I testified. Made the shit up as I went along, he hadn't even given me a copy of the report. Jury didn't buy it. When the trial was over I followed him to the men's room and beat the hell out of him."

"So you still think I shouldn't have gone to Nettle."

"I'm not saying that. But I've got to know you're with me."

"You do or you don't," I said. "I guess we could sit here all night staring at this stuff."

"Hell with it."

We used a felt marker to put our initials on the baggie, and I could hear Dodd's yahoo blasting out of the telephone when Jim called to tell him we had the case.

"Idiot actually thinks Gaines sold," Jim said when he hung up. "He's calling the Chief. They want the report and evidence tonight. Special handling for this one. You want to ride over?"

"To Dodd's? No thanks. I'll sit tight."

"I should call Rob," he said, pointing to the pile of coke on the table. "He'd enjoy some of this."

After he left I lit a candle and set it on the coffee table, brought the mirror over and laid out some lines. I didn't know what was going on inside me. It was as if the numbness in the back of my throat had spread throughout my entire body. I was perfectly, completely empty.

When Rob tapped softly at the door with his three-two-three knock, it startled me.

"Got the call from Jim," he said. "Playing a little hard-ball now, huhm?"

He tapped out some lines and did them quickly before standing up to walk around the living room.

"So," he said, "welcome to the club."

FIFTEEN

T TOOK WALKER A FEW MINUTES TO CLIMB DOWN from the roof. His T-shirt was soaked through with sweat, stuck to his back in a solid sheet. He pulled his bandanna off and wrung it out, then unfolded it and began waving it slowly in the hot afternoon air. Construction workers were everywhere, banging and sawing and carrying around pieces of house.

"What's up?" he asked. His eyes had a flat look, as though he'd just been given bad news.

"Let's walk over to my car," I said. "Too many ears around here."

"Don't matter," he said. "They're all half deaf anyway."

We strolled out toward the curb. Like the street, it had the look of brand-new concrete, almost white. The block was dotted with half-finished houses, some just past the framing stage.

"We'll be through with this baby in a few days," Walker said.

"Walker," I said, "we're busting out this afternoon."

The bandanna slipped from his hands and he grabbed after it as it fluttered to the sidewalk.

"We could prearrange your bail and arrest you with the others. Make it look like you didn't know."

"No way, man, you think I did all that so I could go to jail? No fucking way. Not even for ten minutes."

"Then you better get out of here. Any relatives you could stay with?"

"I'm not going anywhere," he said. "I grew up here, I know these people."

"And they know you. And they know where to find you."

"Let them," he said. "I ain't running."

"You've got no idea," I said. "It's going to get bad. And you're not a cop, Walker, you got no shield. At least they'll think twice before trying to take Jim or me out."

"This may sound weird," he said, "but I'm not ashamed of what I've done. I mean, okay, I'm a dope dealer, in the sense that I take care of a few friends. That doesn't mean I like burglars and thieves. You got a lot of them, and that's fine by me. I'm not ashamed."

"Rob would set you up in Houston."

"I'm not a big-city man. I'm staying."

"What do I have to do," I asked, "threaten you? Tell you that if you stick around I'm gonna put a case on you and you'll wind up in jail anyway?"

He took a step back and looked at me hard, winding the bandanna around the knuckles of his right hand.

"You wouldn't," he said. "I know you. I'm staying."

"You're out of your mind," I said. "Crazy."

"Just enough to get by. I can take care of myself."

"If there's trouble you call the station and tell them that they are to find me immediately, no matter where I am or what's going down."

"I said I can take care of myself."

"Well, watch your back," I said. "You can't stay awake twenty-four hours a day."

He slowly refolded his bandanna and tied it around his head.

"That's why I sleep next to a twelve gauge," he said. "And I'll fucking use it if I have to."

When I got home, Jim was sitting on the edge of the couch, bent over, holding a towel full of ice on his arm. His eyes were shut tight and he rocked slowly back and forth, moaning quietly, humming low tones in the ancient rhythm of pain.

When I shut the door he saw me and stood up, still bent at the waist.

"I took care of it," he said.

A battered black-and-chrome iron sat in the middle of the dining table, its cord trailing up to the electrical outlet next to the phone. I looked at him and looked at the iron and looked back at him, and felt a wave of nausea wash through my body.

"You didn't."

"Had to do something."

I walked over and lifted the towel from his arm, and where the track had been his skin was disgustingly maroon, bubbled with blisters.

"How could you?" I asked.

"I had to."

"Christ, Raynor, you've got a second-degree burn!"

"It's okay," he said. "It'll be okay." He replaced the towel and began walking in circles around the coffee table. "Look, I was pressing a shirt and the ironing board tipped over and I grabbed for the thing and it landed against my arm. That's all. That's the story."

"We don't even *have* an ironing board! I don't believe you did this. I mean you could have gotten a tattoo or something."

"I'd rather be in Hell with a broken back," he said. "Tattoos are about a no-class deal if ever I've seen one."

I poured a couple of shots of scotch and brought one to him.

"I'll have to bandage it before we go in," I said.

"You're not supposed to bandage burns anymore."

"You can't have your shirt rubbing against it. Let me take another look. I'm calmer."

He pulled the towel back.

"Jesus, that's nasty."

"It's ugly all right," he sighed, "but it does what it's there for."

The Vice office was tucked away off a hall near the back door of the police station, away from everything but the evidence vaults. It was small, square and windowless, full of fluorescent light, with two metal desks and a back wall solid with file cabinets: black, beige, army green, covered with stacks of paperwork, arrest ledgers, various files.

Jim had his legs crossed, his arm resting in his lap, and rotated one foot in a small tight circle while he furiously smoked a cigarette. Dodd walked four steps across the room, his boot heels hitting the beige linoleum with rhythmic, rubber-clad thuds, about-faced at the north wall, and clomped back four steps to the opposite side of the room. There he turned and began his journey again.

I sat behind one of the desks, my stomach squirming like a netful of live fish, and paged through the Bust-Out Book, a big, blue, loose-leaf notebook full of names, addresses, photos, descriptions, and offenses. One hundred and twelve citizens, one to a page. Head 'em up, move 'em out. The arrests would begin in another two hours.

I couldn't believe it was actually over. Snap. Just like that. Jim had been under for almost nine months, I for a little over seven. Now, in the space of a few hours, we were expected to slip back over to the other side, the straight world. Jim had done it so many times that he never quite made the transition anymore, regardless of which direction he was shooting for. And me? I was just there, my body was there in the station and I was doing my best not to lose it and run screaming out the back door.

El Jefe, Dodd, the D.A., the grand jury—they would want to see Officer Kristen Cates, clean-living, brave, honest. She hadn't been around in awhile. I liked being Flo, I *was* Flo, I loved getting wired and staying out all night, staggering from bar to bar to private home, peeling hundred-dollar bills off my municipal bankroll to buy dope. Smoke it, snort it, swallow it, fix it, mix that dope, go up, go down, go sideways, go so fucking fast that your tongue can't keep up with the neurotransmitter Ping-Pong championship popping in your brain, go slow and easy, watch your eyelids come down in a twenty-minute blink, go Quaalude crazy, swallow those pills with Cuervo, Lone Star, or that essence of East Texas corruption, Wild Turkey liquor. Just like a fucking senator.

I felt cramped within the pale green cinderblock walls of the Vice office, as though I had just returned from a long journey in a foreign land and was looking with new eyes at the customs of my native people. The so-called straight world.

In a few hours all hell would break loose and more than a few people would be looking for Jim and me. And Walker. I didn't know how many of the threats would be real, there was never any way to tell until something actually happened. For a few redneck assholes it would be a matter of defending their manhood; no woman was going to get away with busting them. I was not looking forward to my required appearance in a briefing room full of the uniformed cops who would be making the arrests. A room full of harness bulls chafing to get out there and swoop on the dealers, eager to kick a little ass. I could see it in some cases, wanted it as much as they did in *some* cases, but the street cops I had known, well, discretion had never particularly been the better part of their valor. Attitude hung in the building like some high-pressure system that promised weather. Cops moved about quickly, efficiently, eagerly. And I needed help.

I walked to the ladies' room twenty minutes before the briefing was to begin and took a good healthy snort of FNU LNU's pink-white Bolivian and then tucked the vial away in my boot.

Handle it. Right. There was the momentary paranoia that always undercut that cool surge of cocaine confidence, heightened, no doubt, by the fact that I was standing next to a clean porcelain bowl in a red metal stall in the ladies' room of the police department. I didn't know what I was doing, I was just there, just standing there breathing, afraid to think, knowing that the good guys were out there, in offices, in hallways, in the lounge. For some reason I wondered if they had policemen's balls in Beaumont, if once a year they sold tickets to a benefit or something like that. I was surrounded by cops who thought I was one of them. Legally, I was, and I had a brand-new nickel-plated badge to prove it. Vice officer. Badge number 714. Seven one four, it was too good to be true. Rorer 714, the identification code stamped on every Quaalude tablet that rolled off the assembly line. Ah, excuse me, Officer, is that your badge number or your recreational drug of choice? I slammed a hand against the metal stall door just to hear it echo in the bathroom, leaned toward the wall mirror to check my nostrils and walked back toward the Vice office.

I felt a tingle spreading upward from the point where my

skull met my neck, my hair stood on end. What if someone noticed, knocked me off as high? I told myself to relax. They wouldn't even be looking at me. They just wanted to knock somebody in the head. Wanted any reason at all to scream resisting arrest and pop someone with their goddamn nightsticks, slap their handcuffs on a pair of bruised wrists. And so what if they snapped? Even if some patrol goon got suspicious, his accusation would wind up in El Jefe's office, and it sure wouldn't be news to Nettle that his narcs were running around wasted.

Jim was leaning against the wall outside the office. "Tonight's the night . . ." he sang quietly.

"You okay?" I asked.

"I feel like shit," he said. "Fucking bust-outs make this whiteboy plenty nervous. Where you been?"

"I went to the ladies' room to powder my nose."

"I hear you, babe. I'm chasing the old yellow dog myself."

"How's your arm?"

"Feels like I stuck it in a hay baler." He put a hand on my shoulder. "Damn, girl, you look plenty scared. You're pale."

"That's what I am. I am plenty scared."

"Look," he said, "don't be getting all drove up here. Lot of folks gonna be screaming a lot of shit about they've seen us do some things. Never, even if they're dangling the goddamn evidence right in your face, never admit anything. Nothing."

He leaned close to me and in a Richard Nixon voice said, "Don't cop out."

"The things we're gonna get accused of?" I shook my head. "You think anyone would even begin to believe it?"

"You got it, baby. That's the whole goddamn reason things get done the way they do."

When he said that I heard a song in my head, "The Way You Do the Things You Do," and it would not go away. It hung there, the chorus repeating itself over and over. Rita Coolidge, no less, singing in her mellow-drenched, drawl-tinged voice, with the white girls in the background doing "oooh-ooohs" trying so hard to sound spiritual and failing miserably.

I railed at myself for getting stuck on such a stupid song and then finally walked back into the office and plunked down behind the desk to sweat.

Court was going to be a regular roller coaster. When these scumbags got up there and began telling their tales, heads would turn for sure. The jurors would sit there listening to each side try to out-lie the other, all the time thinking, "This couldn't have happened. Not *here*. Not in Beaumont, Texas." Like Jim said, everyone would lie. Court. Fucking right-wing absurdist theater with its black-robed critic perched up high on the bench. Justice R Us.

Soon all those defendants would be downstairs in cages, then lined up to be photographed, fingerprinted, tagged, labeled, and filed, then handcuffed again and chained together and transported in windowless white vans to the county jail where they would be photographed, fingerprinted, tagged, labeled, and filed again, and then the lawyers and bondsmen would come to take their money, ill-gotten or earned, and secure for them a temporary freedom, a county-size make-believe universe wherein they could walk and talk and eat and sleep just like regular citizens, but where their dreams would be of the district attorney's office, the district court, and the Texas Department of Corrections.

The Drug War. Tell me about it.

*   *   *

Dodd led the way downstairs to the briefing room. Jim and I didn't even know our way around the station yet.

Confronted by row after row of scrubbed, close-shaved, healthy-looking men in dark blue uniforms with shining badges pinned precisely one-half inch above their left breast pockets, I wanted only to flee to my apartment, to call the defendants and tell them to get the hell out of town, fast, no questions because I couldn't possibly explain even if there were time, just go, go far away and never come back, go and live the freedom that I could only dimly perceive, but pretended so well to have.

I remembered a night in Pasadena, in the briefing room before deep night shift began. I'd been talking with an officer who had worked undercover a year or so before I was hired. We had traded war stories, and then, from nowhere, he said, "Yeah, I met some pretty good people. And the thing was, well, I don't know. Did you ever get the feeling that *they* were the ones who were right?"

The cops rose to attention when El Jefe entered the room. Standing in the back with Jim and Dodd, I was somewhat awed by this semimilitary display of discipline. I could not picture myself snapping to when the head of the department, especially this fish-faced creep, entered a room. Things at Pasadena had been rather less formal.

The Chief introduced Jim and me as the two newest members of the department, explaining that we had been undercover for months. A harness bull in the third row sat staring open-mouthed at us until I got tired of his glaring appraisal and winked at him. He snapped his mouth shut below its tight little mustache and turned to listen to Nettle's instructions.

El Jefe, still only acting chief until the City Council approved his nomination, stood there telling everyone to be careful, to avoid unnecessarily harsh procedures, to use courtesy whenever possible. Then, in his smooth, oil-slick voice, he said, "Of course we all know there are going to be some real dangerous characters out there, the agents have documented well over fifty-seven percent of them as carrying weapons either in their vehicles or on their persons, so do what you have to in order to protect yourselves."

I loathed the man completely, could find nothing about him that I did not despise. El Jefe. The Chief. HMFIC, Dodd called him. Head motherfucker in charge. So calm, so meticulous, and suffering from the worst case of tunnel vision I'd ever seen. Forward ho! (But cover your ass.) Come on now, men, push me up this ladder. He stood there with his vest and tie and shoulder holster, his flabby white arms sticking out of short sleeves. I have never been a slave to fashion, but I just couldn't deal with a man wearing a vest over a short-sleeved shirt, especially this man. It was pathetic somehow. And he had that mustache, that tiny dab of whisker above the upper lip that made me want to remove it with tweezers, hair by hair. He didn't take care of his troops. He cared about nothing but his own petty advancement. He was in the world for Donald Nettle, for nothing, and nobody, else.

That night on the roadside, near the church, his boneless hands grabbing my jaw, his shapeless lips pressing toward my face. I should have slapped him, could have shot him. I jumped from his car and ran.

I pictured the back portion of his skull splattered behind him there in the briefing room, gray matter stuck to the chalkboard. A single red hair driven clean into the ceiling. Imagined what it would feel like to slip my pistol back into the waistband of my jeans, the barrel still warm from firing.

"They've done a hell of a job," Dodd was saying, his

voice booming in the room. "Jim, Kristen, would y'all like to say anything?"

Oh, what I would like to say. Jim looked at me.

"I can't tell you how good it is to be back in civilization," I lied. "All I can really say at this point is that you folks have a lot of respect on the streets." Did that sound good? Did I pass? I wanted more cocaine.

The officers nodded, a few puffed up visibly, some even laughed with delight. I scanned the room. There were six of them with those piss-ant mustaches, almost a fifth of the men in the room unwittingly paying hairy homage to El Jefe, growing miniature tributes right there above their stiff upper lips.

"I've had a few run-ins with some of you dudes on the street," Jim added, "and I can damn sure tell you that *I* was plenty nervous. You're doing a hell of a job out there."

More laughter. The narcs were doing good.

"Take a look at the special notes on the bottom of each page in your notebooks," Dodd said, "concerning suspects who carry weapons. Be sure you check it before attempting any arrests. The radio will probably be pretty damn busy tonight, so keep traffic to a minimum. Call in when you've got one in custody, otherwise, try to keep the airwaves clear."

The briefing broke up and the harness bulls milled toward the exit. Dodd pushed his way through the crowd to where Jim and I stood waiting.

"Okay," he said. "Kristen, you're with my group. Jim, you'll ride with Group One, Chief's in that one. Ya'll got one arrest to make, and that's Gaines. If you want more action after that, radio me and I'll get someone to swing by and pick you up."

Jim walked toward Nettle, who was standing next to the lectern at the front of the room.

"I'll be right with you, Sergeant," I said. "Let me just pop into the ladies' room."

I had anticipated the moment for such a long time that I was actually almost relieved when it finally happened. Relieved and terrified. The squad cars surrounded Drillers, officers blocked the front and rear exits. Dodd walked into the club with his troops behind him and me at his side, mounted the D.J.'s stand, and zipped the needle across the AC/DC album that was playing. He badged the D.J. and grabbed the microphone, his beer belly sagging over his Texas-shaped belt buckle as he paraded back and forth on the stand.

"Don't nobody get alarmed," he drawled into the mike. "I'm Sergeant Dodd of the Beaumont Police Department and we're here to execute arrest warrants on several suspects who are believed to frequent this establishment."

People began looking at one another, suspiciously, a sudden buzz of conversation filled the club.

"If you'll . . . If you'll . . . EXCUSE ME, I'D LIKE TO HAVE YOUR ATTENTION. WE DON'T WANT ANYONE GETTING HURT HERE!"

The club grew quiet but for one or two whispering voices. I could see the bartenders looking toward the back door. A couple of clients headed for the restrooms but were stopped by uniformed officers. The bartenders sighted me, stared uncomprehendingly.

"If you'll just produce some form of identification and file in an orderly manner toward the front door, officers will check your I.D. against our list and if there is no warrant outstanding on you, you'll be free to leave."

He stepped from the D.J. stand and began herding people toward the front door. Then he walked over to me and said, "See anybody?"

"Both the bartenders," I said. "That guy over there in the red shirt, that's Douglas. The waitress in the black tights is one of Jim's cases."

Dodd ran off to grab the defendants and I sat down at a table. The people who had lined up at the front door were staring at me, at Sergeant Dodd, who was also in street clothes, and at the harness bulls who were sweeping through the club, looking under tables and behind the bar, checking for stowaways.

Douglas and the two shag-headed bartenders were marched past, hands cuffed behind their backs. When they neared me, Douglas slowed, leaning back against the officer holding him by the cuffs, looked over at me, and silently mouthed the word *cunt.* I knew that I should do something, but I sat quietly in the chair, tapping my index finger on the tabletop, watching as Douglas was dragged to the parking lot and the waiting squad cars.

He had trusted me. They had all trusted me. It hit me then in a way it never had at Pasadena. There, I'd been such a rookie that I couldn't feel anything but fascination. This time was different. I hadn't counted on growing close to so many of the defendants. They'd believed I was their friend. I had pretended to be their friend. I felt like a snail, spreading ooze in front of me so that I could slither ahead another inch or so, not really getting anywhere, just going for the sake of moving forward.

I sat there wondering if there was any way in the world I could rationalize all one hundred and twelve arrests, knowing that I couldn't.

Dodd drove back to the station about ten that evening, when the bust-out was well under way and close to sixty suspects were in custody. He led the way downstairs, to the holding cells in the basement.

At one point I lost him and a jailer tried to push me into the fingerprint line.

"I'm one of you," I said, and the suspects standing in line turned to look at me. I recognized many of them, had been in their homes, had met them at clubs, at parties.

"You a cop?" one said. "I thought you was Jim's old lady. Man! It ain't right."

"What about old Jim?" said Cowboy. "Man, I fucking knew things wasn't right. I fucking *knew*! I fucking told you I knew, didn't I?"

"Yeah," I nodded, "but here we are. You got the rules all messed up."

"Maybe I do," he said, "but your old man done turned me on a lot more times than I sold to him."

The jailer stared at me.

"Let it ride, Cowboy, tell the D.A."

"Yeah," he said, "we know how that goes."

The holding cells were packed full. Each of the three four-man cells had twenty or thirty defendants in it. Standing room only. The first ones in had grabbed space on the double-decked metal bunks attached to the walls and now sat with their legs dangling over the edges. In the middle cell, only one bunk had fewer than six people on it. That one was occupied by Mr. Gaines, who lay propped up on one elbow, leaning against the wall, his feet hanging over the end of the bunk.

"There's that bitch!" someone screamed when I entered the hall leading to the cells, and the rest of the defendants quickly joined in, yelling loudly in voices full of rage. A few of them climbed onto the bars at the front of the cells and hung there like monkeys, screaming and spitting. Through it all Gaines just lay there, his eyes half closed, like the head gorilla at some zoo, bored with watching his spectators.

In the first cell, a figure stood silently at the front, grasp-
ing the bars with white-knuckled hands. It was Monroe,
the Charles Manson look-alike who had nearly killed me
with those Blue Ringers, Carbital they turned out to be,
and Coors.

He stood silently, staring at me with such hatred that
it made it seem as though the rest of the defendants were
wishing me happy birthday.

Around three, Dodd took Group 2 to an all-night Mexican
restaurant. I sat surrounded by harness bulls eating plate-
fuls of enchiladas and rice and beans. I went to the ladies'
room and bumped up, went back, and moved some food
around on my plate.

"Folks here take good care of the police," Dodd whispered. "You'll see, now that you're out in the open and all.
Shit, I'm just real proud of you two."

I looked at him, too tired to talk. Even the blow wasn't
helping.

"We done kicked ass and took names," he continued.

"I'm kind of beat," I finally said. "Think you can finish
up without me?"

"Hell yeah. Old Jim done turned in several hours ago.
Chief told me he had some kind of weird reaction, just went
into the lounge and laid down on the couch and started crying. God knows he's been through a lot."

"Where is he now?"

"Either at the station or at his place. I'll go call and find
out." Dodd was riding an adrenaline high, pumped up from
kicking down doors and dragging people off to jail. It
showed in his eyes, lots of white visible beneath his thick
blond lashes.

He grabbed a praline from the counter on his way back
from the phone.

"Dude's crashed out on the couch in the Chief's office."

"I could use some sleep myself. Drop me off?"

"The station?"

"No," I said, "my apartment." I did not want to be around cops.

He pulled right up to the front door. No need for secrecy anymore.

"You're sure you'll be all right?" he asked.

"Fine," I said. "Call me if you need anything."

I pulled my gun and watched the shrubbery on either side of the walk as I edged toward my apartment. Inside, I locked the door and shoved a chair under the knob, set up a pyramid of glass tumblers behind the curtain of the patio door. *Light the candle, get the coke.* I loaded five new rounds of double-aught buck into one of the hot shotguns and propped it against the wall. I set my pistol within arm's reach on the couch, laid out some rails. It seemed as though that was what I had been doing since the day Dodd had sworn me in. That and filling out paperwork.

I sank into the soft velour cushions. My bones felt hollow, like something had been inside them, chewing at the marrow.

This was home now, no longer a dealer's crib. It seemed oddly empty. The fictional debutante of the Beaumont Police Department had survived her coming out and been laid in the grave all in one brief evening. Flo, my former self, existed now only on paper, on all those offense reports. I was Kristen once again. Officer Cates. At least that was the theory. Change your identity, jump into the slime and play at cleaning up the streets, then come out and take up right where you left off, supposedly as a decent human being. Only I didn't feel so decent. And I damn sure didn't feel like any cop.

I tooted a couple of lines and picked up my pistol.

It's almost convenient, having a gun so close at hand. I thought about it that night, for a long time, sitting alone in the candlelit living room. Maybe it was the coke. Or maybe I was afraid of what Gaines would do when he made bail. Nettle had his big case now, Gaines was sitting downtown, locked in a cell. It'll be us or him, Jim had said. I picked up my revolver and set its cool blue barrel against my forehead. Placed my thumb over the trigger. I would squeeze slowly, so slowly that I could feel the tension pulling the hammer back, back, feel it in the trigger, slowly. I slid the gun down my nose, pressed it against my lips. I rubbed my thumb, gently, on the trigger, felt the crisscross cut of the metal. I pulled the gun from my face, shut one eye. Stared down the barrel.

When women finally reach the point of shooting themselves, most of them do it in the heart. The experts, the people who study such things, say it's because women are too vain, they don't want to think of themselves lying in the casket with a plastic face.

I don't know how long I played. I remember wishing the thing would just go off while I was staring down the barrel, simply discharge without my having to pull the trigger. I don't know why I didn't do it. Maybe it was because I felt that things were out of my hands completely. Maybe I wanted to see who would come after us. Or maybe I just didn't have the guts.

I stuffed the pistol down into the cushions and sat back to wait, staring at the small gray crack of dawn between the edge of the curtain and the frame of the sliding glass door.

SIXTEEN

WE WALKED PAST POLICEMEN AND SECRETARIES TO
the Vice office. They looked at us furtively as we
passed, and a few offered formal hellos.

Dodd was kicked back in his chair, his boots up on his
desk, yakking on the phone.

"Well, darlin'," he drawled, "have you even read the papers? I couldn't get away last night, things were kind of
busy around here."

Jim rolled his eyes and lit a cigarette.

"Yeah," Dodd said, "I promise, tonight. I'll be by at
nine." He cradled the receiver and swung his feet down
from the desk.

"It's four already? How the hell are you?" he boomed.
His eyes were solid red.

"Shit, boss," Jim said, "you ought to split down with
your partners here."

"Huh?"

"Hell, town's dried up, I'm smoking squares, and your
eyes are the color of rare roast beef."

"Aw, no, man. It ain't like that," Dodd grinned. "I just
ain't been to bed yet. Look at all this shit." He waved a
hand across the swamp of paperwork on his desk. "Still got
all this to log in. I'll be here till Christmas."

"How many'd we wind up with?" Jim asked.

"Eighty-nine in custody. Not bad for a night's work."

"Gaines out yet?" I asked.

"Fuck no," Dodd said. "Judge set his bond at a smooth seven hundred and fifty thousand. His lawyer is appealing it this afternoon. But right now his ass is in the county jail. And look what we got."

He stood up and patted a stack of VCR tapes on top of a file cabinet behind his desk.

"They found it in the trunk of his car after y'all popped him." He looked at Jim. "You shouldn't ought to have taken off so quick."

"I didn't see much sense aggravating things. We nearly had to kick his ass as it was."

"Yeah," Dodd said, "I heard he was kind of pissed. Claiming you'd framed him."

"Yeah," Jim said, "sure. Just like he was a fucking Rembrandt."

"What's with the tapes?" I asked.

"We'll have a look-see in a few minutes," Dodd said. "Right now I got to show you something." He dug in a drawer for a moment and came out with two sets of shiny brass keys, dangling them in the air for a moment before handing one to each of us. Then he leaned back and kicked one leg across the corner of his desk, rolling his head back and forth, stretching his neck.

"The big one," he said, "is the back door. The one with that funny hook in it opens the basement door downstairs, into the booking area. And that third one . . ." He stood up. "Come on, I'll show you."

Directly across from the Vice office was a huge, heavy wooden door. When we had passed it on the way in, I'd thought it was a broom closet.

"Your key?" Dodd said, holding out his palm. I handed him mine.

He worked the lock and led us inside, turning to pull the door shut behind us. The room was small and shelf-lined, packed full of bongs, water pipes, packages of syringes, ancient apothecary bottles, boxes and bags of pills and powders, bricks of pot.

The streets might be dry, but the police department had stuff stockpiled.

"The evidence vault," Dodd said.

Nirvana. Jim picked up a brick of pot and examined the markings on its plastic cover.

"This isn't from our cases," he said.

"No," Dodd said. "We took most of that straight to the lab. This is leftover from cases that got pleaded. It's just waiting to be burned." He stuck his hands in his pockets and looked at the ceiling. "Yeah," he sighed, "we're just so damn busy, we ain't got around to it yet. You know."

Jim looked at me with raised eyebrows. I shrugged. There was no way to know if it was a trap. But then, on the way out, Dodd kicked a box of pills on the floor and said, "Shit, y'all just make yourselves at home. It's been done before."

El Jefe, Dodd said, was out to lunch, and an important one at that. Nettle's desk was huge, easily eight feet across and four deep, and not a paper was out of place. In the center was a walnut nameplate/pen holder with DONALD NETTLE etched in a brown wood-grain plastic insert. On the right side, stacked in-out trays held a couple of papers. To the left was an eight-by-ten of Mrs. Nettle in her beehive and four beaming children, three girls and a boy, all with their father's even white teeth and tight-lipped smile. Behind the desk was a huge Beaumont P.D. shield flanked on the right by Old Glory and on the left by the red, white, and blue of the Lone Star State.

Dodd wheeled the VCR he'd borrowed from the booking room over to the Magnavox against the front wall of the office. The television, he said, was there so Nettle could keep up with the news.

"That and 'Guiding Light,' " Jim said.

"Speaking of which, get them, will you?" Dodd said.

Jim hit the switch and sat down on a leather couch that ran at a right angle to Nettle's desk. I leaned next to him, against the arm of the couch. A big silver *X* gyrated on the screen to the sounds of synthesized horns, then expanded into *X-tra Special Video,* then disappeared into a small white dot in the middle of black. Marching music began, and the dot grew into gold script letters: *The Beat of a Different Drummer.* The screen went black again, and then, an empty white room. A girl entered, moving mechanically, her head swiveling sharply, left, right, left, as she marched in step to the music. She had on a gold-plumed helmet and wore a short black skirt, gold bloomers shining beneath it, and a sleeveless black-fringed gold shirt. Her feet were in gold boots and she carried black-and-gold pompoms.

"Where's the Chief?" I asked.

"Meeting with the D.A.," Dodd said, his bloodshot eyes never moving from the television.

The girl danced snappily, a drill-team routine, tossing pompoms skyward, bending to catch them inches from the floor, flashing her tight gold bloomers. Her face was layered with makeup, her lips painted deep maroon, almost black, around her yellowed teeth.

"Oh, boy, here we go," Dodd said.

Three men marched in, wearing black-and-gold band uniforms, pounding away on snare drums.

"It's Sousa," I said.

"A defendant?" Dodd peeled his eyes from the screen and turned to look at me. "Which one is he?"

"The music," I said. "John Philip Sousa."

"Who gives a fuck," Dodd replied, turning back to the set.

Harness bulls began creeping quietly into the office, edging along the walls and standing silently.

"Heard you were looking at some evidence," one of them whispered when Dodd looked around.

"Gaines case," Dodd said. "Ain't you supposed to be on the streets?"

"Shift change. Just got off."

"Stick around, watch this shit, you'll see what getting off is," Dodd said.

One of the patrolman edged over and stood next to me. Jim sat, ignoring the television, his legs crossed, his left foot jiggling rapidly. He took out a pocket knife and began carving his fingernails.

"Hey," the patrolman whispered, "isn't that girl wearing a Trojanette uniform?"

"Damn right," Dodd said.

"Baytown?" Jim asked, looking up. "He was recruiting from the Baytown University Trojanettes?"

"Maybe so," Dodd said. He stared open-mouthed at the screen. The Trojanette, still with drill-team precision, yanked off her shirt and tossed it off-screen. The harness bulls around me hooted and clapped, and one of them took out his handcuffs and began twirling them on his finger. The dancer swooped up her pompoms and marched around the drummers, then raised one finger and invited them to follow her as she marched through a doorway toward another room.

"I'll be damned," the patrolman said quietly.

"What," Dodd said, "she's not that hot."

"No," the bull said, "but I know her. She's Willard Freeman's daughter. Went off there to school just last year. I'll be a son of a bitch."

"Who's Willard Freeman?" I asked.

"He owns about two-thirds of this town is all," the patrolman said. "Calls the damn president of the United States Jimmy. His little girl better hope he doesn't ever see this shit. He'd kill her for sure, and everyone else involved in it, too."

The lights came on.

"Turn that thing off," Nettle said from the doorway. "I want this office cleared. Immediately. Sergeant, I'll see you when you've returned that equipment to its proper place."

The grand jury room had a huge conference table in the middle and a coffee machine on a tiny metal stand in one corner, brought in especially for the marathon session. Around the table sat the twelve upstanding citizens who, with no small encouragement from the D.A., would determine whether or not to indict the defendants we had rounded up.

"State your name for the record please."

Vincent Carthage, the assistant D.A., looked about my age, but very bookish, very court-clerkish. His brown hair curled over the collar of his suit and he wore heavy black spectacles.

"Kristen Cates," I answered. My voice sounded calm enough.

"And how are you employed?"

"As a police officer for the City of Beaumont."

In spite of the prep session by a whole herd of attorneys, I was apprehensive about how these people would receive my testimony. I shouldn't have worried.

Nettle had timed the bust-out to coincide with the empanelment of a brand-new grand jury for Judge Hammit, known as a tough, law-and-order kind of guy who would choose his jury commission carefully. The jury commission, in turn, selected the grand jurors, and the defendants they chose to indict would wind up in Judge Hammit's court. It was one big circle of appointments, looping from Judge Hammit to his commissioners to the grand jury and back to the judge again. These twelve good citizens sitting around the table might want to know a thing or two about drugs or weapons, but they were team players. They would not dare question the facts of the cases.

There were nine white males, two women, and a token black. They were wearing their Sunday Best; one of the women even had on a woven straw hat with a bouquet of silk flowers pinned to the wide brim. Their qualifications were spelled out in the *Code of Criminal Procedure.* You had to be a citizen qualified to vote, of "good moral character," you had to be able to read and write, you couldn't have any felony convictions or be under indictment "or other legal accusation for theft or any felony."

It boiled down to a matter of speaking passable English and avoiding getting caught for a crime.

Vince kept his questions simple, asking the same things about each case: What did you buy, where did you buy it, how much did you pay, how did you I.D. the defendant.

Jim had already given four hours of testimony. It was my turn now, to talk about the cases I'd made alone and verify the facts on the cases I'd made with him. Sitting there in my court clothes, a conservative suit, skirt over the knee, sling-back pumps, wearing a shoulder holster for the first time in months, I answered quietly, with yes or no, as Vince went over the cases.

I had a stack of case reports in front of me, but rarely looked at them. It was as though I were talking to a long-

lost friend about events that had gone on during her ab-
sence. But seeing it on paper, the times, dates, descriptions,
faced with the clinical rendering of the events, I tried to
draw a line down the middle of my emotions and convince
myself that I had never been a friend to any of them. I had
gone on the streets to make dope cases, and that's all I had
done. If some of the defendants were foolish enough to
think I actually cared about a dope dealer, it was their own
delusion, not mine. I tried to maintain that attitude as I
spoke to the God-fearing citizens at the table. Their faces,
the pinched eyes, the drawn mouths, told me that they were
terrified of what they were hearing. Their town had been
invaded, and with the Lord's help they were here to do
something about it. It scared me. And even though I knew
that I was supposed to be disinterested, the truth was that
I had gotten close to some of the defendants, and so I
played down their cases, tried to portray them as decent
people who really didn't deserve to go to prison. It didn't
seem to help.

Vince saved the big one for last. By that time, the jurors,
all but the woman in the hat, looked tired, bored with going
over the same details case after case. She was into it, fists
clenched neatly on the table, but I couldn't get my mind
off my feet, which were hurting from the contortions forced
on them by high heels.

"Okay," he finally said, "your partner has already testified on this case involving Will Gaines, but I'd like to just
run over it with you."

I pulled the report from the stack in front of me.

"Let me direct your attention to the twenty-sixth of
April, 1978, that's a month or so ago. Do you recall that
date?"

"Yes sir, I do."

"Sometime after six P.M. on that date, did you have occasion to speak to Officer Raynor in your apartment?"

"Yes sir, I did."

"Did the two of you discuss a Mr. Will Gaines?"

"Yes sir."

"What was the nature of that conversation?"

"We discussed the possibility of making a cocaine purchase from Mr. Gaines that evening."

Yes we did, Mr. Assistant District Attorney, ladies and gentleman of the grand jury, we did indeed discuss the possibility of buying coke from Will Gaines. We decided it couldn't be done.

"And where did you go to make the purchase?"

"To the alley behind the Drillers Club."

"What time did you arrive?"

"Shortly after eleven o'clock."

"What was your assignment?"

"I was to wait in my car, near the back door of the club while Agent Raynor bought the cocaine."

"When he bought the cocaine."

"Yes sir."

"From Gaines."

"Yes sir, from Will Gaines."

"And what did you see while you were sitting in your car that night?"

"I saw Will Gaines step out back, and there appeared to be a short conversation, and then Gaines handed Agent Raynor a manila envelope."

I had solemnly sworn that my testimony would be the truth, and so I made my words true. I lied with conviction, I made myself believe it. I had to. I pictured the whole thing as I lied to the jurors, I saw it happening, saw Gaines make the delivery, just as he would have were there any justice in the world. He had to be taken down, and so, to appease the remnants of my tortured little Catholic-girl conscience, I took the long view and gave the jury the words they needed to indict Will Gaines for a crime he did not do.

One statute, another statute, it didn't matter. Jim and I were turning it around on him, discarding all the rules that he chose not to live by, and somehow, it was right. Our action was Justified. Q.E.D.—almost.

When Vince stood up, I thought it was over, but just then the woman in the hat raised a tentative hand.

"Excuse me," she said timidly, "but I'm not used to all this, and I'm confused about one thing."

Vince shot me a glance and then told her to go ahead with her question.

"Earlier today," she said, "there was a sergeant in here, Sergeant Dodd, I believe, and he mentioned something about a young man, I believe his name was Walker, and I'm just not sure what his part was in all of this. Could you explain?"

I looked to Vince, but he apparently had nothing to say.

"I'm not sure what you're referring to," I said.

"What I'd like to know," the woman said, "is whether or not this young man was one of the ones selling drugs. It was never made clear by the sergeant."

I had no idea what Dodd had said or how much Vince knew about our informant. If I said the wrong thing, Vince would know it was perjury, and I didn't know how he would react to that. I phrased my response carefully.

"All I can tell you about that," I said, "is that I never personally bought any narcotics from him and I never witnessed him selling any narcotics to anyone."

The woman fingered the flowers on her hat and cocked her head to one side. Vince jumped in quickly and dismissed them for the day.

I wondered why the videos weren't mentioned.

Outside the jury room, having received accolades from Vince and nods of gratitude from the jurors for my courageous sally into the world of crime, I stood leaning against the wall wondering where Jim had gone. Dodd walked up, nodding respectfully to the jurors as they passed along the wide, high-ceilinged hallway.

"He's in the men's room," he said. "Asked me to wait on you."

"What's the deal with Walker?" I asked.

"What deal?"

"What did you tell them about him?"

Dodd was standing there trying to look confused when Jim walked up.

"How'd it go?" he asked.

"Problems," I said. "They asked about Walker."

"Let's go outside," he said.

It was almost dark as we stood on the sidewalk in front of the courthouse, a pink granite art-deco tower that sat in the middle of the town square. The row of parking spaces in front of the building was filled with a line of S.O. cars, white Pontiacs with black-and-gold emblems on the doors. Most of them had the new red-and-blue Visibars, but there were a few with the old double-cupped red lights on top.

"So," Dodd said. He sat down on a fender and lit a cigarette.

"What'd you tell them," Jim said.

"And why," I said. "Why'd you burn him?"

"I didn't have a choice," Dodd said. "Don't ask me how they knew. But they did. Anyway, I took care of it. Ran straight to the office after I testified. His paperwork is right here in my boot."

"You mind if I hang on to it?" Jim took Dodd's cigarette to light his own.

"No problem." Dodd reached to hike up his jeans but

stopped suddenly and straightened. "Oh, man," he said, "here comes just the person I do not want to talk to right now. Thinks he's another Melvin fuckin' Belli or something."

Waddling toward us was a short, dark-suited fellow with a thick strip of black hair that ran around the back of his partly bald, partly shaved head, from one ear to the other. His tie was pulled loose and he carried a large satchel stuffed full and overflowing with papers.

He nodded at Dodd, stuck his hand out at Jim. "Charles Sommier," he said, grabbing Jim's hand and shaking it vigorously. He stepped toward me, stood barely a few inches away, and offered a dishrag handshake. "Friends call me Chuck. I've heard so much about you both. I'm representing, at the moment, forty-three of your defendants. I anticipate that number increasing as the trials begin." He stepped back two measured steps, pulled his satchel to his chest.

"I don't expect we'll have many trials," Jim said. "Most of the defendants will see the light and cop a plea."

"I'll withhold judgment on that," Sommier said. He stepped in close again. "But from the stories they've been telling me, I think I have good reason to anticipate some lively courtroom encounters." Again, back two steps.

"Hey, Chuck," Dodd spat, "how'd you wind up with forty-three defendants anyway? You get advance notice or something? Wait at the jailhouse to sign them up?"

"You know my reputation in the community, Sergeant, I'm sure."

"Is that reputation good or bad?" I asked.

He smiled and said, "It's simple. I'm without peer. And, as your good sergeant is well aware, I make it my business to keep tabs on Beaumont's Finest." As he stepped forward, I stepped back a couple of paces. He smirked at me.

"God knows," Dodd mumbled.

"Well, Chuck," Jim said, "we've got to be somewhere. Nice of you to introduce yourself."

"My pleasure, I assure you. Let's face it, thanks to the duo of Raynor and Cates, I'm going to have an especially lovely Christmas this year. Might even take the wife on a cruise. Business, as they say, is booming."

He did an about-face and walked away, still clutching the satchel to his chest.

"What an asshole," Dodd said. "Son of a bitch decided he was real smart when he won a civil suit against the department. Got two million dollars for a punk who claimed some harness cops kicked his butt one night."

"Did they?" I asked.

"Hell no," Dodd said. "All's they did was knock on the front door to serve a warrant. Unfortunately his old man was sitting in the living room watching 'Saturday Night at the Movies' when it happened."

"So how'd he win the suit?"

Dodd smiled at a memory and scuffed at the pavement with his boot.

"They knocked with a sledgehammer."

"Well," I said, "Chuckie sure has got his priorities lined out. Good Christmas, a cruise. Wonder what his clients will be doing?"

"Picking cotton," Dodd said.

Jim was still watching Sommier waltz across the parking lot when Dodd handed him the files.

"Yeah," Dodd said, "that's what it'll be. Jump down turn around pick a bale o' cotton."

"I'm not so sure," Jim said. "Dude's probably one hell of an attorney." He tossed away his cigarette. "He's about a cold-blooded bastard."

SEVENTEEN

ICILY COMPOSED WAS HOW THEY DESCRIBED ME IN THE newspapers. Valium calm would have been more accurate. Eight or ten of the defendants had jumped out and insisted they wanted a trial. I took light blue pills and got on the stand and said what the prosecutors wanted to hear, trying to answer in a manner that would make the defense attorneys cringe.

Nettle was loving it. He trooped us around to every civic organization in town, showing off his prize narcs, feeding us mashed potatoes and roast beef before standing us up in front of the Elks so we could talk about "Drugs in *Your* Town, Mr. Citizen."

Jim would stand behind a podium in his three-piece suit, his hair neatly trimmed, looking, as the papers said, "handsomely All-American," and tell the businessmen of Beaumont that they should thank God that their police department was doing everything possible to fight the drug epidemic which had, through no fault of theirs, infected their town.

One by one we gathered up the defendants who had tried to run. By July, there were only seven at large, all either FNU LNUs or people we knew by first name only. Sometimes that was enough. We would feed someone's street name into the computer, get a printout of each one on record, check the birthdates, and pick out those within range. Then we would send for D.L. photos and see if we recognized anyone. Though most of the pictures in the state's driver's-license file were pathetically blurred, we usually managed to find the person we were looking for.

Nettle took a personal interest in each and every case, and used the computers for other purposes. He checked out prospective jurors as if they were applying for a position with the CIA. He had everything from voting records to traffic tickets, he knew where they went to church, what organizations they belonged to, how many kids they had, and whether those kids were Boy Scouts, Girl Scouts, or delinquents. I felt like asking him what color toothbrushes the members of the jury panel used, but I was afraid he might know the answer.

Foolish little Douglas led the charge of the sacrificial lambs. He was the first defendant to go to trial, ran right out front. They gave him a life sentence. Jammer got thirty years. Cowboy went down for seventy-five. Lester the Mo was up for the Big Bitch, habitual offender, three strikes and it's life with no parole. He got it.

Lawyers began making appointments to see Vince and the other A.D.A.'s who were helping with the cases. The words *plea bargain* were whispered behind his office door. Chuck still hadn't brought a case to court. He was lying back, perhaps waiting to see what the others got, and in the meantime his clients were showing up at our office claiming that he was costing them everything but their pocket change.

A few of them even offered to snitch. Butch Cravin, a shag-headed blond fellow with a scar that ran down the left side of his huge nose, said he was desperate, he would do anything. He sat across from Jim's desk, sweating like a hog in a sauna, his T-shirt growing dark around his armpits as he spoke.

"I just can't afford that Mr. Sommier," he said. "Hell, he's got the title to my car, he's taking twenty percent of every paycheck I get, and I still owe him thousands. I got to have a little relief. I can get you a guy down in Port Lavaca who deals pounds."

"Pounds of what?" Jim said.

"Pounds of pot."

"Not interested," Jim said. "We want cocaine."

Cravin sat there for a moment staring at the floor, and then wiped his hands across his thighs.

"All right," he said. "But you got to get me off completely, no probation, 'cause I'm gonna have to leave the state if I want to stay alive."

"We can't promise anything," Jim said. "But we'll do what we can."

I'm from the government, and I'm here to help you. The guy had sold us some prescription diet pills and a few grams of coke, small-time deals. But he was looking at big time, anywhere from two to ten on each case. If the juries continued their hang-'em-high ways, Cravin would get an even thirty years.

I sat at my desk, staring across the hall at the evidence vault while Jim bargained with him. I had Valium in my purse, pot at my apartment, there was no telling what Jim had stashed away, and here we were, part of the system that had Cravin's head in a vise and was tightening, tightening.

He made the calls from our office, actually put Jim on the line to talk to the connection. We could get a kilo in two weeks.

When he hung up, Jim scribbled down the straight-line number and handed it to our newest informant.

"Call in every day at four-fifteen," he said. "I'll let you

know how we make out with the D.A. Your paperwork's in his office, so we've got to go through channels now."

"Thanks, man," Cravin said. "I mean, I wouldn't do this, only I got a family, a couple of kids, you know, I just can't pay what Sommier is asking."

"You could try for a court appointment," I said.

"I don't qualify. I have to get broke before they'll give me one."

"What about it?" Nettle said. He pulled a paper from his in-box and began reading it. His office was as cold as December, but the air conditioner hummed away. I pulled a chair up to his desk.

"It's a kilo of coke," I said. "A good bust." I wanted to add, "for a change."

"I don't see where Port Lavaca has anything to do with what's going on in here in Beaumont." He cleared his throat.

"It's a step up the ladder," I said. "We bust a local's connection, et cetera."

He put the paper down, pinning it to his desktop with his fingertips.

"Look," I said, "Jim's already talked to the guy. We can make the buy next week."

"It's out of our jurisdiction."

"What about the State?"

"Not interested," he said. "They have a bad reputation."

"Chief," I said, "our defendants are starting to talk, they're giving up sources. I just spent three hours visiting with Jammer in the county jail. He said he'd go to work for us tonight. If you won't do the Port Lavaca deal, what about getting Jammer out?"

"Unless I misunderstood you, the only thing he can do is a speed lab in Dallas. That's not our problem either."

"It is our problem," I said. "It's a damn crank lab. Crystal meth. You know how much of that we bought. They're all over the state. This is a source."

He reached beneath his desk and brought out his briefcase, centering it carefully on the polished mahogany before he stood up.

"Officer," he said, "it's late, and I'm tired. Good-night."

It was almost midnight when I got home. There were lights on in my apartment. Standing outside the door, I heard the twanging guitar of Willie Nelson. I slipped my gun out and worked the key with my left hand.

Jim and Walker were sprawled on the couch. In the center of the coffee table was a pyramid of empty beer cans, next to that a bong and a bag of weed.

"Hey, baby," Jim said, "how'd it go? You flip that bastard?"

"He going to cooperate?" Walker slurred.

I ignored him and pulled a chair over from the dining room.

"He says he can do a speed lab in Dallas."

"All right then," Jim said.

"No, it's not. El 'Keep-my-ass-on-the-promotion-track' Jefe says no way. He wants deals in this county or no deals at all."

"Man," Walker said. "Some fucking cop he is."

"Shut up, Walker, you're drunk," Jim said.

"You're both wasted," I said. "Lock the door when you leave." I flipped the stereo off as I walked to the bedroom.

"By the way, Raynor," I said, "could somebody explain to me why I'm out working until midnight while my partner is at home getting loaded?"

"Damn," Walker said, "I think I'll hit the road."

"Good idea." I shut the bedroom door, slipped off my

shoulder holster, stuck my gun under my pillow, and passed out.

When I woke the next day around noon, Jim was lying next to me, also fully clothed.

I was showered and dressed and scrounging around the kitchen for something to eat when he wandered in.

"What time is it?" he asked.

"An hour and a half before work. You want some lunch?"

"Sandwich sounds good. Think I'll shower."

I dug around in the refrigerator and slapped a couple of sandwiches together. When I opened the box of saltines, I found a rig tucked in between the wax-paper packets of crackers. Used. A thin film of red inside, coating the cylinder.

I heard the shower running and began searching. Tore the kitchen apart. When I'd finished, I'd found three more. All tinted red, one still with a few fresh drops of bloody liquid in it. I lined them up neatly on top of Jim's sandwich and slipped back into the bedroom to get my badge and gun before I drove to the office.

I could have hit the highway and kept on going. I should have. Put the top down on the 442 and just kept on driving.

I went to the office and sat at my desk. A harness bull stuck his head in the door and asked if Dodd was around.

"Not yet," I said.

"Tell him to find me in the lounge."

"Will do."

I sat there. I took a kit from Dodd's desk and cleaned my gun. I cleaned and didn't think and cleaned some more. Finally I holstered it and began reading the quotes on the desk calendar. "The supreme happiness of life is the conviction that we are loved." Victor Hugo. "In the choice of a horse and a wife, a man must please himself, ignoring the opinion and advice of friends." George John Whyte-Melville. "There is nothing in life so exhilarating as to be shot at without result." Winston Churchill. I sketched a horsehead on the desktop.

It occurred to me that I had been looking in every direction but one, and it was only then, in that moment when I forced myself to recognize that I was not, and could not be, responsible for Jim's life, in the instant when I made myself give up on him, that I realized I would make it. The evidence vault was across the hall, loaded, and the key was on my desk.

I did not want cocaine.

I remembered a night, about halfway through the investigation, when a pot dealer had showed up at my door at two in the morning. He stood on the landing, shaking, his nose swollen and dripping blood. When I brought him inside, he sat down and stuck his bruised arm out at me and said, "My nose is gone and I can't find a vein. Can you fix me? Please?"

I'd asked him how long he'd been shooting and he said, "I don't know. Three days. I was at this party, you see, and I couldn't get my nostrils cleared, so I, you know . . ."

He handed me his dope and I fixed a syringe and hit him. And then I did my own arm, hating myself for loving the rush, pity-hating the helpless, slobbering fool of a human being who'd just finished begging me to pump him full of cocaine and now sat across from me, supercharged, his eyes so wide they looked like they were about to pop out of their sockets, cartoon style, and start orbiting his head. Weren't we having fun. I felt like a monster that night.

The evidence vault was across the hall. I wanted to be far away from it, in a house somewhere out in the country-side, far away from the mess I seemed so capably to have made of my life. If Jim was going down again, he would do it alone. I was finished. I understood this. I felt it.

When he finally walked in he was all business, whistling briskly as he began digging in a file cabinet. I watched him; I felt him in the room with me, remembered that first day, his hand across the desk, wrapped around mine, his strength, his eyes.

"You seen the case reports on Jackson?"

"No," I said.

"He's up. We're meeting the D.A. tomorrow morning. Ten o'clock."

I sat there.

He yanked a file out of the packed drawer. "If he pleads that means Gaines is up."

"Fine," I said.

"You should look over the reports."

"Maybe I should just run a little speed, get really fired up for the trial."

"I'm walking into this office five days a week and doing my job, baby. It's nothing to get crazy about."

That was it, he had it down cold. It was nothing to get crazy about. It would not do either of us any good at all.

"The trials should be over soon," I said. "What do you think, another three or four weeks?"

"If we're lucky." He slammed the cabinet shut. "Why do you bring that up?"

"I'm not up to finding U-80s in the cracker box."

"It's not a problem."

"You're right," I said. "It is definitely not a problem. When we're through in court, I'm walking."

"Do what you have to," he said.

I knew I was pushing, and that sooner or later something would give. I didn't know what direction it would take, only that I was being a genuine bitch, trying to make Jim hate me. I did my paperwork and followed Dodd's orders and took my meals alone. I didn't ask Jim for his advice or his company; I answered his questions with as few words as possible. I kept to myself. It was easier that way not to care.

He had the burn on his arm, he would be careful about tracks now. That necessary scar, in all the right colors. The colors of puncture, the colors of bruise.

I knew his anger, shared it to a degree, the frustration when some spit-bucket defense attorney managed to walk a defendant. I felt the same rage as he did at the incompetence of idealists. Who could believe that playing by the rules would even begin to work against people who had no rules?

As a Law Enforcement Officer, my fundamental duty is to serve mankind; to safeguard lives and property; to protect the innocent against deception, the weak against oppression or intimidation, and the peaceful against violence or disorder; and to respect the Constitutional rights of all men to liberty, equality, and justice.

There was big satisfaction in beating the sleaze at their own game, at having persuaded them that I was one of them and then facing them in court.

I will keep my private life unsullied as an example to all; maintain courageous calm in the face of danger, scorn, or ridicule; develop self-restraint; and be constantly mindful of the welfare of others. Honest in thought and deed in both my personal and official life, I will be exemplary in obeying the laws of the land and the regulations of my department. Whatever I see or hear of a confidential nature or that is confided to me in my official capacity will be kept ever secret unless revelation is necessary in the performance of my duty.

They had told me about everything, they had sold to me,

they had bragged of criminal exploits. I quoted their damning words from the witness stand and grinned at them when
the jury wasn't looking.

*I will never act officiously or permit personal feelings, prej-
udices, animosities, or friendships to influence my decisions.
With no compromise for crime and with relentless prosecution of criminals, I will enforce the law courteously and ap-
propriately without fear or favor, malice, or ill will, never
employing unnecessary force or violence and never accepting
gratuities.*

I played both roles, I was both sides. I comprehended
their longing, I shared their needs. And I despised us all.
The difference between them and me was that I understood
there was no difference.

*I recognize the badge of my office as a symbol of public
faith, and I accept it as a public trust to be held so long as
I am true to the ethics of the police service. I will constantly
strive to achieve these objectives and ideals, dedicating myself
before God to my chosen profession . . . law enforcement.*

I knew, in each case, every trial, even as I was saying
"so help me God," that I was about to get up on that stand
and lie like a thief in the name of the law. Because that was
how it worked. I had given up on Jim; I just wanted out
of there as fast as possible. I had abandoned any hope of
my own salvation. And that is why I was so good at what
I did.

EIGHTEEN

I THINK HE WAS PROBABLY AS RELIEVED AS I THAT THE struggle was over. Partners we were, and would be, for a few more weeks anyway. But we were lovers no longer, had no future, and both of us seemed resigned to doing our remaining time as painlessly as possible.

When Walker told me that there was a mobile home for sale in the park he'd moved into, I went to take a quick look and bought the thing right away, not liking it, but seeing it as something I could drag onto a couple of acres at some future date and use for temporary shelter while I built a cabin. I wanted to live in something simple and clean, uncluttered, something I had put together with my own hands. I would have watchdogs, which I would train myself. I would work at some sort of manual labor, perhaps look after horses at a stable. In the evenings I would garden or listen to music, perhaps study toward becoming a park ranger. Animals deserved protection. Protecting animals would be worthwhile. I had not decided on a place, but knew it would be somewhere west of the Rio Grande, outside of Texas and far away from Jim.

The rental truck had a large green elephant painted on either side. Jim and Walker and I loaded my living-room furniture and hauled it to the new place Wednesday afternoon.

Jim was quiet and helpful, and neither of us mentioned to Walker that I would be living there alone.

After we fit the big L-shaped sectional against the back and side walls of the living room, we sat sweating and trying to decide whether to make another load. It was almost dusk, and I was in favor of going ahead, getting the move done under cover of darkness.

"I thought I would go clubbing tonight," Walker said.

"I don't get it," Jim said. "Why the hell do you want to sit in a dark noisy room with a bunch of drunks, especially when half of them are probably looking to kick your ass. Or worse."

"No trouble so far," Walker said.

Jim pulled a baggie out of his pocket and found a shoebox top. He used his business card—Beaumont Police Department, Jim Raynor, Vice Officer—to separate the seeds from the leaf, and stashed the boxtop under the sectional while we smoked.

"I've got the truck until five tomorrow," I said. "I guess we don't have to finish it tonight."

When Walker had gone, Jim and I set about cleaning the place up. The previous owner had left odds and ends of furniture lying around, and what looked like most of his dishes. We found a rolling tray and a power hitter in the kitchen and a bottle of mannitol in the medicine cabinet.

"Looks like we missed one," Jim said.

The trailer was set low to the ground and felt so flimsy that I was sure if I jumped up and down I would find myself standing on the sandy earth beneath the thing, in among the underpinnings. A front door entered onto the living room, with the kitchen to the right, separated by an open bar. There was a long, narrow hallway off the living room, and down the hallway were a small front bedroom, a washer and dryer set back in an open space, the bathroom, a door opening onto the back lawn, and, at the end of the hall, the larger bedroom. The wall-to-wall was a ratty orange color, and there was a gold globe swag lamp in the corner of the living room. The walls were wood-grain paneling. But there was a roof, and there were doors I could lock.

When I opened the refrigerator the musk-drenched smell of mold knocked me back a step.

"Downright nasty," Jim said.

Greenish-brown blotches covered the interior, like some kind of parasite that thrived on plastic.

"Make you a deal," he said. "I'll clean this thing out while you buy some groceries. We got to get this place livable."

Like there was still a *we* to talk about. There *we* were, the happy couple moving into the lovely new home. I wanted it to be that way, and the illusion was mine for the asking, but I knew that sooner or later Jim would throw me a fistful of reality.

When I got back from the store, he was standing on the front patio, whistling "Red River Valley" and hosing down the shelves. I tried to imagine what it would be like if we both left the department, what kind of home we would have. I couldn't.

The trailer had been vacant for some months, and late summer rains had washed soil onto the patio. It mixed with the water as Jim sprayed the shelves, turning into a thick reddish-colored mud that coated the patio. I stepped around the puddles and went to the kitchen.

Here's the happy homemaker, preparing dinner for her loving husband, things are just great. I assembled some roast beef sandwiches and considered taking cooking lessons.

On Monday, we would meet with the D.A. to begin preparation for the Gaines case. But tonight, Jim wasn't wired, he was giving me a break, doing everything he could to say he wanted to work it out. Just like he did every time I said I couldn't handle it anymore. I thought about waking up in my cabin somewhere out in New Mexico or Arizona, watching the sunrise before I began the day's work.

We sat on the couch and ate off paper plates.

"Maybe I should move this thing against the other wall," I said.

"Least you've got something to sit on," he said. "I'll have to break down and buy some furniture. Anyway, if you move it it'll block half the hall."

After dinner, Jim stretched out on the longer section, against the back wall, and I took up my place on the short part, under three large windows that overlooked the patio. We had the kitchen and living-room windows wide open, and although crickets were starting their evening calls and the screens were missing, no bugs came in. It was cool for the the first time that year, and I was loving the peaceful sound of the breeze in the trees, the calm of evening, the clean, rusty soil scent of the countryside.

Nobody but Walker and the guy who'd sold me the place knew where we were. The phone wasn't even hooked up. For the first time in long months, I felt I could relax. Just plain rest.

"We could crash here tonight," Jim said, lighting a joint.

So he was staying. He was lying on my couch, close enough to touch, and he was staying.

"We could make another trip," I said. "Get the bed and a few towels and things."

"This is fine," he said. He got up and locked the front door. "Sledgehammer could pop this open first stroke."

He brought the shotgun from the kitchen bar and propped it between the wall and the couch, just at arm's reach from where he was lying. The Colt .25 he had given me during our first investigation, almost three years ago, was on the coffee table next to the hillbilly's rolling tray. I moved my .357 from the kitchen table to a place on the floor, next to the corner of the couch, where the two pieces of sectional met.

We were where nobody knew we were, and the breeze felt good and the air smelled clean, and when Jim took a Quaalude and handed me a Percodan I thanked him and swallowed it. Since the bust-out, the county doctor had kept him steadily supplied with legal prescriptions.

After Jim turned off the patio light and checked the doors one more time, we lay back on our respective sections of the couch to watch the local news. We were in it, usually, some way or another.

El Jefe had leaked a story about Gaines being a pornographer with ties to organized crime, but it said nothing about any pending indictments. It sounded as though the Beaumont P.D. had him cold for delivery of cocaine. Even the D.A. seemed to believe our offense report, and I wondered what the nature of his attack would be. The background material was all in our favor, and I knew they would find a way to bring it in. Pornography was about as popular as cancer in Texas.

"I should close the windows," I said.

There was no answer. He was curled on his side, passed out. I gazed at the open windows, but the Percodan had me feeling warm and sleepy. It was such a beautiful, beautiful night.

It's a moth. It must be. A moth, fluttering in my hair. I do not want to open my eyes. Sleep is heaven. Percodan sleep, full of dreams, soft, solid, and warm. The lamp has drawn in a moth, attracted it. I brush it away.

It comes back, tickling my forehead, dancing in the light.

The open window. I didn't shut the windows. Crickets will come in, and june bugs, let them. Moths can come in. Everything is fine.

Something taps, taps hard against my forehead. It is not a moth. Hard like metal. Tapping. Tap tap tap. With purpose. I feel the blood drain out of my face. I must open my eyes. I can't open my eyes. I must.

I am looking into the black holes of a double-barreled shotgun. This is not happening. This is happening. This is realer than life. This is life ending. This is shotgun death.

He's smiling at me. From miles away at the other end of the shotgun, from just outside the window, he is right there, braced on the windowsill, leaning in, aiming a shotgun at my face, smiling at me. I've-got-you-now-bitch sneering. Sticking it under my nose, forcing the stench of metal up my nostrils.

I am awake and this is happening. He is tapping the shotgun at my forehead. I am had. I am helpless. I am about to die.

I push myself up, watch my body move so very slowly, I am sitting, and my blood has burst from its veins, it is loose within me, swirling, washing, crashing like waves against the inside of my skin, trying to break loose, gush from my pores. I raise my hands to shoulder level. He's got me. Make it quick. But mercy is not his, he wants to watch me suffer. Wants it slow and sensual, wants to feel it, wants every loving minute of it.

He teases, plays with my head, caresses my cheek with the cold hard steel of the shotgun, touches my bloodless lips with the shotgun. How long do I have? Jim sleeps. Stretched out next to murder, he dreams Quaalude dreams.

In this instant it is Gaines and I. Blond hair. Big. Filling the window. Smiling. I think it is Gaines, I can't see past the shotgun, black holes, I am staring into them. I feel it

is Gaines, feel his hatred, his joy at touching the trigger, at
knowing he will soon pull it. I am begging with my eyes for
a single minute of air, life is out of the question, I am gone,
I don't even know what is on the other side, if there is anything, please let there be something. I close my eyes. Just let
me feel for a few more seconds. Give me a minute to jettison
my existence. To say good-bye. To try to make sense of it.
I close my eyes and wait for the blast. A few seconds more,
I just want to keep breathing. Just air.

Behind closed eyes I see a grave. Perfect in its dimensions.
Cut into bare black earth, straight and solid as polished mar-
ble. A blank headstone, no casket, just bones. A measly half
skeleton, rotting, remnants of something human. Animals
deserve protection. I could protect the animals. Am I still
breathing? My hands are up, I have no weapon. Please, just
let me be here for a few more minutes. Please, God, am I
talking to you or to myself?

I feel Jim stir, his foot presses my thigh as he straightens
his legs.

A blast, a roar that fills the room with heat and slams my
ears and my eyes are closed, am I here?

The smell of gunpowder fills the room. I hear Jim scream,
I smell, I am breathing. I open my eyes and the shotgun is
pointed past me, aimed at Jim. He is reaching for the hole
in his leg.

The barrels are warm-hot against the skin of my hands,
I grab, I push up, try to force the shotgun toward the ceiling,
I am on my back, why was I sleeping, Jim is rolling off the
couch, another blast, I feel the explosion blowing out of the
left barrel toward Jim, it's happening so slowly, I can't stop
it, so quickly. Jim screams again, still rolling, falling from
the edge of the couch toward the floor, I am hanging on to
the barrels and kicking out through the open window, trying
to take the shotgun, screaming bastard-son-of-a-bitch-

motherfucker, screaming into air, kicking at air, he yanks the barrels from my hands, I see Jim rolling, see him rolling off the couch onto the floor, I roll behind him, I am crawling, crawling on the floor and the sounds coming from Jim are animal sounds, wounded, dying animal sounds, from deep inside, from pain, from fear, and I can't listen, I don't want the sounds, we are crawling on the floor, I feel carpet burning my hands, I hear those sounds and I feel pain in my gut, in my stomach and lungs, a wrenching, and those sounds are coming from me, from me and from Jim, the same sounds, the please-God-don't-let-us-die sounds, the begging moans, the bellowing coughs, the crawling-on-the-floor sounds, it hurts to make those sounds, it tears something loose inside, those moans, those cries for mercy from the bastard who is blasting eternity in through the window, gunsmoke and helplessness, we are crawling on the floor, it can't end this way, it has to be worth something, not crawling on the floor, not begging, not this way. Please, God, not like this.

The sounds keep coming, I don't want them, I can't stop them, slaughterhouse sounds, I see blood on the floor behind Jim, I feel warm on my arm, I see blood on my arm, God damn the man who is making us crawl, God damn him. I am on the floor, I see my pistol, I reach for it and know that I will kill him, I will kill the bastard who is murdering us, I reach, I grab, I feel the grip in my hand, my finger on the trigger, I am looking for my target, looking for Gaines's chest, Gaines's head, anything, the curtains hang between us, I look and the shotgun comes back through the window, at me, at my face again, double barrel, two shots, has he reloaded? I can't know, I pull back, half kneeling, raise my hands, Jim is crawling, the room glows gold, Jim is behind the couch, I feel the stringy shag carpet in my hands, I grip it, feel it pull loose from the floor, Jim is almost safe, I am looking at the shotgun, aimed at my face. It disappears out

*the window. I duck, I crawl on the floor like a beggar, like
a sinner, like a soul in hell, I crawl. I crawl for my life, waiting for an explosion in my back. I hear the sounds coming
out of me, I hate myself for begging, I beg louder.*

*I round the corner of the couch. Jim is in pieces. A chunk
of his arm is missing. A perfect crescent of flesh and muscle
and bone, gone from his forearm. He has the shotgun, trying
to put a round in the chamber.*

*The back door. We are at the end of the hallway, behind
the couch. The back door. Straight shot. How many are out
there? Where are the windows, we're surrounded by windows. How many? Where? Jim's hand flops helplessly. He
looks at me and at his arm, his eyes dull with horror. Where
are they? How many?*

I grabbed the shotgun, the cool and solid of it, jacked
a round into the chamber as I raised myself to kneel behind
the couch, the hard crack of metal, salvation. Aim at the
window and fire, eject, fire, eject, fire, eject. I did not feel
the recoil or hear beyond the blast of the first shot. It was
silence, smelling of smoke. How many were out there and
would they come back? Jim was on the floor, blood everywhere. I jerked a pillowcase and wrapped his arm. He
screamed pain.

"Press it," I said. "Press it hard."

He couldn't stop moaning. There was a fist-sized hole
in his leg. Tendons floating white-loose in the dark red of
his muscle, his tissue, I saw bone.

I yanked the couch away from the wall, pulled the plug
on the lamp. Darkness. Precious darkness, the sound of
Jim's hand flopping against the phone as I crouched across
the floor toward the front door, how many are out there,
where will they be, slapping the TV off as I passed, grabbing
my pistol from the floor, kick the front door, go out shooting, gunfire flame above my head, shooting at the sky,

shooting at air because I had to shoot something, anything, wanted bullet into flesh, bullet into bone.

Then there were headlights in the drive and I crept along the edge of the trailer and jumped out aiming at darkness, sighting on the driver, prepared, but too late, willing but tardy, and it was Walker and a woman, a girl with terror in her eyes, it was Walker, it was help. I ran to the car. "Jim's hurt, get an ambulance." The girl nodded, Walker dragged his shotgun from the back floorboard, "I knew as soon as I heard gunfire," he said. We approached the front door, three blasts, windows shattering onto the patio.

"Jim," I called, "we're coming in."

He was on the floor near the front door, holding the shotgun with his good arm, saying, "Please. Please." I knelt over him, Walker went into the kitchen and stared at the sink, walked back to the front door.

"Watch," I said. "They may come back."

"I thought water was running in the kitchen."

"It's his leg."

I knelt over Jim, took the shotgun from him. Heard the blood pouring from the hole in his thigh, pumping in time to his heartbeat. Found the pressure point in his groin, knelt over him, pressed hard with my hand, heard the blood flow slow. I could smell it over the gunsmoke. The blood smell. The smell of Jim's muscle and bone, the smell of his wounds. It was blood and dirt and sweat and sex, life smells mingled, rising up to me as I knelt over him feeling the carpet grow soggy beneath my knees, trying to stop the goddamn blood.

"I'm gonna puke," he said.

I turned his head. Please. Who do I pray to? Please don't. It meant shock, it meant death close by, minutes away.

"Walker." *My voice is calm. I hear it talking, but I am choking, I need air.* "Go next door, get help."

He ran crouched across the patio, across the lawn to the neighbor's trailer, banged on the door. I saw him huddled against the thin aluminum wall, searching the darkness, his fist pressed hard on the locked-tight door of my anonymous neighbor's home.

A scared man's voice trembled from inside the trailer, said, "Go away! We done called the police. We called for help. Go on now! I've got a gun in here. Get away."

Walker came back, stayed on one knee in the open doorway, holding his shotgun, waiting.

"How is he?"

"Not good." *He needs a hospital.* "I'm afraid to move him."

"They said they called." Walker nodded at the neighbor's trailer.

It was forever before I heard sirens, too far away. I pressed Jim's leg, my arm shaking. I pressed.

It took the sheriff's office over half an hour to get there. I knelt over Jim, aching and waiting, terrified that the assassin would come back to finish his job before help arrived. Jim's blood was everywhere, Jim's flesh was splattered on the wall. I felt heat in my arm, I pressed his leg. I heard engines roaring, tires squealing, saw headlights and flashing red lights. Walker stood and held his shotgun ready to fire.

"Sheriff's office, we're coming in," a voice said.

The lights went on, the paramedics stooped over Jim. White bandages flashed as they wrapped his wounds. I stuffed my pistol in my jeans and walked outside. In circles. Breathed the pine smell. I walked in circles and tried to form a thought.

I turned to see six or eight deputies trampling around the patio. There would have been footprints in the mud.

This much I could understand. There would have been footprints.

One of them turned to me and said, "Looks like you got into a real shitstorm here."

"Ever heard of a crime scene," I said. They stared. I walked away.

From somewhere came Doak Jones, standing before me in his uniform, and I knew him, I'd seen him in court, he was people.

"They're taking him on over to the hospital," he said. "Let's go over here and talk."

He led me to the next-door trailer. Now that the sheriff's office was there the man had opened his home. His wife offered me juice, water, coffee, she would not let me alone.

"Can't I get you something?" she kept asking.

I wanted nothing, I wanted to breathe, I wanted to feel, I wanted to be with Jim.

"Who was it?" Jones asked. "Did you see who it was?"

We were in county jurisdiction, outside the city limits. It was the S.O.'s case.

"It was Gaines," I said, certain that it was he, I saw the blond hair, I saw the sneer and the look in his eyes. I felt him there outside the window.

"Are you sure?" Jones asked. "Absolutely sure you saw him?"

I was not sure I was still alive. I was sure of nothing.

"If it wasn't Gaines," I said, "it was his twin brother." It had to be Gaines. He had reason. Out on bail. He had right.

"Come on," Jones said, "I'll drive you to the hospital. You're bleeding."

I looked at my arm. A bruise had started to form. There

was gunpowder, a black stain out of which blood trickled slowly. I couldn't feel it.

I lay on the X-ray table with my gun in my hand. When the technician came in, he saw it and jumped back.

"It's okay," I said.

The machine hummed above me and from somewhere in the room came the sound of a heartbeat.

"Lie still," he said. There was a click and a short, louder hum. I had only two bullets left. I needed to reload.

He worked the machine and I lay on the table, the air around me buzzing, until he finished and inspected my arm. He poked at it with a probe and wrapped it in bandage, said I could leave.

I walked through glowing corridors until I found the emergency room. Jim was laid out on a steel table, yelling such pain that it hurt to listen. There was a bag of blood and another of clear fluid hanging above him, the I.V.'s plugged into the back of his left hand.

"It hurts!" he moaned, then screamed, "GODDAMN IT, IT HURTS! Get me something for the pain! It hurts!" His eyes looked as if something were trapped in them. He saw me and reached, tubes dangling out of his hand. "Make them give me something," he said. "They won't give me a thing because of the Lude."

The doctor came in and told me I must leave. I felt myself lean to kiss Jim and told him I'd be waiting. His lips were cold. His face looked plastic. I wanted to know he would live. The doctor stretched surgical gloves over his hands and stared at me impatiently. I leaned over Jim and heard my voice say, "I love you."

In the hallway, I found Walker and the girl and we grabbed each other and something gave inside and I was crying, trying hard to stand up and holding on to both of them and crying, and then we were all crying. I saw Bachman, Nettle's assistant, Nettle's wing man, standing near the wall, staring at me with disdain. Tough cop. I didn't care. I sobbed.

I sat wrapped in a blanket, in a waiting-room chair outside surgery. *They are trying to save Jim. It's all right, I think he will live, there is blood here, blood in bags, they can keep him alive. I do not know about his arm or his leg, if he will have them when he comes out of surgery, but I know he will be alive. I think he will be alive.*

Dodd came in, his wife in tow. She plopped herself down across from me, snapping her words like bubblegum. I watched her mouth push them out, something about being in bed having the time of their lives when they got the call. I wanted to tell her to go home, go fuck her brains out, no great loss.

Rob arrived. Drove from a meeting in Austin in less than three hours. Nettle lived twenty minutes away, but Rob was there first. Rob knew, he'd been through it. He sat next to me and held me, telling me I was safe. I couldn't believe him.

I sat in a chair, wrapped in a blanket, and rocked. Rocked back and forth.

"He'll be okay," Rob said. "I thought Denny was gonna die too. He'll be okay."

I hope he keeps his arm. He deserves to have his arm. And his leg. He deserves his arms and legs.

My blouse was sticking to me and I looked down at it. I was covered with blood. My own blood on my blouse, Jim's blood all over my jeans. Everywhere.

Nettle made his entrance, his suit perfect, his tie neatly knotted, his hair combed. He walked over calmly and looked down at me.

"You're sure it was Gaines," he said. Jim didn't matter to him. Gaines mattered. The case mattered.

"Pretty sure," I said.

"No," he said. "The sheriff needs your statement. You'd better go with him."

"I'm staying here until they finish with him."

"That's not possible," he said tightly.

I felt Rob's arm on my shoulder.

"I'll be here," he said. "I'll wait."

Nettle puffed up like an adder, sucking air into his suited chest.

"You go with the sheriff," he ordered. "We want it on paper. It was Gaines."

NINETEEN

SAW HIS BOOTS FIRST, WHEN HE WALKED IN THE door and shut it quietly. Full quill ostrich, custom-made Lucchese's. Burton Cash, twelve years a Ranger, stood behind the old wooden desk in the center of the room and stared down at me with implacable gray eyes. *It's a goddamn shame the good old days have disappeared, we ought to just toss a fucking rope over the old oak tree in front of the courthouse and hang the son of a bitch right there on the town square. The good old days. What the hell is going on, anyway, got fucking cunts thinking they're the police, bad enough the law's fucking around with goddamn narcotics enforcement at all, now they done dragged some broad out of the kitchen and hung a badge on her tit. What the hell is it? Goddamn locals can't hold their mud, ain't worth a shit, and here's some bitch thinks she's tougher than a nickel steak, I know what she needs, cure her ass of that goddamn liberation bullshit just right quick.*

He was tall, up around six three. He was, except for his belly, lean. But then he was expected to be a hard-drinking man, the belly could be excused. It wasn't excessive, wouldn't get in the way when he reached with lightning quickness for that real live pearl-handled six-shooter with the raised gold initials slung low on his hip. He wore boots and khakis and Stetson, he wore leather vest, he wore string tie. He had a diamond pinkie ring, fourteen stones set in the shape of a revolver. He even had the voice, deep and drawling. Slow-talking man, made in the image of Lone Wolf Gonzaulles. Texas Rangers. The governor's assassins.

The interrogation room was tiny and square, with no windows and too much light. I sat shivering in a molded plastic chair, waiting for I don't know what. I was still bloody, it had dried in dark purplish stains on my clothes, under my fingernails.

After a moment, Cash set his Stetson on the desk, ran one large hand through his thick white hair, and said, "Tell me how it happened."

I'll admit that I didn't tell him about the drugs, but I told him everything else, exactly as I recalled it, with as much attention to detail as I could muster in that nightmare morning. I laid it out, sat there all balled up in the chair and talked to the man. He'd already heard the tapes from the P.D.—a frantic voice yelling, "Somebody's shooting!" and then the sound of three shots in the background. Jim blowing the windows out while I was edging back into the trailer after Walker drove up. The whole thing was estimated to have taken less than three minutes. Three fucking minutes.

"Write me out a statement," Cash said, and handed me a few sheets of legal paper. "I'll be back in awhile." As he walked out the door, I heard him mumble, "Must be a hell of a period this month."

Jim's blood on my jeans.

I watched my hand from somewhere far away as I wrote down the words. Shaky, very shaky, I couldn't calm myself, couldn't get the smooth, even script that was normally mine. I wrote and watched the pen form in scribbly, deficient letters the words that told what had happened, and while I looked at the words, my hatred, my realization of

just exactly what had been done to Jim, to me, took form
and grew until I felt that if I never did another single thing,
I would find Gaines, and face him, and make him feel what
I had felt only a few hours before.

Doak Jones stood next to me in front of Judge Hammit's
desk while I swore to the truth of my statement. The sheriff's office was asking for an arrest warrant on Gaines.

When I got back to the hospital, Nettle and Rob were
standing in the hallway of the intensive care unit, outside
the door to Jim's room.

"He's not awake yet," Rob said.

I wanted to ask him something. I wasn't sure what.

"They didn't amputate," he said. "They're not sure yet,
but so far they haven't amputated."

"You gave your statement?" Nettle asked.

"I want to help find him," I said. Some rules Gaines
would know.

"Absolutely not," Nettle said. "You are to stay right
here." He rubbed a hand over his jowl.

I tried everything short of begging to persuade him to
let me be one of the arresting party. When I realized I was
getting nowhere I shut up and and acknowledged his order.

"I mean it," he said.

"I heard you, Chief." He didn't believe me, but left anyway. When he was around the corner, Rob pulled out his
pistol and checked the clip.

"Pussy motherfucker can't tell me to stay away," he said.
"I'll call you when we've got him."

"Before," I said. "Call me the instant you get him put
down somewhere."

Jim woke up from surgery around three. I sat by his bed,
watching his eyelids flutter in the afternoon light until he

managed to open them. His arm was in a cast to the elbow and suspended from a shining chrome contraption attached to the bed. There was a single, thick metal stitch, like barbed wire, embedded in the front of his thigh, and beneath the stitch, his open leg wound. Ringer's lactate laced with antibiotics drained drop by drop from its clear, bulging sack into the I.V. needle in his left hand.

His eyes went to his arm, and then over his body to his right foot, which lay helplessly flopped at the end of the bed.

"I can't feel it," he said.

I started to talk, I tried, and then things went scrambled in my head. I slipped my hand under his, careful not to disturb the I.V. I did not know what to say, and even had I known I don't think I could have said it. The doctors did not know if he would walk. They did not know if they could avoid chopping his arm off. It was too soon to tell anything. And I had walked away from it with a deep rectangular gouge and a bruise, and a few tiny holes where pellets had skipped across my arm on their way to Jim. He took it, he took all of it. It did not seem right to me that I should be able to walk in and out of his hospital room while he lay wondering how long he might have an arm. We sat there, just looking at each other, not sure why we were still alive.

Finally, he spoke, softly, almost in a whisper.

"You did it right," he said. "You saved my fucking life, girl, and I have to tell you that you have never looked better than when you grabbed that shotgun and cranked off those rounds." He paused for a moment, swallowed, took a breath and continued. "The form was just right. Weight forward, leaning into the shot, so damn precise. It was beautiful. Don't you feel bad for a minute, girl, you saved my life."

But he must have known what I was feeling. It was working inside me like venom: the awful, aching guilt of the part-ner who'd been spared.

It was dark, gloomy dark, and smelled of ammonia-scrubbed cement. Cold, I remember it always being cold in there. The cell I lived in was haunted by Will Gaines. I couldn't close my eyes because each time I did I saw shot-guns. I couldn't keep them open because the face of Will Gaines edged around corners, slipped out from under the bed, floated, shimmering, in the gray light of the cell. Smiled. Always smiling.

Protective custody. The word around the department was that Melton Stack was fond of the bottle, that his trans-fer back to our quiet little office, supposedly to help Dodd run things, was actually a measure taken to keep him out of harm's way. He greased his dyed-black hair straight back and wore white slip-on shoes. It would be four years before he was pensionable, and El Jefe seemed happy to let him ride it out behind a desk in the back room. This was the man Nettle put in charge of keeping Jim and me alive.

Jim's situation was easy, Stack put a twenty-four-hour guard outside the door of his hospital room. But it was late in the afternoon before good old, scotch-smelling Stack came up with a solution for me, sweet-talking me into a holding cell in the basement of the P.D. There was a small kitchen down there, and a shower. I would be required to wear a bulletproof vest whenever I left the station.

In the cell, he laid a large sheet of heavy plywood across the center, resting it on the bunks bolted into opposite walls, and laid a mattress on the plywood. He stood box springs upright against the metal end of the bunks to block the view of the stainless-steel toilet from the camera in the corner of the cell. I had to climb across the bed and squeeze around the edges of the box spring to reach the toilet, but it was worth it for some kind of privacy. After Stack left, I put tape over the intercom and tied the cell door wide open, looping the rope repeatedly around the bars and tying triple knots in it. Chain would have been better, but Stack had refused that request. There was a camera that surveyed the hallway, broadcasting its signals to monitors in the dispatch office upstairs, offering a twenty-four-hour view of the goings-on in detention.

I piled some clothes on the upper bunks, hauled my stereo and television into the hallway, and set about the business of waiting, for what I did not know. I breathed and my heart beat. I listened to it, was amazed by it. I spent long hours sitting in the middle of the mattress in my cell, staring through the open door at the TV, washing down Seconal with scotch and 7-Up, premixed in a two-liter green plastic bottle.

I wasn't locked in. I could roam as I pleased, provided I did not leave the station except in the company of a uniformed patrolman. Yet I stayed in the cell, how many days, sitting on the mattress staring out at the silent TV screen and listening to Steely Dan. *Agents of the law. Luckless pedestrians.* Hour after hour. I brought a tiny brass incense burner from the evidence vault and hung it from one of the bunks to cover up the pot smell. I knew it was 12:30 A.M. when the local station stopped broadcasting, and I knew it was 5 A.M. when they came back on the air with the "Farm and Ranch Report." The rest of the time was filled with television voices or jittery gray light and white noise, all of it in an attempt to keep Will Gaines away.

I watched, I kept watching. His ghost was there with me, floating around my cell.

Some days after the shooting, I don't remember how many, Lieutenant Stack stumbled downstairs and said I had to go with him to the trailer. He was drunk enough that two miles down the road he pulled over and asked me to drive.

My vision went yellow at the edges as we turned onto the winding drive at Pleasant Oaks Mobile Home Park. I thought for a moment that I would pass out. Something was wrong, the sun was shining and the lawns were mown, two kids rode by on bicycles. Everything was calm, but I felt as though my blood had gone viscous.

I kept telling myself, as we walked toward the open door of the trailer, "It's all right, it's safe, it's safe."

I don't know how long I stood outside, staring at the shattered windows, remembering. I felt a hand nudge my shoulder and heard Stack slur, "Let's go in."

"Why are we here," I said.

"Just go in. Let's do it and get out of here."

Sitting in the living room, pointing a broomstick at a couple of deputies who sat at the other end of the L-shaped sectional, was Ranger Burton Cash.

He started when he saw me, but shrugged back his shoulders and reaimed the broomstick.

"It would have to be this angle," he said. One of the deputies wrote something on a notepad.

"You've got it wrong," I said. "We weren't sitting that way. I was on this section, Jim was there. We were asleep, lying down."

"No," Cash said. He leaned the broomstick against the couch and stuck his face out at me. He needed a shave. He needed a brain. "I figure there was a second shooter involved," he drawled. "The evidence don't quite agree with your story."

"I know what I saw."

"You think you know what you saw. There's an awful lot of unanswered questions."

"I've got one," I said. "Why wasn't the crime scene protected?"

"We sealed it," one of the deputies said.

"After you walked all over it."

"Look," Cash said, "up here you've got flesh on the ceiling, and some blood over here, and back on that wall. It can't be that way if things happened like you say."

"I told you the truth in my statement," I said.

"There was a second shooter, and he was inside."

I moved toward the couch. I wanted to touch it, to know that it was real. I needed some kind of physical confirmation that I was really in the room and this was happening. Cash would have his theories and wasn't about to believe anything said by anyone who worked narcotics, especially words that were being spoken by a twenty-four-year-old female.

"Never mind," Stack mumbled to me, "you want to get anything while you're here?"

"No," I said, "nothing."

Stack turned to go. Cash stood up, kicking the broom onto the floor.

"Hold on there," he said. "I've got some questions and I'll get some answers, whether your chief of police cooperates or not. What about this Walker fellow."

"You're wasting your time," I said. "He lives up around the block."

"Now, ain't that convenient. Y'all being neighbors and all. How many times did you fuck him? Ol' Jim like to watch?"

I looked around the room, at the dried blood and flesh on the paneling and ceiling at the end of the couch. Pieces of Jim, there on the wall.

And one dumb son of a bitch sitting right on top of exactly the kind of evidence he wanted, the boxtop that held marijuana and Jim's business card there under the couch, maybe four inches from the heels of his boots, but he wouldn't find it. He wouldn't even look, wouldn't move a thing. He was busy with theories.

"Who needs hard evidence?" I said. "There's a feeling in the gut when things aren't right."

"That's for damn sure," he said. "And I'll tell you right now I don't appreciate the attitude downtown."

It was almost funny. El Jefe was holding fort against the Rangers and the sheriff's office, trying to keep everything running smoothly and under control even where he had no jurisdiction.

The couch cushions lay scattered around us, blasted full of holes and crusted with blood. Cash saw me looking and said he wanted to take them.

"Anything," I said. "Follow the goddamn yellow brick road."

I went to the hospital each afternoon and stayed to watch Jim eat dinner. He ordered guest trays of tasteless hospital slop, and got furious when I had to cut the meat up for him. The harness bulls hated us. Hated escorting me to the hospital, to the doctors' offices, to the pharmacy to fill my generous prescriptions. They especially hated it when I sent them to pick up a pizza. But they did it. Nettle's orders. Keep her happy. Keep her calm. Do what she asks.

Hours crawled past while I sat in Jim's room, whispering to him when he was awake, but mostly just sitting there. He lay on his bed, dosed on painkillers, hollow-eyed and pale, and looking so fragile I was almost afraid to touch him.

I returned to my cell each night around midnight to take up my watch. Even after Gaines surrendered, two weeks after the shooting, I watched. Sitting on the mattress with my back against the wall, I would smoke a joint, eat some Seconal, and settle in for the long night of staring at the visual static on the TV screen, peeking, every few minutes, at the edges of the cell.

It was dusty, I remember that. Big gray dustballs in the corners. And I remember Nettle himself, only a couple of days after Gaines surrendered, driving me over to see a shrink, and the two of them sitting in the walnut-paneled, Persian-carpeted office trying to persuade me to take sodium amytal.

"This was the standard treatment for shell shock after World War Two," the shrink said. "And it may help you to recall more fully what happened."

"It might be a good idea," Nettle said. He sat smugly in his jacket and tie, his legs crossed and his hands in his lap.

"The Ranger thinks I shot Jim."

"We know that's nonsense," Nettle said. "But it would look better if you took the treatment."

What would look better? Nettle tucking a tape recording of my voice while I was on truth serum into his office safe? Another precautionary measure? I didn't know why he wanted it, but the simple fact that he did was enough to make me say no.

"If he thinks I shot my partner, let him. Let him investigate until he drops dead. Gaines already surrendered."

"And pleaded not guilty," Nettle said.

"How are you sleeping?" the doctor asked.

"Behind Seconal," I answered. "I get a couple of hours from a hundred milligrams. Too much adrenaline."

"I'll give you something for that," he said, his teeth yellow behind his Freud-like beard. "The Placidyl is for sleep.

The others are Azene and Inderal. They'll stop the anxiety. Think about the treatment. It might be just the ticket."

"I'd like to go now," I said. "Jim's expecting me."

When I got to the hospital, the intern who came to the room each day around three to clean Jim's leg wound was already at work. I sat watching and second-guessing myself, wondering what action I could have taken. I shouldn't have put my gun on the floor, I should have had it down in the cushions, right next to me, where I always put it before going to sleep. Or I hadn't realized quickly enough that Gaines's shotgun was empty; in that instant when I was kneeling on the floor, reaching for my pistol, I could have gone ahead and picked it up, stopped him. But Jim was already hit by then. I didn't know. I looked at the hole in his leg. I felt that I should.

The intern was saying something.

". . . it'll have to be done every day, even after he's released."

I took a pair of surgical gloves from the box and pulled them over my hands.

I swallowed everything the shrink gave me, on schedule and sometimes ahead of it. The fear came each night, a sudden surge that exploded from somewhere down around my stomach and turned my body into a thing of rock and jelly, unable to breathe until the last second, until I thought surely I would choke to death, curled on my mattress in that cell. Only then could I draw a breath, and after that first one I couldn't get enough. I would sit up, gasping, my wet-sponge lungs filling with the dark, ammonia-filled air that pressed the concrete walls around me.

Each afternoon, I poured the peroxide into the hole in Jim's leg, took gauze in my gloved hand, and swabbed out the wound. It was so deep that it swallowed most of my finger. Jim would lie staring at the ceiling, his face tightened.

I couldn't tell him, right away, that the Ranger thought I was lying, thought I was the one who'd shot him. But when I did, he laughed out loud.

"Isn't that just like a woman," he said. "Blow her lover's arm and leg half off, manage to wound herself in the process, and then keep the guy she just tried to kill alive until the ambulance finally gets there. Makes perfect sense. Did you do it?" He pressed his head back onto the stack of pillows behind him and rolled his eyes. "Come on, you can cop. I won't get mad."

I finished cleaning the wound and stripped off the gloves. It made me shake, every time I stuck my fingers into his leg, left me squirming inside, but I did it. It became a ritual, a way to pay for my negligence the night of the shooting.

"Help me slide up a little?"

I leaned over him and slipped a hand under his arm, put the other around his waist.

"On three," he said.

His body was soft where it had never been soft, the muscle tone disappearing daily.

"Twenty-nine days on my back." He winced. "God, if I could just turn over."

"Cash is sure I did it."

"Maybe we ought to get married so they can't make us testify against each other."

"Some proposal." I laughed.

"Hey," he said, "if I hadn't stayed that night, I wouldn't have got shot, would I. And if that ain't true love I don't know what is." He got serious suddenly. "You saved my life, girl. What are we going to do, just kiss everything we've been through good-bye, pretend none of it happened?"

He wasn't kidding. He was proposing marriage.

"Everything's changed now," he said. "Everything. I got a good solid look at my life when Gaines pulled the trigger."

He ran a finger over my cheek.

"Look at me," he said. "I'm all shot up, missing most of one arm, don't even know how I'll walk. Got my fifth surgery coming up next week. Here I am. I want you to marry me."

I bent over him and carefully slipped my arms around his neck. I had loved him and I had given up on him, and on the very night I had tried to leave, the first time I really thought I'd be able to make the break, we had been bound together and thrown headlong into a place where we needed each other to survive.

It was in his voice, and I felt it in the way he put his arm around my shoulders and pulled me to him. He was willing, finally able, to love me now the way I'd loved him from the very start. I had proved myself.

I kissed him and sat up, took his hand. I wondered if the drugs the shrink had prescribed were the reason I couldn't feel anything.

"If they don't lock Gaines up," I said, "it's only a matter of a few months before we're both dead anyway."

"You'll get over it," he said. "I know you don't think so now, but you will. I'll get medical retirement and we can get the hell out of here."

For some reason, the term shotgun wedding came to mind.

We were married the day they indicted Gaines on two counts of attempted capital murder. The bride wore beige silk and no shoes so that she might lie next to the groom in his hospital bed during the ceremony. The groom wore blue gym shorts with a tux collar and matching blue tie. The ceremony was performed by a local justice of the peace. After the traditional kiss, the bride was heard to say, "Is this the part where we start living happily ever after?"

I spent the wedding night at the hospital, massaging Jim's right calf, trying to get some circulation going. It felt as though there was nothing but mud beneath the skin.

"They'll give him some time," I said at one point. "Ten years, twenty, maybe fifty."

"The less, the better," Jim said, "far as I'm concerned. I want him on the street."

TWENTY

HEY BROUGHT JIM TO THE COURTHOUSE THAT MON-
day in an ambulance. Outside of the thick oak door
leading to the 252nd District Court, Nettle took a long
look at him and rubbed his hands together like a miser with
a new stack of cash.

"This is just great," he said, "just great. You look like
a sick whore in church, the jury will love it."

Jim rolled his morphine-loaded eyes over at me. He was
in an old wooden wheelchair, his stitched leg extended
straight out in front of him, his arm still bandaged thickly
from fingers to elbow, propped on pillows on the wide pine
armrest. He wore a dark green bathrobe, a get-well gift
from Rob and Denny.

"I'm not up to this," he said.

"You have to be," Nettle said. "You made the buy."

The bailiff came out and rolled the chair into the courtroom. It was beautiful, with oak wainscoting on the walls
and huge windows running along two sides of the room.
Etched-glass light fixtures hung from an incredibly high
ceiling. We walked across shining marble-chip floors toward the judge's oak bench, and then I saw Gaines.

He was sitting next to his attorney at the counsel table,
dwarfing the captain's chair that held him. We locked eyes
instantly, and it was as if there were a malevolent, almost

supercharged current flowing between us, pulling and repelling at the same moment. I pressed my arm against my side and felt my gun in its holster and thought how easy it would be to yank it out and just blow him back over the cherrywood bar and into the pews of the gallery, put an end to the fear, return his sick little midnight favor. Rob had tried his best to put the man down, but in the end, Gaines made it back into custody alive, taking the safe way, calling his attorney to arrange a surrender. But this wasn't the shooting case. This trial was on the delivery charge.

As the bailiff positioned Jim in front of the bench, I turned from Gaines and stood next to the wheelchair. In line with us were Dodd, Nettle, and a lab technician from the Department of Public Safety, there to testify that the powder submitted as evidence in the case was in fact cocaine. The bald-headed bailiff, wearing a five-point star the size of Texas on his pocket, stepped between the witnesses and the bench and raised his right hand.

"Do you solemnly swear or affirm that the testimony you are about to give will be the truth, the whole truth, and nothing but the truth, so help you God? Answer I do."

We answered in unison. I looked straight at Judge Hammit while the oath was given. He leaned across the top of his huge bench and looked at the lot of us, frown lines creasing his face.

Jim would be the first witness. The bailiff wheeled the chair around to face the gallery and ushered the rest of us from the room. Both sides had agreed to invoke "The Rule"; witnesses were allowed in the courtroom only while they were testifying.

I followed the bailiff to Judge Hammit's chambers and sat down on a red leather couch to await my turn. A few minutes later I stepped into the judge's private bathroom to swallow another Valium.

* * *

"I will remind you that you are under oath," Judge Hammit said. I took my seat in the witness stand.

I nodded and looked straight ahead. Vince, the same A.D.A. who had taken me through the grand jury, tugged at his earlobe to remind me to make eye contact with the jury. I looked to my left, tried to catch their eyes. Only one of them, a young man about my own age, refused to return my glance.

Gaines crossed his hands on the defense table and stared at me. I stared back, and he mouthed the word *liar*. I looked back at the jury.

Vince stood up, said something, and began walking toward me.

As he approached the witness box, I wondered whether he believed the case he was prosecuting. Though he had given no indication that he doubted our report, I wondered. There were judges all the way up the line—the street-cop judges deciding whether to arrest or release after questioning, the D.A.'s office judging whether to present the case, the grand jury choosing whether to indict, and finally, finally, it all wound up in a courtroom before a group of citizens who didn't have a clue.

They paid their taxes, and portions were allocated to law enforcement, to the keepers of the peace. That was what cops and courts were for, to ensure that the taxpayers were not disturbed. I didn't know exactly what Gaines had done to bend the city fathers so far out of shape, only that he had. I didn't know who all he had on film. There was no telling what kind of insurance he carried. The tape with the Trojanette on it would sure have made Daddy mad, and from what that patrolman had said, Willard Freeman was the kind of Daddy who could always get the chief of police on the phone. I didn't know. I simply didn't know.

But this was it. The end result of that quiet meeting with Nettle behind the grocery store when he'd said, "When are you going to make the big case?"

Early Sunday morning, the gospel music was blasting from Jim's hospital room. He had the bed raised to sitting position and was snapping the fingers of his left hand in time to the music.

He smiled when I walked in and then said, "Ain't no white woman in the world can sing like that. Listen to them."

"They're good."

"Goddamn right. Beautiful."

"You getting religion here or what."

"I just like the music," he said. "A person can't fake adoration."

Around noon he switched the station to listen to the news. Still no decision. A solid week of trial and two days of deliberation. No verdict. I washed his hair and shaved him and gave him a sponge bath.

"Watch out," he said, "I'm beginning to feel like a human being again."

Each hour, all afternoon, we listened to the news. Around six, they announced that the jury in the Will Gaines cocaine trial was hopelessly deadlocked.

I pushed the cart loaded with the remnants of Jim's hospital stay and an attendant pushed Jim's wheelchair. Almost two months after the shooting, they were releasing him. He wore a leg brace and rested his new cane across the arms of the wheelchair.

Stack had found a safe house for us, off a highway on the west side of town. We loaded the trunk with the potted plants that had been given to Jim during his weeks in the hospital. The D.A.'s office had sent one, there were several from local churches, a few from various judges, even a cluster of marigolds from Chuckie the Lawyer. He could spare a few bucks for flowers and still manage his Christmas cruise. Stack stood leaning on the car door while the attendant and I eased Jim into the front seat.

When we pulled into the drive, I leaned up to whisper, "It's okay. I don't expect you to carry me over the threshold."

He smiled at me, but he looked nervous at being out in the open again.

At night, that first nightfall, the roaches came out. Hundreds of them. Big ones, with wings. South American cucarachas.

I had stacked the mattresses from the three beds in the house in one corner of the living room and put Jim up there. I pushed an old, heavy dresser in front of the front door, threw a blanket down on the floor next to it, and gathered our guns around me. I sat in the corner, keeping an eye out for roaches that might approach Jim's bed and staring at the huge plate-glass window in the middle of the living-room wall. A safe house, Stack called it. There was a squad car parked in the backyard, complete with a dozing patrolman. A two-lane highway ran in front of the place. Anyone could cruise by and lob something through that window, or let go a shotgun blast.

For the first day and a half, they left us there without food. I called Stack several times at the five or six numbers he'd given me. Someone answered at each one, but no, Melton wasn't in. They sounded like they might be girlfriends, just the sort of charmers who would be attracted to a guy like Stack.

"Forget it," Jim finally said. "Where'd that Jack Daniel's go?"

We ate Placidyl and drank whiskey, but even with that I didn't sleep much. Little naps in the afternoons. At night I sat in the corner, cradling the Ithaca .12 gauge against my shoulder, watching the window and waiting. Jim lay on the mattresses.

I don't know how many days passed before Nettle prissed his way into the living room and sat gingerly in a chair. His nostrils flared with disgust as he looked around. Jim still smelled of open wounds, but I had gotten used to it.

"You might want to get cleaned up," Nettle said. "You'll be having company this afternoon."

"Who?" Jim asked. He lay atop his mattresses, staring at the crusty brown edges of the water stains on the ceiling.

"A Mr. Berthe," Nettle said. "He's been appointed chairman of a new committee, the governor's Committee Against Drugs. He'd like to meet you."

"CAD?" I asked. "What kind of action is that?" Disdain dribbled onto Nettle's lips when he looked down at me. I sat on my blanket in my corner, next to the front door, surrounded by our arsenal—the Ithaca pump action, my Colt .357 revolver and .25 automatic, a Browning 9 millimeter and Colt .45. And a couple of Buck knives, in case it came to that.

"Clean up," Nettle said. "He'll be here in a few hours."

Stack had not bothered to furnish our honeymoon suite with sheets or dishes or any of the simple amenities that make it possible to exist with any comfort. We had a package of paper cups and plates. Jim rested on bare mattresses. We didn't complain. It wasn't important. We took medicine and drank and watched each other's backs. All we wanted to do was stay alive.

I got up to shower when Nettle left. The bathroom tile was pink and cool and layered with dust. I checked to make sure the window was locked. There wasn't a towel in sight.

I reached into the stall to turn on the water. There was a sickening whoosh, then a blast, and the room went pink as I dove to the floor, scrambling; it was happening, and I heard, for an instant, the sound of a faraway waterfall, so very far away, so distant, and then everything went black.

Something was cool against my forehead, cool and hard, like glass, like tile, and then I could smell dust, I was breathing in dust. I heard water running, forcefully, splattering loudly against something. I pulled myself up, afraid to look at the narrow, frosted-glass window, terrified that Gaines's face would be there. The shower was running, hot water gushing against the back of the prefab stall. There was a crack in the plastic where the shower head had hit it.

I rested against the wall until my back and buttocks had warmed the tile against me. At some point I leaned over the toilet and tried to vomit, but nothing would come. I pulled my clothes back on and turned the water off before going back to the living room.

Jim was asleep on his mattress, zombied from Placidyl. I went to the kitchen and swallowed a Seconal. The patrol car was still parked in the backyard, the cop inside reading a paper. I wondered if he liked his job.

I don't remember the arrival. I remember sitting on the blanket on the floor, amazed to see a man who was not afraid to sit in front of the window. The chairman of the governor's Committee Against Drugs was afraid of nothing. I knew that it was only a matter of time before something deadly came through that window, but he sat there calmly, ignoring Nettle and talking with Jim about the investigation.

He was wearing a pinstripe suit with a pale blue shirt and dark tie, and wing tips. His bright silver hair was cropped so close to the scalp that it seemed almost flesh colored.

I did not say much. The Seconal had me struggling to keep up with the conversation and watch the window at the same time.

He stood up suddenly and paced back and forth before it. Finally he turned to Nettle and said, "Chief, this is ridiculous. Let me take these people to Houston, get them some good medical care, keep them safe until they're through testifying. I'll guarantee they'll be present in court whenever you need them."

Nettle cleared his throat and shook his head no. In that sickeningly smooth, calm voice he said, "I'm sorry, Mr. Berthe, and we do appreciate your offer, but it's impossible."

Berthe's eyes narrowed. He was obviously not used to hearing the word no.

"They have to be available for trial on very short notice," Nettle said. "It's not feasible to take them anywhere right now."

"That's ridiculous," Berthe said. "Just plain nonsense. I can have them here in under two hours. Day or night."

Nettle shifted in his chair and plucked at his suitcoat.

"They have to stay within the county."

Jim and I were still looking at each other when Berthe stood up abruptly and reached down to shake my hand, then Jim's.

"You people take care," he said, looking at me closely. "Here's my card in case you find yourselves in Houston."

They were barely out the door when Jim hobbled to the kitchen. Neither of us could think of a reason in the world why Nettle was demanding that we stay inside the county, unless it was that he wanted us found dead within the boundaries so he could have some control over the investigation.

While I gathered our weapons and the few clothes we had brought, Jim made a call.

"Get here now," I heard him say. "As fast as you can. We're not going to sit around here and wait for somebody to come blow us away."

Rob pulled up out front a little after ten. We waited until almost midnight and then I went to the kitchen window and checked the backyard. The patrolman was asleep, his head against the headrest, his mouth hanging open. We moved the dresser away from the front door and hauled our things out to Rob's Wagoneer. Jim crawled into the backseat; I huddled down in front. Rob waited until we were down the road to turn on the headlights.

Rick Carrio didn't ask a question when Rob delivered us to his doorstep in Houston. It was nearly three in the morning, but Rick brought us inside and said, "I guess we could use a fire," and went out to the balcony to get some wood.

He got it started while I settled Jim in the upstairs bedroom. The drive had exhausted him. When I came out, Rick was just putting the poker away.

"Make yourself at home," he said. "I've got to work in a few hours. I'll say good-night." He clumped downstairs and everything was quiet.

I propped the shotgun against the edge of the mantel and sat down cross-legged in front of the fireplace while my husband slept in the next room. I would call Mr. Berthe in the morning.

*   *   *

The first thing he did was get us an apartment. The second
thing, a few weeks later, was to get Jim back into the hospital. Mr. Berthe's security chief had dropped by to check
on us one afternoon, and the next thing I knew Jim was
installed in a private room in the maternity ward, registered
under an alias. They operated that afternoon, opening his
leg to cut out infection.

They kept him almost a week for observation. I slept on
a cot next to his bed, in a room that had huge, colorful
storks painted on one wall, their beaks holding blankets full
of newborns.

The apartment Mr. Berthe had provided for us was a split-
level two-bedroom place, complete with alarm system, tear
gas, and an AR-15 with a laser sight. We were instructed
to knock the phone off the hook if there was trouble. The
troops would be there in less than three minutes. But we
knew the inside of three minutes like nobody's business.

We were briefed weekly on the activities in Beaumont.
Mr. Berthe had his sources and, though he didn't go into
detail, said that if and when we did have to return, we
would do so under guard. We were to consider everyone,
even the people in the D.A.'s office, as potential assailants.

He took care of everything. Our belongings had been
gathered from the mobile home, the two apartments, and
the jail, and placed in storage. Our cars were parked in a
garage somewhere downtown. We were to try to stay in the
apartment unless it was absolutely necessary to go out.
That meant if we started going stir crazy. Jim slept a great
deal.

*   *   *

I don't know how Nettle got the number. I answered the phone one night, expecting it to be a security check, and his sick-sweet voice said, "When are you coming back?"

I wanted to throw the phone into the fireplace. I wanted to smash something. His sugar-coated venom drooled out of the receiver and I sat there, no words, unable to communicate my rage. I remembered how I'd felt the time speed-freak Lester said, "My philosophy of life is slit thy neighbor's throat and pimp his kids." I'd wanted to gut-shoot him, just rid the community of a maggot.

"You can't be serious," I said. "You know damn well I won't be back."

"Well, that presents a little problem." He cleared his throat. "Not for Jim, his retirement paperwork will be through any day now." He cleared it again, with that obnoxious dry little cough of his. "But your circumstance is different," he said.

"How is that?"

"You are to return to Beaumont immediately or you're off the payroll. If you're not coming back, I'll need a letter of resignation. A couple of lines will do fine."

"Chief," I said, "I'll write you a fucking book."

I don't remember waking up. The first thing I knew I was standing at the top of the stairs aiming at darkness, watching Jim bounce down the staircase in his underwear, step by step, waving a gun in his left hand, his right arm in a sling.

"Come on, motherfuckers!" he screamed. "Come on!"

I tumbled down after him, feeling the noises working down in my chest, trying to hold them in, terrified, certain that it was happening again, and wishing, after staying ready for such a long time, that it would.

The apartment was empty. Something, maybe the rumble of traffic from the expressway, had caused the alarms to go off. The tiny plastic boxes aimed at the front door and the patio sliding-glass entrance shrieked obscenely in the empty room. I stumbled past Jim and yanked the plugs from the wall.

When I turned around, he was sitting on the stairway, his head in his hand, rocking slowly back and forth.

"God damn them," he said. "God damn them."

We held each other until we could think again and then for some reason I went to the patio and brought logs to the fireplace. We lay there in front of the fire for the rest of that night and well into morning, wrapped around each other, trying to rest.

After that night, the fireplace became my talisman. I made myself believe that as long as I was in the circle of its warmth, I was safe. Day after night I sat watching the flames, concentrating only on shades of orange and yellow and blue, on the shapes that flamed so briefly, changed so quickly, that I wasn't sure they had even been there. I think I was trying to let it hypnotize me.

What sleep I got came when I was there, wrapped in the blanket, hidden behind a row of brown corduroy cushions that I took each evening from the couch and stacked in front of me.

All that winter, I sat before the fire. I saw the way Jim looked at me. I didn't say much. I put food in front of us and listened to him tell me I had to eat. I spent my afternoons massaging his leg, trying to get some feeling back into it and hoping to prevent the cramps that seized him in the middle of the night. I sat in front of the fireplace, cooking my back until I couldn't bear the heat, then turning to face it.

I ate my pills and took care of Jim when I could manage it and I waited for shotguns.

It was that way until April, and still there was no word on any trial. No constables came to the door waving subpoenas. Then Jim was able to walk without the brace, with a decided limp, but still able to walk, and he was starting to use his damaged arm again.

We thanked Mr. Berthe and traded our cars in on a used Blazer.

TWENTY-ONE

OPENED THE FREEZER TO ADD JIM'S LATEST HAUL. The chill air cooled my ankles, swirling like heavy white smoke in the afternoon heat. Catfish fillets were stacked three deep and six high on all four shelves.

He walked up and hung his chin over my shoulder.

"We could give some away," he said.

"I don't care what you do with it," I said. "I'm burnt out. No more catfish for me."

Jim's retirement held us over, paid the rent on a wood-frame house a few miles from Canyon Reservoir, not quite halfway between Austin and San Antonio. We went fishing and trimmed the yard. We had candlelit dinners on the screened-in back porch. He stopped getting mad at himself when he had to ask me to help him with something he could no longer manage alone. But he fought it, he tested his body every time he got the chance. He painted the garage. He built bookcases in the small second bedroom. We went fishing often, trying to pass time while we waited for the subpoena. Gaines had walked on the cocaine case, but the D.A. said he would pursue the attempted murder charges. He would reach us through Mr. Berthe.

"That's it," Jim said, "lob it out easy, land it there in the deeper water, where the big ones are hiding."

We'd left Beaumont late in the morning, right after the closing arguments. Mr. Berthe's men had delivered us safely to Houston Hobby and we managed to catch a one thirty flight to Austin. We kept the radio on while we drove to San Marcos, on the chance that there might be news of a verdict.

When we got home, we were too tired to do anything but sit down in the front porch swing. I was wondering what would happen to Gaines when Jim said, "Let's go fishing."

"Again?" I asked.

We sat on the grassy bank of Canyon Reservoir, wearing cutoffs and T-shirts, holding cane poles and waiting for a nibble. I was almost lulled into sleep by the red-and-white plastic bobbers floating on the murky green surface of the lake. It was one of those hazy May days when the air seems to match exactly the temperature of your body. I felt as if I could close my eyes and evaporate into the afternoon. Across the lake, on the side that fronted the FM306, a lone skier was hot-dogging behind a long, low-slung speedboat.

"He won't walk on this one," Jim said.

I pulled my pole up and let the bobber slap the water.

"Topwater floater," Jim said. "Attempted murder. He's not gonna slide."

"Righteous case," I said. "He might."

"No way." He pulled his own pole up and flipped the line farther out in the water.

"Even if he goes down, he'll get out eventually."

Jim was quiet for a long time. Then he turned and looked at me and said, "The bastard better hope they find him guilty and send him somewhere for a long, long time."

When we got home from the lake, Rob was sitting in the rocker on our front porch, smoking reefer in his corncob pipe. He would take a lungful of smoke and hold it while he took another mouthful and blew smoke rings toward the wooden porch canopy.

"Where you been?" he called, walking toward us.

"Fishing," Jim said.

I pulled the ice chest from the back of the Blazer and Rob took it from me.

"Sure is an ugly ride," he said. "What color is that, puce?"

"It motors," Jim said. "It motors." We walked across the lawn to the front porch and sat down on the swing.

Rob struck a match on the sole of his boot and leaned against the wall, puffing quietly.

"They gave him forty years," he said finally, keeping his teeth clenched against the pipe. "Came back with a verdict in fifty-five minutes."

"Almost enough," I said.

"Happens real quick when you say it," Rob smiled. "Serving it's another matter entirely."

"I hope they have that bastard on his knees in the cotton field first thing tomorrow morning," Jim said.

"So." Rob shifted away from the wall and moved to lean on the railing. "You catch anything?"

"Three," Jim said. "Kris got the big one."

"She only thinks so," Rob said.

"If you'd like to stay," I said, "I can show you what a lousy cook I am."

"Be kind to yourself, baby," Rob said. "It's hard to ruin catfish. Maybe I'll drive into town and get some wine. I don't have to be back in Houston until late tomorrow afternoon. What goes with catfish? A sweet wine, some Piesporter maybe?"

"A man ought to spring for champagne on special occasions," Jim said. "Get some of that stuff they use at presidential inaugurations."

Rob drove off in his state Plymouth and Jim went around to the back porch to clean the fish. I sat with him while he sharpened his knife.

"I think you got a four-pounder there," he said, staring at the lone fish I'd pulled in. "Not bad."

"I think I'm still not real keen on fishing."

"Give it up," he said. "You've been threatening to quit since the first day I took you."

"I'm not much for baiting hooks."

"Hell, baby, it's the worm that gets the fish. Besides, didn't you hear Rob? He says you only think you got the big one. Better stay with it."

"He's stoned, for a change. You really think it's four pounds?"

"Easy."

I looked at the catfish, on ice now with the two smaller ones Jim had caught. Its smooth blue-gray skin was slick and shiny. Somewhere off in the woods a dirt bike buzzed harshly in the dusk. Other than that, the only sound was the rhythmic rasping of Jim's knife blade against the whetstone and the locusts whirring in the trees.

I picked up my fish and held it with both hands at arms length.

"Could be," I said. "Might be four pounds."

"Yeah," Jim said, holding his knife silently for a moment.

I laid the fish back in the ice chest and sat back down.

"Forty years," I said. "They give a little freak like Douglas life for selling a few grams of speed and Gaines gets forty years for trying to kill cops. Go figure it."

"The jury system, babe. Throw them bones."

I brought a pan out and Jim laid the fillets in and wiped his knife.

"Forty," he said. "He might do seven on that. I can wait."

It was about a month later, I think, when Rob dropped by again, this time with his new partner. Jim's catfish stash was on the verge of overflowing the freezer.

Rob didn't introduce anyone; he pulled a computer printout from his pocket and shoved it at me as soon as I answered the door.

"It's for real," he said. "The snitch on this deal ain't never done me wrong. Says the dude's got some kind of exploding bullets that even the goddamn FBI can't get ballistics on."

"What the fuck are you talking about?" Jim asked.

"Take a look," Rob said. "Came in this morning."

Jim looked on as I read.

AZAV 0111 16.17
08.17 06/27/80

652 TXDPS HOUSTON 06/27/80
ALL STATIONS TEXAS

WANTED FOR BOND JUMPING, CONSIDER ARMED AND EXTREMELY DANGEROUS.

WANTED FOR BOND JUMPING CAPIAS 407296 AND 407297
TAYLOR COUNTY SHERIFF OFFICE, ABILENE, TEXAS

RICHARD BOYD FOXWELL AKA DICK W/M DOB/12/04/40 6/2" 200# LT BRO HAIR BR EYES.

LAST SEEN DRIVING BLACK VINYL TOP/BLACK CAD-
ILLAC EL DORADO TXLIC/TLC556. SUBJECT HAS PRE-
VIOUSLY BEEN CONVICTED OF MURDER AND HAS
BEEN QUESTIONED BY A FEDERAL GRAND JURY RE-
GARDING THE MURDER OF A FEDERAL JUDGE IN SAN
ANTONIO. SUBJECT IS REPORTEDLY ARMED WITH A
44 MAG REVOLVER AND SHOULD BE CONSIDERED EX-
TREMELY DANGEROUS.

AUTH AGENT BOB KEAGON UNIT 830

TXDPS HOUSTON KBH 10-0817CDT

"I got a snitch who says the dude's holding a paper on
Kristen," Rob said.

"I know him," Jim said. "Dick Foxwell, yeah, I met him
years ago when I was working cases in the old Rancho
Milagro Hotel down off 45 in Houston. Old-time character.
Hell of a gambler."

"Man, you got that," Rob said. "And I'll bet you a nickel
he did that judge."

Rob's partner was staring at me like I was already dead.
I introduced myself and reached to shake hands.

"Bill Watson," he said.

In the living room, Bill sat on what remained of the sectional we'd had in Beaumont, the part that had no armrest
on the left end. He looked about thirty, tall and slender with
curly red hair just going gray at the temples. His beard was
coming in almost solid gray.

"I'm telling you," Rob said, "snitch says the dude's been
hired to kill the chick cop."

"Who's behind it?" I asked.

"Who the fuck knows," Rob answered.

"I'd wager a guess," Jim said.

I went to the kitchen and mixed a batch of margaritas, toying with the blender while I pictured Dick cruising north from Houston in his big black Caddy, his .44 under the front seat and my description in his shirt pocket. He would have the center console pulled down between the front seats in the El Dorado to accommodate his gangster lean. He might smoke a tiny cigar. He would drive the speed limit and avoid drinking while he was on the road, though it was perfectly legal. Who the fuck knew.

Finding me would not be easy. The house, the phone, the car, everything was under an alias, courtesy of Mr. Berthe.

Rob came into the kitchen while I was pouring the drinks.

"You all right?" he asked.

"Never better."

"Listen, my rookie out there, he's really green. I mean I think the dude's cool and all, but, you know. Haven't taken him on a deal yet."

"Not sure he'll come up for it?"

"I got some jam-up blow here. Be good to find out where his head's at."

"So we should do some."

"It's cool?"

"Everything's cool," I said. "Nothing is not cool."

"Hey. We'll find him. He won't even get close."

"I'm not worried." I wasn't. At least now there was a name.

He dug into his pocket. "You want a bump?"

"It's been awhile," I said. "I'll trade you a margarita."

By five the next morning Bill Watson, assigned to narcotics for six whole days, was lying in the backyard puking happily, too wired to know he was drunk.

I sat next to him, shivering in the cool predawn air.

When he'd stopped retching, I turned the spigot next to the back porch and brought the garden hose to him.

"Drink," I said.

He raised himself on all fours and took the hose, gulping convulsively.

"Damn," he said. "This beats pulling bodies out of car wrecks."

The sky was starting to streak pink against the gray of morning, revealing tiny drops of moisture on the flat blades of St. Augustine grass that covered the back lawn.

"Rob's been around," I said. "He can show you what's happening."

"I can't believe some of the shit he tells me."

"Believe it."

"You're out for good?"

"Forever and ever."

"Rob said you two pissed a few people off."

"They needed it."

"Well, me and Rob will be looking for him."

"I appreciate it."

"Yeah, Rob will have the whole office out after the guy. You know he's senior agent-in-charge now. He'll have the whole section out. Most of them's new."

"The beat goes on," I said.

"What do you mean?"

"Nothing that wouldn't sound pretty damn stupid, pretty naïve."

"Y'all took some nasty dealers off the street."

"Hey," I said, "we didn't do shit. We kept the numbers rolling through the D.A.'s office. We helped a genuine bastard secure his future as chief of police. That's all we did."

"You put dealers in prison. You got to do what you can."

"No question about it. So you get out there and bust dope

dealers. Take down some genuine fuckups. Just try to take care of yourself. Try not to get hurt."

"I can't afford to," he said. "I've got family."

"Well, darling," I said, "if that's the case, you are in the wrong line of work."

He stood up and tucked his shirttails into his jeans before he said we should go back inside.

"Hey, Bill," I said as we walked across the lawn, "do you like catfish?"

We slept in shifts. Jim at night, I during the day. I sat on the sectional, backed into the corner of the room, holding my pistol, and listening for the click of a door latch, staring into the shadows of our home, waiting for someone, maybe Foxwell, maybe just some pissed-off speed freak, to come after us. For the rest of summer, and on into the fall, I sat up nights, waiting.

Jim hung up the phone, walked to the refrigerator, and took out a beer.

"Dodd's in town," he said. "Wants to come visit."

I asked him what for.

"Said he's on vacation, just wants to say hello."

"He could do that on the phone," I said.

"I told him to come by."

I stood in the shower trying to make sense of things. I couldn't know why Dodd had suddenly decided he wanted to see us. I couldn't understand it.

When I stepped from the stall, I heard his baritone drawl floating through the house. I eased into the hallway.

"So how's she doing," he said. "Hell, I can see you're fucked up."

"I got scars. I hurt sometimes. But Kristen, she's plenty

messed up herself. She wanted to get dogs, Dobermans. Hell, we don't need them. She hears things that nobody else can."

"Like what?"

"Like last week Rob and a friend are over and she's just sitting there in that chair saying nothing and all of a sudden she whispers, 'There's someone at the door,' and a few minutes later there *was* someone at the door. A couple of Mormons. Hell, there was music on and Rob was going on about some bust or other and you couldn't hear anything outside the room. But she did."

"Nothing wrong with paying attention," Dodd said. "She's got a pretty good reason."

"I'm not getting down on her," Jim said. "Jesus, she's hainty and it's a blessing. I'm thankful. I'm just saying it's a little strange."

"I don't think so," Dodd answered. "It sounds perfectly normal to me."

I tiptoed back to the bedroom to dress. What was he doing? Why was he in our home? I made some noise in the hallway as I walked back out.

He hadn't changed much. Put on a few more pounds in his belly. His hair was longer, but still curly and pale blond, the color women pay money for. He was standing in front of the fireplace, one boot resting on the hearth.

I said hello and curled up in the corner of the couch.

"How you doing, girl?" he asked.

I wanted to know why he was there.

"I'm doing," I said.

"Looking good."

"Considering what."

"No, really," he said. "Retirement's agreeing with you."

"I don't mean to be rude," I said, "but it's my time to sleep. Don't be offended if I nap off on you."

I stretched out on the couch and slid my pistol down in the cushions. There was something hard inside one of them. I turned it over and reached inside, probing into a two-inch rip that had been there since the night of the shooting. Whatever was in there was tube-shaped, like a half-inch piece of a nickel roll. I unzipped the cushion and scooped out a couple of handfuls of shredded foam.

Jim and Dodd stopped talking and watched. I pulled a chunk of white plastic from inside the cushion and handed it to Jim.

"I'll be damned," he said.

"What is it?" Dodd asked.

"Shotgun wadding. Must have been there since the shooting."

It explained my wound. A simple piece of plastic, stuffed into the base of a shotgun shell to propel the pellets out. That was what had hit my arm, ripped into the flesh and left such an odd, rectangular scar.

"That Ranger," I said, "Cash, drove around with these cushions in his trunk for the better part of two months."

"Well that makes him a dumb-ass, then, don't it," Dodd said eagerly. "Proves you told the truth about the shooting. I'll be happy to run it back to the D.A. for you."

"That's okay," I said. "We'll hang on to it." I didn't see where it proved anything. It matched the scar on my arm, was one more piece of corroboration for my story, but Cash wasn't looking for that kind of evidence, and I had the feeling that if I gave it to Dodd it would quietly disappear. I straightened the cushion and lay back down, closed my eyes.

"Hey," Dodd said, "Gaines is doing the time."

"You know there's supposed to be a paper out on Kristen?" Jim asked.

"I heard," Dodd said.

One of them struck a match.

"Hell," Dodd said suddenly, "both of you look damn good. Healthy. I'm glad to see it."

Their droning voices filled my head.

"What's Nettle up to these days?"

"Oh, hell, Jim, you know, he's same old shit, finally got his appointment. He's there being the chief of police. Drinking with the city manager and the city attorney, having a good old time. Still talking about the bust-out."

"That'll be grist for the mill for years."

"Yep, yep it will. Myself, I may quit policing one of these days and go into the private sector. Got an offer to do some oil field security. Pays good, decent hours, low risk. I might do it. Damn, I'm glad to see you folks doing well."

"Take it easy, boss," Jim said. "If you want to stay for lunch I'll cook up some catfish."

An oil field offer. Dodd would do well there. Well-intentioned Dodd. Good old boy. Always seeming to try so hard to get the punchline, but usually left scratching his head while everyone else laughed at the joke. He wasn't even sure what it was he wanted to be part of, but he knew he wanted in. He worshiped Jim, and Jim got off on it. One afternoon soon after the bust-out, Jim had told Dodd that old-time street characters always wore lots of diamonds, and the next day Dodd showed up at the office with rings on his fingers and a big dent in his Sears card.

From somewhere in my half-conscious brain, I wondered if Dodd had been sent to kill me, but I was doubting myself before I even finished the thought. Dodd didn't know about the stash. He knew the rules had been bent, he knew Jim should have been pulled up, he knew we'd lied in court. But I never got the feeling that he understood why. Or questioned it. He was faithful to Jim, and tried to hide his discomfort at being that way. Not Dodd. He protected himself by refusing to look closely.

But Gaines was in Huntsville and Gaines wanted out of Huntsville. He would do what it took. He would find a weak link and pull until the chain snapped. Dodd might be a weak link, he was certainly where I would start, but it didn't make sense. I couldn't measure the extent of my disturbance, but I felt I was approaching a danger zone. At the edge, ready to lose it. Paranoia. It had to be. Dodd didn't have it in him to kill anyone. I couldn't think. No. Wait. Listen. Everyone has it in him to kill. Paranoia. But Gaines needed me alive. I had been at the meeting. I knew. He needed me alive. Wait. Pay attention. It is only a question of circumstance.

I gripped my pistol and lay there with my eyes closed, waiting, wondering just how twisted I'd become. I heard Dodd's heavy bootsteps follow Jim out of the living room and into the kitchen. I heard voices, not words. A few minutes later there was the sudden crackling hiss of fish being laid into hot grease. I gripped my pistol and slept.

Pain had a lot to do with it. I told myself that, making excuses. Jim lived with pain, in his shoulder and his leg, it slept with him, he woke up with it, it was always there. He would go weeks with it and then cave in, swallowing legitimate pills. For the pain, he said. To get rid of the hurt that was like acid burning inside his leg, eating away what was left of the muscle.

I sat in my corner and hoped that he would get through just one night without getting ripped from his sleep. He slept from around midnight until just after daybreak, I from after breakfast until mid-afternoon. This was our pattern. Evenings we spent at Canyon Reservoir. I wondered what Dodd was doing.

When winter came and the weather broke we stayed inside, staring at the television or reading.

I didn't recognize it at first, I was off guard. It may have been happening for months before I knew, before I was sure.

Rob was working a big case in Austin, and Jim began running with him, leaving me to wander our home well into the morning, checking windows and doors, listening. I knew every creak the old frame house made, the rush of gas flame igniting under the hot water heater, the tin crack of the stove cooling after I'd boiled water for tea, the pickup that blattered down the road each night at ten thirty. The deep-chested dog some acres away that howled for six minutes at moonrise.

I'd been expecting what I found. It wasn't that I looked for anything. It would present itself; I was only biding time. I didn't want to know.

The phone rings, you answer, the calling party listens for a moment and hangs up. You dismiss it. It happens again a day or two later. And yet again.

Rob drops by at nine. Offers a joint. I decline and Jim leaves with him. He comes back around four in the morning, wide awake, hyper.

"Get some rest," he says. "I'll watch. I'm not sleepy."

I lie on the couch and listen to him fidget, cleaning a gun, sharpening his knife, polishing his shoes. This happens more and more frequently. The phone calls follow the nights out. Patterns take shape.

"I am your wife," I said one morning. "You are my husband. Make your choice."

He went out that night with Rob. The phone rang, the caller hung up.

I poured a scotch. I sat down on the couch and lit one of his cigarettes. I listened.

Just after the first rays of sun came through the slats of the blinds, filling the kitchen with spring morning light, Jim stood up from the table and threw a bowl of Cheerios against the wall.

"You're out of your mind!" he yelled.

The bowl shattered, pieces flying to the floor. The milk dribbled unevenly over the bluebonnet wallpaper.

"Out of your fucking mind," he said. He sat down and flopped his hands onto the table. I poured a cup of coffee.

"Would you like some?"

"No. I mean yes. What in holy hell is going on?"

I gave him a cup and sat down across from him.

"I hope milk doesn't stain," I said. I took a sip from my mug.

"You can't just leave," he said. "You can't just do that. Just leave."

"What do you want me to say, Jim? I forgive you the girlfriends? I forgive you the dope? Again? I forgive everything? Just please let me love, honor, and obey? What do you think I am, a goddamn fountain overflowing with love and kindness? I'm on empty."

"Where you going?"

"I have no idea."

"What are you going to do?"

"It doesn't matter," I said. "Something. All of a sudden you're worried."

"There's a paper out on you."

"And I could die crossing the street. What do I do, go introduce myself to the guy and get it over with?"

"I'm plenty worried. Plenty."

"Save it." I got up and opened a cabinet, tossed a brown paper bag onto the table. "You worried about this?"

I picked the thing up and ripped it open. Rigs scattered everywhere, a pie-tin-size chunk of crystal meth clattered onto the tabletop. It was fresh from a lab, a perfect circle, white and waxy, like paraffin.

"I'm worried about this," I said. "You get it from Rob? Blessings and best wishes to both of you."

I sat toward the back of the bus and watched San Antonio roll by in the dark. I should have been hurting, should have been wondering if I'd made the right decision. But all I could feel was blissful solitude, a sense that, after years, *years*, I was going somewhere, it didn't matter where, it mattered that I was no longer running in place.

I was alone, away from Jim, away from all of it, and the bus was almost empty, rolling down night highways, taking me somewhere.

TWENTY-TWO

GOT OFF WHEN WE HIT CORPUS CHRISTI. I BOUGHT a Dr Pepper and sat down on my suitcase in a thin strip of shade next to the front door of the depot. I got everything but my feet out of the sun, and sat there dripping from the humidity and feeling the late April heat on my toes.

I wondered where Dick Foxwell was, what he was doing. I imagined him sitting in a back room somewhere, having lunch with Nettle. Maybe the city manager would be there, maybe the city attorney. Maybe Willard Freeman would attend, his face drawn into a confident smile as he thought about his daughter and listened to quiet talk about how Nettle had finally managed to put Gaines away. He would consider his financial investment to have been worthwhile, after all. Gaines was paying for it, paying dearly for having put Willard's Trojanette daughter in porn films. They would be there, all of them, discussing structure and planning, speaking obliquely of pornography and damage control, of how to tie up loose ends. I was a loose end. Justice, Texas-style. Just-Us. The tight little circles. The good old boys. It hadn't started with JFK or LBJ. It was a tradition, and it had been going on since long before Lone Wolf Gonzaulles strapped on a gun and went to take care of the governor's business. One riot, one Ranger.

I told myself I was being paranoid, that the part of my

brain dedicated to reason had been eaten away by white powder. The sun was burning my feet. I would have sandal-strap tan marks. Foxwell would be told to look for them, to remove my shoes after he was sure I was dead and look for the tan marks. Paranoia. He would check for the scar on my left biceps. He would rifle my pockets, my purse, maybe deliver my driver's license as proof that the job was done. I began to believe that I might have twisted off some-where along the line, that I might still be in the jail cell in Beaumont, only imagining that I had escaped. I took off my sandals and pressed my bare soles against the heat of the concrete beneath me. I could feel it, so hot it almost burned. I licked sweat from above my lip, tasting salt. I could feel and I could taste. I wasn't imagining.

I looked carefully as the second hand on my watch ticked over the tiny slashes that marked the passing of seconds. It moved in short jerks, one line at a time, exactly, precisely, one-second echoes. I watched, it took forever, it took no time at all. Three minutes gone, one hundred and eighty seconds down the tubes. It satisfied me somehow, it felt like a sort of victory, to see time passing and know I was still there.

I could do this. I knew how to hide.

The sun was burning my feet. I pulled on my sandals and took Mr. Berthe's card from my purse and walked to the pay phone.

A pickup wheeled to the curb, catching a piece of gravel with the edge of one front tire. There was a loud hollow pop and a tiny stone shot out and pinged against the wall a few feet from my suitcase.

The man driving had one large arm dangling out the win-dow. Mr. Berthe had said a green Ford pickup. I stood up.

"Kristen?"

I nodded and walked over, tossing my bag in the back as I climbed in. He turned toward me, leaning against his door, studying me. "You're all right?"

"Yes," I said. "I'm fine. I mean, I'm okay."

"Roland told me to get here immediately."

"You work for him?"

"A little security now and then. Nothing terribly exciting." He put the truck in gear and pulled away from the curb.

"I appreciate this," I said. "I just need a few days to sort some things out."

"Stay as long as you want. And don't worry about Foxwell. He won't come around."

"I'm not so sure."

"Like I said, I work for Roland Berthe. Call me Marshall."

"Okay," I said. I did not ask questions.

He was big-boned and muscular, with a thin waist that left his Levi's hanging low on his hips. His jeans were bagged out in the seat and had a large oval spot on the right calf where the material was worn thin, almost white, as though he'd spilled bleach on it. He had silver-gray hair that he wore pulled back in a short ponytail that reached in a curl to the broad space between his shoulder blades.

We drove past rows of white stucco houses with palm-treed yards. The air smelled of ocean and soon we turned down a road that ran along the beach.

He cut the rattling engine as he made the turn onto a gravel driveway and we coasted to a stop in front of a squat wood-frame house that had splotches of light blue clinging to its walls.

"Been meaning to paint the place," he said, slamming his door when he got out.

There were dozens of small Mexican rugs scattered over

the wood floors of the house, and bookcases stuffed to over-flowing lined two walls of the living room.

"We'll put you right back here," he said, and he carried my suitcase to a small room across from the kitchen, at the opposite end of the hallway that led to the front bedroom. There was a twin bed against the wall beneath a large window, covered with a multicolored Mexican blanket. There was no closet, but a row of clothes hooks were fastened to a board on the wall. The opposite wall was almost obliter-ated with drawings done in colored pencil, some on plain gray cardboard. Most of them were frameless, held in place with thumbtacks pressed through their corners.

"During the season," he said, "I draw people. I go across to the beach there and set up my easel and people come around to get their portraits done. I use colored pencils, mostly, though occasionally somebody will insist on char-coal. I've gotten quite fast at it, it's almost rote now. I prefer to use color though."

He put my suitcase on the bed and turned to see me star-ing at the wall.

"Some people are disappointed with the way I see them," he said. "They refuse to pay for their portrait. But it doesn't happen often. That's twenty years' worth hanging on the wall. My monument to rejection." He stared at the draw-ings for a moment and then clapped his big hands together. "What the hell," he said. "Let's get some chow."

I woke late the next morning, in a sweat, and the house smelled of saltwater and coffee. When I opened the window the breeze was hot. I could hear Marshall humming in the kitchen, something that sounded like opera.

He was at the stove, stirring eggs while he sprinkled jack cheese over them.

"Wait'll you taste this," he said. *"Migas.* It's got eggs

and tomatoes, onion, a little cheese here, a few pieces of tortilla, jalapeños . . . Can't beat it."

I found a pitcher of iced tea in the refrigerator and drank a glassful quickly, pouring a refill before I sat down.

The table was set with mix-and-match dishes and paper towels in place of napkins. Marshall brought the pan to the table and spooned huge portions of eggs onto the plates.

"Go ahead," he said, "eat. I'll be right there." He stuck the pan in the sink and ran water into it, staring over his shoulder at me. "Well?"

"Delicious," I said. "You call it *migas*?"

"Got the recipe from a Mexican gentleman who had me draw him. Talked me into a barter, and I think I came out the winner on it. You're soaked."

He flipped a light switch as he sat down, studying me. The overhead fan buzzed loudly and then got quiet as the blades began turning.

"What did you do, keep that blanket on the bed all night?"

I pushed the wet hair off my forehead, embarrassed.

"I have a thing about windows," I said. "Since the shooting. I'd rather sweat."

"Nobody's going to come around here and try to shoot you," he said quietly. "Believe me."

He had no idea how much I wanted to believe him, or maybe he did. I just wanted to be able to trust someone. I wanted someone to promise me that I didn't have to be terrified anymore, that I was safe, that I could fall asleep without wondering whether I would be awakened by a goddamn double-barreled alarm clock.

His eyes softened and he looked, for a moment, like he would pull me close and do just that, comfort me, assure me. It would have been wonderful, that morning, just to fall on his shoulder and cry.

I wished that I could. I blamed it on the pills, the Azene and Inderal. That had to be the reason why my feelings were trapped. It was as though they were playing hide-and-seek, darting around inside me, hiding, afraid to be found. I picked up my fork.

"You'll have to show me how to cook this," I said.

He leaned on the table and started eating seriously, his eyes rounding larger before each bite, a look of infant bliss spreading over his face as he chewed. Halfway through the meal, the table began to jiggle. When I peeked beneath it, I saw that Marshall had one foot twisted behind the leg of his chair, and his heel was bobbing rapidly up and down, like a piston in action. The white spot on the calf of his jeans was against the metal chair leg, rubbing.

He saw me looking and raised an eyebrow.

"What is it?"

"I can't get a bead on these eggs," I said. "They're moving around."

"Oh," he said, straightening. "Nervous habit." He took another bite and we ate in silence for awhile. I assumed he was nervous about Foxwell.

My tongue was still burning from jalapeños while I washed the breakfast dishes. Marshall stood next to me, humming, carefully drying each dish I gave him.

"You know," he said at one point, "I run every morning on the beach. It might do you a world of good."

It scared me to be without a weapon. I would jog for as long as I could, trying not to think about the fact that my gun was wrapped in a towel under Marshall's umbrella and I was getting farther and farther away from it. Too, there was the pain of it. I had forgotten how to push past that point where I knew I would stop hurting and start to enjoy the run. Each day, I dropped out and walked back to the

umbrella long before Marshall made his U-turn at the surf-
board rental shack a few miles down the beach. I dreaded
it, railed at myself, called myself a topwater floater each
time I had to stop and watch his massive back drawing
away from me while I stood bent over on the sand, gasping.

By the time he returned and took a quick swim, I would
be almost dry, sitting on a towel next to his easel.

"Keep after it," he would say. "You're doing better.
Starting to look almost healthy."

Almost three weeks passed before he strolled into my
room one morning and took the pill bottles from the nightstand. I was bent over, tying my tennis shoes, and found
myself tripping after him as he walked to the bathroom and
began dumping the pills into the toilet.

I stood in the doorway, not believing that he was flushing
my medicine. He tossed the containers into the wastebasket
and leaned against the sink.

"Give yourself a chance," he said.

He shuffled me out of the doorway and retrieved his easel
from the living room, stopping at the front door to call,
"Let's hit the beach. And no dropping out today."

Give myself a chance. I tied my shoes and grabbed my
bag and walked after him, tasting panic on the back of my
tongue, scared at the prospect of functioning without drugs.

In the afternoons, I would lie under the umbrella, watching
as Marshall whistled and sketched tourists. Some of them
looked at us oddly, wondering, I suppose, what the relationship was.

I would sit watching him while his eyes went back and
forth quickly between his subject and the sheet on his easel,
his hands so large that the pencils looked miniature in
them. But no matter how much he seemed to concentrate
on his drawing, I had the feeling that he was intensely

aware of everything around us, and would know in an instant if something wasn't right, if there was some kind of danger approaching.

I was still uneasy when I took off at his side each morning, heading down the beach toward the surf shack, but I'd stayed with him the morning he'd dumped the pills, gutted it out until I thought my lungs would explode, and then suddenly I was breathing easy, able to do the full four miles.

I began to feel safe in his custody.

I was trying to fall asleep when he came loping across the beach, a paper bag in one hand, a newspaper in the other. I got close, actually managed to doze, on some of those afternoons. The shushing of the Gulf's small waves and the noises of children shouting across the sand made it almost easy for me to close my eyes.

He sat down in his canvas chair and dropped the paper next to my towel, pointing to a small article near the bottom of the page. Dick Foxwell was in custody in Austin. They had him for bond jumping and he'd been caught with a Walther PPK under the front seat of his Caddy. He was being held without bail, and it looked like he would be indicted for murdering a federal judge.

I sat up and dug my feet into the glorious warmth of the sand. There were teenage couples scattered about, eating popcorn and rubbing each other with oil. The water was full of would-be surfers, paddling desperately for position when something more than a meager wave rolled across the water. Gulls walked awkwardly across the beach, pecking at bits of shell until they realized it wasn't food and took to the air.

"I told you not to worry," Marshall said. "Roland doesn't put up with much nonsense."

*   *   *

Sometime during the months I spent with Marshall, I
began to realize that I was still alive. My body was stronger,
that was part of it, but more than that it was a certain sense
of unease, a feeling that I was a total stranger to the thing
beating inside my chest. I felt like I was on hold, and wasn't
sure how long I could endure the discomfort. But I was
scared to death of the alternatives. It was easier, under
Marshall's care, to believe that one day I might feel whole
again. There was no risk involved. For the longest time, he
demanded nothing from me except that I run with him each
morning, and serve as an audience while he drew portraits.

I'd made spaghetti, Marshall's recipe, with loads of pepper.
The dishes sat scattered across the table. I'd told him, over
dinner, that I was thinking about going back to school.

"I'm all for it," he said. "But it costs money."

"I managed before," I said. "Student loans and waitress
tips."

"What about your family?"

"I don't see them often. Hardly ever." I began clearing
the table.

"Leave that for now," he said. "I think we should talk."

"I don't want them hurt, that's all. I get concerned that
somebody might decide to get even while I'm visiting." I
tested the dishwater with my fingertips, found it too hot
and ran more cold into the suds.

His chair scraped against the floor and then I felt his
hands on my back. He turned me to face him and covered
my wet hands with his.

"You can't live the rest of your life thinking this way,"
he said. "Foxwell's locked up. No one is after you."

I was almost ready to believe it.

"I could leave any time now," I said. "You've done a
lot, and I'm grateful."

"I'm not asking you to leave," he said. "Roland told me to take care of you; that's what I'm trying to do. Truth is I'd do it now anyway, whether he wanted me to or not."

"I'm checking out schools."

"That's great, but you shouldn't be so isolated. You're twenty-four, for God's sake. You should be going on dates, enjoying yourself."

"Marshall," I said, "I am still married."

"I haven't seen any husbands around here lately," he said. "You think you owe him the rest of your life or something? Go out. Have some fun. If you won't go alone, I'll take you out. You know how to two-step?"

I slipped my hands from his and turned to the sink. I couldn't explain why I felt no attraction. Not for him, not for anybody. And I could no longer blame it on the prescriptions. It had been almost two months since Marshall had poured them into the toilet. Maybe Jim was part of it. But I think it came down to Gaines. I felt as though he had robbed me of my emotions, my ability to feel, as surely as if he'd murdered me that night.

"I'm not trying to push you," Marshall said quietly. "I just think you ought to socialize a little. You really should go see your family. It's summertime. Maybe you could join them on vacation or something."

"The last time we had a family vacation I was in sixth grade," I said. "We went to San Antonio."

"Ah yes," he said. "Every young Texan must see the Alamo."

"It was kind of fun. We pulled up in the parking lot and there it was. My sister Michelle wasn't impressed, said it looked like it might fall to pieces just any minute. My father launched into this tale about the war with Mexico, and Valerie, who was about five then, was soaking up every word. Her eyes were getting bigger and bigger while my father talked on, Davy Crockett, Jim Bowie, the thousands of Mexican troops, and as she's listening to him she's getting lower and lower in the back seat. So he finishes up with the Texans all getting killed and Santa Anna on a rampage and says, 'Okay, let's go have a look.' By this time Valerie was all the way down on the floorboards. She came up very slowly, peeking over the seat, and then she looked over at the Alamo, suspiciously, and said, 'If they're having a war, I'll just wait in the car.' "

Marshall chuckled quietly. "I'd wager they'd really like to see you."

"I don't know," I said. "I think my sisters feel like I ran out on them." I tossed him a dish towel. "So, are you going to help me or do I have to dry them, too?"

He was stacking the last plate when the phone rang. He said yes and listened a minute and a change came over his face. He stiffened and began snapping the dish towel against his thigh.

"All right," he said. "I'll tell her." He swelled his massive chest out and held it that way, nearly popping the buttons from his denim shirt, staring at the receiver for a long moment before replacing it.

"That was Roland," he said. "Your partner will be down tomorrow morning to pick you up." He propped a foot on a chair and leaned on his knee. "The FBI wants to interview you."

My head felt suddenly as though it were full of termites. Buzzing. Chewing. Swarming.

"About what?" I asked. "What for?"

"The drug bust," he said, sitting down. "Don't panic," he added, "they pull stunts like this all the time."

I sat on the seawall, my overnight bag at my feet, watching the gulls coast on wind currents. Waiting for Jim.

He pulled up at the appointed hour and leaned across the seat to pop the door lock. I'd forgotten, or at least hadn't remembered, how fierce his eyes could look, how cold blue-gray.

"You look good," he said. "You got tan and all."

"Thanks," I said. "How's your leg?"

"Okay. I've been riding a bicycle to strengthen it. Still hurts a lot."

"Sorry to hear."

He pulled onto the road and flipped on the radio, began tapping his fingers against the steering wheel, nervously, not bothering to keep time to the music. We drove in silence until we hit 37 North. I tried for awhile to quiet the droning in my head, but my effort was wasted.

"We need a lawyer," Jim said finally. "I talked to Nettle about it."

"What on earth for?"

"He's in this thing as deep as we are, deeper I'm sure. Said the city would provide one for us. No charge."

"Maybe we should call Sommier."

"Like we could afford him. Besides, he wouldn't come near us. The one they got for us is supposed to be the best in San Antonio."

"Why San Antonio?"

"Hell, it's the feds, baby, why do they do anything?"

"I'm serious."

"They want to keep everything well outside of Beaumont, for awhile at least."

"I'm lost. What exactly is going on?"

"Dodd called me Friday, told me the FBI would be getting in touch. Said they knew everything. No sooner did I finish talking to him than the phone rang again. It was the feds, wanting to set up an interview. Then Nettle called and gave me this lawyer's name."

"What happened? Did he say what they know?"

"He said Gaines's lawyers had managed to get a habeas corpus hearing. They put Dodd on the stand and he ran off at the mouth for a good hour and a half. Told about how you came to him, tried to stop the investigation, about how strung out I was. Everything. He told them everything. Put it on public record."

"What," I said, "he suddenly got a case of Christian conscience? I mean, where was this attitude when I went to him in the first place?"

"In his back pocket, baby, right next to his paycheck and badge."

I didn't believe it. I couldn't. Three years later and here came the feds. I was trying, at long last, to go back to school. I didn't smoke dope, I barely drank beer. The first time in my life that I'd started to get any kind of grip on things and here came the feds. Investigating the investigation. But Gaines hadn't gone down for cocaine, he'd gone for trying to murder us. That part was simple.

And so was the rest of it, if I'd been willing to allow myself to think about it. I don't know how many times I had seen Jim cock his head back and assume the lanky stance of a cowboy philosopher, staring off at the sky. It had been his favorite phrase from the start: What goes around comes around.

"They're saying the shooting case was wrong?" I took one of his cigarettes and punched the lighter. "Is that what they're saying?"

He let his hands slide around to the bottom of the steering wheel and rolled his head sideways and back, until he was looking straight at me, slowly shaking his head no.

"Dodd admitted that you tried to stop the investigation, told them I was strung out, that Nettle stonewalled you. That's all I know."

"And now Nettle's providing us with a lawyer."

"Technically it's the city. But you can bet he's behind it. Hell, he's got no choice but to tell the truth or cover his ass. What do you think it'll be?"

"So what's the drill?"

"Like always, baby. Deny, deny, deny."

I stared out over the big yellow hood of the Blazer while the scenery crawled past in a blue-and-green blur.

We were about an hour out of Corpus when Jim asked me to drive.

"I'm sorry," he said. "It's cramping real bad."

"You didn't have to come all the way down," I said. "I could have taken the bus."

"I wanted to," he said.

He pulled over and walked around in the bar ditch, stopping every few steps to bend and massage his thigh. I climbed over the gearshift and adjusted the seat, while trucks roared past, the wind gusts in their wakes slamming against the Blazer, rocking it on its wheels. I tried not to watch him, tried not to feel too responsible.

He went to sleep almost as soon as we were back on the road.

When we reached San Antonio, he said he would drive again. There seemed to be construction everywhere, detours abounded. We moved slowly in heavy traffic, past dozens of bright orange signs printed with black-lettered commands. As we approached an underpass, I saw a heavy rope with six or eight black-and-white striped cans hanging from it, strung tautly across the roadway about twelve feet up. A sign between the dangling cans read LOW CLEARANCE: IF YOU HIT THIS, YOU WILL HIT THE BRIDGE. The concrete underside of the bridge itself was cracked and scarred where more than a few truck drivers had ignored the warning and peeled the tops from their rigs.

"Look to your right just after we pass this hill," Jim said.

There in the middle of several acres of pastureland was a large square brick building, attached to it a giant chain-link cage, almost as large as the building itself, filled with baboons. The sign in front said SOUTHWEST FOUNDATION FOR BIOMEDICAL RESEARCH.

They sat hunch-shouldered on tree limbs, metal railings, the ground, some in small groups, others alone. Several swung on metal rings suspended from the top of the cage, looping easily, gracefully, through the air.

"It's some kind of primate research center," Jim said. "We should visit sometime. Did you read about that thing where experimenters strapped a bunch of monkeys into cages and ran I.V.'s into their arms?"

"When was this?"

"I don't know, some time ago. The monkeys could press one button and get banana chips, or a different one and get a hit of cocaine, straight into the vein."

"You don't have to tell me."

"Only one survived. The others pressed that magic button until they had heart attacks or starved."

"We're supposed to be a higher life form."

"Says who."

"So what do you do, keep pressing the button?"

"I haven't. Not a day since you left. Not once."

"Works every time. I leave, or threaten to leave, and suddenly you're okay. It seems to be the best for both of us."

"Except that I love you."

I think, by that time, he actually did. I like to believe it, that at some point he really loved me. I try to pin down the moment, the instant when he might have realized that what I had asked of him all along was something so extraordinarily plain that it was hidden, buried beneath ornamentation, like the pine tree at Christmastime that is wrenched from its place in the earth and stuck in a window, draped with things plastic and shiny. Always, when I look for the moment, it comes back to the shooting. I think that was the first time in his life that he'd ever *needed* anybody, and I happened to be the one who was there. I'd stopped the blood, the life flowing out of his body, and finally, finally, he'd realized that I loved him. But he'd fought against it for such a long time, and even after it had happened, that neither of us were sure how to overcome it.

I couldn't answer, and he said nothing else until we pulled into the lot in front of a large glass-and-brass office tower, the address Nettle had given him, where he shut off the engine and sat staring out the windshield.

"I've got it together now," he said finally. "Once and for all. And the one thing I know in the world is that I love you."

I sat looking at the gleaming front doors of the tower. The door handle was cold against my palm.

"It's a nice building," I said. "So new and all."

"Let's go then."

I felt an incredible lethargy pressing my body to the seat, as though gravity had suddenly doubled. I ached. I simply ached. I thought about drinking gasoline and swallowing a lighted match. That might feel good.

There was a rush of cool air as Jim opened his door and put his foot to the pavement. Halfway out, he turned to look at me.

"Well?"

"I think if they're having a war," I said, "I'll just wait in the car."

TWENTY-THREE

SAN ANTONIO'S BEST WAS MANNY GONZALES, A tall, husky Mexican-American gentleman with striking Aztec features. The high cheekbones and arrow-straight nose of that tribe had, in this man, survived through the centuries. He was truly beautiful, with wavy dark brown hair, deep brown almond-shaped eyes, and golden, almost whiskerless skin.

Beautiful, he was. Involved in our case, he was not. When he introduced himself, he covered my icy hand gently with his own warm, soft palms and said, "Don't be nervous. Just go in there and tell them your side of the story."

"What, specifically, are we being investigated for?" Jim asked.

"The charge they're considering is Violation of the United States Code, Section 241."

"Could you translate?"

"Civil rights."

Jim sank into a leather chair next to our new lawyer's desk.

"They're saying you might have put someone in jail with-out due process of law."

"How much time?" I asked, not believing my own question.

"Up to ten years and a ten-thousand-dollar fine."

"Same as for kicking ass," Jim said.

"Or stuffing a ballot box," said Gonzales. "It's a very broad statute."

"Everything they do is broad," Jim said, shaking his head. "So why exactly are we here?"

"You've done nothing wrong, am I correct?" Gonzales folded his hands on the desk before him.

Jim gave him a short nod.

"Just go in and talk to them. You have nothing to hide."

"Supposing," Jim said, "speaking hypothetically of course, that we *had* committed an indiscretion here and there? What then?"

"The investigation is preliminary at this point," Gonzales said. "I've been hired by the City of Beaumont to represent you while you're down here, only because the FBI will not interview you unless you have representation. I've spoken at length with your former boss, and I really think you should discuss things with him. Your defense strategy is a matter for counsel in Beaumont."

I sat down next to Jim.

"I believe they would like to speak to you separately," he said. Then, looking at me, "They want to see you first."

I glanced at Jim and he shrugged.

"Give 'em hell," he said flatly, almost in a whisper.

I don't know what I expected to find when I walked through the door, or even if I had enough presence of mind to be able to expect anything. I turned the ornate brass knob on the door and took a deep breath and walked into the room.

The first thing I saw was a tape recorder on a long mahogany table in the middle of the small room. It leaped out at me like a sudden close-up in a film, and I had to force myself to sit down before it. There was a flowing, hollow noise rushing into my ears, like the sound that had hit me so many years before, the first time I'd really done cocaine.

The Federal Bureau of Investigation. Three years late. A matched set of feds. One short, one tall. The short one had brownish-gray hair combed in wispy, slanting bangs that reached about halfway down his forehead, leaving a strip of waxy skin between there and his heavy gray-flecked eyebrows. He was wearing a gray suit and a red tie. His nose was pink with sunburn below his small brown eyes, and he was smoking one of those long, thin, dark brown cigarettes. The tall one had on a white sport shirt with ep-aulets on the shoulders and a breast pocket with a plastic insert full of felt-tip pens. He had mounds and mounds of thick black hair, combed in a style reminiscent of the fifties, and large, slow-moving green eyes with thick black lashes. His lips were so thin as to be practically nonexistent.

As soon as I sat down, the short one looked at the tall one and said, "Well, Fearsome, shall we begin?"

The tall one flipped out a badge case and hung it for a brief moment in front of my face, then slipped it back into his jacket.

"This is Agent Maygrett," he said. "I'm Agent Mc-Phearson."

Maygrett shifted forward and casually flicked his ciga-rette in the direction of the ashtray. McPhearson pressed a button on the recorder and I watched as the plastic reels began turning. Like my insides, twisting and reeling and turning. A dizzying wave of nausea rolled through me. I took a glass from the table and poured some water.

"September fourth, 1981, three forty P.M.," he said, speaking more to the recorder than to me, "interview with subject, Kristen Ann Cates, conducted by Special Agents Walter McPhearson and Thomas Maygrett in the offices of Berg, Lonner, Hoffman, Rosenthal, Wulf and Gonzales in San Antonio, Texas, concerning subject's participation in the 1978 undercover narcotics investigation by the Beaumont Police Department." He looked at me. "Is that correct?"

"Yes sir," I said.

"Now, since you are a former police officer, I assume you are aware of your rights."

How many times had I said it? Now it was my turn: I had the right to remain silent. And the right to be considered instantly guilty by doing so. The only ones who don't cooperate are those who have something to hide. We were talking FBI, talking J. Edgar, secret files on God knows who, on Martin Luther King, on every half-baked sixties radical who ever strapped on a headband and jumped on a park bench and said Fuck the Establishment. I did not know how much they knew.

"Yes sir," I said, "I know my rights."

"And you are here voluntarily."

"Yes sir."

McPhearson leaned back in his chair and Maygrett leaned forward.

"Did you take drugs while you were working undercover for the Beaumont Police Department during the winter and spring of 1978?"

It was like being in the starting blocks, crouched over the white chalk line, so hyped, so psyched, that when the gun went off I would either set a new record or fall over and land with my face in the cinders, just pass smooth out.

"No sir," I said. "I have, as my application to the department indicated, smoked marijuana on three or four occasions when I was in high school. That's the extent of my drug use."

It went downhill from there.

*　　*　　*

"Damn it to fucking hell!" Jim screamed. He hit the brakes at the intersection and slammed his hand hard against the dash. "Son of a bitch!" The rage in his voice seemed to bounce off the windshield.

"Easy," I said. "It's only a red light."

"We are fucking getting hung out to dry," he seethed, "and Nettle's behind it. The bastard's gonna give us up like a damn ten-cent donation to United Way."

"How can he," I said. "He can't. He was giving the orders."

"Fucking feds! They've talked to everybody. Did you get the impression that they know everything that happened during every godforsaken instant of that entire investigation? Did it seem that way to you?"

"They knew what to ask," I said. "They definitely knew what to ask."

"There's so many tongues flapping in Beaumont right now you can put your laundry on the line and the goddamn hot air will dry it in three minutes flat."

The light changed and Jim ground his way into first and popped the clutch, leaving short black patches on the pavement behind the Blazer.

"It's not right, man," he said. "It ain't fucking right. I'm not going to hang for that bastard."

"So what, we're supposed to tell them the truth? That would go over like nuns at a Klan gathering."

"They know," Jim said. "They've known for years. They can't afford to hear it. You can bet your ass the feds would like to take down the local boys, and the state as well. Fade some of their own heat by turning up the burners under the locals."

"And leave the DEA to carry on? Like they're straight?"

"Ask me about the feds," he said. "Ask me who trained me." He punched the cigarette lighter and glared at nobody. "First goddamn undercover work I ever did was with the DEA. Bastards taught me everything I know. And I," he said, turning to look at me, "taught you."

"I met one once," I said. "At Rob's house. He was ushering people back to the bathroom one at a time, all afternoon. There were three or four state boys over, and noses were running, you know. Finally I got Rob alone and asked him why I wasn't included in the split-down, and you know what he said? The fed was hainty of local cops. I couldn't believe it, that fucker, strutting around looking like a cross between Waylon Jennings and a top-dollar gigolo. Had this big black Stetson on, and a bright red rodeo shirt, and he had a long brown beard. Know what was on his feet? Tassled Italian loafers. I don't know how he ever managed to buy any dope. Somebody must've felt sorry for him."

"Where was I?"

"Who knows," I said. "It was during the investigation. We were both pretty much down and dirty by then. You wouldn't have believed this Yankee DEA bastard, trying to play urban cowboy. Saying you-all this and you-all that. Right before I left I told him it was y'all, man, like yawl."

"Well, we ain't talking DEA here, babe, this is FBI, accountants turned cop. These boys do it with paperwork and tape, you know, and they've got us on the record now. You can bet they're on their way back to Beaumont to talk to a grand jury and indict our little white asses. We go to trial? We'd be rolling bones on ten years. Smartest thing we can do is cop a plea and hope we catch the judge on a good day."

I remembered the night of the bust-out, Jim standing outside the office doing his Tricky Dick imitation: Don't cop out. I felt my insides go wormy and heat shot up the sides of my neck to the top of my head and spread slowly back down, as though it were being poured over my skin. I tried to make sense of the words rattling inside my head.

"We could run."

"Run?" Jim said. "You ready to disappear? Live the rest of your life wondering when you're gonna get caught? Man, I've got so many fucking scars on my body that they'd find me in no time. Some goddamn bounty hunter would be on our ass and steady looking for a dude with a fucked-up left arm. You don't see a scar like this every day."

He waved his arm at me, turning his hand so that I could see his forearm. It had gone white, over the years, puffy and white, but the tiny ovals from the steam vents in the iron were still visible. And there were the other scars, the ones hidden under his clothing. The mass of stitch marks on his arm. The metal where bone had been. The fist-sized crater of sunken skin on the front of his thigh.

"Look," Jim said, "everybody's got at least one probation coming. We can do that. If anybody goes it'll be me. They aren't going to put you in the joint. Hell, you tried to do right. Nettle stonewalled you. You got nothing to worry about."

"Right," I said. "Nothing at all. I'll just skip into the Federal Building and tell them I'm sorry, I got fucked up on dope and wasn't thinking straight. Good luck with your case, Mr. Prosecutor, and have a nice afternoon."

"You'd better cut the bullshit," he said. "And concentrate on saving your ass."

"Hey," I said, "Raynor? Why don't you tell me what you suggest. I'm wide open here, but I also know that the truth didn't go over so great the last time I had occasion to tell it." He tightened his grip on the wheel and pressed himself against the seat back.

"Step one," he said, "is we get on the horn to those feds and tell them we'd like an appointment."

*   *   *

The FBI kept its Beaumont agents in the Jack Brooks Federal Building, a limestone Neo-Gothic number that stood next door to Sears and smack across the street from the old red brick Baptist church. Maygrett led us to his cluttered desk, situated near the back wall in a windowless corner.

"First," he said, "let's find you a lawyer. Before we talk, before we do anything."

"Two-thirds of the lawyers in town were involved in our cases," Jim said. He sat with his legs crossed, his left foot nervously tapping the floor. "Who does that leave?"

"I suggest someone with experience in federal court." Maygrett's chair whined as he leaned toward the floor to grab the Yellow Pages.

The Honorable Melvin Francis Hardwick, esteemed member of Beaumont's tight-knit circle of practicing attorneys, would do his best to keep Jim's sentence to probation. The Honorable Mr. So-And-So. Mr. So-And-So, Esquire. Lawyers in Texas could choose their adjective. Frank liked Honorable. The word *Esquire,* he said, reeked of feudalism.

Titles aside, Frank was our lawyer: thirty-five hundred for me, and absolutely no way he would plead me if there was the remotest chance I would do time. Seventy-five hundred for Jim. We would empty our account of Jim's remaining retirement money, and Frank would bill the rest.

After we'd signed, he handed the papers to his secretary and ran a hand through the few strands of hair that sprouted from his crown. Then he looked down his long slender nose and took one step back from his bed-size desk.

"Tell them everything you know."

Jim's mouth dropped.

"Shouldn't we discuss this?" he asked.

"You did it, right?"

"We don't even know for sure what Dodd said."

"Doesn't matter. You've got one shot at it. Cooperate every way you possibly can."

I heard Maygrett's pager beeping out in Frank's waiting room.

I didn't want to talk. Out of fear. Out of shame. But when I thought about the investigation, about what had been done, about what I had helped to do. . . . Nothing that happened in Beaumont had been about justice. Now, maybe, there was a shot at it. A chance, finally, to take a witness stand in a court of law and actually tell the truth, no punches pulled, just lay the entire ugly mess out there in the open. Let someone else decide. Let *them* put Nettle away.

All that self-righteousness sounded good bouncing around in my brain while I sat in the Honorable Frank's office. Honorable Mr. Lawyer. Mr. Lawyer, Esquire. I couldn't count the number of times I'd heard them whispering in the hallways outside of courtrooms, making deals with people's freedom.

Hanging on the wall behind the Honorable Frank's desk, next to his diplomas, were three framed needlepoints: WITHOUT JUSTICE, COURAGE IS WEAK. THERE IS NO LITTLE ENEMY. WE MUST ALL HANG TOGETHER OR ASSUREDLY WE WILL ALL HANG SEPARATELY.

Dodd had snitched, and God knew why. I sure didn't. To clear his conscience? Because someone had enticed, or perhaps insisted?

The Honorable Frank's high-pitched voice was fluttering around my ears. ". . . the only thing you can do," he was saying. "It's like this, boys and girls, the immunity train pulls away from the station one time, one time only, and whoever's the first on board gets to take the ride. Dodd's the one who gets to drive the engine and toot the horn."

Had I had seen some other way out, I might have taken it. Then again, I had Nettle in my sights and the United States of America was begging me to pull the trigger. *THE UNITED STATES OF AMERICA* v. *James Michael Raynor and Kristen Ann Cates.* All hail to the Red, White, and Blue.

Thy banners make tyranny tremble.

Some days Jim went first, some days I got the morning session. The Holiday Inn in South Houston was only a few miles from my parents' home. I had driven past it daily on my way to work at Wild Bill's in the Alameda Mall when I was in high school and after. Now I was, in effect, under house arrest there. Debriefing, they called it. We would stay in Houston until they were through asking questions. Less security risks that way. We could go nowhere without the agents. We went nowhere period.

When I wasn't sitting in a puffy brown chair in the agents' room answering questions, I was sitting at the table in our room, staring out the window at the traffic on the Gulf Freeway, wondering if I would actually go. Incarceration.

"You're looking at probation," Maygrett would say at least once every session. "No promises, but as long as you tell us the truth, my opinion is it's definitely a probation situation we have here."

I sat across from him at the small table in his room and listened to him assure me. Or maybe he didn't say anything about it. Maybe I imagined it. McPhearson didn't look so confident, but I didn't question Maygrett. I couldn't bear to.

They had charts and diagrams and names and places and dates. They dressed neatly, in shirt and tie, each day. Maygrett smoked his brown cigarettes and reminisced about other cases before he started the morning interrogation.

"Yeah," he would say, "had a bank robber over in Port Arthur, popped that fucker like a grape. Popped him just like a grape. Took two hours, he told me everything."

We went over each case. Was it legitimate? Did you turn in all the dope or cut it? Did you testify in court on this one or was it a plea? When did Jim start shooting up? How much dope were you taking? When did you first meet with Dodd about Jim's problem? With Nettle? What about this Denny fellow, and Rob? When did they meet with Nettle? What was said? What really happened the night of the shooting? And so forth, and so forth, and so forth.

When we finished telling them, they didn't believe us.

We followed them back to Beaumont and they set up the polygraph in an empty lecture room in the Federal Building, one flight up from their office. I sat in an injection-molded blue plastic chair, facing rows of scattered tables and vacant seats. The examiner was strictly business, short and light-skinned, with spiky brown hair. His card said OF-FICE OF ENFORCEMENT OPERATIONS, CRIMINAL DIVISION, DEPARTMENT OF JUSTICE. He had an almost cybernetic air about him, moving superefficiently as he attached gadgets to my body. I felt as though I were being prepped for surgery.

The drill was the same as it had been when I took the exam in Houston, only this man was obviously a professional.

When he'd hooked me up, he sat down at the table, to my left and slightly behind me, and I heard the familiar sounds of switches flipping and needles scratching against paper. It occurred to me that if the examiner in Houston had been any good at all, or hadn't been on Nettle's payroll,

I did not know which, I would never have passed that test, and I wouldn't be sitting where I was. I wondered if the defect was in the examiner or in me, if I'd played so many roles that I could no longer distinguish one self from the other.

I don't remember very much about the examination itself, except that I was honest. I listened to his voice, which, unlike his manner, was gentle and soothing. He spoke softly, with quiet rhythm.

"Just relax," he said, "and answer truthfully with a yes or no only. If you have problems with the way I phrased a question we can discuss it afterward and I'll ask it again later. The test is about to begin. Be very still now and relax."

I stared at the wall, tried to empty my mind. The paper was rolling.

"Is your first name Kristen?"

I recall that he focused, during the first hours of the examination, on the meetings with Nettle and on drug use. I recall worrying that he was being too nice to me.

"Have you taken any drugs today?" he asked near the start.

"No," I answered.

It didn't seem as if any time at all had passed before he told me that was all for the day, we would continue tomorrow. He quietly removed the metal plates from my fingertips, undid the blood-pressure cuff, and disconnected the tube wrapped around my chest. I stood, anxious to get out of there.

"Did I pass?"

"You can talk to the agents about that," he said. "I really shouldn't discuss results with you."

But then he pulled a couple of chairs up to a table near

the back wall of the room and motioned for me to sit down.
I hadn't realized until then that the sun had gone down,
the room was growing slowly darker as dusk arrived.

"I told you the truth," I said. "I know I shouldn't say
that to you, that it will make you suspicious and all, but
it's important to me. I'm telling you the truth. I told the
agents the truth."

"Don't get all uptight," he said. "I want you to relax.
That's it, just lean back. Relax." He sat quietly across the
table from me, in the faint shadow cast by a portable film
screen near the window.

"Who shot you?" he said.

"Will Gaines."

"You're not sure of that, are you?"

"It's impossible to be positive," I said. "Certainly it
looked like him. He had a reason to want us dead."

"What I'd like to do," he said, "I'm going to hook you
up one more time today. I'm going to ask you 'Do you
know who shot you?' and I want you to answer yes. Then
I'm going to ask the same question again and I want you
to say no."

He hooked me up and I did it just the way he asked. Yes
I knew. No I didn't know. He unhooked me and looked
at his charts. He spent some moments staring at the paper.

"You don't know," he finally said.

"What do you mean?" I asked.

"You're not certain. The readings are identical for both
replies."

"And?"

"Did you take anything during that lunch break, have
you taken any drugs?"

"All I've had today is fried chicken and Dr Pepper.
That's all."

He shuffled a couple of charts around, the paper rattling loudly in the empty room.

"Sometime between the first test I gave you and the one you just took, on the shooting, your polarity reversed completely." He pushed the graphs across the table. "The slope of your answers. Look at this. All during the first test, your answers sloped to the right."

The lines curved just as he said, sloping to the right, a series of small waves.

"And this," he said, "is the test we just finished."

Thin red lines troughed and crested across the paper, rolling to the left.

"I've never seen anything like it." He slumped back in his chair and began pulling at his eyes. "You didn't take anything?"

"Nothing." I had answered as honestly as I knew how, and even the instrument was unable to distinguish which answer was the lie.

"Would you give a blood sample?"

"If I have to," I said. "I'm not on anything."

"I know."

"Are we finished then?"

"I think what we should do is we should go downstairs and tell Jim that you don't know who shot him."

I didn't know why he was suggesting it, what could possibly be their motive for wanting Gaines completely off the hook. I wasn't sure why I agreed to do it. There was the confusion, from answering both ways and having the polygraph indicate no stress. And there was the unspoken threat that if I didn't cooperate fully I might wind up worse off at sentencing time. But there was also this: I hadn't been sure that night, hadn't been absolutely positive. I *believed* I had seen Gaines. It happens all the time. Cops running around everywhere, demanding reliability, demanding absolute, positive identification, and the witness wants to perform admirably, wants to *know*. And once I'd gotten to the hospital, once Nettle had arrived, I no longer felt I had a choice.

I will admit that during the interminable ride down the elevator, I thought about splitting. I remembered Pasadena, and how confident my schoolgirl witnesses had been when they pointed to the photo of Mr. Ashbey, picking him out of the lineup. That was what I lacked. Certainty. I would be labeled a liar.

It made me itch all over, this interrogation business.

Jim was sitting on top of the desk in the interrogation room, Maygrett was propped next to him, flicking ashes at the gray metal can in the corner. McPhearson was leaning against the wall next to the door, tapping the heel of one shoe against the toe of the other.

The examiner said, "Jim, Kristen has something she wants to tell you."

Jim sat quietly, his arms folded tightly across his chest, and when he looked at me his eyes were barely narrowed, the way they had been the night we'd flipped Walker. His jaw was tight, the muscles in front of his ears flexing ever so slightly, hardly noticeable.

It clicked suddenly, all this attention to the shooting, and I realized for the first time exactly how vulnerable we were. They were looking for something to split me and Jim up, something that would cause us to talk against each other and make their task easier.

If they managed it, things would get unbearably nasty. We would start laying things off on one another, and it would all boil down to a couple of junkie narcs. The feds wouldn't have to upset the city fathers by indicting Nettle, and Nettle would have no cause to talk about where his orders had come from.

I looked straight at Jim, then folded my own arms and leaned back against the wall. I saw the shift, he became witness-stand calm: eyes alert, lips relaxed, hands folded quietly in the lap. Unshakable.

"I'm not sure who shot us."

I said the words. I didn't know, at first, if I was lying. And then it hit me. I was telling the absolute truth. Even if Gaines was the trigger man, I did not have the first fucking clue who was behind it.

Jim looked evenly at me, while the agents stared at both of us, holding their collective breath.

"That's all right," he said calmly. "I understand." I turned to the examiner.

"Can we go now?"

He shrugged at Maygrett.

"Yeah," Maygrett said. "Let's get out of here. We'll escort you back to the hotel."

When we parked in front of our room, Maygrett rolled down his window.

"Tomorrow at nine," he said. "We'll be at the office late tonight if you need anything."

We went to the motel coffee shop for supper. The counter was lined with salesmen, and tucked in among them were truckers in jeans and boots. A few of the booths held local teenage couples, sitting closely and sharing french fries.

"Could be," Jim said, "that it's the feds who want Gaines out. You saw his history. Not a single conviction. Could well be that he's done some snitching for them."

"What are you having?" I asked.

"Son of a bitch probably turns cases for the DEA."

"I don't see catfish on the menu."

"Talk to me, girl," he said.

"It doesn't matter," I said. "He's a snitch? He's not a

snitch? The feds leaned on Dodd? Dodd was overwhelmed by guilt? Doesn't matter. All I know is we can't do a thing about any of it. We are dealing here with a higher authority."

The waitress came over and pushed the chili until Jim glared at her, then gave up and took our order.

"I just want to know," he said when she left. "I want to know who's behind all of it."

"Hey," I said, "Perry Mason is in reruns."

TWENTY-FOUR

T HE COURTROOM WAS COOL AND SMOOTH, CARPETED blue, ceilinged with tiles that soaked up noise and hushed even shouted words. The judge's bench, the jury box, the witness stand, all the furnishings were of cold, dark wood. Above the bench, centered high on the wall behind it, hung a huge seal: Department of Justice. It was the United States versus Nettle, El Jefe against the feds.

Dodd was to be the first witness. Followed by Jim, then me, then Rob and Denny and a couple of Beaumont patrolmen. The defense had subpoenaed Mr. Berthe, but he chose not to show, sending Marshall in his stead. It was a nonsense defense move anyway, Mr. Berthe hadn't done anything but try to keep a couple of cops alive.

I was sitting in the witness room, pretending to read a magazine, when he walked in, tan and fit as ever, and I managed to be calm until he walked over to face me. I stood to shake hands and then Marshall was hugging me, and I him, and there were tears. We were both trying hard not to make some kind of scene, trying to wipe our eyes and somehow be discreet about it.

"Always give yourself a chance," he whispered, and then he was gone and I was sitting in the chair again, thinking that he didn't understand. I was dependent now upon the mercy of the Court.

I spent the next two days sitting in a chair in the witness room, leafing through magazines. When the bailiff walked in finally and called my name, I felt like the bottom had dropped out of my skull and my brain was sliding down the back of my throat. I forced myself up and followed him to the courtroom.

They were all at the prosecution table. Maygrett and Mc-Phearson sat next to D. Lang Howell, the special prosecutor from D.C., across the table from a couple of local assistant U.S. attorneys. When he saw me, Maygrett's left eye twitched in a kind of half wink, a gesture I found ridiculous. *Pop me like a grape.*

The Honorable Frank was nowhere around. He had walked Jim and me into the courthouse, offering a "no comment" to the reporters outside, and disappeared after leaving us in the witness room. He'd said we knew what we were doing. "I'll be at the office," he'd said. The Honorable Frank. Head Wiener-in-Charge.

Nettle's defense attorney was named after a genuine Texas hero, Sam Austin. He was neighborly, a regular sort of fellow from right there in Jefferson County, sitting directly across from Nettle at the defense table. He was big and pear-shaped, wearing a string tie and cowboy boots, his hair slicked into a neat brown wave atop his large head. Nettle was his usual meticulously groomed self, wearing yet another pair of new shoes, these in maroon patent with gold clasps. I remember thinking they clashed with his red hair. His wife was next to him. I could not find it in me to feel sorry for her, although she'd had nothing to do with anything. She was supporting her husband, being his woman, trying to show that he was really a good family man, persecuted by the national government. Maybe she believed it.

Though they called it "preparation," the prosecutors had, for several days before the trial, rehearsed us as to what our testimony would be. We went over our parts again and again. I knew what they would ask, they knew what I would answer. When it came the defense attorney's turn, anything could happen.

Howell, the special prosecutor, was a petite fellow. Not short, but somewhat dainty by the real-man standards of Texas. He wore a bow tie and red button-on braces. His hair was cut in a John Denver special, over the ears and with bangs, but neatly. His appearance was not that of one who could ever even hope to win a case involving a redneck Texas jury.

He opened with the usual questions: where did I live and what did I do, Corpus Christi, school, etc., etc.

A juror who looked like a farmer dressed in his best Sunday-meeting suit scrawled his face up the first time Howell spoke, but seemed, after a few sentences, to begin listening to the words instead of to Howell's marked Yankee accent.

"Mrs. Raynor," Howell said, "you and your husband have entered into a plea agreement with the United States, have you not, in which you have agreed to cooperate with the FBI and tell them the truth concerning the undercover narcotics investigation which you participated in here in Beaumont in 1978?"

"Yes sir."

The gallery of the courtroom was completely full. There were people standing at the back, leaning against the wall, waiting to hear the cops' confessions. I recognized a few defendants in the crowd, sitting there with itchy smiles etched on their faces.

"And you have met with the FBI and told them the complete truth about everything that occurred during that investigation. Correct?"

"Yes, it is." In my mind, I heard the sound of children

singing, "Here We Go 'Round the Mulberry Bush." Early in the morning.

"Mrs. Raynor, did you tell the FBI that you and your partner had falsified a case on Will Gaines?"

"Yes sir, we did."

"Did you also admit to them that you had used drugs during that investigation?"

Sam Austin stood up, turned halfway to the jury, and said, "Your Honor, I object to this business of asking the witness what she told the FBI. I have no protection over that hearsay testimony of what she told the Federal Bureau of Investigation."

The judge didn't even blink. "She's available for cross-examination. Overruled."

Howell nodded his appreciation and continued to ask his damning questions. On and on and on. I sat in the chair and tried to concentrate, *Here we go 'round the mulberry bush,* but I answered mostly by rote. We'd been over it so many times.

I felt a burning in the back of my throat, I tried hard to swallow, sat there gagging silently, answering Howell's questions. *Concentrate, concentrate, don't throw up. Swallow. Just one swallow will make it go away. I am choking to death in front of these people. Yes sir. No sir. I don't recall, sir. I wanted to save Jim. Sir. Swallow.*

I saw Maygrett, his eyes squeezed half shut, as though he didn't want to see what he was looking at. I hated him sitting there all smug and comfortable, defender of justice. *Pop me like a grape, pop me like a grape. Just swallow. Squeeze me right out of my own thin skin, Nettle's on trial but I'm the one copping out, up here telling the FBI's truth and being stared at and examined and praying for just a little relief when sentencing time comes around.*

I swallowed. I answered Howell's hard, polite questions.

Suddenly he was saying, "Pass the witness, no further questions at this time," and heading for the prosecution table.

Sam Austin grabbed a fistful of papers and marched up to the podium in the center of the courtroom like he was bent on crucifying me. I felt like getting down on my hands and knees, crawling across the miles of carpet between me and the door.

"Mrs. Raynor," he drawled tiredly, "you don't really expect this jury to believe that you and your partner accomplished one of the biggest drug busts in this state while you were addicted to cocaine, do you? Let me just read something into the record here."

He had news clippings, letters from D.A.'s and judges and city managers, citations from the Peace Officers Association. He praised me, *praised me,* as a fine upstanding police officer who had gone above and beyond the call of duty in the struggle to wipe out drug traffic.

"Do you think any reasonable person will believe that the chief of police of this city, a fine citizen, and good father, a churchgoing man who has spent his life fighting evil for the benefit of the community, you wouldn't expect anybody to believe that he ordered you to falsify any case now, really, would you?"

I felt suddenly tired, exhausted with all the courtroom tactics. I was trying to catch the direction of his argument, but at that moment the whole bizarre proceeding lost significance. It was only another show, "Corruption and Conspiracy," Now Playing at a Courthouse Near You. I wanted to give Austin a workout, to be a hostile witness without seeming so to the jury. The farce had drained me to that level—I was tired of prosecutors putting words in my mouth, tired of being handled by the FBI, tired of living on the same planet as Donald J. Nettle.

"Mrs. Raynor?"

I was tired of being Mrs. Raynor.

"Answer the question please." The judge's voice jarred me back to the courtroom.

"I'm sorry," I said. "Could you rephrase the question?"

Could somebody, *somebody,* please rephrase the question. I looked to the prosecution table, hoping for an objection, I didn't even know to what, but an objection, please. Somebody object. Somebody rephrase the question. Somebody do something here. Howell sat doodling on a yellow pad. Austin was talking.

". . . and you got upset at the way the department handled the shooting, that you had to live in a jail cell, that Jim's wounds were not properly attended to, and you got upset, rightfully, that this fellow Gaines only got forty years. He tried to kill you. If he were free on the streets, you and Mr. Raynor could even things up. And if Gaines came here to Beaumont to gain a foothold for organized crime . . ."

Howell looked up, suddenly aware of what was happening, and stood.

"Objection, Your Honor, this is nothing but outrageous speculation on the part of the defense."

"Sustained. If counsel has questions, let him ask them of the witness. Otherwise, we can move on."

Austin flipped through his papers and tossed back his head.

"Mrs. Raynor, did Will Gaines or anyone associated with him offer you money to recant your testimony as to who did the shooting?"

I wanted to scream. I sat there, my face crawling with heat while the rest of me froze slowly, until I felt like my skin would crack any minute into a million little pieces and crumble off my bones into a squat mound of powder on the floor. There was no money involved, there was no payoff to Jim or to me. Dodd? I didn't know. The shooting? I didn't know. Yes, I was a junkie, yes, I helped stash on Will Gaines, and yes, somebody shot us. I thought it was Gaines, I believed it was Gaines, I wasn't sure, I didn't know *absolutely*, even the goddamn polygraph was inconclusive. I didn't know *anything*. I simply wanted to scream.

"No sir," I said. My answer was given quietly.

"Did the FBI offer you money to recant your earlier testimony?"

"Objection!" Howell leaped from his chair, swung his pad in a wide arc toward Austin. "The question is totally and completely irrelevant."

"Overruled." The judge peered at me over the edge of the bench, his glasses low on his nose. "The witness will answer the question."

"No sir."

"Then why did you recant your testimony," Austin shouted, "why did you suddenly say that you weren't sure who shot you?" He turned to the jury and raised his palms, like a preacher at a tent revival.

I looked to Howell. He was writing something on his pad. I looked up at the judge.

"I'm not sure I can answer that question."

Howell's head popped up.

"Your Honor, may I approach the bench?" he asked.

"You may."

The judge leaned forward while Howell whispered something to him. I heard the word *polygraph*.

"Thank you, Mr. Howell. The jury will be excused for ten minutes."

The bailiff escorted the jury through a small door at the side of the courtroom. Austin walked to the defense table and rested a hand on Nettle's shoulder.

"What's the difficulty, Your Honor?" he asked.

"Mr. Austin, please approach the bench."

Austin rounded the podium and stood before the judge, who spoke in a near whisper. Again, I heard something about polygraph, and something about "indicated she has been truthful," and Austin shook his head no.

When the jury had filed back into the box, Austin continued his questioning.

"Mrs. Raynor, you expect this jury to believe . . ."

"Objection as to the form of the question." Howell was on his feet again.

"Sustained."

"Mrs. Raynor, am I to understand that what you are telling this jury is that in the space of six months or so you went from being a fine upstanding officer of the law to being a dopehead, a liar, and a thief? That you skimmed evidence, you lied in court, you took drugs, and you accused Will Gaines of selling to you when he hadn't? Is that what you're telling this jury?"

"Yes sir," I said.

"Pass the witness for redirect." Austin took his seat.

Howell carried his legal pad to the podium.

"Mrs. Raynor," he said, "you had started a new life for yourself after you left Beaumont, had you not?"

"I was trying to. I was planning to enroll in college."

"And you knew if you came forward all that would go down the tubes, so to speak?"

"Yes sir."

"You've pled guilty to a conspiracy to violate the civil rights of Will Gaines, a conspiracy involving you, Jim Raynor, Larry Dodd, and Donald Nettle."

"Yes sir."

"Will you identify, for the jury, the man you went to when your partner, Jim Raynor, was strung out, addicted to drugs? Will you point out please, the man who told you and Jim Raynor to make a cocaine case on Will Gaines, whether he was dealing or not? Point him out please."

I pointed at Nettle.

"That's him," I said.

"Now at this meeting, when you met with him to discuss Jim's addiction, after this meeting, did he ask you to follow him down the road to talk things over?"

"Yes sir, he did."

"And you complied?"

"Yes sir."

"And what happened then?"

"He pulled over near a church and I got in his car and we talked."

"What did you talk about?"

"He told me he was glad he could trust me to come to him when there was a problem and that he hoped I would always feel comfortable doing that."

"Anything else?"

"He said he would remember my loyalty come promotion time."

"And did anything else happen that night?"

Howell knew about it. I'd told him, and that was why he was now asking the question. He'd said during preparation that the decision about how to answer would be up to me. It wasn't a criminal matter, it had no bearing on the case. It was personal, between me and Nettle. I don't know why Howell's attitude made me feel that to admit what had happened would somehow make me a topwater floater, a lightweight.

Nettle was staring at me, and for the first time since I had met him I saw him squirm. A bright red flush crept up his neck, over the perfectly knotted tie, and into his cheeks. He slunk down, just barely, but enough that I noticed, and pulled his hands into his lap. He squirmed.

I waited, wanting to enjoy the moment and angry at myself for feeling that way. I thought about it. I savored it. He squirmed and I enjoyed it.

"No sir," I said. "Nothing else."

It was quiet in the witness room, centrally heated and deadly quiet. The trial went on for another two days after I'd finished testifying. Rob and Denny had finally managed to get excused immediately after they testified, and did not stick around for a verdict. Dodd sat against the wall, Jim and I at the table. There wasn't much to say.

I kept having this daydream, while I sat there waiting for the end of the trial. It took place out in the hallway: Nettle would walk up to me, and I would pull out my pistol and point it at his arm and squeeze the trigger. I could feel it. It took away the exact same section of bone that Jim lost in the shooting. Nettle would scream and fall to the floor, blathering on the white tile while phosphorescent blood spilled out of his arm. Then I would aim at his leg and put a bullet precisely where Jim's wound had been. And even though I was using a revolver, the wounds were those of a shotgun, just like that night. Nettle would squirm on a floor slick with his own blood, crying out, begging me not to kill him. I would put my gun slowly away and say, "Jefe. Jefe, you little sweetheart, you." In my dream, I took out a quarter and tossed it on the floor next to him. "Here, Jefe," I said, "call yourself an ambulance." And walked away.

The jury was out for sixty-six minutes. Maygrett and Fearsome and the rest of Team Fed were ecstatic. Sixty-six minutes. It had to be guilty.

But I felt it when we were standing in front of the elevator, waiting to ride up to the courtroom. He would walk. He would go back to his office and live his life and be the chief of police. Fight crime with crime. I felt the jury saying, "This is Texas, not New York City. This kind of thing can't happen here. Leave us alone. We have bills to pay, children to raise; you took the job, now just do what you have to to keep the drugs out. And do it quietly. We don't want to hear about it. The lawn needs edging."

I felt it, and then a few minutes later I was standing at the back of the courtroom, listening as the jury's verdict was read aloud, for all good citizens to hear.

Not Guilty.

All I could think about were the simple weary words said by every Catholic who has ever knelt before a priest: Bless me, Father, for I have sinned. This is my first confession.

TWENTY-FIVE

IM TOOK MY ARM AS WE APPROACHED THE BENCH. I don't remember what we did during the week that passed between Nettle's acquittal and our sentencing. I remember reading quotes in the newspaper: Nettle was back in his office, talking to reporters about putting the incident behind, about moving forward and doing the best job he could.

He didn't attend our sentencing. Different courtroom, different judge. The Honorable Frank said he'd done his best for us. It was out of his honorable hands.

It was the only time ever I saw Maygrett look helpless. He was there, sitting at a table, fingering the wood-grain top.

We stood in front of the bench while the judge shuffled papers. There were presentence reports. There was a letter from Will Gaines stating that he did not demand incarceration for us, that we had told the truth, the real party responsible had gotten off. I couldn't figure why he'd written it, but found it obscene somehow, that he had taken it upon himself to ask for mercy on our behalf. Pornography redefined. Or perhaps the feds felt bad about taking down cops, perhaps they had encouraged him.

Maybe Gaines realized that the wrong people had been shot.

I could see the top of the judge's scalp shining beneath his side-combed gray hair. When he finally raised his eyes, he was looking past us, out into the courtroom, off into the space where judges' minds must go before they send a human being to be locked away in a cage. He stared that way for unending minutes, perhaps only seconds, and then looked at the Honorable Frank.

"Proceed," he said.

I thought my knees were going to let me fall. I leaned against Jim. He was shaking the same way I was. I felt the trembling of nerves in his arm, the ancient fluttering, like the tremors in the skin of a small animal trapped, captured in the horrible grip of human hands.

Honorable Frank started to do a song and dance about leniency in sentencing, but anybody could see that the judge didn't want to hear it. He was pleading for me and I didn't want to hear it.

We could have gone to trial. As a result of our "coming forward," every single case we made in Beaumont had been dismissed. Every fucking case. We could have continued the lie and been blessed by the jury. Nettle would have backed us, we could have walked away from it and left Dodd standing there like a fool with his immunity grant in one hand.

Gaines would have gone back to jail, and the rest of the dealers would have stayed there. Jim might have been able to do it, might even have seen it as the right thing to do. I like to think not.

When Frank's voice finally trailed off into a dribble and he folded his notes, the judge looked at Jim and me for the first time and cleared his throat. I remember thinking that his ears were incredibly small. I remember the black robe and large green eyes, sitting beneath the blue-and-gold seal of the Justice Department.

"This," he said, "is a most difficult sentence, perhaps the most difficult that I've had the responsibility of imposing during my fourteen years on the bench."

I could not hope. But I did.

"Your past contemptible actions have affected lives in this community. Had you not voluntarily confessed, those actions would have continued to adversely affect those lives. Despite your turnaround, those crimes cannot go unpunished."

I heard these words and thought I was going down, thought I would simply crumple to the floor.

"James Michael Raynor, it is the order of this court that you shall be confined in a Federal Correctional Institution for a period of four years, to begin on February 15, 1982."

I felt his arm tense beneath my fingers. He didn't move, didn't nod. Nothing.

"Kristen Ann Cates, it is the further order of this court that you shall be confined in a Federal Correctional Institution for a period of two years."

Half the time. Two years. It could have been ten. But they were doing this to punish us? To punish? Crawling on the floor, begging, that hadn't settled things?

The Honorable Frank looked at us and nodded his head and Jim and I said, "Thank you, Your Honor." It just came out, like we were a couple of trained dogs or something. Thank you, Your Honor.

We walked from the courtroom. Probation, Maygrett had said. He'd been certain I'd get probation. That was his unofficial opinion, not a promise. But I couldn't help feeling that I had been lied to yet again, by yet someone else. Or was it only that I had needed desperately to believe there was a chance?

Outside, there were reporters shouting questions. Honorable told them to come to his office at three for a conference and then he drove us to lunch. On him. He insisted.

I don't remember where we ate or what we ate, or even if I ate at all. I was there at the table, watching Frank stuff food into his mouth. I looked up at one point and saw Maygrett and McPhearson at a table across the room. Maygrett walked over to us, resting his hand on the back of my chair.

"I didn't expect this," he said. "I don't know what to say."

"What the hell can you say," Jim whispered. "We're being punished. I guess blood isn't enough."

"We'll find who shot you," Maygrett said. "That's one thing I promise."

"Tell me one thing," Jim said. "Gaines snitching for you guys?"

"Like I told you," Maygrett said, "we'll find the man who shot you." He walked back to his table.

We stood near a boarding ramp in the Houston airport. Jim's flight would depart in an hour. I was awaiting final call.

"Hey, girl." He took my face in his hands. "Just remember, you're doing Nettle's time."

I pulled away and looked at him and then down at the carpet.

"That makes it a hell of a lot easier, Jim."

"Hey," he said softly.

I sat down on his suitcase.

"I shouldn't have stopped in Corpus Christi. You know? Should have just kept on going. But I couldn't quite make myself give up. I'd find myself looking around the beach every afternoon, hoping to see you walking toward me. I just couldn't give up."

He was silent for a long time, and then he said, "You

act like I took you when you were goddamn sweet sixteen or something and turned you smooth out and put you on the streets."

He blinked suddenly and his eyes got big. I thought for a moment he had recognized someone in the crowds rushing from gate to gate. He looked away to the departures screen and then back at me.

"I need you to be there for me," he said. His eyes were clear, and focused on my own. He needed me. He needed me. The airport carpet was red, almost maroon.

"Ain't that the way," I said. "I'm feeling really thin just now. I don't think there's enough left of me to go around. Do you know?"

He sucked in a quick breath and took a step back.

"We've both had a pretty big chunk carved out of our asses, so what do we do, check out, say 'it's been real,' see you later? You're my wife."

"I just honest-to-God loved you. But I . . ."

"You'll have time to think."

"I will indeed have that," I said. "Right now I'm not even sure where to start. Ask me anything. The answer is I don't know."

He stood there looking at the gate until a steward-smooth voice called boarding.

"That's me," I said.

"Right."

I stood and turned to go.

"Hey," he said. I looked back at him, tried to see only a man standing next to his luggage in an airport. "You'll handle it."

I walked down the ramp. The carpet became navy blue.

On the plane, I bought a headset and stared at the screen and took a Valium and drank a vodka tonic. And another.

*   *   *

There was a transportation desk near the main entrance to the airport.

The cowboy behind the counter had black hair slicked with oil and a Superman curl on his forehead. He stapled something and asked where I was going.

"To the prison." The words seemed to come from behind me, slipping over my shoulder and into the stale air that surrounded me.

"We got state and federal, which one you want?"

"Federal."

"The limo leaves in about ten minutes. Right out there." He pointed out the window to a plain white van with AIRPORT LIMO painted on the side in bright orange letters. I paid four dollars.

There were five other passengers. I sat toward the back, sweating quietly. We wound through the hills, past miles and miles of whitewashed fence glaring in the afternoon sun. Horses grazing. It looked calm.

The driver turned onto a thin gravel road and we passed a small sign, raised metal lettering on a brick slab: UNITED STATES FEDERAL CORRECTIONAL INSTITUTION, LEXINGTON, KENTUCKY. He pulled around a circular drive to the front of a huge red brick building dotted with hundreds of small-paned windows.

The middle-aged, business-suited man sitting next to me in the van followed me out toward the entrance.

"Are you going in?" I asked.

"Only for a visit," he said. "I'm an attorney."

I stood before the locked glass door and looked into the lobby. There were a couple of men in uniforms sitting behind a control panel on a platform in the corner of the room. One of them looked up, and then a buzzer sounded. I pushed open the door.

EPILOGUE

The Beta Unit

KNOW THAT I AM CRYING, BUT I CANNOT FEEL IT IN-
side, and I do not know why it is happening. It is simply
a matter of water leaking down my face, which jerks and
twitches and jumps about, as though there is corn popping
inside my head, beneath my skin. I wipe under my eyes and
put wet hands back in my lap. I am sitting on an examination table, and each time I move the paper beneath me crin-
kles loudly.

The doctor walks in and stands before me. He is a blur
of pale skin and baggy suit. He puts a hand on my knee,
and I can feel the cool of his palm through my jeans.

"You'll be fine," he says.

My lips twist into a shape that I cannot imagine. I feel
them jerking, but it is not something I can control.

"Try to relax," he says. He turns to the guard and says,
"I'll take this one with me. Send the papers to my office."

The guard shrugs and leaves. I follow the doctor out of
the hospital past people staring and down a long corridor
that dead-ends into a dull yellow steel door. He presses the
intercom and a man's voice says, "Yes?"

"Dr. Mossman," he replies.

* * *

In his office, he prepares a shot. "This will get you over the worst of it," he says. "How long have you been here, two days now?"

I don't know.

"Three, I think." I see the syringe and right away I can taste the smell of cocaine in the back of my throat.

"And you were taking medication? How long."

"Off and on," I say. "Since the shooting."

He looks up at me. "How long is that?"

It takes me a minute.

"Almost four years."

Until now I have measured time in increments which fell either before the shooting or after it. Now the center will shift forward, to my release date.

I can't think about it. Now, it is all still with me. *Past contemptible actions.* I should sleep. There are no guns here. No one can get in.

I feel the pinch of the needle in my arm and wait for the drug to wash into my system. What he's giving me isn't important. I will be put in a room somewhere in this place and I will sleep without a gun under my pillow.

Past contemptible actions.

I am sure of nothing.

I will sleep. I will rest. I don't know for how long. I simply don't know.

Give yourself a chance.

I don't know when, or even if. I don't yet know how. I am sure of nothing. But maybe it will come.

Maybe.

I will fold back the covers.

And I will get up on my feet and walk.

Acknowledgments

My heartfelt thanks to:
Jennifer Ash, Raymond Kennedy, Betsy Lerner,
Gordon Lish,
Pat Mulcahy, David Rosenthal, Dr. Robert Towers,
Amanda Urban,
Terry Wozencraft and Deirdre and Mel Wulf.